A

Wild

AND

Heavenly

Place

ALSO BY ROBIN OLIVEIRA

Winter Sisters
I Always Loved You
My Name Is Mary Sutter

A

Wild

AND

Heavenly

Place

A NOVEL

Robin Oliveira

G. P. PUTNAM'S SONS
New York

PUTNAM
— EST. 1838 —

G. P. PUTNAM'S SONS
Publishers Since 1838
An imprint of Penguin Random House LLC
penguinrandomhouse.com

Library of Congress Cataloging-in-Publication Data

Names: Oliveira, Robin, author.
Title: A wild and heavenly place: a novel / Robin Oliveira.
Description: New York: G. P. Putnam's Sons, 2024.
Identifiers: LCCN 2023044747 (print) | LCCN 2023044748 (ebook) |
ISBN 9780593543856 (hardcover) | ISBN 9780593543870 (ebook)
Subjects: LCGFT: Novels.
Classification: LCC PS3615.L583 W55 2024 (print) |
LCC PS3615.L583 (ebook) | DDC 813/.6—dc23/eng/20231005
LC record available at https://lccn.loc.gov/2023044747
LC ebook record available at https://lccn.loc.gov/2023044748

Printed in the United States of America
1st Printing

Book design by Ashley Tucker
Interior art by New Line/Shutterstock

This is a work of fiction. Names, characters, places, and incidents either are the product
of the author's imagination or are used fictitiously, and any resemblance to actual
persons, living or dead, businesses, companies, events, or locales is entirely coincidental.

For Drew, who loves boats

A

Wild

AND

Heavenly

Place

Part One

✣

1878–1879

GLASGOW, SCOTLAND

Is it fearful to think that in many cases large tenements of over-crowded houses were visited by fever from top to bottom; and in some instances not a family, in some scarcely an individual, escaped the disease? A simple-minded person would at once inquire why such places were allowed to exist in the midst of our advanced civilization. Would it be offensive to reply that these "tenements of death and hell," as they have been called, are owned by Christian gentlemen, who make a comfortable living by letting them to their heathen brethren, who might also be Christians, if it were not for their poverty, their moral debasement, their numerical concentration, and their consequent horrible surroundings?

~*GLASGOW HERALD*

1

Samuel

SOMETIMES AT NIGHT, SAMUEL FIDDES RESUR-
rected his fading memories of being wanted. His mother's soft
touch, her tired, insistent goodness, his father's patience as he
showed Samuel how to cut a straight angle, lay a shiplap, sand a
recalcitrant plank. He dreamed of his parents long after the
memory of their faces blurred into oblivion.

But upon rising, Samuel remembered, and girded himself
for the day ahead.

On this cold autumn morning, he brushed his sister's strawberry red hair from her cheek. She lay sleeping on a makeshift
mattress made of straw he had pilfered from the city stables.

"Alison," he whispered, tucking a strand of her hair behind
one ear. "Wake up, wee one."

Alison wasn't stirring. Exhausted five-year-old girls, Samuel
had learned, could sleep through anything. The others slept on,
their bodies still as ghosts. Samuel and Alison shared this airless
tenement room on Argyle Street with five people: three sisters
awaiting word and money from their brother in America, and an
anguished couple whose infant son had died the previous winter
from some mysterious pestilence. Everyone kept to themselves,

guarding their meager possessions with the tenacity of the needy. At six-by-six meters, there was barely enough room for everyone. The square-cut stone walls wept with cold, and on this late September morning, the oncoming Scottish winter threatened a premature appearance. Samuel dreaded the thought. Glaswegian winters could be arctic terrors.

"Wake up, Ali, it's Sunday. We can't miss kirk."

Alison's eyes fluttered open. She was an ethereal sort of child, all cheekbones and skinny limbs, with a pointed chin and that cascade of russet hair.

"Will the kirk ladies have food for us again?" she said.

"I certainly hope so."

She sat up and rubbed her eyes. As always, Alison had slept in her clothes: her black uniform dress, dingy white smock, and the woolen jumper he had bargained for last week from a shop on Finnieston Quay, shoveling their coal delivery in exchange for the jumper. Her woolen coat doubled as a blanket. Samuel feared he didn't know half of what he ought to know to take care of her. She looked a mess. Her face and dress were smudged with dirt, her fine hair was tangled with straw, and she'd recently lost her comb. But more worrisome, over the past few months her skin had turned sallow with a rapidity that had shocked him.

Samuel pulled her onto his lap, and she balanced on his legs, light as a bird. They hunkered by the lifeless stove, sharing a heel of stale bread and eating leftover porridge they'd cooked the night before. In July, when they had fled Smyllum Park Orphanage for Glasgow, they'd slept under a clump of bushes at the eastern end of the green, away from the bustle of the Saltmarket and the confusion of the river quays. The annual fair was on, and the lurid carnival shows featured desiccated mummies and the fattest man alive and even an Indian sword-swallower.

They bathed *doon the water* in the River Clyde because they didn't have money for the public washhouse, and ate meat pies and potato scones and bowls of Cullen skink he filched from the fair booths. When the fair closed, Samuel was forced to branch out, foraging near the Saltmarket, and occasionally begging at the giant cathedral gates and the Trongate. He even ventured to the houses near the dank close where his family had once lived, but he didn't know anyone anymore. In August, he got a job shoveling coal at the Govan Shipbuilding Yard and they'd moved into this damp cell. Alison worked doffing bobbins and spindles at the Wilkie textile factory in Calton. Only young children were small enough to fit underneath and in between the great looming machines to change out spent spinners for new. Every night, she came home covered in tufts of wool. Their combined wages almost kept them in food.

Alison nibbled her chunk of bread slowly, in that way she did when she wanted it to last. Five years ago, when their parents and siblings died of diphtheria and the parish council committed them to the orphanage, Samuel was twelve, but Alison was just an infant. In their five years there, sustained on solid Catholic fare, Samuel forgot the gnawing hunger of his early childhood, though other cruelties took its place. His memories of starvation faded. Until this past July, Alison had never known hunger. Now she was hungry all the time. Recently, though, she had stopped complaining, a worrisome sign. Last night, Samuel had consulted the contents of his pockets. Money enough for three days' food, but it was six days until he would be paid. There would be food at church today, but after that, he would have to ration. Again.

Samuel stroked Alison's hair, knowing it comforted her. "Do you want to go back to Smyllum, wee one? I'll take you back if you want. You'd be warm there, and there'd be plenty to eat. You'd have a bed. You could go to school."

When the nuns expelled Samuel from the orphanage, he had taken Alison with him. *Stolen* might be more accurate, but he had refused to leave her behind, not after what they had done to her. Still, there were days when he feared he had made a terrible mistake.

Alison stopped eating as she considered. Samuel hoped she would tell him the truth so that he would know what to do, because he'd been trying so hard, and they were still in this wretched room on this wretched street, and he didn't know anything about anything.

His sister gazed at him with profound stillness. In the thin light, her blue eyes appeared gray.

"Everywhere is sad," she whispered. "I want to be with you."

Samuel exhaled. He vowed never to ask her again. No matter how hungry and cold they got, it was better to be together, better to fend for themselves.

"Kirk?" he said.

"Kirk."

THE WIND WAS a dervish in the courtyard, and rain had collected in brown puddles around the privies. Samuel shed his coat as Alison danced beside him, trying to get warm. All the boys at the orphanage had worn the same black woolen coat of no distinguishing feature except warmth. At least the nuns hadn't stinted on wool. Today, Samuel took extra care with his spit bath at the standpipe, digging under his fingernails as water ran over his blistered hands. But not even lye soap could conquer coal dust. It clung to everything and set up residence in every crevice of his body. There was only so much a cold bath from a spigot could do. And his clothes no longer fit. Manual labor had broadened his shoulders so that his shirt strained at the seams. His ankles showed from under his pants legs. At six feet, he was bigger than most men. Walking about Glasgow, he'd grown aware that sometimes women stopped and stared. The nuns had mocked the symmetry of his face, the locks of black hair curling around his forehead, his dark eyes. They tried to make little of his intellectual capabilities, too. Inmates of Smyllum were educated to be cobblers or farmers or domestic servants. But when Father Davis, who taught math, noticed Samuel's aptitude, he insisted on tutoring Samuel privately in engineering and advanced math. Samuel believed the spiteful nuns would be pleased to learn that he had been reduced to shoveling coal in order to live.

He combed his fingers through Alison's hair, pulling out the last bits of straw, and then they hurried away from the gray streak of river along the Broomielaw, past the scaffolding surrounding the new train station, and up Pitt Street, the dun-colored buildings casting shadows onto the sidewalks. Rivers of humanity were going about their Sabbath, the wealthy warm and dry in their fine carriages, the poor afoot—squat mothers trailed by ragged children, rail-thin men scurrying past, clutching the lapels of their threadbare coats. Samuel and Alison trudged on. As always, they stopped in at the cemetery of the Presbyterian church to visit their family's graves, today laying only a handful of straw as tribute.

They climbed to the top of Pitt Street, where Samuel turned to survey the city, chilled and sullen on this gray day. From here, Glasgow's elegant George Square, the Trades House, and the city's many churches all cut away to the River Clyde. In Glasgow, all roads and desires led to the river, where the greatest industry of Glasgow prospered. Around the globe, the descriptor "Clyde Built" heralded shipbuilding excellence, and from Glasgow all the way out to the Firth of Clyde, men pounded rivets into iron skeletons, and ships miraculously rose from nothing.

It was Samuel's great desire to build ships. A hundred yards below the orphanage, at the base of the hill, had lain a shimmering loch. Samuel had often imagined it as a great sea, and that he lived on its shores in a stone cottage and built ships—fast, fleet things that could outrun memory.

"I'm cold," Alison said.

"Come on, then, let's go."

"Will that lass be at kirk?"

"Which lass?"

"The one you watch all the time."

Alison, Samuel thought, sighing, missed nothing.

AT ST. VINCENT Street Church, a disapproving usher took one look at Samuel and Alison and herded them upstairs to join the rest of the poor in the gallery mezzanine. Samuel claimed a place in the front row overlooking the sanctuary floor, where the monied citizens of Glasgow milled about, greeting one another in hushed tones.

Even in such elevated company, the girl stood out. Today she wore her fitted blue coat, which he preferred to her others. Beautifully formed, trim, with a narrow waist and flared hips, the girl had a good-humored, plump, smiling face, with dimpled cheeks and pale, smooth skin. Untamed ringlets of thick black hair spilled from underneath her feathered hat. Maybe it was this unruliness that charmed him, or maybe it was that everything about her radiated happiness, but Samuel felt as if he had always been aware of her—as a dream conjured during the long years of his loneliness.

Her younger brother, clad in a tweed coat and shorts, younger than Alison by a year or two, climbed onto the pew beside the girl, and she corralled him with a laugh. Her father and mother were resplendent, he in top hat and tails, she in an elegant fur-collared dress. As the organist struck the first notes, the girl reached for her hymnal and glanced idly up, her wide-brimmed hat tilting back to reveal the fullness of her face, which lit with frank and startled pleasure when she caught Samuel staring at her. Before he could stop himself, Samuel raised one hand in salute. The girl blushed and turned away, fumbling with the pages of her hymnal, and didn't look up again for the rest of the service. Samuel could think of little else but her glance.

When the service ended, Alison hurried ahead of him to the assembly room, where the kirk ladies had spread today's charitable offering of two thick slabs of fatty, warm beef sandwiched between slices of buckwheat bread slathered with butter. Samuel helped Alison to one, and himself to another, and shooed her into a corner where they could eat unobserved. It was one thing to need charity, another to be on display, and he didn't want anyone to see how hungry he was. Around them, other charity recipients scarfed their sandwiches, too, but the wealthy segregated themselves on the other side of the hall, chatting over cups of tea and slices of gingerbread. Soon they would go home to a full dinner table, while Samuel and Alison would retreat to the indifferent shelter of their tenement. Samuel bit into the sandwich with pleasure. The last time he'd eaten meat this good was in the orphanage. Shutting his eyes, he let the fat melt on his tongue, relishing the savory taste of the beef, while Alison made little noises of pleasure.

As Samuel brushed bread crumbs from Alison's coat, word came that sunshine had broken through the dreich day. Members of the congregation, including the minister, still clad in his ecclesiastical robes, streamed out of the assembly room. Rather than going home, everyone lingered in the sunshine, chatting. A spontaneous football game erupted, a tricky endeavor given the steepness of the cross streets. Whenever a carriage passed, someone yelled, "Out the street," and the children scattered. Alison hopped puddles on the wide sidewalk with a group of girls. Samuel, basking in the sunshine, shed his coat and leaned against a lamppost, one eye on Alison and the other on the girl of the blue coat.

A group of people were listening to the girl's father talk about a town on the west coast of North America. A new city, he said, barely cut out of the wilderness, with coal in its hills, timber like weeds, and money for anyone who had half a notion how to make it.

"If you've a plan to invest, don't be coy," someone said. "Tell us everything."

The girl's little brother tugged at her arm, begging to play, and she released him with instructions to stay close. Samuel watched the boy edge farther and farther away, entranced by the exuberant players, until he had migrated to the middle of the street.

At first, no one heard the frantic cries of a runaway lorry careening down the cobbles from the heights of Pitt Street, its failed brakes smoldering, the horse struggling to keep pace, the whites of his eyes bared. Only the harness prevented the carriage from running the horse over. Casks of whisky sailed out of the wagon to crash onto the steep street, spraying amber liquid everywhere. The football players froze, then scattered, but the little boy went rigid, his frightened gaze fixed on the oncoming wagon.

Samuel bolted toward the boy and dove, scooping him into his arms and rolling out of the way just as the carriage caromed past. It rocketed down the street for several more blocks, scattering people and carriages until the road flattened out and the horse, still harnessed and whinnying in terror, veered onto the sidewalk. The cart overturned, smashing to atoms and throwing the driver onto the cobbles, finally tumbling to a dreadful, ear-crunching stop.

For one moment, the crash and the smashed whisky barrels and the football bouncing down Pitt Street absorbed everyone's attention. Then parishioners rushed toward Samuel, among them the boy's father, who snatched his son from Samuel's arms, crying, "Geordie, are you hurt, are you hurt?"

The boy broke out in a wail, overwhelmed by the attention, and buried his head in his father's shoulder.

Samuel felt only his pounding heart. The right sleeve of his shirt had torn at the shoulder, and his left elbow was scraped and bloody. His leg ached a little, but that was normal in this kind of weather.

Down the hill, the horse was unharnessed as the carter was carried away. People pounded Samuel on the back, praising him for his quick reaction. Alison pushed through the crowd to reach him. He kneeled down and she flung herself into his arms.

"I'm all right, wee one. See? I'm fine."

She released him, and he kept tight hold of her hand. The incident played over and over in Samuel's mind. If he had died, Alison would have been left all alone.

Now the boy's father was gripping Samuel by the arm. He was as tall as Samuel, but stooped in the shoulders. He had a neatly trimmed beard and mustache. "The boy's fine. Not a scrape. Our Geordie would have been gone if not for you. May God keep you."

The girl of the blue coat, her cheeks flushed and eyes wet with fear and relief, appeared. "Are you hurt, Geordie? Oh, why did you do that? I told you to stay nearby. I told you."

She came only to Samuel's shoulder, if that. She seemed near his age. This close, she proved even more exquisite. Her skin was the color of alabaster, with soft curves and a bright flush to her cheeks.

Her mother finally made her way through the crowd. She had stronger cheekbones than her daughter, and a clear, high forehead. She inspected her weeping son with brisk efficiency. "All is well. You're fine, darling. You're fine."

The girl apologized, trembling. "I shouldn't have let Geordie go, Mama. I'm so sorry."

"Oh, Hailey, you know what a rascal he can be."

Hailey, thought Samuel. *Her name is Hailey.*

Hailey turned to Samuel. "Thank you. This is all my fault. What you did—oh, no. Look. You're bleeding. Mother, he's bleeding."

"It's nothing," Samuel said, though the wind had picked up and he could feel it grazing against his raw skin where the shirt had torn away. He craned his neck, searching for his coat, which he remembered dropping when he ran after Geordie, but the coat was gone. His heart fell.

Her mother surveyed Samuel, looking him up and down. He was painfully conscious of his ruined clothes, his blackened fingernails.

"We owe you a debt of gratitude. I am very grateful to you, young man. Thank you very much."

Alison was tugging on Samuel's torn shirt.

Hailey asked her, "What is your name?"

"Alison Fiddes," she whispered, suddenly shy.

"It's a pleasure to meet you, Alison. I am Hailey MacIntyre. Who is your friend?"

"He's not my friend, he's my brother."

"Is your brother always so brave?"

Alison nodded solemnly.

"That's the best kind of brother to have, isn't it?"

Alison nodded again as Samuel introduced himself. "Samuel Fiddes. How do you do?" Even if she never spoke to him again, Hailey MacIntyre would know who he was.

Hailey rewarded him with a solemn, direct gaze, then she whirled on her parents, who were already turning to leave.

"Mother, Father, may I invite Mr. Fiddes and his sister to dinner?" Sensing resistance, she tried a different tactic. "Father, please? Persuade him. We have to have them to dinner. Mr. Fiddes saved Geordie."

Mr. MacIntyre glanced at his wife, who looked away with an impatient, resentful sigh.

"Very well, Mr. Fiddes. It appears that Hailey Rose would like you and your sister to join us at table. Come along, the carriage is waiting."

"Wait," Hailey said. "Where is your coat, Mr. Fiddes?"

Samuel tried to hide his dismay with a shrug. "I appear to have lost it."

2

Hailey

IT WAS A LONG RIDE TO THE MacINTYRES' HOME in Glasgow's west end. Both Samuel and Alison gazed out the windows with such rapt expressions that Hailey wondered whether they'd ever ridden in a carriage before. Her father made sporadic conversation, but it lagged in the chill of her mother's displeasure. As the carriage jostled over the cobbles, Hailey stole glances at Samuel, who sat opposite her on the maroon velvet bench. He was so tall that their knees almost touched. It was impossible not to stare. Even in his torn shirt and dirtied work breeches, he was beautiful. He resembled, Hailey thought, the images of Roman soldiers pressed into ancient coins. His broad shoulders winged outward, his black hair flowed in waves, and his searching eyes were the color of coal, with a profusion of even darker eyelashes. Near perfection.

Her mother nudged her, and Hailey reluctantly looked away.

Theirs was a grand, curved street of attached houses, far from the heavy coal smoke of the industrial east end. None of Glasgow's dingy limestone here. Bright with newness, each house had wide, matching stoops, wrought iron railings, and pillars of alabaster. As usual, a waiting footman greeted them in the foyer. Marooned in this land of checkered marble floors and high ceilings, Samuel carried himself well. For the first time, Hailey saw the bounty of their life through his eyes, and as his gaze swept over the rich interiors Hailey remembered with chagrin the look on his face when she'd asked him about his coat.

"Papa?" Hailey said.

"Not now, Hailey," her mother said, handing her coat to a footman. She gave custody of Geordie to the nanny, who waited at the foot of the stairs. "Take him upstairs to the nursery and give him his dinner right away, won't you? He had a bit of a fright today."

Taking advantage of the distraction, Hailey led her father up the wide stairs and down the hallway to his dressing room, leaving Alison and Samuel with her irritated mother. Her mother was always telling Hailey what to do. Lately, especially. She had taken a keen interest in who Hailey danced with at balls, and had implored her to begin thinking of who she might marry. If marriage was on her mother's mind, what was on Hailey's was something else entirely. It was vague as yet, but Hailey knew for certain that she wanted a life far different from her mother's constrained rounds of lunches and dinners and balls—seeing the same people and doing the same things and going to the same places year after year, always smiling to keep up appearances, always pretending to listen raptly when she was really dying of boredom. The conversation was always about money—who wore which expensive dress where, who had a new carriage, and who had purchased a house in the country. The gossip was endless and petty, and there wasn't an authentic word spoken at any dinner party or dance that Hailey had ever attended. At the very least, she was determined to escape a life of mind-rattling pettiness. What that would mean remained shape-less as yet, but Hailey bristled every time her mother said, *Not now, Hailey.* If not now, then when? When would her life be her own? When would even the choice of talking to her father in private be something her mother had no say over?

"Those two waifs are in desperate need of a bath," her fa-ther said.

"Papa, you must give Mr. Fiddes one of your shirts. He can't sit at dinner in his wretched clothes. He needs to be bandaged, too. And I think he lost his only coat when he was helping Geordie. Don't you have one you can spare? The one you've complained the moths have gotten into at the elbows?"

"You can't adopt people, Hailey Rose." Only her father called her by that endearment, and she loved it when he did.

"It never does anyone any good," he continued, but he began to sort through his collection of fine cotton and linen shirts. The closet shelves were filled with top hats and silk scarves and lea-ther gloves. He kept this personal space immaculate, eschewing the doting services of his valet. He pulled the moth-eaten coat from a hanger. Camel colored, perhaps too narrow at the shoul-ders for Samuel, the coat had braided leather buttons and a wide lapel. "Take this to a footman to brush, but we will wait to give it to Mr. Fiddes until he leaves. We don't want to overwhelm him." He took a white cotton shirt from another hanger. "This will do. But this is all, Hailey, do you understand? We can't clothe all of Glasgow, much as you'd like."

"He saved Geordie, Papa," she said, draping the coat over her arm.

"Call for some hot water, too, would you? Mr. Fiddes can wash and change in here."

Hailey lingered. Her father had turned pensive again, as he

often did these days. Neither of her parents would tell Hailey if he was really back to work again. He left later in the mornings than usual and returned early in the afternoons in search of tea and hearth. Hailey and her father had always been close. He had taught her to swim as a child up in Loch Lomond—defying her mother's wishes, Hailey wanting the adventure, her father pleased with her courage, the two of them a secret society within the family. Even more so lately, after the explosion at the coal mine at High Blantyre, and the subsequent deaths of hundreds of miners, and her father's overwhelming guilt. It had happened a year ago, but her father revisited the memory every day. Hailey often listened to him talk about it, sometimes late into the night. Everyone said it was an accident. Her mother was growing increasingly impatient with him. Hailey resented her mother for her frustration, and for her intolerance of any hint of frailty, especially in her father.

"I think Mama's miffed at me."

Her father made a face. "Of course she is. How did you think she'd feel? She'll think you invited those two just to inconvenience her."

"They're no different from anyone else. And they're hungry. We have food. *And* he saved Geordie. But for Mr. Fiddes, Geordie might be dead right now."

"I know that as well as you do, young lady. And I'm grateful to him. But it doesn't make it easier for your mother." He dismissed her with a flat smile. "Now go, daughter. You have guests."

After handing off the coat to a maid and arranging for the hot water and bandages, Hailey returned to the foyer, where the thick silence made it apparent that her mother hadn't said a word to their guests since Hailey had left.

"Mr. Fiddes, my father has something for you. At the top of the stairs, turn right, down three doors. You'll find him in his dressing room."

Samuel glanced at Alison.

"I have her." Hailey squeezed Alison's hand and smiled at Samuel, who returned her gaze with a look of confused gratitude. Light was filtering through the windows, illuminating flecks of gold in his dark eyes. She wondered if he had any idea how beautiful he was.

Her mother waited until he had turned the upstairs corner and then hissed into Hailey's ear, "You never think, Hailey. This isn't a good time. Your father can hardly get through dinner with friends. And one meal won't save these two. Now, take off your hat."

"Father seems fine today," Hailey said, but she unpinned her hat before she led Alison into the dining room, where two footmen were shifting chairs and adding place settings to the mahogany table. One had stacked large books on a chair, and they helped Alison to climb onto it. Alison eyed the bread basket and Hailey snuck her a roll, which she inhaled.

The footmen put Samuel straight across from Hailey, and Alison next to her brother, Hailey's parents anchoring the ends. In her father's crisp shirt, Samuel Fiddes seemed almost at home. The transformation startled Hailey and seemed to startle her mother, too, whose appraising glance registered reluctant approval and somehow missed the rings of coal dust embedded in the lines around his wrists and the thin ebony crescents under his fingernails. The footmen served the soup course, a viscous green pea concoction her mother loved. Alison, though, stared at her bowl with deep apprehension. One of the footmen took pity on her, removed her serving, and slipped her a second bread roll, which Alison greeted with a dazzling smile. Upstairs, they could hear Geordie's fast footfalls, restored to exuberance.

"Hailey, your hairpins have failed you again."

"Mama, you know my curls have a mind of their own." But Hailey combed them back with her fingers, conscious of a covert glance of admiration from Samuel. Her father was flicking his right earlobe, a newly acquired gesture of agitation, which her mother despised. Usually she put a stop to it with a sharp word, but she refrained now. Generally speaking, Davinia MacIntyre was a woman who liked to police her family's perceived defects.

"Mr. Fiddes," her father said. "You mentioned in the carriage that you work at the docks. Are you in shipbuilding?"

"For a brief time as a boy I apprenticed to my father. Now I shovel coal at the Govan shipyards, near the graving docks."

That explained the coal dust, Hailey thought. "My father is in coal, too."

Her mother gaped at her, appalled. "For goodness' sake, Hailey. Being chief engineer of a coal mine is not quite the same thing as shoveling it." She set down her spoon and tried to gain control of the conversation. "Tell us, where do you live, Mr. Fiddes?"

"On Argyle Street, near the St. Enoch train station. But before that we lived at Smyllum Orphanage."

Her father's hand still floated in the proximity of his ear, a disembodied thing that Hailey's mother eyed with distaste. In a voice bright with nerves, she said, "Your hand, dear."

Startled, he laid his hand in his lap. "I thought the nuns at Smyllum were keen on education. Didn't they teach you to read and write? Surely you could get a better job?"

Samuel's gaze was steady. "I learned Latin and read all the classics. A priest from the seminary taught me physical matter, calculus, and engineering. There was a woodworking shop, too. But no one will give me a job that requires any of it."

"Didn't the nuns provide you with monetary resources or referrals when you left?"

"No, sir. We left in a hurry."

Mrs. MacIntyre's interrogative gaze blazed with distaste. "At least they educated the east end patter out of you, though I still hear it a little."

Samuel ignored the insult. "Before my parents died, we lived in the wynds near the cathedral."

Hailey stole an imploring glance at her mother, which her mother ignored.

Her father said, "Thank God those have been torn down. Such a blight on the city. Young man, I notice that you walk with a slight limp. I hope your physical work isn't made more miserable by the fact of it."

Her mother touched a napkin to her lips. "Yes, Samuel, what of your limp?"

"I broke my leg once going down the stairs at the orphanage. The cold bothers it."

Alison came instantly to life, eyebrows raised, back straightening, abandoning her bread roll to say, "But that's not what happened—"

Samuel shot her a look and she quieted.

Hailey's mother looked aghast at the nature of the conversation unspooling around her dining room table. She sighed and consulted the grandfather clock in the entryway, just visible though the archway, her usual signal to the footmen to speed up service. Having already whisked away the soup bowls, the footmen filled plates from the sideboard, forsaking the time-consuming ritual of carrying platters to each diner to let them serve themselves. It was one of her mother's little tricks to speed along service when she was unhappy with the way a dinner was proceeding.

In her high, bright voice, she seized the reins. "And where do you go to school, Alison?"

Alison was busy eating yet another roll. Hailey had lost count of how many the girl had already eaten. She beckoned to a footman and whispered to him to pack a basket of food, along with some bread.

Samuel answered for his sister. "She's a doffer at the Wilkie textile factory."

This, Hailey could tell, horrified her mother. It horrified her, too. When she was five, she spent her days in the nursery upstairs, where four-year-old Geordie was playing now, overseen by their nanny.

"But factories are terrible places!" her mother said. "Wouldn't it be much better if she learned her sums?"

Alison gave a startled lurch of terror, which Samuel countered with a reassuring shake of his head. "Ma'am, please don't alert the nuns or the parish council. They'll only send her back. And I won't let that happen."

"But something has to be done. Your sister can't work—"

Hailey pulsed with embarrassment. "Mother, can't you see they'd rather starve than go back? Something must have happened. You can't just take over other people's lives."

"Forgive me, ma'am, but children can, and do." Samuel's voice was kind. Her mother's prying had not ruffled him. "I worked as a child. You must trust me that Alison is safest with me, and far safer in a factory than the orphanage. Until I can find a better situation for us, she works. And she stays with me."

Her mother exchanged a reproachful glance with her husband, which Hailey knew contained a whole debate about what needed to be done about their difficult guests. In the ensuing silence, Samuel stole a look at Hailey. She mouthed an embarrassed apology.

Samuel took up the reins of conversation. "You are in coal, Mr. MacIntyre?"

Ignoring Samuel's question, her mother said, apropos of nothing, "Hailey, how was your dancing lesson this week?"

Hailey's father turned to face her mother. "Stop trying to protect me, Davinia. I'll answer the lad. Yes, I am in coal. At High Blantyre."

Samuel's face stilled with compassion. "High Blantyre? I'm sorry, sir. I didn't know."

"I blame myself."

"You know you're not to blame, Papa." said. Even the newspaper declared him guiltless. Coal mines exploded all the time. Miners died.

"Stop excusing me, Hailey Rose. Too many people have. I know very well how things go wrong in a mine." He bestowed Samuel with a professorial gaze, a rarity of late. "The High Blantyre mine has firedamp. It's a known issue. That Saturday and Sabbath before the explosion, the barometer dropped precipitously. That's been known to back up atmosphere into the shafts. It also concentrates the damp, you see. And it can snuff the ventilation fires. That impedes circulation when it is most necessary. I should have paid better attention, posted workers on the Sabbath to keep the fires going. Usually, no one goes down the mine on Sundays. On Monday morning, just as the miners began their shift, we believe one of the miners struck a match to relight one of the fires. The miners all have Davy lamps, but sometimes they don't listen about the dangers of an open flame. I was in our office in Glasgow. We heard the explosion here, a distance of some ten miles."

Her father glanced away, and a heavy silence followed. Samuel cleared his throat. "Yes, sir. We heard it at Smyllum, too. It rattled all the windows. We didn't know what it was until the afternoon train arrived and the engineer passed along the news to the nuns."

"Some in Edinburgh claimed to have heard it, too. That's how powerful it was. Two hundred seven miners died that day. Two hundred seven men and boys. I'll never stop thinking of them."

"Please," her mother said. "This isn't a subject for the dinner table."

Harold MacIntyre held up his hand to forestall his wife, his eyes gleaming with a strange intensity. He turned again to Samuel. "You understand, the world is a beautiful thing, Mr. Fiddes, a great wonder, a story of pressure and change. All eternity is contained in firmament deep beneath the ground. Everywhere, lost epochs have been compressed into rock—*rock*—and residual ghosts of plants and animals appear like phantoms. But here is the special thing. Flora becomes coal. Do you understand? Plants—*life*—become coal. So coal is living stone, with a memory. The forgotten past. What miners really do—what their job really is—is to extract time." He lifted a heavy silver knife and regarded it. "But it's dangerous. You have to take care." Abruptly, he set down the knife and resumed eating. Hailey glanced at her mother, who was struck into uncharacteristic silence by her husband's sudden eloquence.

Alison's quiet voice lilted across the table. "Are you very sad, sir?"

He was solemn, considering. "Yes."

The lamb had turned cold, the potatoes grainy. Dessert was a chocolate cake, every crumb of which Samuel and Alison seemed to savor, but which Hailey could not even taste.

Later, at the door, a maid handed Samuel his shirt, which had been patched and wrapped in brown paper secured with twine. The footman presented Samuel with the brushed camel coat. Her father looked on with bemused approval as Samuel tried it on. In comparison to her father, Samuel looked enormous. Surprisingly, the coat fit. An indication, Hailey thought, of how much her father had withered this past year.

"A token, Mr. Fiddes," her father said, gracious as always. "Thank you for what you did for Geordie."

"I'll return your shirt."

"Absolutely not."

The maid had been concealing a package behind her back. Hailey took it from her and knelt down to speak to Alison. The girl's blue eyes grew wide with anticipation. "We found one of my old dresses. Somehow, it avoided the church barrel. It's gray with blue edging. It was one of my favorites. I hope you like it."

As Alison clutched the package to her chest, Samuel prompted her to say thank you, and then he thanked them, too. He cleared his throat one more time. "I apologize, sir, if my question brought back memories—"

"St. Enoch's is quite far, isn't it?"

Hailey observed the flicker of comprehension in Samuel's eyes. Her father no longer wished to talk about High Blantyre.

"It's easy enough for us to walk, sir."

"Heavens no." He told the footman to bring the carriage around, and when it arrived they all walked outside to bid them farewell. At the carriage door, her father reached into his pocket and withdrew a fat purse and pressed it into Samuel's palm.

For a brief minute, Samuel stared at the offering, then he said, "This is very kind, sir, but I couldn't," and handed the purse back with grace and insistence.

He did accept the basket of food, though, which a footman handed into the carriage. Samuel gave Hailey a brief but searching glance before he clambered up the carriage steps. The lingering look was just long enough to prompt her mother to slide an arm through Hailey's. Hailey waved as the carriage departed down the cobbled street.

"You have to admit, Mama," Hailey said, "Mr. Fiddes is an extraordinary person."

"Hailey, he shovels coal and lives in a tenement." There was cold disdain in her voice.

"He returned Father's money."

"That boy put your father in a state. *Extracting time.* He's never uttered such nonsense before. You cannot bring strangers home, Hailey. Do you want to make things worse for your father? And that boy is not for you, do you understand? We've thanked him, and now that's all. And don't you ever speak to me again as if you know more than I do. I won't tolerate it."

"Mother. He *saved* Geordie."

Ignoring her, her mother stalked inside as the carriage turned toward the river, carrying Samuel and Alison away. Hailey shuddered. It was terrible to think of them living amid the soot and fumes of the train station.

The sunshine had fled, and dark clouds blackened the sky. Chilled, Hailey lifted her skirts and went inside, but not before a gust of wind sent fallen leaves tumbling down the street.

3

Samuel

THAT NIGHT, LYING NEXT TO ALISON IN THE DARK, Samuel's shoulder and elbow ached, but for the first time in a long time, he wasn't hungry. At the MacIntyres', he had taken in the marble pillars and high wainscot and groaning sideboard laden with platters of food, trying to cover his unease. He had not known there was such comfort in the world. Their dining table stretched a good ten feet and was attended by servants trained well enough that the surprise addition of extra guests, even those of such questionable background and dress, was concealed by a well-choreographed dance of shifting chairs, a quick addition of more place settings, and an unobtrusive covering of the damask dining chairs with toweling to protect against soiling. Samuel had felt conspicuous in his borrowed shirt, but grateful that he hadn't had to sit at such a fine table in his tattered one. He wondered what it was like to sleep in a house like that, to never worry about food, to always be warm. Marble busts adorned the mantelpiece with blue-and-white vases, brass candlesticks, little china dishes. He didn't think the MacIntyres even perceived the abundance. And the food. Even cold, the lamb had tasted delicious.

For a moment, he regretted returning the money, but he'd not been able to take it, not even for Alison. He hadn't saved Geordie with a reward in mind. He'd leapt out of instinct. It had been the right thing, the necessary thing, to do. And he hadn't wanted to take the money in front of Hailey. He didn't want to be an object of pity to her. The food hamper, the meal, the clothing—it was more than enough.

A chasm separated the MacIntyres' haven of gentility from Samuel's impoverished life. Samuel and Alison were two of five surviving children born to his parents in a cold stone room. His father had worked in the shipyard and his mother had taken in washing, and they'd lived a life of grubby poverty, scraping to eat along with thousands of other east enders trying to survive in the damp privation of the ancient wynds near the cathedral. At eleven, Samuel had left school and joined his father at the John Elder shipyard as an apprentice in order to earn more money for the family. Then the diphtheria raging through the tenements came for his father, then his two little brothers and sister, then Samuel himself, and finally his mother, who gave birth to Alison in the throes of the disease. Were it not for a neighbor who braved their pestilence to sweep Alison away, she would have died from neglect. And then all of them did die, except Samuel and Alison. He had just turned twelve. He remembered tossing clods of fresh dirt onto the graves of his dead family and walking blindly away from the bricked lane of the Glasgow churchyard, his ungloved hands numb with cold, sleet needling into the gap between his neck and stiff jacket collar, the icy fog of his breath adding to the dismal gray of that February morning. He'd stumbled over the Glasgow bridge across the Clyde and along the Govan Road to the John Elder shipyard, where he begged to be taken on as an apprentice by another man. In his fog of grief, all he could think was that he needed money, because he needed to take care of Alison.

But no one was willing to take him on.

The next day, someone turned him and Alison in to the parish council. Samuel never discovered who, but he suspected it was the neighbor caring for Alison, who was overwhelmed by her own eight children. He and Alison were sent to Smyllum Orphanage. Five long years there, suffering the violent whims of the nuns, whose crimes ranged from beating the young ones for bedwetting and crying, to far worse. And now here he was, back in the tenements, worse off than before, still responsible for his little sister and dreaming of Hailey, who lived a life he could never lead in a world he would never know and could not reach.

He didn't want to disappear as his family had. Catch some disease in this wretched corner of life, work himself to death, watch Alison starve slowly into nothingness. He knew things. The nuns had educated him, cruel as they had been. It was as if Samuel had been stunned these past months, unable to do anything but think of how to get food and how to get warm. He had forgotten himself. Forgotten even his dreams of the little stone house on the loch that became the sea.

With this glimpse of a different life, he remembered himself.

He turned quietly so as not to wake Alison. Purpose seized him, and in its grip, he slept.

THE COAL YARD had a washhouse, and after work the next day, Samuel scrubbed the black residue of the day's labor in the pump's icy stream, changed into Mr. MacIntyre's clean shirt, and set out for the John Elder shipyard, hoping they would remember him.

The new clerk said they had no work and turned him away.

It went like that the rest of the week. Each day after shoveling coal, he scrubbed himself of coal dust, donned Mr. MacIntyre's shirt, and tried a different shipyard. During service the next Sunday, Hailey glanced at Samuel once from the sanctuary floor, but the MacIntyres dashed away immediately afterward, as if to not have to speak with them. In the assembly room, Samuel was greeted by the other parishioners as a hero, and the kirk ladies gave him and Alison a second helping of the meal of boiled sheep's heart, but afterward they walked back alone to their room under a sleeting September sky.

That afternoon, the three sisters were waiting for him. They'd finally received their long-awaited letter from their brother in America, which none of them could read.

Milly, the eldest, handed it to him. "What does it say? When does he want us to come?"

Samuel scanned the bad handwriting and terrible grammar. Their brother wrote that he was lonely, and nothing made any sense to him about why he'd gone to America in the first place. The general character of the American people had worn him out. He was treated with suspicion. He'd used up all his money. They should give up thinking of immigrating, or of ever seeing him again.

The sisters turned to one another in cold confusion and wept. The life they had been hoping for would never come.

Tacked to every lamppost in Glasgow were posters encouraging people to emigrate. Steamship lines advertised steerage passage to New York. There were good prospects for miners, domestic female servants, and farmers. All others were warned away. The cold Scottish honesty: emigrate, but only if you have the right skills. Yet, people left willy-nilly from the Clyde for

America all the time. Even Mr. MacIntyre's imagination seemed to have been captured by a dream of the American continent. But the sisters' dream had ended.

THE NEXT EVENING, Samuel applied to the John Brown shipyard in Clydebank, a six-mile walk from Glasgow. It was already late, and Samuel would have to walk back home and find something for dinner. He'd left Alison a slice of cold porridge. He didn't hold out much hope. The previous interviews had lasted only five seconds.

In the inner sanctum of the Brown shipyard office, several men were poring over a set of plans. In heated discussion, they did not notice Samuel standing at the dividing counter. A stove glowed red. Samuel wanted to shed Mr. MacIntyre's fine wool coat, but because it lent him an air of greater presence, he kept it on. His hands were chapped and dirty from shoveling coal, and he thrust them into his pockets. On the clerk's counter lay the unfurled plans of a new steamship. Copy Two, it said. Samuel studied the oversize papers, his eyes hungry for the complicated math of construction. The engineer's meticulous lettering appealed to Samuel, whose instincts went to order and precision. At odds with the chaos of his life, math provided a sanctuary of structure. There were answers in math. Problems could be solved.

The ship was to be 150 feet long, with a beam of twenty-five feet and an elegant design. A river steamer, by the looks of it, like the ones that plied the Clyde, but altered in the pilothouse and bow.

In the back room, the men were making rapid calculations and disagreeing with one another. Samuel studied the inked measurements with care, his eyes methodically absorbing the representations on the page. His gaze rested on a set of figures at the bow. He looked again, calculating twice to make sure.

Inside the office, the conversation was growing more heated. One of the men was fiddling with a slide rule. Father Davis had taught Samuel how to use one before the nuns expelled him.

A clerk in a leather apron and ink-stained fingers tore himself from the group and leaned out the door. "What do ye want, lad?"

"May I speak to the man who drew up the plans for this ship?"

The clerk drew his chin back in scorn. "Get off with ye."

"There's some faulty math. In a calculation at the bow."

The clerk scowled and peered at Samuel as if he were staring down a rat. "Who did ye say ye are?"

"Samuel Fiddes. I've come after a job."

"Doing what? Reading things you've no business to?" But the clerk jutted his chin into the back room and called, "Lad here says he has your answer, Mr. Hathaway."

Mr. Hathaway, an eagle-nosed man of rail-thin build, sporting a pair of half spectacles, craned his neck around the doorway and waved his slide rule. "You've got something to say?"

"The calculations in the bow are off. It seems this line here should read seventy feet, and instead it reads thirty. I think it's thrown off the figuring for the whole section."

Hathaway narrowed his gaze and stalked to the counter. He seized the plans, one finger skimming the drawing, lips moving as he made calculations in his head.

"By God, there it is." Peering up at Samuel, he said, "Uncanny. Who are you?"

"Name is Fiddes," the clerk inserted.

Hathaway studied the pages again. "We've been pounding our heads against the wall. How did you notice this?"

"I see numbers."

"You see them?" Hathaway turned to the smirking clerk. "He sees them." He scrutinized Samuel. "You're too young to be an engineer."

"At school, I learned complicated maths. I can do calculations."

"Is that so? Can you read and write, too?"

"I can." Samuel fought to keep desperation from his voice. "I like numbers, Mr. Hathaway. I like that they bring things to life. Beautiful things, like ships."

"*You like numbers. They bring things to life.*" Hathaway sniffed. "Young man, we don't employ poets."

The clerk snorted with derision.

"I want to build ships," Samuel said. He had never voiced this desire aloud before. "I want to know how to make one, from beginning to end. I want to understand how to fashion lines, how to make a ship float, how to propel it through the water. I want to build the most beautiful ships in the world."

The clerk abandoned mockery and leaned against the doorframe as Hathaway cocked his head and said, "Design them or build them?"

"Both."

"Well, if you want to design them, you'll need to study engineering at university. A three-year certificate in inorganic chemistry, natural philosophy, civil engineering, mathematics, advanced geology. You would attend classes all day."

"What does that cost?"

Hathaway shrugged. "Forty pounds or more."

Samuel sighed. A fortune.

Hathaway turned contemplative. "I suspect you don't have that money, do you? No. Can you draw, though? Trace a line?"

"I can."

"Then I'll hire you to copy these plans. I'll fix the calculations. But you must be exacting, do you hear?"

Hope stirred. "Yes. Thank you, sir."

"Should take you a few months. There are pages and pages to this. It'll keep you out of the autumn wet. And after you're done cleaning up my error, Mr. Fiddes, I'll send you to the yard and apprentice you to our dinghy shipwright. An education of sorts. It's a comprehensive building of a ship, albeit a wee one. After that, everything will be up to you. Remember, though, you can't get very far building ships unless you're an engineer."

The job paid twenty shillings a week. A single pound. A lot more than shoveling coal. He and Alison would be able to bathe once a week in a steam bath down by the river, and there would be more to eat, enough that they would no longer live on the edge of starvation.

And after that, the same remarkable pay for learning to build dinghies.

It was a beginning. More than a beginning. It was a chance.

4

Hailey

HAILEY REMEMBERED ONLY, *ON ARGYLE, NEAR the St. Enoch train station.* Night had fallen, and under a cold drizzle the gas streetlamps yielded little light. An arriving train broke the nocturnal hush, its brakes squealing. Another locomotive rumbled away, pulling a long train of rocking cars. The cacophony unsettled her. People lived here, in the roar and soot.

The family driver, a shadowy figure against the flare of the streetlight, said, "I ought to be driving you right back, miss."

"Which building?" she repeated. The driver had delivered Samuel and Alison home from dinner just over a week ago.

Reluctantly, he indicated one of the dingy tenements along Argyle.

"You're certain?" Hailey said.

"Wish I wasn't."

A second, thin-lipped footman doubling as coachman helped her onto the cobbles, lit a candle, and glued himself to her side. She had bribed them both with her pin money after discovering them stealing a silver tray from the family larder.

She was furious with her parents for shunning Samuel and Alison after church. All week, she'd been looking forward to seeing them, Samuel especially. But her parents had rushed her into their carriage with an excuse of how fatigued she must have been after the previous night's ball at the Great Hall.

It wasn't as if she had danced till dawn. She hadn't even enjoyed herself. Her mother had ordered a new green silk dress for her from the seamstress and seemed bent on introducing her to as many young men in their circle as possible, even though Hailey already knew them from dance class and had dismissed them all as uninteresting, privileged boys whose idea of scintillating conversation involved the balance sheet of the businesses they would one day inherit. The wealth of Glasgow's highborn families was rooted in the Caribbean sugar and tobacco trade, or in shipbuilding, or coal, like her father. But her mother carried on as if Glasgow society were landed peerage. *It matters who you marry*, she said. *Money matters.* Her mother's eagerness that night was, Hailey knew, in direct reaction to Hailey's admiration for Samuel, whose dark eyes shone with a deep intelligence that was more attractive than any balance sheet.

Hailey shuddered. She wasn't ready to marry, and she certainly wasn't going to marry any of the lumbering boys who'd stepped on her feet since she was thirteen. She wanted honesty, intelligence, beauty—in whatever form it presented itself. She'd seen all three in Samuel Fiddes.

She hoped to help the Fiddeses. She'd tearfully begged her parents to keep sending hampers of food to Samuel and Alison, but even her kindhearted father had turned her down. *They have to stand on their own two feet, darling. We can't save all of Glasgow.*

Hailey had asked why they couldn't at least save Samuel and Alison.

Your charitable activities at church are enough, her father had said this morning. *Take heart in that.*

ROBIN OLIVEIRA

In her father's eyes, *enough* was the coat drive the church ran every year at Christmas and giving out food in the Gorbals, which Hailey did every Saturday afternoon. But it wasn't *enough* now that she knew Samuel and Alison.

Yet now, navigating cold tenement halls after dark Hailey doubted herself. The din of quarrels and slamming doors reverberated throughout the building.

"Let's go home, miss," the coachman said.

Hailey began to knock on doors, her queries meeting with disbelief, sly whistles, and outright snubs. Women slammed doors in her face. Stooped men leered. She climbed mud-slaked stairs to the second floor, and then the third. Minutes dragged by. There were endless doors and endless people and endless ways to be poor, it seemed. It was ugly and daunting, especially the blighted faces of the ill-clothed children already exhausted by living.

On the fourth floor, the coachman protested, "Miss Mac-Intyre, your father will dismiss me if anything happens to you."

She pushed on, door after door, catching glimpses of things she'd never imagined.

"Miss, I beg you, let's go home."

Six floors. She'd lost count of how far she'd come, but not of what she had seen.

"This is past belief, miss. You must stop."

At a door at the end of the top-floor corridor, Samuel answered. He was wearing her father's shirt, holding a spurtle dripping porridge in one hand and half a loaf of bread in the other. He reddened as her gaze darted around the cell. Others in the room gaped at her. She'd thought they lived alone. A coal stove barely radiated heat. There was no furniture. A flickering oil lantern threw shadows on Alison, who lay on a bed of straw. Her strawberry hair had escaped its ties, and she wore the dress

Hailey had given her, its long sleeves rolled up. Alison rose and sidled next to Samuel, and he laid a protective hand on her head.

Too struck by Samuel's beauty to speak directly to him, Hailey shifted her attention to his sister. "Hello, Alison. I loved that dress. Do you like it?"

Alison rubbed her eyes. "I'm hungry."

"The throstle jobber pushes her too hard at work. I was just making her some porridge," Samuel explained.

Hailey gathered courage, oddly hesitant now to see her mission through. "Will you and Alison come with me on a carriage ride?"

Samuel gazed at her in surprise for a long minute before he gestured with his loaf of bread. "We need to eat."

"I brought food. You can bring what you have, too."

Outside, the driver exhaled with relief when he saw her. "I thought you were dead, miss."

"Kelvin Drive, please. Along the Royal Botanic Garden."

She climbed with Samuel and Alison into the carriage. Samuel seemed wary. Hailey felt suddenly shy. She'd packed a wicker hamper with cheeses and cold meats and bottles of ginger beer, and she busied herself awkwardly as the carriage wobbled along, distributing small plates and slicing their bread on a board in her lap. She spread mustard and piled beef and cheese and handed the first sandwich to Alison, who took it solemnly. Hailey made several more, handing one to Samuel, who never dropped his guarded reserve. They rocked along, eating but not talking. Alison finished first and wiped an excess of mustard from the corners of her mouth. Hailey handed her an opened bottle of ginger beer and a biscuit. Traffic thinned as they left the heart of the city and entered the lanes of the expansive new park near the MacIntyre home.

Finally, Samuel broke the uncomfortable silence. "How did you find us?"

"I bribed the driver."

He let out a startled laugh eyeing her with what seemed to be admiration. "What did you tell your parents?".

"That I'm delivering food in the Gorbals."

"And the coachmen? Won't they say something?"

Hailey shrugged. "I caught them stealing silver." She shoved her gloved hands between the folds of her voluminous skirt. "The things I have seen tonight, the squalor—I didn't know. I didn't know how people lived."

"Nearly all of Glasgow is starving," Samuel said evenly.

Silence again fell between them. Inside the park, the carriage passed over the Kelvin River, percussing the wooden slats of the bridge. Patinaed statues of mothers and sleeping children anchored the bridge at either end. Alison pressed her face to the carriage window to look out at the shimmering, gaslit haze.

Samuel said, "Why did you come to find us?"

"Because—"

"I don't want your pity. I don't need pity."

Was it pity that had compelled her? Watching Alison eat a second sandwich, her eyes closed with pleasure, fed something inside Hailey that she feared might be ugly. Lady Bountiful, come to the rescue. She said, temporizing, "It's hard to see someone starve."

Sam glanced at his sister, then back at Hailey, dark eyes boring into hers. "If this isn't pity, Miss MacIntyre, what is it?"

Embarrassed, confused, she said, "Hailey."

"Pardon?"

"Call me Hailey."

"Hailey. I need to know what this is."

He was impossible to read, with his black eyes and insistent gaze.

"If you didn't want Alison to starve, then why did you return my father's money when you clearly need it?"

"I didn't save Geordie for money. And I didn't do it for food, either."

Hailey colored. She had insulted him. "I'm sorry I came to you. I've made a mistake. I'll take you back directly."

She lifted the trapdoor to speak to the driver, but Samuel snared her wrist.

"Why?"

She felt herself blush. "Because—yes, I admit, I was sorry for you. But what you did—saving Geordie—I still can't believe it. You did my family a great service. And someone like you, with your courage and intelligence—" Her voice dropped to a whisper. She could not take her eyes from his beautiful face. She could not admit that she had come looking for him for reasons that had nothing to do with Geordie.

"So you are sorry for me?" he said, dropping her wrist and fisting his hands in his lap.

"No," she said, aching for him to touch her again. "I wanted— the truth is, I needed to find you. I want to know you."

Alison stopped eating to stare, aware that something momentous was afoot.

Samuel's hands unfurled, his gaze newly soft, his defenses finally lowered. His hands were large, and she saw that the crust of coal dust he had tried to hide before had vanished, replaced by splotches of ink.

"So, this isn't pity?" Samuel said.

"My father would say that it was."

"I think you're lucky to have parents who worry about you."

"Perhaps I am ungrateful. I want to know you, Mr. Fiddes. And you're not unattractive to look at." She blushed again; it had just slipped out.

"To look at? In wretched clothes and heavy boots?"

"Don't tease me. And you don't have wretched clothes. You're wearing my father's shirt and coat."

Outside, the park passed in hushed darkness. Samuel said, "I watched you."

"I beg your pardon?"

"At church. I watched you from the mezzanine. Every Sunday, before we met."

"You did?"

"I know things about you."

"You do?"

"I know that you mumble the reading along with the lector and play games with Geordie to keep him quiet. I know that you unfasten the top button of your coat when it gets too warm, and that your mother makes you button it up again. I know that you shift in your seat when you are bored with the sermon and tug at your gloves when you grow even more impatient. I know the color of your eyes and the cant of your shoulders. And I know that you wind a finger in your curls when you're thinking, just like you're doing now."

"Well, I know something, too."

"What do you know?"

"That you love your sister. I think it's what I like best about you. That you'll do anything for her."

As if to confirm Hailey's conviction, Alison laid her head on her brother's chest, a deeply contented smile on her lips.

Samuel pulled her closer, an instinctive brotherly gesture that further proved Hailey's words. "I have news."

"Oh?"

With obvious pride, he said, "On Monday, I found a job as a copyist at the John Brown Shipyard. I started today."

"How wonderful. Congratulations! But will they—pay you? Will you be able to move out of that—place?" She heard herself and stopped. It was none of her business how much money Samuel was paid for his work. Bringing him sandwiches gave her no right to pry.

But he seemed unperturbed by her lack of manners. "Alison won't be hungry anymore. And we'll have a hot bath once a week. That's all."

It was as if he were trying very hard not to exaggerate his turn of good fortune, trying hard not to misrepresent himself.

"I'm impressed, Mr. Fiddes."

"Samuel. If I'm to call you Hailey, then you must call me Samuel."

"All right, then. Samuel."

"I have plans, Hailey. I won't tell them to you now. I'm suspicious of luck, and I've only come into it recently. But I have plans, I do. And what you said before? I want to know you, too, Hailey MacIntyre. I have wanted to from the moment I saw you."

Her cheeks flushed. She was surprised to see that the carriage had turned back to the city center, that they were already approaching St. Enoch's. She didn't want Samuel and Alison to go. Outside, all was ghostly, the gaslights flickering yellow in a heavy fog. Alison, sleepy, was dazedly watching Hailey pack up the hamper.

Hailey said, "Alison, will you meet me every Monday? We can go for a carriage ride and talk and eat, and maybe we can get to know one another better."

To Hailey's delight, Alison's face brightened. "Oh, please."

Samuel said, "Am I invited?"

Hailey nodded, pleased to be teased now.

"Thank you for dinner," he said, carrying Alison through the carriage door, her head lazing on his shoulder. She was already half-asleep. "See you on Sunday?"

"We can't talk at church."

"Your parents?"

She nodded.

"At least I'll still have the pleasure of watching you," he said, smiling.

She dared to return his smile.

"Next Monday, then. Ann Street might be a better meeting place. It's just behind us—hidden from the main thoroughfare. Meet you there at seven?"

As the carriage rolled away, Hailey leaned against the seat and shut her eyes, thrilled. She'd done it. She'd found Samuel. She could hardly believe the things she'd said to him. He was the opposite of every boy she had ever met. She felt a thrill for her future, once so stale and predictable, now promising something else entirely. The mournful wail of a foghorn rolled up the Clyde, a low note under the rhythmic clopping of the horses. Echoes of other places and other lives. Even as Hailey fell asleep that night, she could still hear it.

5

Samuel

THE FOLLOWING MONDAY, THE FIRST IN OCTOBER, Samuel and Alison waited nervously on Ann Street for the MacIntyre carriage to appear. Alison was half-asleep against his shoulder when the carriage drew up. They sat as before, Hailey opposite Samuel and Alison. Hailey opened the hamper and again made a meal of the meats and cheeses packed inside, acting as hostess as their conversation flowed in fits and starts about the part of town they were moving through, about the coming winter, about anything except themselves. When they finished eating, Alison laid her head on Samuel's lap and was soon asleep.

All week, Samuel had thought about seeing Hailey again. Tonight, she wore the beautiful blue coat, with its regal black fur collar and cuffs, magnifying the startling depth of her hazel eyes. From time to time during the service, she had glanced up at him, quick, surreptitious peeks that her mother put an end to with a hand to Hailey's wrist. Now that they were finally together, though, he found himself tongue-tied. She felt out of reach. All those confessions that had stirred his heart stymied him now. Each of Hailey's small gestures rendered him weak with longing. Her deft unbuttoning of a glove, the way she tilted her head when she listened to him, her unconscious habit of brushing her curls from her cheeks. He didn't know what to say or do.

Samuel said, "Hailey, I—"

"Will you come sit beside me?"

His heart thrilled at the invitation, the boldness in her voice. Samuel shifted Alison's head from his lap and covered her with a carriage blanket. Maneuvering around the hamper in the crowded coach, he took the seat next to Hailey. Her nearness intoxicated him. Her dark curls, the fragrance of her perfume, the softness of her body jostling up against his; he weaved an unsteady line between disbelief and desire.

She faced him, the glimmering streetlights highlighting the curve of her cheekbones. "Talk to me. Tell me about yourself. Tell me what you love, what you want. Tell me everything."

The carriage was venturing up High Street, past the cathedral.

"My stories won't be like yours."

"I want to hear them. Tell me about the orphanage—how did you come to be there?"

His gaze wandered her face, wondering what she wanted from him.

"Please?"

He told her then, about the diphtheria, losing his whole family. He left out details about Smyllum because Hailey had already lifted her hand to her mouth, tears welling. "How terrible."

"I won't tell you any more. Someone like you shouldn't have to hear it."

She stiffened. "Someone like me?"

"I mean, someone who has lived a different kind of life from mine."

"I haven't lived any kind of life yet."

"No?" Samuel said.

"Well, I've lived a kind of life. Before Blantyre, Father promised we'd travel to Paris to visit the Louvre. There are new artists in Paris, too—I believe they're called the Impressionists. But we haven't gone yet. I don't know if we ever will now. I want to see everything that is new, everything that is beautiful. I feel most at home in Loch Lomond and the Highlands, though. Have you ever been?"

Samuel shook his head. He'd been nowhere. "What is it like?"

"It's so alive—the glinting light on the water, the wind sailing over the heather in the valleys, the rocky shoreline dipping into the sea. I love Glasgow, but that wild place—it feeds something in me, something different from this." With a chagrined smile, she made a gesture out the window to the city street. "But, truly, my life is ordinary."

"Tell me more. I want to know it all."

Shyly, she eased into a description of her day-to-day life— her former governess and her weekly dancing lessons and the society dinners her mother hosted for friends. She described her schooling, how she'd read Shakespeare and Robert Burns before her mother put a stop to her education because a girl didn't need to know more than how to read and write. There had been a trip to Edinburgh to see the castle high on its sheaf of volcanic rock at the top of the Royal Mile.

"I want to see that."

"The castle is glorious, but the Mile smells of cesspools and offal. There are so many people, more even than Glasgow. The closes and wynds are like a honeycomb. New Town is far prettier than Old Town or Glasgow. Once at Holyrood Palace, we saw Queen Victoria depart in a parade of carriages, and then we visited the castle gardens. And I've been to London, too. It's such a long rail trip, and the city is filthy, you can't imagine. But it's marvelous, too."

"Is it?" he said.

"Do you know that you can whisper something against the wall in the dome of St. Paul's Cathedral and it races around and comes back to you? Hyde Park is lovely when the gardens are in bloom. And we stayed in a suite at the Grosvenor Hotel and went to the horse races and ate ices at the Crystal Palace and—"

She broke off, a self-deprecating smile crossing her lips. Their differences had crystallized. She was a girl of wealth, who lived a life of hotel suites and train rides and wild lochs and dreams of Paris. Samuel had never set foot beyond Glasgow except for the orphanage, thirty miles away. His only train ride had been in the care of the nuns on the way to Smyllum, long ago, an infant Alison asleep in his arms.

Such a wide chasm to bridge.

As if she, too, realized this, she said, "Mostly I'm here, though, in Glasgow, doing needlepoint and being bored out of my mind."

"You've already lived so much, and I—"

Hailey unconsciously seized his hand, entwining it in hers. "We are not so different, you and I. Please, tell me what you love," she implored. "I want to know. I need to know."

Her daring gesture spread a startled warmth through Samuel, along with a deep pleasure at the intensity of her interest. No one had ever asked him anything like this before. Words tumbled from him. "I'm interested in ships. I'm only a copyist, but I trace copies of ships' schematics all day. So many workers

need the drawings—carpenters and ironworkers and painters—
that I have to make many precise, accurate copies. Mr.
Hathaway—he's the shipbuilder—he asks me to recheck his calculations, and I do. By drawing and redrawing, I've started to
absorb hull design and structure. In my mind I've begun to design simple ships, trying to sort out the correct dimensions—the
shape of a bow, the hard angles of a stern, the balance of a boat
in the water. Everything works together. If even one dimension
is off, a ship will fail."

Hailey's gaze remained eager, interested, her grasp in his.
He talked on.

"It started because of my father. I told your family at dinner
that I was his apprentice for a few months at John Elder building hulls before he died. Father wasn't an ironworker. He worked
shiplapping wooden boats. But we used to walk around the yard
to look at all the boats being built, and he would talk about
lines and elegance and how a ship was God's gift to man—so
that we could see all the wonders of the world. He wasn't an
educated man, but he wasn't ignorant, either. And the priest at
the orphanage—Father Davis. Some said he turned priest after
a heartbreak. Before that he was an engineer. He's the one who
taught me complicated math and engineering principles. I used
to dream at night about escaping the orphanage, and it always
involved building a boat and sailing away from Scotland, taking
Alison with me. I love the idea of making something. Of figuring out a puzzle, of building something myself, of conquering
the world. I'm tired of it conquering me."

He left off then, fearing he had talked too much.

"That's beautiful," Hailey said, her eyes shining.

She released his hand then, suddenly aware of the intimate

way she had been clutching him. Her cheeks flushed and she gazed at him, a question in her eyes. He wanted to kiss her, but he held back. Then the carriage stopped and it was all over, and he stepped out, carrying Alison.

IT SOON DEVELOPED that on Mondays, Hailey retrieved Alison from the Wilkie factory after her shift so that she wouldn't have to walk all the way back to Argyle Street, while Samuel made a hasty bath at the pump in the tenement's back courtyard. By the time the carriage arrived on Ann Street, Alison had eaten her fill from Hailey's hamper and had been snugly wrapped in a blanket and lulled to sleep by the rocking of the carriage, giving Hailey and Samuel precious time alone.

Samuel had to remind Alison again and again not to say anything to Hailey at church.

"But Mr. and Mrs. MacIntyre were nice to us."

How to explain? "Will you trust me, Ali? Say nothing to anyone."

AT THE END of October, the City of Glasgow Bank failed. People talked of it everywhere—on the docks, in haberdashers' and butcher shops, even in the closes of the Saltmarket. The catastrophe rocked all of Scotland, because the failure of one of the biggest banks in the country boded ill for everyone. The failure would trickle into ordinary society and decimate Glasgow's economy. Hailey and Samuel, however, did not speak of it. It meant nothing to them. Their life together existed inside the bubble of the carriage, and on Monday nights they floated through Glasgow on various routes—in and out of Glasgow

Green, through Kelvingrove Park, along the river quays, always talking, hands entwined. They had not yet kissed, though it took much of Samuel's concentration to keep from trying. Whenever he thought of it—which was all the time—he feared the gulf of class between them. Better, too, not to frighten her.

Time sped into November, when night fell earlier and earlier, and the city was cloaked in darkness from three in the afternoon.

On a Monday evening late in November, they were sitting very close together, their hands intertwined, shoulders touching. Samuel brushed Hailey's curls from her eyes.

"Why did you take Alison from Smyllum?" Hailey said.

Samuel did not want to tell her. He'd never told anyone. Sometimes even he couldn't bear to think about all that had happened.

"I want to know," she said. "Please?"

"I'll tell you. When the children first come to Smyllum, they cry a lot. The nuns lose patience and beat the homesickness out of them. I used to shield them, get between the nuns and the little ones, especially as I got older. The nuns didn't like that.

"One day, when Ali was three—I was fifteen, getting big by then—she wet her bedsheets. The nuns made her parade through the dining hall wrapped in those dirty linens, and then they denied her breakfast while everyone else ate. The nuns did that a lot. The humiliation was supposed to teach us something. I took Ali's sheets from her and stood guard over her while she ate my porridge. When she finished, five of the nuns dragged me to the stairwell and booted me down the stairs. They broke my left leg. I was in bed for three months."

Hailey looked aghast.

"But after that, the nuns kept away from her. The orphanage

releases boys at sixteen, but I was useful, so they kept me around to work. My strength and height came in handy. I built bookcases, repaired broken stair railings, things like that. We had a wary truce, the nuns and I. I would have left, except for Ali.

"Then one morning last July, I turned a corner and found Sister Mary Margaret whaling on Alison, beating her about her head, shouting and calling her a worthless, godforsaken, no-good thing. I grabbed the sister and Alison scrambled away, but somehow the sister got free and caught hold of one of Alison's ankles and pulled her back. I hit that nun square in the face. Alison shot into my arms. Sister Mary Margaret was on the floor, blood dripping from her lip. Right then, the superioress cornered the hallway, and I was told to leave the orphanage for good. That night, I came back and stole Alison out of her dormitory. She was too bruised to walk, so I carried her all the way to Glasgow."

"Thirty miles?"

"It took us four days. We slept in haylofts. I haven't struck anyone since." He wasn't violent. He needed her to know that. "Are you afraid of me now?"

She shook her head. "No."

Relief flooded through Samuel, and they both studied Alison, asleep on the opposite bench, her limbs dangling over the side. The extra money he'd recently earned had made a difference. Between that and Hailey's weekly hamper of food, she'd grown, and her skin had lost its sickly pallor.

Now Hailey's gaze locked with Samuel's, her watering eyes filled with recognition. *There you are*, she seemed to say. *I don't know anyone better than you.*

He had never kissed anyone before, did not quite know what to do or how to do it, but in an instant his hands were in her hair, and he drew her close and touched his lips to hers. Outside, the hush of night dampened the city tumult. Time and space rioted around him. Nothing was urgent, and then suddenly everything was. He took her face in both his hands and kissed her again. His lips softened into hers and kissed her deeply, reveling in the closeness, the endless well of Hailey—a revelation of tenderness and want that nearly shut out reason. What a strange thing desire is, he thought. The moment you give in to it, it teaches you all you need to know. He drew Hailey closer and she melted against him, her hands combing through his hair. His hands drifted to her shoulders, then her neck, then her breasts, instinct guiding him. He calculated nothing. At night, when he was certain that their roommates slept, he took care of himself, as quietly and unashamedly as he could. He felt no shame now. He had never imagined the softness, the yielding of Hailey's body, or what it would be to be so close that he could feel her hips through the multitudes of her petticoats, the swell of her breasts above her rigid corset. Once, he had seen these underthings displayed in the back room of a shop, its door propped open as a seamstress sewed on a dress frame. He'd stopped to stare, puzzling out the laces of the corset and the tiers of cotton, until the smirking seamstress shooed him away. Now he wondered how he could get even closer to Hailey, what it would be to tear the clothing from her so that every part of him touched her.

She pulled away. They were breathing hard, staring at each other, bashful discovery lighting up her face. Her hair was disarranged, unruly. Her lips were swollen. With difficulty, he held himself back. She was a revelation.

"Please help me," she said, seizing his hands. She still wore her gloves.

He was conscious of his own need, wondering if she understood. "I should not have—"

"I need to get my bearings. I didn't know about—I didn't know."

For several moments, they sat in wonder.

"Are you frightened?" he said.

She shook her head. "No. Do you feel what I feel?"

He could not put into words what he felt. It was a thing that did not need words. "I imagined, but I never—"

"You must button my dress," she said.

Hailey lifted one hand and held up her hair, revealing that two buttons were undone. He had no idea he'd undone them. The inches between them sizzled as she held together the two plackets to make it easier for him to fasten them. At the nape of her neck were shorter hairs, fluffy like down. He wondered whether her back was as straight and true as it appeared. He wanted to kiss her neck, undo the buttons all over again.

He turned her to him and touched her face. "All I think about is you. I think—I know—I'm in love with you."

He waited as she stared, her mouth slightly open, her beautiful eyes wide. For a moment, she did not speak. He drew back, wondering if he had spoken too soon, if he had scared her.

But then she smiled, and the coach filled with warmth, and she leaned in and kissed him. Then Alison stirred and they had to pull apart.

Outside, it began to snow. Everything turned white and beautiful. Stair stoops, iron railings, windowsills, slate roofs— even the alleyways and the shanties—were dusted with white.

Glasgow, transformed.

6

Hailey

AFTER DROPPING SAMUEL AND ALISON ON AR-
gyle Street, Hailey sat in reverie as the carriage clopped toward
home.

He loved her. He'd said he loved her. She could hardly believe it when he spoke. They were the words she had hoped for,
and she knew he had meant it.

She relived the kiss—that one long kiss that had extended
into forever. It had stirred her blood like nothing before. Even
now, her breath came in short gasps. She must calm down. She
couldn't go into the house this way. Hastily, she patted her hair
and re-pinned loosened strands. She ran her hands over the buttons of her dress and was relieved that they were still done. She
straightened her skirts and buttoned her gloves and took a deep
breath.

Samuel had such a sharp mind. He was like her father in
that way. Though her mother had been embarrassed when her
father had waxed on about coal, Hailey had been proud. So
much passion, to connect something as mundane as coal to the
wonders of the firmament. Samuel, too. When he talked about

building ships, how they were gifts from God, it revealed a life in tune with his desire.

And he loved her.

What had she said in reply? She couldn't remember. But she would tell him next Monday, would say it to him first thing. *I love you.* She would shout it if she could. *I love you!* For weeks now, she'd been dreaming of their future together. Surely, her father would see in Samuel what she did. He would see how intelligent he was, how ambitious. What did class matter when there was love? He was better than any of the men her mother wanted her to marry. Douglas McMillan was the latest—stuffy, dull, smugly assured of a life of inherited ease. He'd come for dinner on Friday night and spent the evening staring at her, hardly saying a word. All that mattered to her mother was Hailey's future position in society. She didn't care whether Hailey would be happy. Hailey would convince her father of Samuel's worth, and together they would convince Davinia.

She would help Samuel. She would believe in him. She would be by his side as he worked his way up through the shipbuilding ranks. She wouldn't mind a little poverty—it would be noble, and they would build a life together.

And he loved her.

AT HOME, SHE entered via the servants' door in the scullery, ignoring their knowing looks as she rushed past them. She stopped at the mirror hanging in the hallway. Her cheeks were flushed, and her lips looked bitten and swollen. She went to the pump and cupped water in her hands and splashed her face and pinned another loose lock.

Her parents were in the drawing room, her mother wringing

her hands, pacing along the edge of the Aubusson carpet, her father seated in a wing chair before the windows that overlooked the street. A decanter of brandy stood open on the marble table, a snifter at her father's elbow. Only a single candle illuminated the room tonight. Usually, her mother lit every candle in a room. Mired in an argument, they did not see her come in.

"You can't be serious, Harold. This can't be true. It's impossible."

"I'm afraid that it is very true."

"All of it?"

"Every bit of it."

Hailey said, "What's happened?"

Her mother whirled on her. "There you are, Hailey. Where have you been? The minister should not have kept you. It's far too late. And it's started snowing again. Did you make it home without trouble?"

"What's the matter, Mother? Father?"

"You can't take the carriage anymore, Hailey Rose," her father said. "We can't afford it."

"What do you mean?"

Her father spoke automatically, as if he were reading a list from the family ledgers. "Feed for the horses, maintenance of the carriage, paying the driver, the coachman." He turned. "Davinia. Do you and Hailey have enough frocks to make it through the winter? I don't want to shame you."

"Well, we won't be going to balls, so it doesn't matter, does it?"

Hailey was growing uneasy. "Mother? What is this?"

Her mother frowned, a vein pulsing in her high forehead. "Tell her, Harold."

Her father lifted his head and looked directly at Hailey for the first time. "The City of Glasgow Bank. All our funds were in it. Everything. We've lost it all."

"*You* lost it, Harold. *You*," Davinia said.

Hailey sank into a chair. "I don't understand."

Her father still spoke as if by rote. "The fraud at the bank was so extensive that they loaned out every single penny in their coffers to entities they had no business supporting. Across the world. Terrible investments, all. The result is complete collapse. Loss of all funds."

"Tell her the worst of it, Harold." Her mother had grown hysterical, vindictive. "How long have you known that we've lost everything?"

"Since October."

"*October!*" Her mother whirled again on Hailey. "He has been hiding it from us. *Your father.* What did you think, Harold? That money would magically reappear? That you wouldn't have to tell us?"

"But," Hailey said, trying to make sense of what she was hearing, "Father still has his salary—doesn't he?"

Her father's hand flew to his ear. "They let me go. They think I've become too cautious—too worried about the men. They want someone more—aggressive."

"We have nothing," her mother said.

"Nothing?" Hailey said.

"Nothing."

"But what does that mean?" Her thoughts were churning, the shock of *nothing* reverberating in her mind.

"It means, Hailey," her mother said, "that it's up to you now. Douglas McMillan has enough money to support us all. We'll have him for dinner—we must have enough in the cellars to feed him. Wear your lowest-cut dress. Kiss him, do whatever you have to do to secure him."

"But I don't love him. I hardly know him. I won't."

Her mother's gaze turned sour. "Don't you care about us?"

"Of course, but—"

"Then marry him."

Hailey shot to her feet. "You can't ask that of me. Father, please—"

Her father's voice lost its remote evenness, turning soft, gentle. "I've been thinking through everything. We'll go to America. I'll write the Seattle Coal and Transportation Company about a job. I've been reading reports. They'll be glad to have such an experienced hand. There are other coal mines in the area, if they don't want me. We'll start over. It will be an adventure."

"I don't want an adventure," Davinia said.

"Then the alternative is to stay in Glasgow," Harold said. "We'll need to sell the house, but there is still a considerable balance on the mortgage, so we'll reap only a little. And even then, the bank failure has depressed prices so much that we'll be lucky to break even. It's not good. If we stay, Davinia, we'll have to live in a lesser house. We won't have the money to buy. We'll rent—I don't know where. Something better than the tenements by the train station, where that Fiddes boy lives—a cottage, maybe, outside of town. We won't entertain, of course. The expense. No servants. But I'll do what I can. Perhaps I could clerk. You could take in washing. Hailey can help you."

Her mother's gaze turned wild. "You can't be serious." She seized Hailey by the shoulders, her face wretched with pain. "Save us, my darling girl."

Hailey twisted away. "Mother! Please—I—I can't."

Davinia scoffed. "If you don't marry Douglas, you'll doom Geordie to a terrible life. He's young. He'll have no education. He'll become a hod carrier or a newspaper boy or something horrible. Work in one of those factories. He'll get sick. Oh, my boy."

Davinia knew how much Hailey loved Geordie. "Please— don't put that on me—"

"I won't live in disgrace. I won't tolerate it. I beg you, Hailey."

"Mother, no—"

"Didn't you hear your father? We'll live in some horrible cottage—some awful—I can't stay in Glasgow under those circumstances—" She put her hand to her mouth, as if the full extent of what could occur had finally penetrated her cloak of anger. "My home," she wailed. "My life is here."

Hailey's knees almost buckled, hearing her mother's anguish. Hailey, too, had spent her entire life in this house, which her father had purchased in hopes of keeping it in the family for generations. Its white stone pillars, its stoop of solid granite, and its many mullioned windows had made their home seem permanent, their way of life irrevocable. Hailey had never once come home without a sense of stability. This drawing room had been the center of her mother's social life. She had presided over glittering parties that were the talk of monied Glasgow. Now the walls would be stripped of their art, the mantels of their ornaments. Their former life would be sold to the highest bidder. Hailey turned, mourning everything. The prospect of poverty overwhelmed her. Ruin. Destitution. A sober realization swept over her. Her mother could never consent to living as the Fiddeses did. And she, Hailey, who had just an hour ago thought such a life noble, was ashamed to admit her own fear. She was not as courageous as she had believed herself to be, dreaming of a future with Samuel. The magic of the past weeks with him drained away—the dreams, the sudden, miraculous intimacy, the hopes of a future together. In its place the cold reality of poverty. But she couldn't marry Douglas McMillan. She wouldn't deceive him.

Hailey turned again to her father, imploring him to intervene. "Don't make me, Father. Please."

"I'd never ask it of you, Hailey Rose."

Davinia shouted, "How dare you make me the villain here? You've lost our money, and so you lost any right to have a say. Hailey, I beg you."

Hailey felt her heart tearing in two. By refusing, she would doom them all to leaving Scotland forever, and herself to leaving Samuel. But the last minutes had shown her that a life with Samuel was an indulgent fantasy. She needed to put him out of her mind forever. But neither would she use a man she didn't love.

"I'm sorry, Mama. I can't."

"You stubborn, selfish girl," her mother said.

Hailey's father rose from his chair, his quizzical squint resolving as he pronounced, "America, then, and a better life."

With a scathing look at them both, Davinia stalked from the room and up the stairs, tears trailing in her wake.

"Father?" Hailey said, feeling her world crumble around her. "Is there any hope?"

"It's all my fault, Hailey Rose. Our prospects lie in America now, darling. Good prospects, too. A better future is there, I promise. Your mother is just being dramatic. I'm sorry that we have to cut short your life here—your charity work that you've loved doing. Especially your Monday evenings. Such initiative you've shown, such kindness. Please don't mourn too much. I'm sure in America you can resume your philanthropy. I'm so proud of you. Your mother will forgive you." He patted her hand and drifted from the room, absentmindedly taking the single candle with him.

Hailey, stricken, watched him go.

Outside, the snow continued to fall. A lamplighter set up his ladder and snuffed the streetlight. Midnight. The day was done. All turned dark as pitch.

7

Samuel

ON THE FIRST MONDAY IN DECEMBER, SAMUEL
sloshed through the blackened city snow onto Ann Street to
meet Hailey and Alison. He'd been released late from work and
so instead of going up to the room first, he went straight to their
corner. An hour passed as he paced, head swiveling at each new
clatter of wheels. Trains roared in and out of St. Enoch's, but
Hailey's carriage never came. Finally, he trudged up the six
flights of stairs to find Alison wrapped in blankets in the corner,
eating a crust of yesterday's bread. Samuel no longer stopped by
the grocer on Mondays, in anticipation of Hailey's hamper. Alison had been crying, traces marking her cheeks.

"Didn't Hailey come for you?" he said.

She shook her head.

"How long did you wait?"

"A long time. I was scared."

He could only wonder what had happened to Hailey. Fears
for her safety, her health, raced through his mind.

The following Sunday, he dashed to church, where Hailey
appeared as usual with her family in their pew. In his imaginings,

he had feared the worst, but she did not look ill. But neither did she glance his way. She sat rigidly. Her father moved as if through water, while Mrs. MacIntyre gazed at the altar, never opening her prayer book or hymnal, never tending to Geordie, who took advantage of this reprieve from parental vigilance to scramble in and out of the pew. Woodenly, the family rose and sat with the rest of the congregation.

Afterward, in the fellowship hall, Hailey pulled Samuel aside. "I tried to come, but—"

"Is it because of what I did? What I said? I'm sorry, I shouldn't have—"

"Father lost everything. Everything he had was in the City of Glasgow Bank. Everything. All his money. When I got home last Monday, Mama was raging. I thought she'd found out about us. But she hadn't. He'd just told her. He'd known for weeks. He was hiding it from us, carrying the burden alone."

Samuel could not absorb this.

"We have only the house and furnishings left, and our clothes, but that is all. Father says we have to sell everything. Even our house."

"But where will you live?"

"Father is going to sell the carriage and the horses, too, and—do you know what he said to me? He said he hoped that I wouldn't miss my charity outings too much." Her voice broke. "My outings. All this time, he's been suffering, and I've been lying to him. To both of them. I can't see you again. It's not right what I did." She wouldn't look him in the eye. He knew that if she did, she wouldn't be able to say these things. She cared for him, he was certain.

"What *we* did."

She pulled away. "My father is embarrassed even to be seen.

He says it was another failure of judgment. He believes he failed us."

"But we can still see one another, can't we?"

"Don't you understand? There is no more money for coachmen or carriages or extra hampers of food."

"I don't care about any of that, I care—" Samuel reached for her hand, but she pulled away.

"Please, don't," Hailey said. "All this time, I've deceived them. It's terrible what I've done. Take good care of Alison. Say goodbye to her for me." Finally, her eyes met his and he saw only anguish there.

Then she turned and walked away.

IN JANUARY, THE directors of the City of Glasgow Bank were tried in the High Court in Edinburgh and convicted of fraud. An audit exposed the full extent of their ineptitude. No money remained in their coffers. Not a farthing. The MacIntyres weren't the only ones to suffer. More than fifteen hundred businesses and firms closed. The fallout of the devastating collapse caused widespread suffering in the city. But Harold MacIntyre lost the most.

In the next weeks, Samuel neither spoke to nor approached the MacIntyres. From the mezzanine, he observed what their financial ruin cost them. They gave up their front-row pew with its tithing obligations and migrated to the back of the sanctuary, where by some charity of the rector they weren't banished to the mezzanine. Everyone but the minister ignored them. The social shunning extended even to the class of people they had newly joined. It was as if the MacIntyres' sudden poverty had made them pariahs to the wealthy and poor alike.

They held their heads high, but it couldn't disguise the fact that Mrs. MacIntyre's smile had turned brittle, and that Mr. MacIntyre stared into the distance in bewildered shock. He continued to flick his ear, until his wife forcibly held his hand down. From the mezzanine, Samuel saw in an agony of admiration that although all the light had gone from Hailey's eyes, her strength and beauty did not diminish. Her smile might be less quick, but her bearing was just as upright. The new angularity in her figure only heightened the graceful, easy way she moved. Her calm, defiant gaze when anyone in the congregation dared to stare delighted him. And her lips still provoked in him spasms of desire. But she did not return Samuel's attention with even a glimmer of a look. She held to her word.

Alison kept asking, "But *why*? Did I do something wrong? Doesn't she love us anymore?"

Samuel explained that Hailey had her own troubles now.

At the end of February, the ship's architect at John Brown shipyard extended Samuel's copy position another month and paid him five extra shillings a week. Suddenly, Samuel could afford a new shirt and suspenders. He paid a woman to sew Alison a new dress and a cobbler to make her new boots. He bought coal for the stove and a ticking from a dry-goods store. They ate better, too. He limped only when the damp got to him. They retained their same spare lodgings. Alison still worked at the textile factory. Samuel didn't like it, but they had no choice. She didn't seem to mind. He tutored her as well as he could.

He ached for Hailey. He dreamed that he could help her. But there was nothing he could do. As deprived as the MacIntyres were of their former wealth, they nonetheless were still far above him. And she still would not meet his eyes in church. The family left directly after services. No lingering for the newly disgraced, shamed by something they had no control over.

March turned unseasonably pleasant, a welcome respite after the dark, frigid winter, when the wind had howled down the Clyde in an endless gale. One Sunday after services, the congregation gathered outside. And this time the MacIntyres stayed, mingling among the congregation, moving from one person to another. Samuel caught Hailey's eye and she separated from her family and came toward him. Her face was drawn. She reached his shoulder, but her sadness made her seem even smaller than she was. Her eyes were fatigued, swollen, as if she'd been crying all night.

"We sail tomorrow morning for America. A dawn tide. We have to board this afternoon. We are going to the ship now. The *Circassia*. Father says it is better not to see the house again. He wants us to be brave."

"America?" Samuel said, in shock.

"A place called Washington Territory. Seattle, maybe, I don't know. Father's been formulating a plan. He has obtained a job there as supervisor of a coal mine. He is stoic. I think he might even be relieved. His guilt weighs heavier on him than ever. In these last few weeks, he's said that he believes the bank failure is his divine punishment for the High Blantyre explosion. He says he did not deserve the wealth that came to him, that he had made profits on the backs of broken men and he'd been careless with their lives. He says this will be his redemption."

Samuel heard Hailey talking but could not assimilate the information. It was as though a boom were echoing through his mind, drowning out all other sounds. A hole had been ripped in his heart. Hailey was going to leave him. She was going to America and disappearing from his life forever.

"You can't go."

"Father says we have just enough money for our passage. He says it is our new beginning. Our new hope."

She brushed a stray curl from her cheek. Samuel hungrily studied her face, the slight uptilt to her nose, the wide-spaced hazel eyes, the cupid's bow of her lips.

"When I met you, my life began," she said.

"Please don't go." He seized her hand. He didn't care who saw. "Stay. Stay with me. Marry me."

"Marry you?" Hailey's face lit with incredulity.

Samuel said, "We could marry and find a room together, make a home somewhere. They gave me a raise. Someday, there might be money, if the architect will apprentice me. You could work—"

"I don't know anything. All I can do is waltz and converse at dinner parties and lie to my parents. I don't know anything about how to live."

Samuel groped for answers. She was leaving him. "You could do anything—"

"Wash clothes? Be a maid? A governess?"

"Please stay with me." He was begging, hoping against hope.

"Don't you see? I dreamed of a future with you, Samuel, of a life where nothing mattered but us. But that's not real. My family needs me. Should I break with them so I can stay with you? I would never see them again. Who would take care of Geordie? My mother is distraught and can't see to him. She's been crying for a week. The carters have already come for our furniture. We have nothing and I can't leave them—"

Samuel pulled her to him and kissed her. She did not resist. Her soft lips parted and he tasted the salt of her tears. She was leaving him. Even as her arms wrapped around him, she was leaving him. He went on kissing her, ignoring the gasps and inhalations of people around them. He heard nothing but his heartbeat. He pulled her closer, lost in the kiss, lost in her supple body. She could not leave him if he was kissing her. He would kiss her forever, and then she couldn't go.

A pincer grasp on his neck wrenched him free. The minister was hauling him backward. Hailey lifted a hand to her lips, her gaze locked on Samuel. Hailey's mother was marching toward them. She seized Hailey by the elbow. The crowd had gone silent, titters of disbelief breaking through the shock.

Hailey's mother peered at her, eyes wild. Through clenched teeth, she said, "At *church*, Hailey? This boy is nothing, do you understand? Nothing."

"Nothing?" Hailey spat. "Do you mean like us? Penniless, homeless?"

"We are not like him. We are different."

"How, Mother? How are we any different?"

"In *every* way."

Mrs. MacIntyre's face was pale and lined, her beauty diminished by her worries. Samuel felt sorry for her. He wouldn't want her to have to live as he and Alison did. Nor did he want to tell Hailey that her mother was right. The MacIntyres *were* different. He could never imagine them living in a cold room without food or warmth. There was no nobility in poverty. And Mrs. MacIntyre—even in her fury, even in her downfall—still carried herself like a queen.

Marry me. Impossible, and yet Samuel needed Hailey to stay. A life without her? He would bargain with the devil himself to keep her here, even if it meant only that he would catch glimpses of her from the church mezzanine.

Mr. MacIntyre was shoving aside the crowd, pushing

through, his eyes dark with fury. He paused when he finally reached them, out of breath, hat askew, his gaze darting between the minister and Samuel, his daughter and wife. They had stood like this once before, almost on this very spot, when Samuel had rescued Geordie.

Harold MacIntyre reeled back and punched Samuel across the jaw.

Samuel staggered backward, clutching his chin.

Through blinding pain, he heard Hailey calling, as if from very far away, "Washington Territory. Remember, Samuel Fiddes. Remember! Washington Territory."

Part Two

1879

On: Rambles in North-western America

Though so much literary work is now done, and done so ingeniously, to induce emigrants from Great Britain and Ireland to settle on fixed spots in America or Canada that we frankly acknowledge having doubts as to the bona fides of many of these books of travel and exploration professing to describe new or unsettled districts of old countries which are now issued from the press . . . We have no intention of following Mr. Murphy through his varied wanderings in Washington Territory or his excursions in a strange land.

~*GLASGOW HERALD*,
17 MAY 1879

8

Hailey

IT WAS MID-APRIL, AND ALL HAILEY WANTED WAS to be clean again, to have every inch of her skin immersed in hot water. For more than a month, they had been moving, always moving, with no chance for a proper scrub or launder, only spit baths, her clothes grimy with perspiration and wear. She longed for the day when they would stop traveling, when she could peel away her damp, ruined clothes, her molding, waterlogged shoes, fill a tub with scalding water, and wash away the unholy patina of travel.

The crossing to New York had taken ten days, slowed by a March gale. The ship wallowed in deep troughs and teetered on towering crests. Traveling in second class, the MacIntyres fared far better than the passengers in steerage, though they grew ever more rumpled and uncomfortable. Everyone on board suffered. The crew washed down the decks with carbolic acid to remove the stench of vomit. Three days out, Geordie caught a fever. Restless and plaintive, he clung to Hailey, eyes dull with dread and seasickness. He called for his nanny, but she had been let go with the rest of the servants. He still couldn't manage *h*'s, so his plaintive *Lailey* carried in the screeching air. When they reached New York, his fever cleared, but not the hacking cough.

Their parents occupied their own dismal terrors. It was as if Hailey and Geordie no longer existed for them. Since leaving Glasgow, dour silence had characterized her parents' relationship, and when they did speak, they barked at each other. Only Geordie's fever caught their passing, if desultory, interest. It was as if they couldn't believe what was happening to them.

In New York, her father arranged for tickets on the steamer SS *Acapulco*, bound for Panama. He said they couldn't afford the immigrant train to San Francisco. In Panama, they crossed the forty miles of the narrow isthmus by rail, and from Panama City had embarked this morning for San Francisco, where they would change ships for Washington Territory.

To distract from her seasickness, and when she allowed herself, Hailey dreamed of Samuel Fiddes. Of his beautiful face and stubborn pride. The way he looked at her. His hands on her body. His lips on hers. The scintillating revelations of their closeness. From the moment he had first touched her, she'd wanted him. No. From before that, from the first time she had seen him, upright and strong, his black hair thick and wavy, his deep dark eyes sparkling, his shoulders wide, his jaw firm, he'd communicated a sense of dominion despite his poverty.

Remember, Samuel Fiddes. Remember! Washington Territory.

Back in Glasgow, after her father had struck Samuel, her mother berated her all the way to the ship. "What a display you made, shouting at that boy to come to Washington Territory. A boy like that will never come for you. Never. He isn't capable of such an extravagant gesture. I forbid you to think any more of him. He is nothing, do you understand? Nothing."

It was her mother's refrain. *Samuel Fiddes is nothing.*

"I love him, Mama."

Her mother had sighed and said, "You exhaust me."

Hailey knew now that all she had done by publicly kissing Samuel was to add to her father's overwhelming sense of failure. And her own sense of failure, too, for what kind of daughter disappointed her own father? Impassioned outbursts, no matter how deeply felt, bought no one anything in life. Halfway across the Atlantic, she'd apologized, acutely aware that happy endings—beautiful, joyful happy endings—were the work of fairy dreams. Life could be undone in a moment, and often was. An explosion. A bank failure. A plague. An accident.

On deck, she lifted her face to the sea breeze. The faint wind cut the equatorial heat. The sun was setting over the Pacific Ocean in a blaze of coral and purple. There was no one to see her here. No one to call Samuel *nothing*. It was impossible to think that she would never see him again.

But try as she might, no tears would fall.

THREE WEEKS LATER, in late May, a fine drizzle shrouded the wide Strait of Juan de Fuca as the side-wheel steamer *Louisa* chugged against a turbulent, outgoing tide. For six days, the steamer had labored up the coast from San Francisco under a strong onshore wind, forcing its forty passengers inside the stuffy day cabin. But now, at journey's end, there was only the mizzle, a bit of fog, and a light breeze. The MacIntyres were settling themselves on wooden benches sheltered in the lee of the ship, anticipation driving them to get a look at their future. What greeted them was a riot of sea life. To startled gasps, a school of spinning dolphins leapt in and out of the water, splashing great sprays of foam into the fog. Here and there, eagles dipped into the sea to snatch thrashing salmon from seagulls, left to squabble over a roiling mass of herring. The air smelled like sea and salt and unspoiled beauty. Hailey and her parents gaped in awe. All that remained of their wearying voyage was for the ship to buck the stubborn current, skirt the foggy hazards of shore and sea, and venture into the protected, sinuous drama of Puget Sound in Washington Territory, where farther in, on a jumble of steep hills nearly shorn of their last trees, the little town of Seattle awaited them.

Louisa had left Esquimalt Harbor on Vancouver Island an hour behind schedule, delayed by a bad rainstorm. The captain said it was a sound rule that no good skipper crossed the Strait of Juan de Fuca in the chop and wind of a Pacific Northwest squall, not if he wanted his boat to emerge unscathed from the fight. Captain Dugan Alexander Allaway was a barrel-chested, thick-jawed Scot from Edinburgh. Delighted to encounter Scots so far from home, the captain had invited the MacIntyres to dine at his table every night for the entire voyage. Fighting seasickness, Hailey could eat only small meals, but his kindness was welcome after the rigors of their long trip.

The mizzle and rain faded, the sky cleared, and the captain came down from the pilothouse to act as their tour guide. He stood like a preacher on deck and regaled the MacIntyres. "This is country like you've never seen before. Do you spy those mountains to the east? They dwarf the Highlands in beauty and height. And those two white monsters—to the north there and the south? Volcanoes. The Indians tell tales of those erupting, though I've never seen it." He gestured again, indicating the western range of mountains towering above the water. "That is the Olympic Peninsula and those mountains are the Olympics.

Don't they look as if God himself carved them while he was guttered on whisky?"

Hailey tried to imagine God intoxicated and armed with a knife, busy with creation.

"Over there," Allaway said, waving through a clearing mist toward a ghostly specter of islands barely visible in the distance. "That's the Archipelago de Haro. Och, that's just their fancy name. We mariners call those islands the San Juans. A hundred and fifty or so hunks of rock with a churning tidewater that'll take your breath away. Some so small there's barely room enough to plant the heel of your boot on them, others large enough you'd not be remiss if you mistook them for the continent. There's only two harbors deep enough to take the draft of a ship this big, but there are rocky shores aplenty that'll take the flat draft of a dory just fine. Are they not the image of Scotland, though? Come here, Geordie lad. See those there? You get homesick, you make your father bring you up here." He winked at Hailey's father. "Not long now. Eight hours or so to Seattle. We'll defy customs and skip Port Townsend today. The tide is with us." He returned to the pilothouse, and Hailey's mother and father retreated to the saloon with Geordie, but Hailey remained on deck as Puget Sound unfolded before her.

It was spellbinding country. The air was as clean as heaven, the light as shimmering as the Caribbean. It almost made up for the exhaustion of the past two months. Had her father known how beautiful Washington Territory was when they'd struck out from Scotland? He was a sphinx these days, revealing little, but Hailey felt a surge of hope as the wide waters shimmered before her. The sound's rugged shores and inlets cut a picture of unsurpassed beauty. It was mostly wilderness, but she caught occasional glimpses of sawmills in coves, and here and there wooden houses grouped close to shore, and even a long wooden canoe carrying natives. Everywhere was forest and water and sandy bluffs and rocky shores. Dolphins weaved in and out as silver fish jumped, and she caught sight of more than one whale spout and fin. Seals poked their heads above the water, their whiskers skimming the surface, black eyes assessing before they ducked under again. Hailey spent the whole day on deck, marveling at the wonder of it all. It was like the coast of Scotland, this wet and rocky shoreline, up near the Hebrides, where they had spent one long and glorious summer.

Toward evening, *Louisa* entered a wide bay as behind them a scarlet sunset bloomed over the jagged, snow-covered mountain ridge. Everywhere, land and water rippled in huge waves of bluff and bluster and stupefying beauty: the splendid bay, islands smothered in fir trees, the pleasing eastern mountains, and, at a break in the bay, what appeared to be an estuary fanning from a green river valley whose only reason for being seemed to be to frame the enormous snow-covered volcano the captain had told her was called Mount Tahoma.

Soon, though, the air began to reek of smoke and fish. The whole family joined Hailey on deck as *Louisa* pulled closer to land. A brown smudge appeared on a spit where several wharfs jutted into the bay. But it wasn't until Captain Allaway guided the ship to the longest wharf, an enormous crooked, slapdash thing that housed warehouses and squat shanties, that the smudge came into sharp relief.

Ramshackle wooden buildings tottered along a frontage street that rose on bluffs under scalped hills so steep and streets so misaligned that Hailey felt dizzy peering up at them. Cut logs had been driven into the waterfront bluffs, to keep the eroding land from sliding into the sea. Most of the buildings looked as if they had been clapped together from flotsam. A cupola topped the single building of grace: a white-frame edifice halfway up one hill. Dirt and sawdust paved the roadbeds. Stumps pocked the ground. Several factories and a foundry studded one waterfront cliff. A log boom to one side of the wharf corralled acres of sawed logs, as a sawmill above it whined even at this late hour. An island of ship ballast in the harbor housed tattered tents and a dozen beached canoes. A collapsed pier slumped in the bay, its half-eaten pilings tilting wildly. A pair of towering smokestacks loomed in the distance, and beyond them, a mudflat crossed by a train trestle bubbled with ooze.

Beside her, Hailey's mother gasped. "This isn't Seattle, is it?"

A deckhand throwing a line said, "That she is, ma'am."

It was a town so ugly that it defied belief.

9

Samuel

BILLY JOHN GRIPPED HIS MAUL AND HAMMERED A curve of steamed wood, fitting its grooves into the edge of the plank beneath it.

"You see, Fiddes, even for a boat this small, the calculations have to be just right. We did this one proper."

Billy John, an intense, voluble man two decades older than Samuel, had been assigned to apprentice him. Furrows lined Billy's forehead, his hands were crippled and callused from the cold and work, and his clothes were worn thin, but he knew his craft.

"There's nae much forgiveness in a hull, Fiddes, 'specially a wooden one. It has to be tight. And you hae to commit to a shape. Flat-bottomed, round, sleek, they all hae their purposes. You need to know where that ship is going, what waters she'll ply. Shallow, rough, big. You never want one—nae a lifeboat, nae even a river skimmer—to go down. So ye fit her for her purpose. Water is a mighty force. Have ye been out on the ocean? Ye best go out, Fiddes. Ye'll understand the force of the water then. It can toss a ship like a toy. Spin her like a top. If ye're wanting to build ships, ye need to understand the sea."

On and on Billy talked. On this cold April day they were steaming planks to set in place after their angles were marked, bevels laid, ends scarfed, everything bolted in tight. A steam box wet the wood enough to coax straight planks into a curve. They were building a twenty-five-footer, which needed stringers and a bulkhead, different from the smaller boats, whose hulls did not need the same support. Samuel had learned that wooden boats had to be caulked and soaked, and that the iron and copper fastenings required exacting attention to placement, for the wrong metal in the wrong place could corrode every fastening on a ship, and she would eat herself to pieces. Every day with Billy John was an education.

This dinghy was one of a dozen lifeboats for a new steamer whose iron hulk loomed nearby. Great iron ships in various stages of completion were lined up on stays perpendicular to the Clyde, surrounded by scaffolding and crawling with men. Samuel loved the shipyard's clanging and shouting, the wagons hurtling here and there, horses whinnying, mauls pounding. On credit, he'd purchased an augur, a cant hook, and a planer, and was angling for a bevel and chisel. Billy was generous with his tools, but Samuel wanted his own. They were a concrete step toward his future.

They inserted another plank into the steam box. It was Samuel's job to keep its fire burning, a menial task any child could do. But Billy believed that a shipwright was responsible for every inch of his ship.

In the long month since Hailey's departure, Samuel had thought of her every day. His pleasure at learning shipbuilding fought with his longing for her, and sometimes altered his view of Glasgow. It could be a bilious city, frozen even in April, full of general misery and abiding darkness, choked with coal smoke, slick with the offal of too many humans crammed together in too few spaces. But the Clyde also held promise, which he clung to even as Hailey's haunting refrain hummed underneath: *Remember, Samuel Fiddes. Remember! Washington Territory.*

"Get your head out of your arse, Fiddes, and clamp that plank so I can bend it, or ye'll nae be living tomorrow."

Samuel screwed in the bolts of the clamp.

Where exactly was Washington Territory; how did one even get there? He'd inquired. Twenty pounds just for one ticket in steerage to New York. For two, forty pounds. An exorbitant sum, equivalent to the college fees he could not afford. And the cost of the tickets was only the beginning. You had to purchase some kind of emigrant's kit for the voyage, and then there was the medical test to pass at the emigration station for third-class passengers, where a doctor peered into your eyes and mouth and examined your scalp and skin, on the hunt for diseases like typhus and goiter and trachoma. They would have to buy food, too, and find housing when they got to New York. And after New York, he'd have to get to Washington Territory. How did a person do that? How much money would that take? And there was the matter of Alison. Taking her out of Smyllum had been one thing, but spiriting her across the world, to a place he knew nothing about, was another thing entirely. Recently, she had begun to suffer from a cough. Sometimes she coughed all night. The fibers of the factory were working their way into her lungs.

"Lift it out, now, Fiddes, and let's measure her," Billy said.

They pulled the plank from the box and set it on a pair of sawhorses. Billy whipped out a protractor from his back pocket and measured the degree of curve.

"Bolt your end another two degrees to the right and not a smitch more."

THAT EVENING, ON the ferry back to Glasgow, Samuel stepped on deck to watch it dock, marking every detail of how it moved in the ebbing current. A ship had to manage shifting elements—wind, wave, current, and tide—and design dictated how well it performed. Shipbuilding, he was learning, was both an art and a science.

A thin twilight provided little illumination as Samuel climbed the steps to their tenement, where he discovered Alison lying in the straw, listless and feverish.

Samuel interrogated Milly. "How long has she been like this?"

Milly shrugged. She had been despondent in the months since learning that their brother could not send for them. "The lass came home round midday."

"You should have sent for me."

He knelt beside Alison. She was burning up. Dread swept over him, memories of the diphtheria that had killed his family. He paid a boy to take a note to Billy John to tell him he'd be out. Alison's illness lasted three days, and he prayed the whole time, resurrecting the small amount of his faith that remained. He couldn't lose her. If she died, he'd be alone—and he would have failed her. Despite eating better, this winter she had again grown skinny, hobbled by the cold. Lately, she'd been taking on that dusky, hopeless look he saw in almost every child in the tenements.

For three days and nights, Samuel felt powerless as fever

ravaged Alison's body. He kept watch for the formation of the awful membrane of diphtheria, but, to Samuel's great relief, Alison was suffering from something else. He'd heard that children in Glasgow died of illness at a higher rate than children in the rest of Scotland. He could not lose her. She was his responsibility, his life. He owed it to her to make sure that she survived her childhood.

APRIL BLED INTO May. Because of her long absence, Alison lost her job at the factory, and Samuel brought her to work with him, hoping that by being outside she could avoid the worst of Glasgow's scourges. She earned a pittance carrying notes at the shipyard, dodging the great ships under construction, ducking under scaffolding, and climbing ladders into massive hulls to deliver Mr. Hathaway's missives.

Samuel had built three dinghies with Billy when he graduated to building one on his own.

He completed it in two weeks. Billy said, "Well done, Fiddes. And now make another."

"How long?"

"Same length."

"No, I mean how long before I can build something bigger?"

Billy laughed. "Don't be daft. Ye won't be making anything bigger. Ye're a dinghy builder. That's what ye are now. That's what y'apprenticed to be. Be grateful. They're paying ye a fine wage. If ye keep on at your work, ye might get another few shillings a week in a few years. Half of Glasgow is outta job after the bank failure. Don't ye know when ye've made it good?"

At the end of the shift, Samuel took Alison by the hand and went to Mr. Hathaway.

"Sir, would you be willing to apprentice me again? I want—I need to learn engineering. I can't build dinghies forever."

"That's not the way of things, Fiddes. I told you that."

"But I—"

"Samuel, even if I were to take you on in some capacity, no one's ever going to give you the position you want. It's not about your native talent. You need a certificate. You need to know things I cannot teach you."

On the ferry, Samuel sat in the stern and watched Alison play along the rails. It was one of those rare spring Glaswegian evenings when a bright sun had graced the day, and now evening light lingered in a pink sky. As the boat churned past Queen's Dock, a great stillness overcame Samuel. Five impressive ocean-going steamers occupied the deep, newly dredged slips—bound for ports across the world. Glasgow, as the city liked to boast, was harbor to all the globe. The rational thing would be to abandon hope of ever seeing Hailey again. The world would always need ships. And dinghies. Chasing Hailey to Washington Territory would erase that security. He couldn't even be certain where the MacIntyres had gone.

He laid his head back, the wooden slats of the bench cradling his neck. He had nothing. No money for university. No money for steamship tickets. Nothing to recommend him to America. Just a few unpaid-for tools, his boots, Mr. MacIntyre's coat, and a job building dinghies. And Alison.

Glasgow had become a void after Hailey left. Before, the hope of seeing her, of being close to her, of talking with her, of touching her, had sustained him. To Samuel, Hailey MacIntyre had been home.

The Clyde bubbled away from the stern, flowing out to the firth, and from there to the Atlantic, and on to America, and somewhere beyond that to a place called Washington Territory, where Hailey was. Even as he thought this, Milly's brother's complaints flooded back. *He wished he'd never gone. He'd been a fool to leave. He'd gained nothing and lost everything important.*

It was nearly impossible to hold those two opposing thoughts in his mind at the same time.

TWO WEEKS LATER, in the predawn chill of a late-May morning, Samuel entered the gates of the south basin of Queen's Dock. He carried a bag containing his tools and clothes. Heaving it over his shoulder, he took Alison's hand and skulked from shadow to shadow to the base of the steep ramp to an enormous ship, the *State of Nevada.*

Yesterday, the captain of the *Nevada* had hired him as a fireman. He was going to be paid to shovel endless tons of coal into the ship's boilers to move this hulk of iron through the ocean to New York. Alison, however, was another story. With a cautionary finger to his lips, Samuel picked her up and stole up the ramp and across the deck to the recessed door that led into the working bowels of the steamer. He moved with stealth, fearful of detection by an early-rising crew member or an overeager watchman. Yesterday, he had memorized the decks of the ship when his new boss gave him a tour. Now, in whispers, he coaxed Alison down three ladders to deck four, went through a set of hatchways to the aft, and slipped down a corridor to a closet.

Light flared around the doorjamb at the end of the corridor. He froze midway.

"Samuel—"

"Shh!"

Ten more steps to safety. He took them, holding his breath, then eased the door of the closet open, sidled inside, and let out his breath.

"It's dark in here," Alison whispered.

The large closet stored disused linens and smelled of must. Until they passed Queenstown, the final port of call for ocean-going ships, Alison would have to stay out of sight. After that, it would be only the Atlantic before them, and he could let her loose to wander among the steerage passengers undetected, per-haps even claim a free bunk. He was stealing her passage. Im-moral, perhaps. But what extra fuel would it cost to move a ship with her meager weight aboard? Besides, he was the one shovel-ing the coal. If anyone's back would suffer, it was his.

"It's dark," Alison whispered again.

"It's only for a couple of days. Make a nest of the linens. Be a lady of leisure. I'll visit you and bring you food. When it's safe, I'll let you out. I'll be working. Do you understand? I have to work. And you have to be brave. Braver even than before. As brave as you can imagine. Can you do that, Ali?"

"But what about . . . ?" she trailed off, embarrassed.

"I'll bring you a bucket. It's just for two days. That's all. And I've brought you some bannocks. And some nuts. I'll find you cider, too, if I can."

It was very dark in the closet. He could hardly make out her small frame. He could not, thank goodness, see her fear.

"Can you be still now, Ali? Can you stay in here like I'm say-ing? Promise me, now. Promise."

She nodded.

He fixed a nest of linens around her. "You're safe here. Don't go anywhere. Do you understand me?"

She murmured sleepily in assent.

"I'll come back when I can. Until then, you're to be quiet as a mouse."

He had to report soon, but for now Samuel eased his way back into the corridor and climbed up to the deck. Dawn lightened the sky. Sailing wasn't until three, but a line of travelers was forming at the gate, their barrels and cases and cloth bags kept close beside them, each family an island of anticipation and worry.

Beyond Queen's Dock, beyond the mighty shipyards, up on the hill, the great sandstone edifices and cathedrals of Glasgow stood fast against the whipping winds of Scotland. Samuel studied their grimy beauty. Everything—the screech of the seagulls, the chilly gray of the sky, the distant tile roofs—seemed strange and important to him. For the thousandth time, he weighed staying. Was it madness to follow the whims of his heart, to gamble everything? Was it reckless? No doubt. But all his desires were embodied in this act. To build ships, to find Hailey, to keep Alison safe. If he was a fool, he was vulnerable in the way that all fools were, but life here offered only grim alternatives. And life in Washington Territory, if they ever got there, offered the hope of more, and the hope of Hailey. *Remember, Samuel Fiddes. Remember!*

He took one last look at the towers and domes of the city. He would never visit his family's graves again. Never lay thistles or shed tears to wet the soil that sheltered them. And no one would remember him or Alison after the wake of *State of Nevada* washed them down the Firth of Clyde and into the English sea.

A step forward, or a step backward? Shoveling coal again.

No one had heard anything from the MacIntyres. Not a letter, not a word.

They had disappeared into America.

And now so would he and Alison.

10

Hailey

SEVERAL DAYS AFTER FIRST SETTING FOOT ON the soggy soil of Seattle, Hailey huddled under an overhang in a driving rain with her mother and brother, waiting to board a train of the Seattle and Walla Walla Railroad to Newcastle.

Hailey's body still swayed from their two months at sea. The gray sky was flinging buckets of water at them. Their clothes wouldn't dry. Her mother had worn her best dress to make a good impression, and as she brushed rain from her sodden cloak and studied her muddied hem, her lips moved in silent fury. On the endless voyage, she, too, had been crippled by seasickness and stunned by their change in situation. Now her hazel eyes were veiled with defeat. Hailey's father's fine features had grown ravaged, his trademark warm smile faded. At some point, he had abandoned ear flicking for an unapproachable absentmindedness, and even now, surrounded by strangeness and the pouring rain, he stood apart, his felted bowler hat no match for the deluge.

On *Louisa*, a woman with steely curls at the next table had heard her father talking about Newcastle, which he had revealed to the family as their final destination only after they'd left San

Francisco. A coal town, about eighteen miles from Seattle by rail. The Newcastle mine was important to Seattle, he'd assured them. Aside from timber, coal was Seattle's biggest industry. Their housing would be assured, as he would be the superintendent. There was nothing to worry about. He had arranged everything.

The eavesdropping woman turned a crooked eye on them and snorted, "Newcastle? Cougar Mountain, more like. Big cats over there. Keep out an eye for bears, too."

Hailey's mother turned in alarm. "Big cats?"

"Oh, they're everywhere, but the worst of it is the mud." The woman assessed their footwear. "Get your hands on some rubber boots."

So, yesterday they had purchased the recommended rubber boots, but none of them had thought to wear them to the train.

It occurred to Hailey as she inspected her ruined leather shoes that none of them possessed the common sense they would need for this new life.

A far cry from the relative splendors of St. Enoch's, the S& WWRR depot was a shed at the end of a frontage road called Commercial Street, a dirt avenue of crooked wooden buildings with sagging roofs—mostly saloons and shops and an occasional warehouse. Only one side of Commercial was planked with a sidewalk, which undulated in uneven repair.

The family had spent the previous two nights at the American House, a thin-walled hotel perched on a low rise above the shoreline, with a view of the long wharf where *Louisa* had deposited them. It advertised itself as the "Best and Cheapest House in town for a Poor Man"—small comfort to her mother, who had wanted to stay at the Occidental Hotel, which she'd learned on *Louisa* was the finest in Washington Territory. The rambling white building stood opposite the American House, overlooking a misshapen plot of land called Occidental Square, ambitiously named, given it was a muddy soup where a tall flagpole cast a long shadow and a silver telegraph wire hummed along its edges. Too expensive, her father pronounced, and so they'd climbed the steps to an attic room of the American House, her mother weeping. It was the kind of place where single men paid room and board and considered it home.

They'd gotten no sleep. The occupant in the next room snored the whole of the night and the sawmill whined all day. The first afternoon after their arrival, Hailey slipped away while everyone napped. In the end, she wished she hadn't. Seattle was a thrown-together place, its unpainted wooden buildings weathered and leaning, consisting mostly of taverns with barely clothed women hanging from upstairs windows. Shocked, Hailey hurried past as several men on the street catcalled after her. Painted signs advertised gambling. Drunken men shouted and spilled along the streets. A single shop sold notions and buttons and dress patterns, and another advertised ice cream—but Seattle felt like a place where no woman should walk alone. And it was cold. A south wind had kicked up off the bay, blowing in the kind of damp chill that invaded bones. No worse than Scotland, really, but knowing that a warm fire in a snug house wasn't waiting for her at the end of her walk made the sensation infinitely more disagreeable. The whole place was infused with a fishy, saltwater tang underscored by sawdust.

At one point, she thought she saw Samuel walking toward her. She had seen that beautiful face so often in her mind's eye that now it appeared before her.

But when the man walked past, he looked nothing like Samuel.

It was fatigue, she told herself. Grief. She returned to the

American House. What a silly fantasy she had built in her mind. Samuel would come for her? Such notions could only disappoint. She had seen for herself how large the world was. She had to grow up. She wasn't a naive girl anymore. She slipped back into her room and lay down on the bed next to Geordie, and this time could not keep herself from weeping.

The conductor called for boarding. The train pulled a single passenger car trailed by a dozen empty coal cars, which moments earlier had dumped their contents into bunkers at the pier where *Louisa* was now tied. Hailey looked longingly at the ship, wanting desperately to sail back to Scotland and their old life.

A dozen or so passengers scattered themselves in the car. Hailey and Geordie occupied a wood-slatted bench across the aisle from their parents. Geordie clambered on top of the seat and peered through the rain-streaked windows, eyes wide. Hailey wrapped her arms around him to steady him, taking momentary comfort in his solid weight. She hoped the train ride would distract him and make him forget his nanny, for whom he still cried at night.

They rumbled off, crossing a long, curving trestle above an expanse of tideflats before it entered the river valley, a cultivated stretch filled with farms and, to her surprise, a fenced-in racetrack, complete with viewing stands. The train stopped several times to pick up people on the side of the tracks, and once at a place announced as Steele's Landing, a white house nestled in a bend of the river. After an hour, they arrived in Renton, a town made up of a few houses, empty lots, and a store called Gum King & Co., its English sign underwritten in Chinese characters. Despite the incessant rain, passengers were made to debark because an extra locomotive had to be added.

The MacIntyres stepped under the store's slanted eave to

wait. They heard two men arguing nearby over just who was responsible for building the railroad.

"Gum King ran the Chinese labor for the last of it, not Chin Gee Hee. But people don't know that."

"I tell you, it was Chin Gee Hee."

"Well, you'd be wrong. Chin Gee Hee may run Seattle labor, but down here at the base of the lake, it's Gum King. He ran three hundred Chinamen hacking through the wilderness to lay down that railroad in underbrush so dense you couldn't see two feet. All of them camped out there, sleeping in tents, opium thick as clouds. You think you're in America, and then you turn the corner, and you're in China."

Inside the store, several Chinese men stood in a tight circle, their strange high-pitched syllables and halting speech incomprehensible. Hailey had never seen Chinese before. They seemed exotic and frightening, part of all the newness in her life.

Oblivious to the chatter, her father stared out at the muddied railroad workings. Aside from his air of distance, his temper had grown short over the course of their travels. He had thrown a glass at a waiter in the second-class dining room on *Circassia*, and on the train crossing the Panama isthmus he had raged when he had to stand because so many peasants had crowded their third-class car with their pigs and chickens.

There was a boom as the second locomotive was coupled, and they were allowed to pick through the puddles and mud and climb back into the car.

The train left the depot and crawled along a sparsely logged lakeshore. The lake's surface boiled with raindrops under low clouds that almost obscured an island in the middle of the lake. They began a long, slow rise as barefoot children darted out of a clutch of rough-hewn cabins to throw rocks at the train.

Moss-draped logs and enormous ferns carpeted thick woods. In places, sunlight did not penetrate, but here and there patches of clear-cut let in a glimmer. Geordie cooed at the wild landscape as her father gazed out the window and her mother gripped her reticule in silence. Several times, Hailey had to shut her eyes, because it felt as if the train were flying through the sky over bridges pieced together with twine. In the middle of one endless trestle stretched across a deep gorge—so high a crow flew underneath them when she dared a peek—Hailey feared they might plunge to their deaths. Finally, at a small, tree-rimmed lake, the tracks leveled, made a last turn up a final rise, then exhaled to a stop, brakes and whistle screeching.

They disembarked onto muddy ground circled by fir trees so tall that it was impossible to see their tops. Rain still slashed the sky. In this savage deluge, there would be no keeping an eye out for bears or wildcats. Nor was there shelter, sign, or depot, just a wye junction to turn the locomotives.

But there was industry.

A nearby blacksmith's forge glowered with heat. A sawmill whined behind it, sawdust flying. Elevated sheds housed Chinese men hunched over shifting screens, hands skittering like crabs, sorting coal. It tumbled down an incline into overhead storage bunkers that straddled the tracks. Underfoot, shards of shiny black coal littered the hardpan. As they waited for their bags, engineers detached the locomotive and shunted the empty coal cars they'd dragged from Seattle into position under the coal bunkers. Everything made a racket.

Geordie's legs, protruding from his short pants, streamed with rain, mottling his skin with cold. Rivulets ran down Hailey's neck. She pushed away a wave of self-pity. This would be her new resolve. To refuse to give in. The conductor was helping

Mr. MacIntyre to stack their bags and trunks under the dripping overhang of a large fir. Other passengers, less burdened, streamed away, wielding bumbershoots against the rain.

"Harold," her mother said. "Where is the carriage you promised?"

Her father mumbled something inaudible. The conductor suggested they leave their things and walk to the cookhouse, where they might be able to locate Charlie Bane, a miner who worked the night shift but sometimes hired out his wagon. It was worth trying, the conductor said, casting a doubtful glance at the heap of their possessions.

"Cookhouse?" her father said.

"The lodging. Up the hill," the conductor said, pointing. "In town."

Her father immediately set out, leading them up a muddy gash of road. They'd gone two steps when the bunker chutes opened above the railcars and a deafening hail of falling coal split the air. Geordie burst into tears. Her mother held her hands to her ears. Hailey, slipping and sliding, dragged her little brother up the hill. But her father, inured to the cacophony of coal towns, continued on unperturbed.

The town wound through a bleak, narrow valley shorn of its trees, stumps pocking the ground. A washboarded, potholed main street meandered up to a rise where a church occupied a low ridge. A hundred squat, one-story houses bordered a wide street and side lanes dead-ending in the surrounding dense woods. Coal smoke poured from stovepipes. Slag heaps smoldered thirty feet high, emitting noxious fumes. Unpainted sheds leaned off balance, threatening collapse.

Her mother seemed to take the ugliness as a physical blow. Though she was married to a coal engineer, she had never once stepped foot inside a coal town. Hailey had thought that nothing could ever be as ugly as Seattle, but this gallimaufry of a town surpassed it in spades. Soaked through, teeth chattering, they climbed the rain-slicked wooden sidewalk and mounted the stairs to a crude boardinghouse. Inside, the building smelled of wood rot.

A man brandishing a dripping scrub brush popped his head over the balustrade of an open stairway in the small lobby. "How do? Devil of a day to try to keep things clean, isn't it?"

Her mother was prying her sodden gloves from her hands. "Are you the innkeeper?"

"More like a bed and boardinghouse, but I'm in charge."

"My husband, Mr. MacIntyre, has accepted the position as superintendent. You failed to send a carriage for us, and so, as you can see, we are drenched. Didn't you hear the train whistle?"

"Davinia," her father said. "Let me—"

She ignored him, easing her right glove from its vise grip. "We have been assured that we have housing arranged. We sent ahead that we were coming."

"Is that so?" the man said, climbing to his feet and clomping down the stairs, his canvas pants soaked with sudsy water. At a desk, he fumbled through some notes, then flipped open a ledger. Furrowing his brow, he said, "I'm not seeing—"

"We were promised accommodations. Surely you are aware of that, Mr.—"

"Berg. I assume it was Mr. Shattuck with whom you corresponded? The superintendent?"

"My husband is the superintendent. The new one. We're here now and we're tired and we'd like to be shown to our accommodations."

Mr. Berg narrowed his gaze. Measuring his words, he said,

"This time of day, Mr. Shattuck is usually down the mine. No doubt he'll be up soon and he'll clear this up."

Her father removed his hat and held it against his chest, running his finger along the brim. "A mine this new needs someone like me. They'll be thrilled to have some know-how from Scotland. These Americans—"

"Welsh, mostly," Mr. Berg interjected cheerily. "And English and Scots. Hardly a bona fide American among us."

Her mother trained a sharp eye on her father.

"Davinia," he said. "When I told you that the mine had offered me work, that was not true in the unequivocal sense. I didn't want you to make a fuss about coming—"

"A fuss?" she said. *"A fuss?"*

"This is the place for us, Davinia, I know it is. We can start over here. It's as far from Scotland as can be."

"Harold MacIntyre, are you saying that you have no position here?"

He stared.

"You lied to me, Harold?" she shrieked. "You put us on a ship and brought us halfway around the world to this horrid place on a *lie?"*

Geordie, who had been trailing a long-legged spider on the floor, looked up, startled at this unfamiliar violence. He, too, began to shriek. Hailey scooped him into her arms and took him to the window and its view of the drab little town, the incessant rain, the muddy mess. They had spent two months—*two months*—traveling. On a lie. She'd left Samuel behind because her father had lied.

In the distance, the train screeched and departed. Hailey buried her head in Geordie's neck and clucked at him to soothe him, but she was really trying to quell her own rising panic.

"Hush, Davinia," her father said. "They'll hire me. I know they will. They need me."

A strangled noise erupted from her mother's throat. In one awful moment, she put her hand to her mouth, bent over, and vomited onto the floor.

"Goodness, madam." Mr. Berg's gaze flickered between the mess on the floor and her father, who was focused in a way he hadn't been since they'd left Glasgow. It was as if her mother's collapse had somehow revived him.

"Mr. Berg, where did you say—Mr. Shattuck, was it?— would be? The mine? Can you direct me?"

"Sometimes he supervises the loading of the train," Mr. Berg said. "You may have passed him without knowing. Or you could ask for him at the mine entrance. He usually tells the carters if he is going in. The entrance is down the road, to the right, smack in the middle of everything."

"Mama," Hailey said, setting down a wailing Geordie. She hadn't called her mother *Mama* in a long time. She crouched beside her on the floor. Her mother was shivering now, shaking as if she would never get warm. Hailey had to do something, say something, so she uttered the first comforting words that came to mind, though she did not believe them. "Mama, it will be all right. It has to be."

Her mother sat back on her knees and regarded Hailey with a cold gaze that terrified her. "Don't be stupid, Hailey. Nothing will ever be all right again."

11

Samuel

ALISON SPENT THE VOYAGE FROM GLASGOW TO New York sleeping in the linen closet, unable to find an empty bunk after all. When they arrived in Manhattan, Samuel distracted the immigration official at Castle Garden so that Alison could slink past without discovery, which she managed with all the ease of a girl who'd spent the past year slithering under looming machines and running invisible though the streets of Glasgow. At customs, the officer cocked one eye and informed Samuel that Washington Territory was thousands of miles away yet. Why did he want to go to such a faraway, wild, hardscrabble land that wasn't even anything anyway?

Samuel ignored this and asked about the cheapest way there.

The officer shrugged. "Ship. Through Panama. Cheaper than the immigrant train to California."

With his fireman's wages, Samuel paid a week's room and board at a flea-infested hotel near Castle Garden, bought a newspaper, and scoured the Shipping News for a list of arriving and departing ships. The Pacific Mail Steamship Company's *Colon* was to sail in a day's time to the Isthmus of Panama. Its pier was at the foot of Canal Street on the North River.

They hired him in an instant. Shoveling coal was brutal work. No one wanted to do it.

Since the moment they had left Scotland, every sinew of Samuel's body screamed with pain. The muscles in his back and arms had grown taut as a slingshot, and the shinbone of his once-broken leg ached constantly. He was never clean. And there wasn't enough food in the world to slake his hunger. The heat of the engine room created its own kind of fatigue, but just being at sea was exhausting. The glint of the sun off the water, the rocking of the ship, the endless empty vistas—even the fresh air—wicked the life from him. And yet there was more than another month of the same ahead.

Once again, Samuel smuggled Alison aboard, this time in the deep of night, but soon after leaving New York, the captain discovered her, and in a fury put her to work mopping hallways and rooms to pay for her passage. She slept in steerage on a shared bunk with a family with only one child, and Samuel slept on a rocking hammock in a windowless crew cabin at the stern with the other firemen. As on *State of Nevada*, he worked four hours on, four hours off.

Several days out of New York, Samuel took a break on the aft deck, Alison asleep against his chest. He leaned his head back, feeling the thrum of the engine through the wallboards. Time had stretched. It seemed like months and months since they'd left Scotland, but only weeks had passed. Ocean waters did that, he'd discovered. He'd also discovered that he had launched himself and Alison into a world far more immense than he had known. Beneath this realization lurked the terrible fear that the MacIntyres could be anywhere. Washington Territory had been Mr. MacIntyre's stated destination—but on the streets in Manhattan City, a dozen men had promised Samuel jobs, mostly in mines in a nearby state called Pennsylvania. Had the offer tempted Mr. MacIntyre? Had he abandoned the long voyage to Seattle? Night after night, these terrible possibilities played in Samuel's mind.

He was beginning to understand that America was nothing like Scotland. It was a place that believed in itself, a country that harbored wild optimism. Anyone with determination in his soul and grit in his heart could prosper. That feeling—true or false— was infectious. There would be no turning back, despite his worries. He was determined. But he and Alison were two months behind the MacIntyres, two months during which anything could have happened.

For now, though, the air smelled of salt, the lingering scent of rain, and the clean wash of sea. Samuel shut his eyes and listened to the rushing seawater.

I'm coming, Hailey. I'm coming.

12

Hailey

ANY DREAM OF A BATH VANISHED THE MOMENT Hailey stepped inside the four board-and-batten walls of the house the coal company rented to them. Like all the others in town, it measured twenty-four feet by twenty-five feet and consisted of a long, narrow front room that served as living, dining, and scullery, and two bedrooms separated by a flimsy wall. A layer of grime covered a single table, two bed frames, and the plank floor. Everything reeked of must. A coal- and wood-burning stove occupied one corner of the front room and served as both heater and cookstove. There was no bath. Water had to be fetched from a nearby spring. The privy stood twenty feet behind the house; an open garbage pit lay between them, where two enormous rats were rummaging in the previous occupant's waste.

No one in Newcastle, and certainly not CB Shattuck, the mine supervisor, rejoiced over the arrival of a Scottish engineer with grandiose ideas about educating them. It was clear the moment her father returned from speaking with Shattuck that his expectations had been quashed. He'd been offered the job of fire boss. The previous one had quit the day before, lured north by word of gold in the Skagit Valley. The job paid two dollars a day, a full dollar less than miners equipped with their own tools, and only a little more than the carpenters, tracklayers, and trap boys earned. House rental was ten dollars a month.

Hailey's mother pulled a handkerchief from her bag and wiped the seat of one of two ladderback chairs. She sat down and did not speak for an hour. Her father helped Charlie Bane retrieve their things from the tracks as Hailey took stock. Their trunks were full of fine clothes and Doulton china. Useless now. What they needed was a mop and bucket.

Charlie Bane read Hailey's mind. "The company store is just down the way. It's not as bad as some. Fair prices. They'll keep a credit running for you and take out what you spend from your da's pay. Down the main road. Painted white. Can't miss it."

Against her parents' wishes, Hailey took Geordie and ventured down the lane, still wearing her drenched clothes. The mine, it seemed, worked around the clock. Its timbered entrance lay fifty feet from their house, and coal cars rattled in and out, pulled on rails by trudging mules who blinked and brayed in the sudden light. Another train had arrived, and the grating thunder of coal tumbling down the long chutes reverberated up the little valley. Coal mining seemed to require an awful lot of shouting. Hailey realized that there would never be a moment of quiet here. They lived in the middle of a factory.

She was relieved that the store, at least, was a neat clapboard structure that stood apart from the town and depot. The aproned clerk behind the counter raised his eyebrows at her sodden appearance. She set Geordie down to play with some carved wooden animals for sale while she bought a broom, mop and bucket, a bar of soap, another bucket for carrying water, and a burlap bag of beans, which the clerk told her would make a fine night's supper. Did they have a cooking pot? Well, she'd need one of those, too. A spoon to stir them up? Tin plates and cups? Utensils? What about coffee for the morning? Salt and pepper? She'd have to buy the coal for the stove up at the mine. It was the bad stuff they couldn't sell, lots of clinkers, but it would heat well enough. Did they have bedding? No? Well, they'd need two horsehair tickings. And blankets, too. What about a lantern? Kerosene? Matches? Milk? That she'd have to collect in a bucket when the milk train arrived in the morning. Milk cows wouldn't produce in this racket. The boy would deliver her purchases in an hour. That would be ten dollars. He'd put it on their account. Hailey shuddered. Though she had no idea of the value of a dollar compared to a pound, with the house rental and this, they were already twenty dollars in debt, which seemed a lot.

Before she left, she said, "How do I cook the beans?"

"Beans? You don't know how to cook beans?" A young blond woman with a bouncing step approached before the clerk could answer. "Why, that's the easiest. Just triple the amount of water to the amount of beans. Soak 'em first, though, then boil 'em up till they're edible. If you have an onion or bacon, throw that in."

She had a young baby strapped to her chest and wore a plain muslin dress and thick rubber boots. "We all saw you this morning coming from the train and wondered who you were."

"My father is the new fire boss."

"And you're not married?"

"No."

"Well, the boys are going to be happy. Hardly a single girl of marriageable age for miles and miles." She extended an ungloved, chapped hand and shook Hailey's. "I'm Bonnie Atherton. This is my baby, Angus." She stroked her son's head. "Four months old today. My husband mines. We came from San Francisco."

"Hailey MacIntyre."

Bonnie eyed the pile of purchases on the counter. "Didn't come prepared, huh, even with all those trunks? You can ask me anything. Our house is up by the church, third house on the right. The location keeps us from some of the coal dust, but not all. It's in the air here. You never get used to it. Well, I'm off." And she danced out the door.

Hailey turned to the clerk. "Do you have an onion? And a knife?"

Geordie held up one of the animals, a sleek, beautiful horse, but Hailey denied him. She had already spent far more money than they possessed.

That night, Hailey prepared the first meal of her life, under-cooking the beans over a weak fire while her father attempted to sweep and her mother stared into the distance. Afterward, lying in the bed she shared with Geordie, she listened to her mother weep through the wall as her father snored. She understood that nothing was predictable now, not where they would live or whether they would have enough to eat. Not even in her worst imaginings had Hailey thought that her father would lead them into darkness. Outside, the wind blew, rattling the windows and insinuating itself between the gaps in the batten boards. A steam whistle shrieked, signaling the next shift. Lantern light blotted out the darkness. They would need curtains. And more blankets come winter.

The irony of their circumstances assailed Hailey. They were as destitute as the poorest of Glasgow, mired in the very situation they'd fled Scotland to avoid. They could have stayed, her mother's humiliation be damned, and been recipients of the food hampers she had once distributed, which she, at least, would have welcomed. Or perhaps she should have married

Douglas McMillan, with his stolid, dull eyes, his mind-numbing silences, and his pockets full of money, saving her family from their present calamity. The cost of her refusal now was this. But even if Douglas had been the most charming man in the world, he wasn't Samuel.

Hailey fell asleep to the sound of her mother's hiccups.

HAVING NEVER COOKED, cleaned, laundered, or even dressed themselves without the help of an army of servants, the MacIntyres were mystified by the practical skills of living. Until this moment, neither Hailey nor her mother had any notion of the amount of labor the servants had performed on their behalf. The lighting of fireplaces, the provisioning of the kitchen, the laundering of clothing and scrubbing of floors, the dusting of window ledges and polishing of furniture, the painstaking cleaning of crystal chandeliers, had been accomplished for them by a troop of silent maids and footmen moving invisibly through their home, providing them with lives of comfortable privilege.

Hailey suffered from fewer years of privilege than her mother, but she was equally stunned at the amount of work that staying alive required. Feeding themselves posed perplexing challenges. Coaxing coal to flame in the stove required constant stirring with a poker. They burned a lot of food before they learned the basics. They subsisted mostly on beans and, if they were lucky, eggs purchased from their neighbors who kept chickens. They failed at every attempt to make bread until the sociable Bonnie knocked one day and discovered them staring at a burned, unleavened loaf they had just pulled from the oven. Astonished at their helplessness, she returned the next day to teach them the fundamentals of sourdough, sharing some of her own starter, which had been nursed across the ocean on her mother's sojourn from Norway, and then Bonnie's from San Francisco. Meat? Meat required hunting and a hunting rifle. A domestic pig necessitated a pen and the willingness to hunt it down when it escaped. Chickens needed a coop, and vegetables a garden, all of which required time and even more obscure expertise than any of them possessed. The available fruit was wild berries, but none of those had yet ripened.

Within mere days of their arrival, Hailey's body ached from all the work. But soon it responded to the challenge. Her arms grew muscled, her waist taut, her thighs strong. Knowing that her body could answer the day's demands gave her confidence. She might be marooned in a strange and awful place, but her body, at least, was up to it. But she was also conscious of male eyes following her wherever she went, even to gather water at the spring or to walk with Geordie down to the creek, where for a few moments they could escape the sulfurous fumes of the mine tailings. She knew that at least half of the hundred miners working at the mine were single. A few attempted to introduce themselves, and one even ventured an offer of a walk in the woods. Hailey ignored them all.

NEWCASTLE, HAILEY SOON learned, was surrounded by a wilderness unlike anything in Scotland, filled with the bears and big cats the woman on *Louisa* had warned them about. The bears—huge brutes that showed little fear even in the daytime— had to be run off from the garbage pits with clanging pots and noisemakers. Even the odd, scrappy animals called racoons that stole trash from their garbage pit seemed like terrifying beasts to Hailey. They bit if you ventured too close, an awful prospect because they nested near the privy. At dawn and sunset, a cougar would sometimes slink at the edges of the town, camouflaged in the shadows. Occasionally at night they stole roosting chickens from their coops, and the frantic squawking would wake the town. Hailey could never get back to sleep, because men made a racket rushing into the night with rifles and lanterns, even though it was better to shoot the cats out of the crooks of trees in the daytime while they napped. Hailey shied away from the clearing where hunters hung the carcasses from tree branches. The cats had grim, yellowed teeth and sleek, muscled bodies. And the coyotes! Those wild dogs made a yipping racket at night, calling to one another as they killed prey who cried with primal, sorrowful wails.

Her father had not warned Hailey or her mother what life was like in a coal town, and though Hailey could forgive him, her mother could not. Davinia particularly complained that the slag heaps burned off waste and leaked poison into the air. Everything they owned began to sour, even the primitive furnishings they had paid a mine carpenter to fashion for them. They used their packing trunks as furniture since there was nowhere to put them. And finally, the garbage dump continued to attract rodents. Hailey purchased a single mousetrap and learned to drown the invading voles and field mice in a pail in the corner, distressing Geordie, who wanted to play with them.

Aside from Bonnie Atherton, the six hundred citizens of Newcastle were not welcoming. It seemed that Bonnie was indiscriminately friendly, heedless of the ridicule flung at Hailey and her family. Hailey overheard things, growing aware that their waterlogged passage through town that first day had caused a sensation. It became clear that the fine cut of their sodden clothes and hats, the many trunks carried into their house, and the absurdity of their position were discussed and mocked, especially after the story circulated of her mother vomiting in the lobby of the boardinghouse. At the water pump, women tittered as Hailey approached, shushing their friends and offering knowing looks. Sly questions about how they were getting on did not disguise a certain glee. Hailey was positive that their haplessness might have earned them friendship if only her mother had not snubbed everyone. Or, at least, this was how Hailey believed the wives perceived her mother's reclusive silence after hearing one say, *Snobbery from a woman who doesn't even know how to bake bread? Laughable.* So the women of the town judged them as they floundered through their days, and the young women close to her age who might have offered Hailey friendship made the excuse of marriage and children and houses to keep, even though Hailey often observed them chatting over fence rails. All except Bonnie, whose kindness helped them through the worst of their stumbles, though she, too, had a baby and her own husband and house to care for.

Her mother grew more and more irritable. Mornings, she sat slumped wordless in the kitchen over her morning tea. Even when Geordie woke and padded into the front room, she couldn't summon the energy to greet him. Without a nanny it seemed that she found the chore of raising an energetic boy exhausting. If Geordie begged to be picked up or played with, she snapped at him. Geordie's face would crumple in confusion, and Hailey would lead him away to play with his growing collection of birds' feathers and rocks and shards of coal that he kept under their bed. He had brought with him from Scotland a set of beloved painted toy soldiers, which he played with obsessively. He took to sucking his thumb, and the hideous habit quieted him so much that their mother did not even impose the vinegar cure she would have insisted on in Scotland. The hacking cough he had developed during their voyage persisted. Camphor was available, but expensive. There was never any extra money. So, Geordie coughed.

Her mother went to bed immediately after supper, isolating herself in her room without so much as a *good night,* leaving Hailey alone with her father after she put Geordie to bed. As she washed the dinner dishes and tidied the front room, he rambled on about whatever crossed his mind. These private conversations gave Hailey a terrible feeling of discomfort. He ought to be having them with her mother.

"You know, Hailey Rose, it's right that I lost that money in the bank. It's punishment for neglecting my duty."

He had never revealed the total sum of his monetary losses. That devastation he carried alone.

"But Hailey Rose, I'm grateful for this paltry wage. It's penance for High Blantyre. Being the fire boss means I impose the rules. So there won't be any explosions, not when I'm in charge. I'll keep these men safe."

Two weeks after arriving in Newcastle, he roused them from their beds at dawn, shouting that they needed to pray. He forced them to kneel beside him, even Geordie, who whimpered and rubbed his eyes.

"Oh, God, I beseech you to keep my men safe and my senses sharp. Keep me mindful of my responsibilities. Smite down the forces of the devil, who is eager to see me fail. Give me wisdom as I dole out the daily blasting powder and water the gangways to snuff the explosive coal dust. In my responsibility, I need your divine help. I pray to Saint Barbara, the patron saint of miners, to watch over us all."

This became a daily ritual. Afterward, Hailey and her mother would drag themselves into their day, their knees sore, their hearts haunted by the increasingly vacant look in Harold MacIntyre's eyes.

And always, the perpetual gray skies, the drizzle, and everything wet.

ONE DAY IN early July, the morning dawned with a sky blue as indigo. Shunning chores, carrying a stick to ward off animals, Hailey took Geordie and climbed a path to an outcropping of rock above the church. It was hard work to drag her skirts to the top of the hill. The exertion made her breathless. But from here you could see forever—out to the glistening splash of Lake Washington and the misshapen island that floated in its waters and the gray glimmer of Puget Sound beyond, and the tall, craggy mountains that a drunken God had carved. Geordie sat beside her, building houses of sticks and rocks and playing with beetles and bugs while Hailey turned her back on her intolerable present and gazed out on the beautiful landscape.

She changed the past to what she wished she had done the day of their departure only a few months ago, when they wound along the quay in the interminable second-class line. In this conjured past, Hailey took a last look at her saddened parents and their terrible plan for their future, whisked Geordie into her arms, and ran back along the Clyde all the way to the city, along the Broomielaw to Argyle Street, up the dreadful six flights of Samuel's tenement and into his welcoming arms.

Stay. Stay with me. Marry me.

She had thought then that she would not have been able to live that life. From the revelations of the past several weeks, it turns out that she could. She and Samuel, Geordie and Alison, a family knit from love.

In essence, Geordie was hers already. She was the one who helped him to bathe and dress. She prepared his food and played with him. When he grew particularly peevish, she sang to him. Singing songs of Scotland soothed her. One song, in particular, never failed to subdue her inner pain, though its mournful tones could send them both into a melancholy that no amount of beauty could dispel.

O ye'll tak' the high road, and I'll tak' the low road
And I'll be in Scotland afore ye
But me and my true love will never meet again
On the bonnie, bonnie banks o' Loch Lomond

'Twas there that we parted, in yon shady glen
On the steep, steep side o' Ben Lomond
Where in soft purple hue, the hieland hills we view
And the moon coming out in the gloaming

O ye'll tak' the high road, and I'll tak' the low road
And I'll be in Scotland afore ye
But me and my true love will never meet again
On the bonnie, bonnie banks o' Loch Lomond

With every note, she suffered the endless miles that separated her from Samuel. As she helped Geordie to gather the new treasures he had collected—pine cones and feathers—Hailey hardened herself for the descent into town, for she understood what her mother had meant.

Her life had taken a turn from which it would never recover, and nothing would ever be all right again.

13

Samuel

OFF THE COAST OF OREGON, *LOUISA* WAS EIGHT hours into a July storm—a raging southerly—that was driving the ship northward through twenty-foot waves. Samuel Fiddes, working in the boiler room, heaved coal into the firebox, barely keeping his balance in the heaving sea. He and the other two firemen had been battling for two hours to keep a full head of steam so that the captain could maintain steerage through the boiling waters. Skin glistening with sweat, thirst raging, Samuel hoped to God that someone was taking care of Alison.

They had boarded *Louisa* in San Francisco six days ago. Roaming the docks in search of a job, Samuel had heard someone hollering at him in a Scots burr so thick it was as if they had docked in Glasgow. A man in full captain dress was staring down at him from the bow of a side-wheeler.

"You, lad. Any chance you're in need of a job? We're in need of a stoker. One of ours has gone on a bender."

"Where are you headed?"

The man grinned. "A Scot! Brilliant. I'm Captain Allaway—from Edinburgh. We run between here and Seattle. You have experience?"

"I do."

"Job's yours, then."

Alison, whom Samuel had ordered to hide behind a piling, came out from behind it and took his hand.

Allaway narrowed his gaze and sucked air through his teeth. "Jaisus, boy, what're you doing dragging such a wee one around for? I don't appreciate a swick. Does this mean you're going just the one way?"

Samuel nodded.

"Ah, Christ. This means I'll have to hire someone for the trip back." He scanned the docks, fuming. "I'm desperate. You and the bairn, then. Come aboard."

The trip had been calm up the coast and then the southerly had blown in with a vengeance. Laboring beside Samuel in the fire room were Pruss Loving and John Salvation Loving, black men and coal tenders who balanced the fuel loads to prevent the ship from listing. Father and son, they had toiled for more than a few years on *Louisa* with Sven, the tall Swedish engineer now screaming at them to keep pace.

"Pruss? John? Nice to meet you," Samuel had said when they'd been introduced.

The father was tall and lanky, with a lithe, muscular body and a head of silver hair. His son was wider and even more muscled, with high cheekbones and smiling eyes. "Oh, no," the son had said. "It's John Salvation, all of a piece. I don't answer to anything else."

The fever pitch required constant shouting and coordination. Legs braced, teeth gritted, it was hard going. Samuel's muscles were screaming. Perspiration poured down his forehead into his eyes. The air was sour with sweat. Minutes passed. Another hour. Two.

The ship's shallow draft made it a poor seagoing vessel in a storm. It rolled from side to side. During one precipitous lull, a huge wave crashed over the ship, flipping the boat a perilous sixty degrees to starboard. Coals spilled out and embers flew everywhere. Samuel lost his grip and tumbled toward the opening of the firebox, its gleaming heat searing his arms and face. John Salvation threw his shovel aside and dove to catch him, tackling and tumbling with Samuel just before he would have been flung into the firebox. Pruss piled on, their collective weight stopping his slide, saving Samuel's life.

Above the heavy roar of wind and waves, a sickening crunch shuddered through the ship. Dread flooded through Samuel. Just last night, Sven had told him about the SS *Pacific*, which recently had sunk somewhere in these waters after a collision with another ship, everyone dead but two.

Instantly, a signal came from the helm to dampen the engine fires, and they picked themselves up off the floor and whirled into action, slamming shut the firebox door while Sven diverted excess steam through the safety valve, stilling the walking beam engine. Helpless now, *Louisa* rode the waves. Pruss and John Salvation corralled the loose embers and shoveled them back into the firebox.

"What the fuck are you waiting for, Fiddes?" Sven bellowed, his blond hair plastered to his sweat-slicked forehead. "Go up and find out what is going on. If *Louisa* is going to sink, holler at us quick, because by Christ I'm not going to die in the pit of this damned hulk."

Samuel scrambled into the passageway and up a ladder, fighting his way through the saloon. Chairs were overturned, glass was smashed. Passengers had long ago been ordered to the safety of their cabins, but God knew how they were faring. He went to the pilothouse, where Allaway, clad in a waxed jacket and pants, was peering through the window into the afternoon gloom. Rain washed across the deck, and the seas reached the sky.

"Shut the damn door," he yelled.

"Do you know if my sister is all right?" Samuel screamed.

Allaway shouted back, "You're lucky. I ordered a woman to take her into their family's cabin."

Relieved, Samuel braced himself against the door. "Sven wants to know what happened."

"Log. Tree, more like. Waves tear them off the shores and turn them into torpedoes." Samuel had already learned that of all the causes of Pacific Northwest shipwrecks—burning, wreckage, stranding, foundering, collision, groundings, the explosion of a steam engine—it was the ships that simply never arrived, listed in the annals merely as "sunk," that were most likely to have struck a log. "Is there water below?"

"None in the engine room," Samuel said.

Allaway turned to his first mate, a stolid man of about thirty with a leathered face. "Whatever you do, keep us pointed north. The water's going to strain at the rudder. Fiddes here will help you hold her. I'm sounding the ship."

Samuel clamped his hands on the wheel and with the first mate fought the waves to hold things steady. Foam frothed the swirling waters. After half an hour, a hint of pink glimmered under the driving clouds. The rain grew intermittent.

The captain returned, slamming through the door, soaked through. "Hull's intact. But that damn log smashed a portion of the paddle wheel."

Without a means of propulsion, they'd be unable to go anywhere under their own power. The prevailing current could sweep *Louisa* onto shore. Up and down the coast, hulks of rotting ships reminded everyone of the power of the sea.

Samuel said, "Do you have wood? Saws? Nails?"

"Course. But we lost our carpenter in San Francisco. He took his tools with him."

"I built ships in Glasgow. Small ones, but I can help. I have tools."

"Jaisus, is that true?"

Samuel nodded. "How bad is it?"

"A quarter of the wheel, far as I can tell. And some of the housing, too."

"Show me?"

"God bless you."

SAMUEL ASKED JOHN Salvation to help, and the two tore away the broken housing of the paddle wheel and tossed it into the now flat sea. Samuel clamped the paddle wheel in place so it wouldn't turn as he worked on it. He counted ten broken paddles and a few square yards of outer housing that needed to be replaced. He and John Salvation worked through the night under the light of a lantern and a breathtaking splash of stars. The cool air was a welcome change from the intense heat of the boiler room. They sawed and hammered and steadied each other, leaning out over the water to hammer boards into place. John Salvation had a quiet, calm way about him that Samuel instantly trusted. He had a quick wit, too, which was sometimes unintelligible because of his slippery speech. Pruss and John Salvation came from a place called West Virginia, and it was as if they spoke a different language from Samuel. But they soon developed an ear for one another.

Working with Pruss and John Salvation was the first time Samuel had ever even spoken to a black person. In Scotland, there were colored people, descendants of slaves from the brutal Scottish sugar plantations in the West Indies, victims of the triangle trade, in which Africans were transported to chattel slavery in America and the islands. They had won their freedom at the turn of the century in Scotland's Court of Session and Parliament, not in a war, like in America. In Glasgow, they lived on Jamaica Street and worked in the forges of the shipyards. They kept to themselves, southern strangers in a strange northern land. Mostly no one bothered them. But here—Samuel had already seen enough to know that their war had settled nothing. On a dock in Georgia, Samuel had watched from deck as a foreman had beaten a black man almost to death.

The two worked well together, spurred by necessity. By five a.m., the fix was accomplished. Captain Allaway gaped with relief at his repaired ship and barked at the first mate to send the signal to start up the boiler.

"You two sleep," Allaway said. "Pruss and Sven have had their rest. But I'll need you soon. We're several days out of Seattle and we're already late."

Samuel could barely stumble down the ladder to his room tucked under a stairwell. Alison was sitting on the floor outside the door, her knees drawn to her chest, her eyes wide with terror, a puddle of exhaustion. She took one look at Samuel and burst into tears. He put down his tools and knelt beside her.

"Are we going to sink?" she said.

"We fixed it. I wouldn't let anything happen to you."

John Salvation materialized beside them and handed Samuel two biscuits slathered with honey. "Cook is grateful."

Through a mouthful, Samuel introduced the coal tender to

Alison, who was devouring her own biscuit. He wouldn't tell her that John Salvation had saved his life in the engine room, in order not to scare her, but it was true. The full realization of how close he had come to being seriously hurt finally hit Samuel. He would have ended up in the firebox if not for John Salvation, who had risked himself to save Samuel from being burned.

"He's our new friend," Samuel said.

"Friends? Who'd want to be friends with you?" John Salvation raised one eyebrow and shot a teasing grin at Alison to let her in on the joke. "Why, you look like you just climbed out of the grave after being buried alive for a hundred years."

They burst into laughter, all the tension of the past twenty-four hours releasing in a fit of guffaws.

Before he could stop himself, Samuel blurted, "No one has ever saved my life before."

Alison's voice broke. "What?"

John Salvation knelt beside her, speaking in a soothing voice. "Your brother is the one who saved us all with his hammering and nails. He's a good boatbuilder, your brother."

Alison sniffled, "I don't like boats."

"Oh, little miss," he said. "You and me both. Especially after a day like yesterday. Tell you what. I make dolls. Would you like me to make you one? She'll keep you company when your brother is busy."

Alison pressed her lips together, hesitating, though her eyes sparked with interest. "A doll?"

John Salvation winked. "Yes, little missy. Just for you."

14

Hailey

ON A SATURDAY EVENING IN EARLY JULY, THE Newcastle Odd Fellows hosted a dance. Their hall stood in a clearing a hundred yards north of town on a cliff above the tumbling creek. It boasted no paint and little decoration, but tonight its bare bones had been transformed with bunting and candlelight. An air of anticipation hummed inside, because fifty Seattleites—including several girls of marriageable age accompanied by their parents—had ridden the train to Newcastle. The place overflowed. The visitors would bunk overnight in people's homes and partake of a pancake breakfast at the church before traveling back to Seattle on a special train the next morning. Miners milled around the hall, gawking at the newcomers. In a corner, fiddlers with red kerchiefs tied around their necks tuned their instruments. The room was already warm and someone threw open a window. Nervously, Hailey plucked at the sleeves of her dress. She was sorry she had worn the green silk gown her mother had had made for her last ball at the Great Hall in Glasgow. She had kept it back from the ruin of housework, for it was far too fine. The other women wore simpler dresses of calico or lawn.

She'd been torn about coming, but Bonnie Atherton had insisted. Hailey feared that their family were still the town pariahs, but loneliness had stalked her since Scotland. It had been so long since she'd had anything like fun, and she loved to dance. But now, in the joyous hubbub, she felt out of place. Her father, standing beside her with an air of fumbling nervousness, was her chaperone tonight, since her mother had refused to come to what she called a country dance of no significance.

"Papa," Hailey said. "Let's go home."

"Certainly not, Hailey Rose. It will look bad if we leave now. I need to be here for my men, to show them that I support them."

Inwardly, Hailey shook her head at the things her father took responsibility for, but she took his arm and prepared to endure an awkward evening. Warily, she eyed the milling miners, secretly glad that so many Seattle girls had come so that she would go unnoticed. It seemed that everyone was ignoring her and her father. They had only to suffer through the first hour, and then she could persuade him to leave.

Bonnie, all dimples and smiles, hurried to their side. "You came. I'm so glad you did."

Hailey gave a tentative smile. "Where is baby Angus tonight?"

"Sarah Joos took him for a few hours so Alan can skip me around the dance floor. He does all right, even if he lost his pinky finger to an axe last year. He'll whip me around like no one's business." She leaned in, a conspiratorial twinkle in her brown eyes. "Tell me, who is it you have your heart set on?"

"What do you mean?"

"Which of the boys? They all talk about you."

"Do they?"

"Come on, now, Hailey, don't be coy. You know they do. Is it James Murray you're after?"

"Who is James Murray?"

"Oh, Hailey, you're hopeless. He's the one over there, trying to hide that he's looking at you."

To Hailey's disinterested eye, mining hadn't hardened James Murray too much. He was in his early twenties, maybe, with a short, compact body, and a face that featured a nose a tad too soft, a brow a touch too heavy, and lips much too thin. Studying him, Hailey had the feeling that if she could just alter the coarser features of his face, he might be attractive. The only traits of note were his sparkling blue eyes and russet hair.

"He's a good friend of my husband, and he's Scots, like you," Bonnie confided, as the grand officer—an ebullient Mr. Berg from the boardinghouse—clapped his hands for attention.

"Welcome to the Independent Order of Odd Fellows at Newcastle! We are delighted you are here! And welcome to our guests who have traveled all the way from Seattle!"

Vigorous applause rang out for the intrepid Seattleites. Bonnie patted Hailey on the arm and left to join her husband, who was happily downing a pint of ale from a keg at a checkered-cloth-covered table across the room.

"Let the festivities begin! Gentlemen, claim your partners."

A herd of men detached themselves from the general throng and stampeded toward Hailey. She felt her father pull away from her even as she clung to him. A man who introduced himself as Aidan Cumberbatch reached her first. A Welsh miner possessed of big hands, Aidan wrapped an arm around her waist and drew her onto the crowded dance floor. The lead fiddler tapped his instrument three times with his bow and launched into a polka.

Off they whirled.

How long had it been since she'd laughed? Or forgotten her-self? Hailey couldn't remember. Breathless, she gave in to the sudden sensation of happiness, not minding when Aidan stum-bled on her toes or swung her too vigorously. The sensation was invigorating. When the polka ended, another man claimed her for a Scottish reel. Then came a jig, which she stumbled through under yet another partner's tutelage. Apparently, a waltz was far too staid a dance when you'd spent eight hours underground. Hailey was claimed for every dance. She refused no one. It was liberating. At a break in the music, someone brought her a rum punch, a strong drink that she nonetheless gulped as she tried to catch her breath. She vowed to ask for iced tea from now on.

From the edge of the crowd, James Murray caught her eye, and when the band started up again, he somehow parted the sea of men and requested her hand.

The miner proved polite in his studious steering of her around the dance floor. Unlike the others, he was given to talk, and in sporadic beats reported his life's story. He came from Ayrshire, in the west of Scotland, and had mined since he was twelve years old. He left Annbank when he was nineteen and struck for America. He'd been mining in Newcastle for three years. He wasn't going to be a miner forever. He had plans. These were vague, something to do with a better life, but he reported this intention so earnestly that Hailey believed him. A girl like her, he said, deserved someone who had plans. His eyes conveyed fervent sincerity, and to his credit, he listened intently when she answered his questions about her life. He yielded her hand, but only reluctantly, and cut back in the very next dance, earning glares from his fellow suitors. He managed to win her last dance for himself. He proved himself persistent, steady, affable, and reliable. Not awful in any other respect, not that she could detect. He walked her home.

Her father—pried from the corner where he had spent the evening—trailed them at a distance, despite Hailey's efforts to include him in the conversation. As a miner, James Murray carried more status and made more money than her father, a social turn that still shocked.

When they reached the door, James Murray asked, "Would you allow me to call on you?"

He inspired no affection, no desire. He wasn't dull, but he wasn't interesting, either. He radiated none of Samuel Fiddes's light. Suddenly, she was very sorry she had gone to the dance. She refused James Murray's request and shut the door.

THE NEXT MORNING, her mother, sitting over her cup of tea, said, "You know, daughter, your father told me about last night. That young man could be helpful."

Hailey was tying her hair with a ribbon before she went to the spring to fetch water. "James Murray, you mean? Helpful how?"

Her mother shrugged. "He's lived here a long time. He's established. Your father says he's good at his job."

She stared at her mother. Where was the rapier condemnation she had meted out to Samuel? "Are you telling me to make myself available to a young man who mere months ago you would have forbidden me to even go near?"

"Maybe he can teach your father to hunt. I'm getting tired of beans."

"I can't believe you, Mother."

"Give the man a chance. He might help us. You cannot hold yourself precious, daughter."

Hailey whirled on her. "My entire life you've told me that we are above everyone. You wouldn't let me talk to Samuel. You pushed me at Douglas. And now you want me to court James Murray when you wouldn't even let Samuel look at me? James Murray is nothing to Samuel. Nothing. You can't use me like this. I don't understand you."

Her mother heaved a sigh. "Understand this, Hailey Mac-Intyre. Samuel Fiddes is never coming for you."

Hailey snatched the tin bucket from its nail and stalked into the cool dawn. Mist rose from the bare, trampled ground and hung about the treetops. The sky was barely pink. No one was about. On Sundays the mine was shuttered, so she could hear the birds singing. She made an arc around the mine entrance, heading to the spring. Once there, she worked the pump handle in a fury, angling away to keep her skirts from becoming soaked. The weight of the filling pail tugged on her arm and shoulder.

Of course Samuel wasn't coming. Of course he wasn't.

LATER THAT AFTERNOON at the MacIntyre house, Bonnie came over to teach Hailey how to make a pie. Standing over the kitchen table, Bonnie said to her, "Three parts flour, two parts fat, one part cold water. Mix it with your hands. So. Who did you like?"

"What do you mean?" Hailey said, measuring out three cups of flour into the striped crockery bowl.

"At the dance, silly."

"Oh. No one." She retrieved the saved bacon fat from the shelf above the stove and used a knife to scrape it onto the neat pile of flour.

"No one?" Bonnie said. "Not even Alan's friend? Alan says James Murray's the best of them. As brave as they come."

Hailey looked at Bonnie with raised eyebrows.

Bonnie shrugged. "Okay. Maybe he's a bit dull."

"A bit?" Hailey said, pouring in a cup of water. "He drones on and on. And he looks like—a potato."

Bonnie shrieked with laughter. "No, he doesn't!"

"Shhh," Hailey said, plunging her hands into the dough. "You'll rouse everyone."

Angus, Bonnie's baby, lay asleep in the middle of Hailey and Geordie's bed. After some whispering between her parents, Hailey's father had gone out to hike down the creek bed. Her mother had retreated to her bedroom and shut the door, seemingly disinterested in pie-baking lessons or any of the day's remaining chores. Geordie had hidden himself underneath the table on the floor, curled up with a blanket and his painted soldiers. Hailey hoped he would fall asleep, too.

"Okay," Bonnie said, conceding. "Maybe James Murray does look like a potato. But Alan says he can fire a coal wall like no one else. He's last to leave, sends everyone to shelter. First back in, too, even before the smoke clears. Last week he dragged John Peters out of that rock fall before anyone else could get to him. Saved his life. Alan says he's sweet on you. You could do a lot worse."

She peered at Bonnie. "Have you been talking to my mother?"

"No. Why?"

"Hmmm. Well, I'm not interested in James Murray." Hailey lifted the glob of wet, heavy dough from the bowl. "Now what?"

Geordie popped up from under the table and stuck a finger into the dough and pulled it out and stuck it into his mouth with a giggle. So, not asleep.

Bonnie gave him a playful tap. "Geordie, it's not cake. The pie won't be sweet until it's cooked. You'll get a piece as soon as it cools. Hailey, work in more flour so the dough isn't so wet. Not too much or it will get tough."

Hailey sprinkled more flour and worked it in, doling it out by pinches. She wouldn't waste even a teaspoonful. She had splurged on a cone of sugar for this pie, an expense her father did not yet know about. Bonnie had brought with her some muslin, a rolling pin, and a pie plate, and she showed Hailey how to halve the dough and roll each lump out on the floured cloth. They laid one flattened circle into the pan, cut off the excess, and poured the sugared rhubarb bubbling in a pot on the stove into the unbaked crust. They draped the second layer over, cut slits in the top, and put the pie into the oven to bake. It was hot outside—a rare occurrence—and the oven was making it even hotter inside, but Hailey didn't care. They were finally going to have something sweet.

Thirty minutes later, the crust was golden and the fruit bubbling.

As if on cue, her father, flushed from his exercise, returned from his hike. Hailey balked when she saw that James Murray was with him.

"Ran into Mr. Murray here. I invited him to accompany me home. Is there tea?"

Bonnie winked at Hailey and said, "You can bring me back my pie plate when you've finished." She gathered up Angus and her rolling pin and left Hailey defenseless against her father's machinations.

Hailey poured out the tea her mother would surely resent sharing and cut everyone a piece of pie, making James Murray's slightly smaller on purpose. Geordie climbed into her lap to eat his, blowing on the pie to cool it. Hailey let the sugared compote melt over her tongue.

Murray was quiet, polite. Genial, even. He noticed Geordie's soldiers and said that he carved animals and that he would carve one for him. A horse, for his army. He declared the pie delicious and talked with her father about the mine workings. When Hailey reluctantly offered him a second piece, he waved it off, said he had to be going, and thanked her sincerely for the most delicious thing he had eaten in his life. "Goodbye, Mr. MacIntyre. Goodbye, Geordie. Nice to meet you."

Murray took care to shut the door gently behind him. From the bedroom, bedsprings creaked, and then her mother opened the bedroom door, hair disheveled, a smile of approval on her face.

SEVERAL DAYS LATER, Hailey was up at five in the morning and at the pump again when she heard a rustle from above. She looked up, her gaze combing the vegetation and rock outcropping. Dawn light filtered through the fir trees and alder saplings that sprang up underneath.

Twenty feet above her, in a crevice of a boulder, a cougar simmered on its haunches, readying to leap, its eyes, black as black, trained on her.

She couldn't remember what she was supposed to do. Scare the animal? Hide? Meet its gaze? Look away? She couldn't remember. She stifled a cry and didn't move.

Then, a gunshot.

She dropped the bucket and ducked as James Murray crashed out of the underbrush beside her, his rifle aimed where the cat had been. With his gun, he traced the animal's retreat as it leapt straight up the rocks and back into the forest. He peered after it for a long time, then turned to Hailey, his legs thrust wide, the rifle butt resting on his hip.

She gaped. "How—how are you here?"

"Best time to hunt is early morning."

Murray refilled her bucket and carried it for her to the house. Several people stuck their heads out of their doors, curious about the single gunshot. James lifted his rifle to acknowledge it was him and not to worry.

Self-conscious, Hailey accepted the water from him outside the house. "Thank you."

He tipped his hat and walked away. She stood watching him go. What would have happened if he hadn't been there? Her hands were still shaking. She tried to catch her breath.

She was about to go inside when she heard her parents talking through an open window.

"Charlie Shattuck said a strike is possible, and soon."

Something about the tone of her father's voice made Hailey wait. She lowered the pail to the bed of spent fir needles that accumulated outside their door no matter how many times she swept them away.

"Well, Harold," her mother said, "if you were going to ruin our lives, couldn't we have just stayed in Scotland and been ruined there? Why didn't we just move to High Blantyre? Why did we have to come halfway around the world to suffer the same fate we could have suffered in Scotland?"

Though voicing the same desperate conclusion that Hailey had come to, her mother spoke without a hint of spite or anger, in a languid but unforgiving tone, as if their desperate situation no longer deserved the raw emotion she had expended since they'd arrived.

Her father talked on as if he hadn't heard. "Yesterday, Shattuck sailed to San Francisco to try to get better pay for everyone. But the company has a loan it can't repay. That's the main problem."

Her mother sighed. "It's never your fault, is it, Harold?"

Her father seemed not to understand the danger. He responded in an even tone he'd developed lately, oddly petulant and reasonable at the same time. "That's not fair, Davinia. You know that everything—especially the explosion—is my fault. It was impossible to live in Blantyre. To see the faces every day of those widows—their children. You know I couldn't stand it. But the bank failure was different. They deliberately deceived me, Davinia. They deceived everyone. You know this. That was different. That was bad luck."

"Such a freighted word, *luck*," her mother said, speaking in the dull, passionless voice of a court examiner.

Hailey wanted to go inside, but fear held her back. Lately, she'd become a reluctant referee, never sure whether she was helping or hurting when she interfered. But this argument was different. Her mother had never before resorted to scorn.

"Listen to me," her father said. "If I had known what trouble the Glasgow bank was in, I would have put our money in the Bank of Scotland, but—"

"Tell me, why didn't you know? I ask you, Harold MacIntyre, how in heaven's name didn't you know that you were being cheated? Are you so blind that you can't discern when someone is pulling the wool over your eyes?"

"I'm not responsible for other people's thievery."

Her mother laughed, her voice thick with derision. "We are here because of you. We are ruined because of you. And now, it has happened again. Did you even think to investigate this company's solvency before you brought us here? What do you propose we do next, Harold? Walk to Canada? Sail to China? We could travel around the world chasing your fancies. Of course, we still need to eat every day. Or did you forget that part?"

They fell silent.

After a long moment, Hailey retrieved her water bucket and opened the door. Her mother took one look at her, set down her tea, and went past her into the morning without uttering a word.

"Papa?" Hailey said.

He sat crouched over a bowl of porridge.

"Papa. Are we in trouble?"

"I've got faith in Charlie Shattuck."

"But are we in trouble?"

"I've still got an idea or two."

"But will we have to go somewhere else, like Mama said?"

"Don't you worry yourself, child. Did you get water? I'm thirsty."

Hailey studied her father's lean face, which had turned heavy-lidded with fatigue. She longed for the time her father's lighthearted jests and calm deliberation steered their days. She had always trusted him, but now she didn't. He sat, slowly spooning porridge into his mouth, looking off into the distance, eyes blank. A strike would mean no pay. Suddenly, spending money on sugar seemed the most frivolous thing Hailey could have done. Who would help them if they had no money? How would they eat?

She had a vision of Samuel sailing toward her, coming for her, and then she pushed it away. What had these last months taught her if not to be practical? Samuel wasn't coming. She set down her pail, went outside, and climbed the plank sidewalk to the boardinghouse where James Murray was sitting on the front steps, smoking, his rifle listing against a wooden post.

Silently cursing her mother, Hailey said, "Mr. Murray, you may call on me."

A smile formed on his thin lips, and an unnerving blue sparkle lit his eyes. "Tonight?"

"Whenever you like."

15

Samuel

LOUISA WAS CROSSING THE STRAIT OF JUAN DE Fuca. The sun was burning fast through a lingering mist, and everything had taken on the sparkle of refracted light.

Samuel was on a break, standing at the rail, taking in the astonishing vista of mountains and water. Alison clutched the doll that John Salvation had fashioned for her from braided rope and a scrap of calico. It hadn't left her side. To the surprise of everyone but Samuel, John Salvation and Alison had become fast allies. On his breaks, the coal tender joined her at the bow of the steamer, on the hunt for whales and more giant logs.

Allaway appeared, his gruff voice wistful as he gazed toward a ghostly specter of islands barely visible in the gray light. "Take a look. You've gone halfway round the world, but don't those isles look like our beloved Scotland?"

Samuel peered through the telescope Allaway had thrust into his hands. The islands were hilly, creased with an occasional treed ravine amid wide swaths of dry meadow. The topography may have recalled Scotland for the captain, but it resembled nothing of the grimy closes and tenements of Glasgow. Seen through the lens of the telescope, the islands seemed uninhabited, just a tangle of driftwood and rocky beaches and soaring seagulls.

Allaway claimed not.

"Nothing is ever as it seems, young Samuel, remember that. Those islands are teeming with enterprise. Farmers. Orchardists. Lime kilns. They're just like my lowlands near Edinburgh. I'm telling you, you chose well, coming here."

A pod of killer whales surfaced to race the steamer, their tall dorsal fins slicing through the waves. One breached, splashing into the water with such force that it sent a spray of seawater over the bow. Alison squealed. The whales seemed to have come out of nowhere. The water frothed with their black spines, so many of them rising and falling that they looked like the walking piston of the engine.

"Blackfish," the captain said. "Wolves of the sea. Did you ever see them up in the Firth of Clyde? They venture up the Clyde itself, I'm told. Don't know why, with all the filth in the river. They're everywhere here. Fishermen hate them because they gobble up the salmon."

Allaway returned to the wheelhouse, stopping here and there to answer a greeting, shake a hand, give a clap on the back. He had announced that *Louisa* would soon be shifting to the southern route between San Francisco and Panama, and the passengers had turned nostalgic.

At the entrance to Puget Sound, *Louisa* anchored at Port Townsend to check in with customs. Schooners bobbed in the harbor, and acres of raw lumber, corralled by rope and chain, formed immense floating rafts. The water smelled of sewage and seaweed and wet wood.

On deck, John Salvation said to Samuel, "Cap'n sometimes

skips customs, if the tide is right. We'll be here an hour, at least. It depends on if they find something."

"Find what?"

"Opium."

"What's wrong with opium?" Samuel said.

Opium was sold in every druggist's shop in Glasgow. In Smyllum, the nuns quieted babies with Mother's Friend, a syrup of poppies. The drug was sold everywhere, in sticks and in other syrups at the chemists. They unloaded it raw in droves in Glasgow on the Clyde to be sent to the refining factories in Edinburgh.

"Nothin's wrong with it," John Salvation said. "Except folks here don't want to pay the tax, so they sneak it. Under houseplants. In the false bottoms of suitcases. In tins of tea. Some boats specialize in outlaw delivery. The customs men are bent on finding it all. They auction off the opium and sell it themselves and make a good amount of money for the government. Doesn't seem right, but that's how it goes."

"Like free trading in Scotland. Irish whiskey without the tax."

John Salvation shrugged assent. "If you say so."

A grim-faced customs inspector arrived in a tender, boarded *Louisa*, and rifled through the ship and passengers' baggage. Finding no contraband, he cleared *Louisa* on her way.

After spending the night at anchor, Captain Allaway cast off the next morning with the rising tide. The current would do part of the work of carrying them to Seattle, saving fuel. Samuel thanked the Lord that today was the last day he would ever have to descend into the hell of a steamer's boiler room. Over the week, and since the accident, Pruss and Samuel and John Salvation had developed a rhythm, while Sven maintained his air of grim calculation, all the while heaping abuse on Samuel for his "holiday," no matter that Allaway had sworn that Samuel had saved all their lives.

Now that Seattle was near, Samuel allowed Hailey's face to come to him vividly with each shovelful of coal. Hope flared as he had not allowed it to before. He squashed fears that Hailey wouldn't be in Seattle. She had to be there.

"Won't be long now," Sven said. "I can feel Captain turning in to the bay." He lifted his chin, sniffing. "Is that smoke?"

Even in the confines of the fireroom, Samuel could smell it. Not the usual, acrid bite of smoldering coal, but the over-powering scent of woodsmoke. Fire was the dread of every ship's crew, but in a wooden ship it was more dreaded still, for there was nothing to stop it until the flames consumed the ship to the waterline. But no call came to dampen the fires.

"Forest, maybe?" Pruss said, leaning on his shovel. Pruss Loving's considerable height was unstooped by his years of physical labor, and his posture looked elegant even in this la-conic pose.

Sven shook his head. "Little bit early for the fires to be burn-ing. Been a wet summer. Fiddes, since you like playing the truant so much, go on up and find out what gives."

Calls and shouts of panic were now penetrating the engine room.

"By God, hurry!"

Samuel hotfooted it up the ladder and on deck, but the ship was intact, fire-free, and sailing into a wide bay under a twilit evening tinged with pink. In the near distance, a thin gray column of smoke rose from a point of land at the base of a cluster of steep hills. He couldn't make out much more, but passengers crowding onto the bow of *Louisa* began to wail. One woman dropped to her knees.

No forest fire this. A town had burned. It was still smoldering. There were no flames, but the stench of smoke festered as *Louisa* drifted closer. Samuel could make out several wharves jutting into the bay. At one, a schooner had burned and sunk, its blackened masts poking above the water. He crossed himself automatically, hoping that its sailors had escaped. No ships were tied to any of the wharves, though a dozen lay at anchor in the bay. Allaway was weaving *Louisa* between them.

Samuel said, "Is this Seattle?"

A man answered with an open-mouthed nod of disbelief.

Samuel stared. Seattle had burned, and he hadn't yet set foot on her shores.

He hurried back to the engine room.

Sven, always a fountain of profanity, said, "By Christ, the whole town?"

Samuel recalled seeing intact houses. "A part of it, I think. Along a point."

"Are the wharves still there?'

"Some."

"What about the fuel bunkers? We're damn near out of coal. If they're burned, we're stranded."

"I don't know."

Samuel had come halfway around the world, and Seattle had burned.

The signal finally came to douse the fires, and Sven opened the valves to let off steam. They felt the ship maneuvering as Allaway nursed her to the dock and the bump as the fenders made contact.

"Lines, ho!" came the cry as the line handlers tossed them onto the dock.

IT WAS SAID that Seattle was a place you could smell long before you arrived: to step out onto a Seattle dock after the fresh sea air was to step into a reek so strong and peculiar it took your breath away. Samuel could testify to that. Not even the stench of woodsmoke could cover the odor.

A dozen dockhands laughed as Alison, thrilled to be off the ship, nonetheless shouted, "Everything stinks!"

Samuel shushed her as Allaway pressed money into his hands. Samuel's pay was to have been Alison's passage, but Allaway said, "Something extra, for saving us, Mr. Fiddes. You ever need anything, you ask me. *Louisa* will be back one more time until she shifts south. We'll be staying in port for a few more days than normal to paint your fine work. If you ever want a job as a ship's carpenter, you ask me."

Samuel couldn't imagine ever boarding a ship again. He'd been on ships for two months, his blood swaying in time with ocean swells, and suddenly he felt oddly suspended in space. But as he stood on the dock surveying the town, he realized that he had no solid plan. His goal had been to get to Seattle, but now that he had arrived, he had no idea where to go or what to do or how to find Hailey. He was frozen. And the town was half-burned.

Allaway sensed his confusion. "I have a friend here. The Widow Barnum. She runs a good boardinghouse up the hill, near the university. You go there. Tell her you're my friend. She'll find you a place to stay."

"We'll show him," Pruss said. "C'mon, Scotty." Pruss and

John Salvation had begun calling Samuel *Scotty*. Samuel didn't mind—he considered it a term of affection.

Samuel and Alison walked with the Lovings down the wharf into the town. Samuel counted a total of four wharves extending into the bay. The farthest was lined with coal bunkers, but the nearest, a dogleg jetty nearly a thousand feet long, smoldered, its dubious underpinnings emitting a steady sheet of thin, gray smoke. Though the length of the wharf was drenched with water, an unseen fire still percolated in the materials supporting it. At its foot, closest to town, the wharf's sawmill lay in ruins, as did a few of the structure's nearer warehouses, but farther out a saloon, blacksmith shop, water tank, boiler works, and icehouse still stood.

Pruss said, "Yesler's Wharf. It's the most important one in the city, but, Lord, that man has made a mess. It's a firetrap, a rat trap. I'm surprised they were able to keep it from burning entirely. You see, Scotty, there's not much of a shoreline here. The bluffs rise straight up from the water. And the seabed drops almost straightaway. Not easy to build a pier in these waters near town. Teredos—shipworms—eat the wood, too. So, Yesler's been making land out of nothing for years, piling garbage and ship ballast into the bay and filling it in with sawdust, building his wharf and businesses on top of that. God knows what Yesler put in there. But no matter, the city will march west into the sea because destiny calls. Or so everyone says."

Above the burned town, prisms of water shimmered in the lingering smoke. On this late-July evening, the sun was still high in the sky, outlining a stretch of high western mountains. Another set of mountains loomed to the east. The water of the sound lapped against the shore. In every direction, layers of the world formed like strata: the unruly expanse of the magnificent bay, floating islands covered with fir trees, layers of distant hills, and jagged snow-covered mountains in the far distance. But the town itself looked like the capital of hell planted in the kingdom of God. For several blocks, gray ash lay in heaps, smothering half-burned timbers and fallen storefronts. Twisted metal gave evidence of ruined industry. Sodden piles of wood and pools of water spoke of a desperate effort to save the rest of the town, which had succeeded, because beyond the burned district, houses and buildings lay untouched. The sight was arresting—apocalypse thwarted.

Here and there, people were poking through the mess. Running down the middle of one street was a muddy river of ash and detritus. Mill Street, Pruss informed him. In the ruins, at least thirty men had already begun to shovel debris and char into wagons for oxen teams to haul away. It seemed that an entire block and a half had burned to the ground—a total of twenty buildings reduced to smoking ash and ruin, housing the town's most essential warehouses and stores.

"Commercial Row," Pruss said. "Gone now."

What had he imagined? Samuel wondered. Glasgow's stone permanence? New York's exuberant crush? A pale approximation of San Francisco's sandy hills? What kind of place was this? Where had he come to?

Samuel could not imagine the lovely Hailey here, in this primitive, squalid place. Or her parents.

He realized that in every one of his imagined arrivals, Hailey had been here. Strolling on the dock as the ship arrived, or greeting him at the base of the gangplank, somehow knowing that he was on the ship.

A terrible thought struck him. "Did anyone die in the fire?" he said to no one in particular.

"You all from the *Eldorado*?" A man in a slouch hat and overalls was interrogating Samuel. "The sailors who helped us last night? Who manned the hand pump and put the fire out?"

"No. But did anyone die?"

"A woman on *Dakota* died from hysteria, afraid her house was burning. Another fell from the coal wharf, but she was fished out alive. Burning timbers fell on someone, but he lived. There are a few lost fingers to axes, bucket handles, like that. But we're counting our blessings. Those sailors—the whole town would have gone without their help."

Samuel exhaled. At least, if the MacIntyres were here, they hadn't died.

"Oh, look at that, will you? The mountain's out," John Salvation said.

Samuel peered southward through the pink evening light, beyond the rubble of the fire, to where twin smokestacks stood dormant. Beyond them, above a river valley and estuary spilling into the bay, a single, magnificent snow-covered mountain took Samuel's breath away. He had been too preoccupied at first to see it. He knelt down and pointed out the view to Alison, whose trepidation through the ruins of the fire had increased with every step. Now she gasped at the glimmering peak and smiled at Samuel, who was relieved to see a spark of delight in her eyes.

THEY WERE ALL starving. John Salvation and Pruss led them through town. They passed a muddy square piled high with goods rescued from the businesses that had burned. They went on to a cookhouse a block up one hill. The doorway lintel was so low Samuel had to duck so he wouldn't hit his head. Inside, it was crowded with men hunched over dinner plates piled with food.

"Our House," John Salvation said. "William Grose owns it. Looks like he's cooking tonight. We'll get some food here before we go up to Widow Barnum's."

William Grose resembled a giant. A rotund black man of significant height, he was swathed in a white apron, laboring over a long grill. Despite his girth, he maneuvered around the kitchen with ease, effortlessly ducking under the low beams of the ceiling. He waved at them to sit down and brought them four plates of cooked meat and biscuits. After setting them on the wooden table, he shook hands with Pruss and John Salvation and said, "Who are your friends?"

"Samuel and Alison Fiddes, from Scotland," Pruss said.

Grose nodded at Alison, whose eyes widened as he greeted her. "How do you do, Miss Fiddes? John Salvation make you one of his famous dolls?"

Alison gripped her doll and nodded.

"Some day for you to arrive in Seattle, isn't it? Don't you be worrying. We're all safe now."

Pruss said, "Bill, Cap'n says we'll stay in port two days, maybe five. We hit a log. John Salvation and Scotty here fixed it up, but there's painting to do. And the Inspector of Hulls has to come round. Could be a week. You have room for us upstairs?"

"Always."

After William Grose returned to his grill, Pruss said, "All right, Scotty, what're you doing here, anyway? Why'd you come? You're as secretive as a squirrel hiding nuts. You got family here? You going to make a home here with them?"

Home? Samuel had dragged Alison, his only family, to the other side of the world because home had sailed to Seattle two months ago. "I'm looking for someone."

John Salvation regarded him steadily. "You saying that you

came all that way from Scotland, as far as far can be, just to look for someone? Here? In this place? *This* place that just burned down? And you don't know anyone?"

Samuel nodded.

With a deep breath, John Salvation said, "Well, you got yourself into trouble, now, ain't you, Scotty?"

16

Hailey

IN MID-JULY, THE CONCERNS THAT HAROLD MAC-
Intyre had voiced to his wife became widely known. The Seattle
Coal & Transportation Company—which owned both the S&
WWRR and the Newcastle mine—was in considerable financial upheaval. The company was owned by a San Francisco con-
sortium. The cost of shipping coal to San Francisco—where
nearly all of it went—ate up so much of the profit that there was
little to spare. And miners were agitating for better conditions—
including pay, but mostly safety. Since June, injuries had multiplied. In one week, a miner lost his arm in an axe mishap, a
second died after he broke his back in a rock fall, and a third
knocked his head after falling over a coal cart and lost his sight
for two days.

These mishaps occurred even though the vein they were
mining was one of those beauties: eleven feet thick, uninter-
rupted by faults, angled at just the right slope, dry as a bone, and
with a ceiling of hard rock. The rich deposit was as clean and
bright as one could wish, ripe for the picking and easy to work,
easier than most of the coal mines in the world. The Welsh miners especially loved this new mine in Washington Territory, for

Welsh mines suffered frequent explosions from firedamp and dust, and the malicious threat both posed. But not in Newcastle. It was like working inside a diamond. Clean and dazzling.

Or at least, that was what the company claimed. The thing was, when journalists came sniffing around, the company avoided mentioning pitfalls. They failed to disclose the occasional roof falls where glacial till made the ceiling spongy, the bad ventilation that choked the men deep inside, the suffocating gases that seeped out of the earth, the groundwater that sometimes flowed like rain. Instead, they boasted yields and production, the shiny new railroad, and the flowers that decorated window boxes in town (hastily obtained from Squak and planted when they'd gotten wind that someone was coming).

Still, was it too much to ask to walk into a mine at the beginning of a shift confident that at the end you would walk out alive?

Discontent roiled the town. Complaints multiplied. Petulance reigned.

In late July, the miners defied orders from Shattuck and formed a union. The talk of a strike mushroomed.

In the middle of all this, James Murray called on Hailey.

Most of the miners, married or not, whiled away their evenings in the tavern located just off company property. Not James. Or so he said. He represented himself as a hard worker who lived a sober life and who had ambitions beyond Newcastle. And though in Scotland they never would have met, here her parents turned a blind eye. Hailey and James were free to go wherever they wished. He came for her in the evenings, and they walked to the stables to visit the mine horses and mules, or climbed down the steep bank to the creek, or met in the church to chat in the pews, away from observing eyes.

James Murray was nothing like Samuel, and he stirred nothing inside Hailey. He had this habit of watching her as he spoke, his eyes sharp for her reaction. She would nod along, only occasionally glancing away to pet a horse's neck, or to observe the light falling through the overstory. When she looked away, he would cease talking, and his gaze would grow slightly wounded. On occasion it seemed that he suppressed a spark of irritation. She learned to pay complete attention to him.

But she could not deny his kindness. One day he brought them a cured ham after he'd killed his hog, and the next week several cuts of salted venison from a deer he had shot. He presented Davinia with a cone of sugar for her tea, and Harold a new knife, which he accepted with bemused puzzlement. True to his word, James carved Geordie a horse—the very animal Hailey had been unable to buy in the company store the day they arrived. James's spontaneous expressions of goodwill seemed to bring him a great deal of pleasure.

Just as in Scotland, the summer evenings stretched long into the night. Hoisting Geordie onto his shoulders, James would lead them along the creek in search of toads and snakes. His awkward intensity eased when he directed his attention to Geordie, and then he could be light—jolly, even. He taught Geordie how to fish in a shallow pool beneath a babbling waterfall while Hailey watched from shore, and he even built a lean-to of fallen branches along the stream bank, where Geordie played endless games with his soldiers and new horse while James conversed with Hailey in that halting way of his. Once, he asked what a highborn girl like her thought of this rough life, and she replied that she was grateful to him for giving Geordie all the attention her father could not, sidestepping his implicit request for approval. She wasn't ready yet to give him that. Geordie, though, reveled in James's company, pleading every day for him to "come and play."

More than once, her mother asked, "Are you warming to James Murray?"

"I don't know," Hailey would say, though they had already fallen into calling each other Hailey and James.

What Hailey knew for certain was that her father's increasing imbalance and her mother's vague detachment terrified her. Hailey suffered a growing sense of being unmoored. And James offered a handhold. Was it fair? Perhaps not. But she needed a handhold now.

At night, to the clatter of the mine, Hailey sometimes couldn't help concocting visions of Samuel tracing their same watery voyage, seeing the very landscapes that she had—New York's astonishing bustle, Panama's wild jungle, San Francisco's dry hills assailed by the wild Pacific and the feral waters of the bay. It was as if some unconscious part of her always kept track of where Samuel might be and what he might be doing. But most nights, rationality dampened all hope, and she feared for him in his miserable lodgings in Glasgow and prayed that he was making his way in the world. Perhaps he had earned some real money and found somewhere better to live. Perhaps he had sent Alison to school. *Perhaps, perhaps*—always she hoped for something better for him, envisioning a gleaming future in which he achieved everything he wanted. Then the next morning when she woke, she would feel even more bereft, and loneliness and indecision would lead her to accept James's well-intentioned overtures.

On a Monday evening at the end of July, Hailey told James she could not meet as they had planned. Her mother hadn't stepped foot outside in the past week except to toss rubbish into the pit or to visit the privy. Her gaze had become steely, abstracted, her mood unpredictable. And Hailey's father spent his evenings brooding. They needed to get out, even for an hour, away from the damp little house and its reminder of all that had gone wrong. And Hailey wanted to see if she could see anything of Seattle from the ridge above the town. Apparently, there had been a big fire. When the trains didn't arrive Sunday morning, someone had climbed the cliff and spotted a cloud of dense smoke above the town. CB Shattuck and Mr. Berg had set off on the three-mile hike to Newcastle Landing on Lake Washington on the off chance of finding someone to row them across the lake, to see if anything of Seattle had been saved. They'd returned this morning to say that only a part of the town had burned and that James Colman, the railroad engineer, was checking the tracks to see if the fire had warped any of the rails. No one knew when the trains would run again.

Hailey persuaded her mother and father to climb the hill with her. Though the ground was wet from a brief shower, the clouds had parted and the sky now shone. In a fit of playfulness, Harold swung Geordie onto his shoulders. Up they climbed, following the old Indian trail that ran over the mountain to Squak Valley. In a clearing on the edge of the cliff, they laid down a macintosh. Directly beneath them, the mine tunneled through the mountain, but up here the ever-present din was muffled, the air clear.

In the distance, they could see traces of smoke lingering above Seattle. The view was untamed and alive with the deep greens and blues of forest and sky, layers of light pink and orange above the distant Olympics, the sun a hovering pale globe, everything scrubbed clean by the rain. A warm breeze rippled through the trees, lifting strands of hair from their necks, cooling them after the exertion of the climb.

Geordie, breathing easier in the cleaner air, gathered stray twigs and built a ship.

Her father leaned back on his hands, stretching his legs before him.

"The strike is set for the day after tomorrow," he announced. "It's time for the MacIntyres to leave." Recently, her father had begun to refer to their family in the third person, as if he were narrating their life from a distance. *The MacIntyres will eat now. The MacIntyres will go to church now.* "There's a gold mine up north on the Skagit that's reporting good returns. We'll go there."

"Gold?" her mother said.

Geordie, sensitive as always to the whirling vagaries of mood in their family, stopped playing to stare.

Her father said, "God says he has punished me enough. Now he's ordered me to earn back our lost money in the gold mines."

Davinia's voice turned cold. "God told you?"

"Oh, yes. God tells me all his plans. I'm told they're bringing in twenty dollars a day to the man. Several steamers run up the east side of Whidbey Island into the slough that reaches La Conner. Far easier than an ocean voyage. It's north, sixty miles. A hundred. Maybe less—"

Davinia stared at him. "God told you that he wants you to take us even further into this wretched wilderness?"

Hailey reached for Geordie.

"It's not that far. A sojourn of three or four days. It's into the mountains north of here. I'll purchase the necessary kit in La Conner, the tent and such. Apparently, the MacIntyres will have to hire natives to take them up the Skagit on canoes. It will be an outlay, but I've saved some money. The MacIntyres should be fine."

Davinia began to laugh wildly. "You've saved money?"

Geordie broke free as Hailey stared, speechless.

"Yes. Twenty pounds in gold. From the household accounts in Glasgow," her father explained, as if twenty pounds in gold were nothing, which in their former life had been true.

For a minute everything stilled. All the chatter of the woods died as the sun plummeted behind the Olympics, a swift and breathtaking drop that turned the woods around them into a gray jungle, devoid of color. Davinia seemed unable to catch her breath. "Do you mean to say that all this time you've had money? When we couldn't buy camphor for Geordie? Or pay for a doctor? Or get decent food?"

"I've been saving it."

Her mother gaped for a long minute. Then she said, "Give it to me, Harold. Give it to me right now."

"Mama, don't yell," Geordie cried. He broke into a coughing, wheezing fit and flung himself into Hailey's arms.

"Let's go down, Father. Mother, let's go," Hailey pleaded, rising and carrying Geordie and walking swiftly to where the path descended through the trees, eager to remove him from the explosion she was certain would come.

A sharp observer of her father, Hailey had thought that his new penance of humble work had begun to buoy him. He had taken them all to the other side of the world to reverse the mistakes of High Blantyre, to ablate the sin of whatever misjudgment he believed he had been responsible for, and it seemed as if he might have come around. He'd kept his eye out in the mine for improvements. He'd suggested a redesign of the ventilation fans and the repositioning of the trapdoors. He whistled sometimes as he left for work.

How wrong she had been.

As Hailey made her way down the path, alert for prowling cougars, she heard her mother scream, "I will not look at you, Harold MacIntyre, for one more blessed second of my life!"

ALL NIGHT, HER parents screamed at each other while her mother threw her belongings into a bag. Hailey huddled in bed with Geordie as she tried to make sense of her mother's ravings. *She was going home, and she was going home now.* She tore through the house, overturning coffee tins, rifling through the pockets of Harold's work pants, yelling, "Where is it?" and "Give it to me now," and finally there was an exultant cry, then more struggle. It was impossible to tell how much money her mother had found.

When Geordie finally fell into a fitful sleep, Hailey climbed from bed and went out to the front room. "Mama, stop. Please. What are you doing?"

Her mother turned on her, eyes raging. "Get out of my way, Hailey."

Hailey retreated in horror.

At dawn, her mother dragged her bag out of the house and up the muddied lanes to the boardinghouse, the neighbors gaping and tittering, having heard the whole argument.

"But where is she going?" Hailey said, watching from the open door. "Papa, go after her. Please. You must."

"Your mother is just being stubborn. She'll come to her senses."

The mildness of his reply infuriated Hailey. He looked none

the worse for wear after his night of battle; he was acting as if his wife had stepped out for tea.

"Thank God I held some money back. Another ten in gold. That will do nicely to outfit us for the Skagit."

Aghast, Hailey said, "But surely we won't go without Mother?"

"Of course we will. You can cook for me. It will be an adventure. And when I've made my fortune, we'll see your mother back in Scotland."

Both, Hailey thought. Both her parents had broken.

Frantic, she scanned the house. How long would it take to pack her and Geordie's things? What time was it? If she hurried, they could go with their mother—wherever she was going. Hailey went again to the door. Mr. Berg was leading her mother away on a donkey, her bag slung over the animal's neck. Hailey tore around, snatching up things at random: one of Geordie's toy soldiers, a pair of his underwear hanging to dry from the clothesline above the stove, her hairbrush.

"I need five dollars, Father." Yesterday, an impossibility, today, within his grasp. A sum that would buy two tickets on the railroad. Maybe the train would run today. Any minute, they might hear its whistle.

"Hailey Rose, I need that money for the Skagit. Now, I'm late for work. We don't even have time for prayer this morning. The whole mine is delayed because your mother lost her bearings for a moment. I need to distribute the blasting powder. There's likely to be a mutiny if I don't."

"I can't stay with you, Papa. I can't go to the Skagit with you."

"But I need you."

Something in her father's defeated posture told Hailey that he did need her. Searching for something to say—anything—to shake him from his delusion, she said, "Let's go home, Papa. Let's go back to Scotland. Today. Right now."

But he hadn't heard her. "When we go through Seattle on our way up north, we'll find your mother. She'll come to her senses then."

Of course. They had to go through Seattle to get anywhere else. On twenty pounds, her mother couldn't get far, could she? What was the ticket price to San Francisco? Hailey couldn't remember. But, no, surely her mother wouldn't leave Seattle without her and Geordie. Would she? *She was going home, and she was going home now.* No. She couldn't make it to Scotland on twenty pounds.

Still, Hailey thought of James. Perhaps he would loan her five dollars, take her to Newcastle Landing, find someone to row them away to get her out of here. But would she and Geordie be any better off with their mother? How could she leave their father? The choice was impossible.

Cap in hand, her father patted his pockets, a look of vague distraction on his face. "Hailey Rose, darling, can you cook something other than beans for dinner? I'm awfully sick of them."

17

Samuel

AFTER DINNER, SAMUEL, ALISON, AND THE LOV-
ings stepped out of Our House and into the town's sodden re-
mains. The late-evening air smelled of damp, burnt things.

"Let's get you to Widow Barnum's and get you settled,"
Pruss said, swinging Alison onto his shoulders.

North along the waterfront, in the opposite direction from
the blaze, several factories and foundries studded a gradual rise
to a towering, unwieldy hill, where a few whitewashed houses
clung to its heights. Above the burned district, the rest of town
climbed eastward, higgledy-piggledy, up from the bay. If there
had been any question that Seattle was built on hills, it was answered the minute Samuel began to climb the dusty, clay-packed
streets. He twice had to stop to catch his breath. There wasn't a
spot of level land anywhere. Platted in an approximate grid in
anticipation of the city Seattle wanted to become, the streets
were rutted like washboards and riven with ditches. Some houses
stood on stilts because their lots fell away beneath them. Stray
cows and pigs roamed where they pleased, rooting at vegetation
and lying down in the middle of the stump-pocked streets. A
horse, unharnessed and unmanned, strolled past as they climbed.

All Samuel could think of was Hailey. Finding her in this mess seemed an impossible task. He entertained again the terrible thought that the MacIntyres hadn't come to Seattle after all.

Pruss stopped at a two-story, unpainted clapboard house with a narrow porch. A tiny woman was sweeping ash from the veranda. Barely five feet tall, with a glossy crown of auburn hair and big blue eyes, she had a thin nose, freckles, and a small mouth. She wore an apron and the sleeves of her dress were rolled up. She stopped sweeping and rested her palms on the top of her broom.

"If it isn't the Lovings," she said, speaking in the same long drawl as they did.

"Good to see you, Mrs. Barnum." They all removed their hats.

"Boys, I believed we all might die. My daughter and I spent the night of the fire on the next ridge over, dodging embers. Some folks even went all the way down to Leschi, thinking to submerge themselves in Lake Washington just to survive. Or is it Lake Duwamish? The names of things here don't seem to stick. I returned to this mess." She indicated the pile of ash at her feet. "All my male boarders pitched in fighting the fire. I found their dirty washbasins out back, not even emptied. Lord save me from men." She jutted her chin at Alison and Samuel. "Who are these two?"

"Samuel Fiddes, ma'am. This is my sister, Alison."

Pruss said, "Captain Allaway believes you may have a room for them. Scotty here fired with us up the coast."

"I do indeed," she said in a honeyed voice. "Always for a friend of Captain Allaway. Is he going to pay me a call today?"

"He said to tell you that he is sorry, but he is taken up with *Louisa*. She suffered a bit of trouble on the way up. He'll try to come later."

"Well, then."

Alison yawned.

"That child is tired, Samuel Fiddes," Pruss said. "Put her to bed. And, ma'am, if you'll excuse us, we're going back down to see if we can help in some way. Scotty, come looking for us when you can. We'll ask about pay for helping to clean up the town."

As soon as they disappeared, Mrs. Barnum's honeyed coquetry disappeared. "I'm not a sentimental woman, no matter that Captain Allaway recommended you. If you cannot pay, I will turn you out. I have one room in the back. Room and board is five dollars a week. You got that?"

"I do," Samuel said, though he wasn't sure how much money the captain had given him. "I'll get a job as soon as I can."

She narrowed her gaze. "You'd better hustle, 'cause the miners over to Newcastle might be going on strike. They'll all come flooding into town, hungry for work."

"Newcastle? Is that a coal mine?"

"Yes."

"Is there one in Seattle proper?"

"Oh, now, who told you that lie?"

"How far is Newcastle?"

Mrs. Barnum looked at him quizzically. "You have to take the train. Eighteen miles or so, down to Renton and then over to the other side of the lake. You a miner? 'Cause I like my boarders to stay a long time."

"Not a miner. Is Newcastle the only coal mine near here?"

She sniffed. "Well, there's almost a dozen of 'em. Down to Black Diamond, Franklin, Renton—that's the Talbot—a few up north near Bellingham, down in Pierce, near Tacoma. I can't keep track of them all. But Newcastle is closest."

Samuel swallowed, a plan forming. Newcastle, then. He would go there first, and if they weren't there, he would visit every single one in turn until he found Hailey.

Mrs. Barnum walked them through a parlor furnished with scattered armchairs and continued down a central hall, ending at a door to the outside. Two rooms stood opposite each other. One a bedroom, and the other a scullery where a girl was kneading dough on a floured board.

"This is my daughter, Annabelle," Mrs. Barnum said. "We run this house ourselves. No Chinamen. Won't have them in the house. Annabelle, this is Samuel Fiddes and his sister, Alison. They're looking at number one."

The girl briefly raised her eyes. She, too, had masses of chestnut hair pinned up in a messy crown. Caked in flour up to her elbows, she held herself like a warrior, even in an apron and a plain dress.

Across from the scullery, room number one was as narrow as the kitchen, but tidy, with whitewashed boards for walls and a rag rug underfoot. One bed, a dresser and basin, and a single high-backed chair occupied nearly the whole of the room. Immediately, Alison untied her boots and lay down on the bed. For weeks, she'd been complaining that her toes were pinching her. Samuel wondered if Seattle had a shoemaker.

Mrs. Barnum leaned against the doorjamb, awaiting his approval. "You want it?"

"How long can we stay?"

"Like I said, as long as you pay your rent. Supper is at six. In the summer we eat out back on the sawbuck table, unless it's raining, and then we set up in the parlor. It rains a lot here. If you need drinking or bathing water, we have a cistern in the back. There's a spring up the ridge, with a flume. Just follow the people

ROBIN OLIVEIRA

with the buckets. It's a climb. Privy's out back." She paused and placed her hands on her hips, seemingly waiting for Samuel to do something. Then she said, "I take payment in advance."

Samuel emptied his pockets.

"Silver dollars?" Mrs. Barnum said, sorting through them. "Captain Allaway was generous with you. Of course, that man can afford to be generous." She plucked five of the coins from Samuel's outstretched palm.

That left him with eight—a week and a half more of shelter. He would need a job. How would he do that and look for Hailey? And watch Alison? He'd made it to Seattle, and yet the possibility of finding Hailey felt further away than ever.

"Mrs. Barnum, did you ever rent to some Scots called Mac-Intyre? Would have come about two months ago?"

She squinted at him. "MacIntyre? Can't say I have."

"Have you met them anywhere?

"Not that I remember. Now, Annabelle and I share a room upstairs. We sleep with an axe under our bed, because women are scarce in Seattle and saloons are not. The wilderness lies just over the back of the nearest hill. Beware. Last week a black bear wandered into town and marauded our blackberry vines."

"Don't scare them, Mama," Annabelle called.

"They don't look like they scare easy," Mrs. Barnum said, departing back down the hall without a word of farewell.

"Well, Alison," Samuel said, sitting on the bed beside her.

"I want to go home," she shouted suddenly, kicking him. "I want to go home."

He watched in horror, conscious of Annabelle just across the hall. Alison had never behaved like a wild animal before. He grabbed her ankles. "Stop it. Did you love the nasty cold in Glasgow? Did you love the choking coal smoke and the night soil in the gutter and the endless dark nights? Did you love changing spools in that factory, or getting whacked by the throstle jobber? How about running through the streets by yourself?"

"I don't care! I don't like it! I don't like it!"

He tried to soothe her, but she was echoing all his own terrors. So far, he didn't like it here, either.

"Hello?"

Samuel turned. Annabelle was leaning against the doorjamb, bread dough sticking to her fingers.

"What's the girl's name again?"

"Alison."

"Alison, child," Annabelle said, "hush up and listen to me."

Startled, Alison peered at her.

"Everybody here wants to go home. I want to go home. But you won't get home by pitching a fit. I already tried it." She whirled back to her bread dough and did not look over again.

Alison peered after her, her cheeks streaked with tears. For two months she'd been squirreled away on ships, left to her own devices, and she'd asked for none of it.

"Come on, Ali, time to use the privy and go to bed."

Worn-out, she yielded. He walked her out into the yard. Chickens roosted in a henhouse in one corner. Wire wrapped around a garden of squash and corn and lettuces. The wooden privy stood opposite the henhouse. The sun was setting. The university, a three-story cupolaed building, the grandest in town, stood on a huge lot across the street behind. None of it resembled the tenement courtyard on Argyle Street.

When she was done, he lifted her and carried her inside. He removed her dress and tucked her next to her doll.

Alison drew her legs to her chest. In a low-pitched voice full of sleep, she said, "Do we have to share with anyone?"

Samuel startled, realizing that for the first time in their lives, they had a room to themselves. Right now he could shut the door on the world, and that was more than they'd had in a long time. And it was quiet.

"No, Ali, lass. It's all ours."

Instantly, she slept.

Samuel undressed and lay down beside her.

Tomorrow, Newcastle.

18

Hailey

SEVERAL HOURS AFTER HAILEY'S FATHER LEFT for the mine, a deafening rumble thundered from deep in the earth, rattling the ground, houses, dishware, furniture, bed-clothes. The bunkers went silent. The sawmill, too. In the un-precedented quiet, crows shrieked from high above in the fir trees. Time stopped.

Everyone dropped what they were doing and ran toward the mine. Mothers, wives, children, sawyers, pickers, cooks, bar-tenders, store clerks, everyone. Hailey, washing dishes, snatched up Geordie and ran the short fifty feet to the mine entrance, where the air was thick with dust and confusion.

CB Shattuck took charge, counting and recounting miners as they poured staggering and gasping from the mine. Covered with coal dust, spitting soot, they were unrecognizable. Their wives and mothers and children stumbled between, pawing at them, sobbing in relief, spoiling their dresses as they embraced their loved ones.

Hailey lurched through the crowd, searching for her father. She seized people, screaming, "My father? Have you seen my father?" Man after man proved not to be him. The powder house, where he sometimes could be found, stood padlocked. Her heart dropped. Her mother had abandoned them this morning, and not five hours later her father was missing. She clung to Geordie in her arms, feeling lost. She clamped down on the panic threatening to overtake her.

Shattuck checked and rechecked names against the shift roster. Fifty men in the mine. Miners trickled out in twos and threes until the tide ebbed and Shattuck shouted for order, his voice carrying above the keening of the women still searching, calling, "Where are you? Finneas! Davie, Davie!" joining Hailey's and Geordie's cries of "Father! Father!"

Shattuck totted up the sum again, his index finger running down the roster, his eyes searching the crowd. "Oh, blast it, if you can't find your man, come here, tell me who's missing!"

A small crowd surged forward, women grasping his arms, children clinging to their mothers' skirts. Hailey was close behind. Frantically they shouted names at Shattuck as behind them another cry arose: "The strike! The strike! We should have struck yesterday!" Over and over again Hailey yelled, "Harold MacIntyre," until Shattuck locked eyes with her and nodded.

"MacIntyre?" someone called from behind her shoulder. "He should be here, goddammit."

Hailey cringed to hear her father's name shouted in anger. She spun. "He's lost in the mine!"

Geordie wailed.

James Murray appeared at Hailey's side, covered in soot, a shallow slash across one cheek. He reached for her hand, and she gave it to him. His eyes appeared dazed and alive, electric with the effort it had taken to get out of the mine.

She was surprised to feel relief at the sight of him. "My father. I can't find him."

James looked stricken. She knew he wanted her to throw her arms around his neck and cry like the other women were doing. But she couldn't, and she didn't want to examine why right now.

Blinking, shrugging off the lassitude of shock, James said, "He's not at the powder house?"

"No."

"Sometimes he goes into the mine and waters the dust instead of making the boys do it."

James elbowed his way closer to Shattuck, pulling Hailey along, Geordie's head buried in her neck.

"Everyone hush!" Shattuck yelled. "Listen up. Six men are missing. Five miners and the fire boss. We need volunteers to go back in to search!"

Someone ran to unearth the rescue stretchers from under the cookhouse as Shattuck bellowed orders about assembling at the entrance to form teams. All was bedlam.

"Listen, Hailey," James said. "We can't wait another second. I'm going back in to look for him." He hollered to Shattuck, "I'm going in." He took up a Davy lamp and dashed through the crowd, a bandanna pulled up over his mouth and nose.

"Goddammit, wait for the others," Shattuck called after him, but James had disappeared into the mine.

Hailey found Bonnie Atherton, tears pouring down her face. Her husband, Alan, was one of the missing. The women held hands in stony silence.

A team of twelve men inched into the mine opening, Davy lamps extended, followed by another dozen men who formed a bucket brigade to douse any burning timbers. It wasn't a rock fall, the survivors insisted. It was an explosion. If the coal vein was on fire, the whole mine would have to be closed. The whole mine could be burning now. Their livelihoods were at stake.

Miners lay sprawled on the ground, overcome by their brush with death, fear finally overwhelming them. A few women had fetched water and were offering it to escaped miners with tin cups foraged from the cookhouse. No one knew why the explosion had happened. It was a mine that wasn't supposed to explode. Possibilities were considered, repeated, mulled over. An unanticipated pocket of methane? A careless hand with the blasting powder? Dust? No one knew. Someone blamed faulty blasting fuses. As always, others questioned whether enough care had been taken, a few muttering about whether the fire boss was to blame.

Geordie buried his head in Hailey's neck again. She cradled him close. It could just be the two of them now.

Time crept by. It was like waiting for the dead.

The first of the missing men was hauled out. Bonnie squeezed Hailey's hand tighter.

Burned over most of his body, the victim blinked lashless eyes, his mouth working, chest heaving, his rasps filling the air.

Who was he? Which man was he? He was burned so badly, no one could tell.

One of the mine doctors—Joseph Leary—put his hand to his mouth. Such horror. It seemed it was beyond him. There were two doctors at the mine, but Grant Bryant had gone into Seattle earlier in the week to purchase more medicine and hadn't returned. Relative to Dr. Bryant, Dr. Leary was young, yet his forehead had already furrowed, his hair turned silver.

Leary roused. "Muslin strips! Carron oil! Linseed oil!" He pointed to his wife. "Run home. It's all in the cupboard in the parlor. And you there," he said, nodding to the saloonkeeper, who'd come running. "Get to the store and empty the shelves of vinegar."

A woman melted to the ground beside the injured man. He was her husband. She recognized him by a scar on his exposed buttock. His pants had been burned from his body. Bonnie and Hailey exchanged a fearful glance.

The mine, his stretcher-bearers reported, had not caught fire. That would have been the end of everything. It would have had to have been flooded, shuttered.

An hour never felt so long. Over the course of this eternity, one by one, another four men were carried out. The last of the five was not recognizable except by the lack of a pinky finger on his right hand. It was Alan Atherton, Bonnie's husband, dead on a stretcher at her feet.

Bonnie began to keen.

Hailey couldn't breathe.

Where was her father?

And then James Murray emerged from the mine entrance, leading her father by the hand. James was even more soot-blackened, his pants torn, his face weary. Her father, too, was covered in soot. He was gripping a watering can and a safety lamp. His hands trembled. His whole body shook. Hailey searched him for burns, for cuts. Nothing. She flung herself into his arms. He was all right. He was alive. He raised his arms slowly, belatedly, his embrace perfunctory. Geordie was still wailing, reaching for him.

"I had to look everywhere," James said. "He must have heard the blast and acted quick. I found him in one of the rooms off the main gangway. Smart man. Dove in, missed the fireball. He could have walked out on his own, but he wouldn't move. I had to wrestle him out of there. He isn't talking."

"Papa. Papa, tell me you're all right?" Hailey said.

Her father looked right through her.

People came and shouted at him for answers, but her father said nothing. He was stricken, unable to react, or to help, or to direct anything. Geordie had slipped from Hailey's arms and was clinging to her leg, crying.

Finally, her father brought his mouth to her ear and said, "It's my fault, Hailey Rose. My fault."

"No, Papa."

"I should have stopped it. I should have known."

"Known what? Known what?"

"Everything."

It was then that he left her. She felt him slipping away, out of time, back to High Blantyre, back to the past. There would never be any forgiveness for him now. No redemption. The dust of failure would cover him forever. Geordie was holding out his arms to be taken up. This demand seemed to make her father drop away completely. He had nothing left to give anyone. He was still breathing, still standing, but he had exited his mind.

James took her father by the elbow and walked them all the short way home.

19

Samuel

THAT SAME MORNING, SAMUEL ASKED THE TESTY
Annabelle if she would watch Alison. "I need to get to Newcastle today."

Annabelle raised an eyebrow. "What's in Newcastle?"

"Please, could you help me?" Though Alison had slept hard
and woken in a better mood, she wasn't fit to go anywhere. "She
needs to stay put, just for a day. Please?"

Alison, overhearing, promised to help Annabelle with housework. Samuel supposed that any semblance of home was a comfort to his sister. And the house was lovely—clean and airy, filled
with light.

When Annabelle acquiesced, Alison danced at his feet.
Breakfast had been served outside to all the boarders on a sawbuck table—pancakes with syrup and fried eggs—and just the
bounty of it had further improved Alison's sense of well-being.
Samuel was thrilled to see it.

Annabelle said, "It takes all day to get to Newcastle and
back—and there's only one train, one set of tracks. But I don't
think it's running. They're worried after the fire."

After saying goodbye to Alison, Samuel dashed down the steep hill into town, skirting the devastation of the fire and heading for the tideflats and the train trestle that ran across them. At the foot of King and Commercial, a painted sign on a small shack said, *Seattle and Walla Walla Railroad.*

The clerk informed him that the trains weren't running and might not for days. The engineer feared the fire had disrupted the tracks, and he wouldn't allow the train to run until he had inspected the switches and the rails.

Samuel said, "Can I get to Newcastle some other way?"

The man sniffed, peering at him through narrowed eyes. "I s'pose. Walk, follow the railroad tracks, bushwhack through a few gorges, cross a couple rivers, hike up the mountainside."

"How long would that take?"

"It's near eighteen miles, son. There are no roads. James Colman built that railroad for a reason. Or if you've got the money, you could head on over the ridge three miles to Leschi, hire someone to row you across the lake the six miles to Newcastle Landing. Fight your way through the wilderness on the other shore up to the town, if you figure out which way to go. You're best off waiting for the train. What's a day or two? The trains might run tomorrow, but Colman, he's particular, so we'll see. Usually, we keep a tight schedule."

"What time does the first train run?"

"Six thirty. Then eleven."

Frustration thrumming through him, Samuel turned to downtown, where it seemed that every man in Seattle was crawling over the ashy detritus of Commercial Row. An army of ants, Seattle citizens, bent on rebuilding the town as fast as possible. Everywhere, men were piling wheelbarrows high with burned timbers, trundling them to the tideflats, and dumping them into the muck without ceremony, returning for more. Before a lot was even cleared, other men were hammering together frames and raising them to form the walls of new buildings, everyone shouting and pointing and calling, "Steady, steady."

Samuel ran into Pruss and John Salvation. They'd heard that a man named Bailey Gatzert, who managed the decimated Schwabacher warehouse, was hiring for two dollars a day. He wanted two buildings built as fast as possible—one adjacent to Yesler's Wharf, and another just across the alley along Commercial.

Pruss said, "You goin' to look for your people?"

"I want to, but I can't today."

"All right, then. Why don't you come with us, earn some money?"

Stymied, Samuel figured he might as well. He went with them to see Gatzert and all three were hired for the day.

Because Seattle's sawmill had burned, a shipment of milled timber had been sent over at dawn from Port Blakely. Samuel turned a plank in his hand. "What wood is this?"

"Fir," Pruss said. "Grows here like weeds. Everyone said it wouldn't burn." He gave a short laugh.

"Doesn't anyone use brick? Or stone? Something that won't burn?"

"Scotty, something you need to know about Seattle," John Salvation said. "It's always in a hurry. There's only a few brick buildings in town—Jennings' store for one, and Wa Chong in Chinatown's another. Besides, Carkeek burned. They're the ones who sell brick."

"Chinatown?"

John Salvation lifted his chin. "Past the Lava Beds."

The Lava Beds, they explained, housed brothels. The soggy

few acres of land south of Mill Street and east of the devastation. Chinatown lay beyond that, under the twin smokestacks, which Pruss informed him belonged to the coal gasworks that lit the few streetlights in town. Chinatown's boggy ground housed a few stores, opium dens, cookhouses, washhouses, and more brothels. The Celestials lived in houses on stilts overlying the indistinct shoreland of the tideflats: foul, smelly ground partly submerged at high tide and used as the town's garbage dump.

"Celestials?" Samuel said.

"Chinese. They built this place," Pruss said. "Graded the roads. Built the railroad."

"They came all this way?" Samuel said, feeling instant warmth toward these fellow transplants. If they had found a home here, so far from their native land, then perhaps he could, too—though, by the sound of it, it seemed as if the Chinese weren't really prospering as much as surviving.

He saw no Chinese among the workers. "Why not today?"

"Not appreciated anymore," Pruss said.

"Why not?"

Pruss stiffened and spoke in a near whisper. "People don't like that there are so many of them. John Salvation and me, there are only a few of us black folks. They can ignore us. But the Chinese—nearly a thousand of them. Whites are afraid that there will be more Chinese than them. They think that if the Chinese help, they'll lay claim, settle more into the city. Get too comfortable. Think they belong." Pruss made a vague gesture toward some Indians wading in the tideflats, open-weave baskets tied to their backs, picking their way around the trash to collect clams and mussels from the rocks exposed by the low tide. "Those people were here first, and they don't have any say in what goes on around here."

Samuel had already noticed the ramshackle lean-tos lining the beach where Indian women were drying clams on strings, and the makeshift tents perched on an island of ballast in the harbor, canoes pulled up at sharp angles on the artificial island. Just like in Glasgow, the rich built on the heights while the poor were relegated to the damp.

"Nothing's fair, is it?" Samuel said, coughing. Ash was being kicked up everywhere.

"Not that I've noticed," Pruss said. "Now, let's build Gatzert a new building."

By noon, they had erected two sections of frame. The building would eventually be a long, narrow thing, thirty feet by ninety—all fir. As he worked, Samuel kept looking toward the depot, but there was no sign of a locomotive or a train being readied. He pushed away his frustration. Pruss and John Salvation heaved a pair of sawed-off two-by-fours over their shoulders and ferried them to a new frame and hammered them into place.

A renewed Seattle was springing up around them. It seemed that if you put no art into it, you could rebuild a city in one day. Samuel thought of all the hours it had taken to build just one dinghy—the careful planing and steaming and fitting. The building they were working on would be finished tomorrow. They broke for a meal at Our House, and once outside again, Samuel craned his neck toward the depot.

John Salvation said, "You ever think of asking Captain Allaway about your people?"

"Why?" Samuel said.

"Only way here is by steamer—unless they came up on the Military Road from the Columbia River. Unlikely, though. Most folks come by water. They could have taken any line from San Francisco. The Puget Sound Line, the Pacific Mail. Seven ships between 'em. But maybe they took *Louisa*. When did they come?"

"Two months before me. The father said they were coming to a coal mine in Washington Territory. Seattle, maybe."

"Well, now, you do know, there aren't any coal mines in Seattle proper? And Seattle isn't all of Washington Territory?" Pruss said.

"I know," Samuel said. "But don't most people stop here first? Isn't it the biggest port?" He plunged into a description of the MacIntyres. "A family. They had money—well, once they did. A father, tall, straight back, fine features. The mother thin, dark hair, high forehead. Worries a lot. A daughter—my age—the prettiest girl you've ever seen. Chestnut curls down her back. And a little boy, he'd be about five now, named Geordie."

Pruss and John Salvation peered at each other, eyes narrowing in concentration. Pruss said, "That little boy who liked to look for whales? What was his name?"

John Salvation shook his head. "Don't remember. Cap'n would know better than either of us, though."

Samuel felt another rush of hope. Why hadn't he thought of this? A Scot would remember a Scot. "Let's go now."

"After we finish, and after Gatzert pays us, son."

They raised all the exterior walls of the building by four o'clock, then started on the interior—a partition for an office and a back storeroom, Samuel working through his rising impatience. They finally finished at six and gathered their pay and first went to the depot.

"Not tomorrow," the clerk assured Samuel. "Don't know when yet."

They found Allaway drinking whiskey in his quarters on

Louisa. The tide had dropped so much that they had to climb a wharf ladder down to the deck.

A deep scowl was affixed to Allaway's ruddy face. "Bloody paint's suddenly as dear as gold. And the Inspector of Hulls won't sign off until she's painted within an inch of her life. We're never going to get out of here."

Pruss said, "Scotty here has a question."

Allaway turned with a knowing smile. "Ah, came to your senses, did you? You don't like Seattle? I'm happy to have you back. We'll all adopt wee Ali, won't we? I'll teach her her numbers. No better life than at sea, is there, boys?"

Samuel ignored the invitation. He explained about the Mac-Intyres.

Remember, Samuel Fiddes. Remember! Washington Territory.

Allaway scowled a second time. "I remember them. Darling daughter they had. Too pretty for Seattle. Delivered them to the American House myself."

They were here. The MacIntyres were here! He could hardly catch his breath. "Where is the American House?"

"Burned down. Good thing, too. Miserable place. One of Yesler's tinderboxes—practically held together with string, like this whole town." It turned out that Allaway liked to ramble when he was in his cups. "I heard today that Colman blamed Yesler for the fire on account of the disrepair of his properties. No love lost between those two—"

Samuel had no patience for Allaway's ramblings. "Do you know where they are?"

"I tried to talk MacIntyre out of staying there—he had a nice family—but he wanted to save his pennies. Said he was moving on—"

"Where? Moving on where?"

"I remember him droning on and on about something. God, he was in love with whatever it was. Could hardly get him to shut up about it."

"Coal?"

Allaway's eyes brightened through his whiskey haze. "Jaisus, that's it. I don't know for certain which mine he was headed for, though. So many around here. If it's not timber in Seattle, it's coal. And salmon. That's the lot. That's what Seattle does." He seemed pleased to summarize Seattle's industries so succinctly.

"Would anyone know for certain?"

"OJ Carr, the postmaster. Directory will be no help. They print those in December. You could comb through the newspaper passenger lists, see if they went up to Whatcom, maybe. The *Daily Intelligencer* survived the fire, and they keep back issues, but it would be a hell of a thing, trying to spot them, and those lists aren't always complete. Passengers don't always want to be mentioned. Or you could just ask around. No more'n three, four thousand people in Seattle. Ask at any saloon. Seattle's a small town. Not like San Francisco."

20

Hailey

THE MORNING AFTER THE EXPLOSION, HAILEY woke her father to ask him what to do. But her father would not speak. He answered none of her questions. He only stared. She made tea and when she brought him a cup, he had lain back down. He could move, he could follow directions, but he would not talk. He was hollowed out. Absent. She tried to shake him out of his stupor, but he was no longer himself. She tore apart the house but found no ten dollars in gold. Her father had imagined them into being. Geordie woke and kept asking where their mother was. Hailey gave him a biscuit for breakfast and took him outside to the lip of the treed ravine above Coal Creek so she could think. In the absence of the clatter of the mine, birdsong split the morning. She sank onto the carpet of needles.

They had nothing. Some beans. Some flour. They could live for perhaps a few more days.

Yesterday, when James had helped her to bring her father back to their house, he had eased Harold onto his bed and removed his boots.

"People are saying that your mother went back to Scotland," he said.

"She left this morning. She was furious. Father wants us to go up the Skagit."

"He never."

"He wants me to keep camp for him."

"You're too fine for that."

It was the most personal thing he had ever said to her. She wondered why he thought it. Her fingernails were broken and tarred with the work of living. She had not tended to her hair in some time. Not since the dance, she thought, and even then, it had been only a feeble attempt to re-create what any Glaswegian lady's maid could have crafted in a moment. James offered to stay with her as long as she needed, but he was covered in soot and the cut on his cheek needed attention. She made him go back to the boardinghouse and rest. After all, he'd been in the dark of the mine, crawling around, trying to find her father.

"Hailey?" She turned now and saw James coming toward her. At the lip of the ravine, he stopped and struck one foot out, as if he needed to brace himself against his own urges. He had bathed and dressed in his Sunday shirt and pants. The slash on his cheek had turned scarlet.

He said, "We voted to strike. The explosion was the last straw. They've furloughed all of us."

"I don't know what I'm going to do," Hailey said quietly, checking where Geordie was. "Father is—he's gone. His mind is gone."

They returned to the house. James took one look at her father and went for the doctor. Dr. Leary came and examined him. He shone a light in her father's eyes and down his throat and made him squeeze his hands. Her father was fine physically, but when the doctor asked him questions—"What day is it? . . . What time of year? . . . Who is the mine superintendent?"—her father couldn't answer. Or wouldn't.

The doctor stood gazing down at his patient, who had coiled himself into a fetal position and drawn the covers over his head.

"Your father needs to go to Steilacoom. To the hospital for the insane. It's a steamer ride from Seattle down to Tacoma. He's docile enough that I can take him myself. As soon as Dr. Bryant returns, I can take him there, admit him. The territory pays the fees, so you won't have to worry about that."

Hailey backed against the wall, her fingers crawling at her skirts. She had been the daughter of a wealthy man and had lived a life in which no harm had come to her, and now the whole world had changed.

"No."

"He's struck dumb, Miss MacIntyre. When this happens people can't take care of themselves. I don't know if he will ever be able to take care of himself. Do you understand me? I mean in every way. To feed himself or to use the privy—anything."

Words clawed at Hailey's throat. She looked over at Geordie, playing with his soldiers and animals, and envied him his ignorance. "He'll get better."

But she was arguing with herself. He wouldn't get better. He hadn't been better in a long time. God was telling him things. The gold mines were the answer to their troubles. They had money they didn't have.

Dr. Leary's face softened. She did not want his pity, but, oh, how she wanted his kindness.

"He might get better," the doctor said, though it was clearly a concession he did not want to make. "But he's going to need care until then, do you understand? At the asylum—"

"I can't do that to him."

The doctor spoke gently, his voice measured, his eyes showing greater concern than yesterday, when dozens of men had needed his care. He looked as if he hadn't slept. "A while ago, I discovered him behind the powder house, babbling about something that had happened in Scotland, about an explosion there. He's not well, Miss MacIntyre. He hasn't been for some time."

"I'll take care of him."

The doctor looked around the house. It was in disarray. The morning dishes still needed to be washed and laundry was hanging and a mouse was struggling in a trap. The doctor put on his jacket. "I have other patients to see. You should know, Miss MacIntyre, that I can commit your father without your permission. He isn't violent, so I won't. But you are taking too much on. You don't realize. He will be like a child. It will be too much for you."

The door slammed behind him. Hailey reached for a handhold and couldn't find one. Mad? Her father was mad? Time stopped. Her throat closed. Geordie still played in the corner, but his shoulders were hunched as if he understood everything. He was her responsibility now. Geordie and her father. She was seventeen years old and she needed to make a life in this strange, awful place. She did not know how long she stood there seeing her future unspool before her. Not even these last ungodly months had prepared her for abandonment. What a foolish thing it was to be a spoiled girl without tether or skill or means.

She turned to James, who was now, suddenly, at her elbow. She'd forgotten that he was there.

He took her by the hand.

"Hailey MacIntyre, marry me," he said. "This proposal is not the way I envisioned it. Nor perhaps the way you did—if you did. I know it's not romantic in the least. But I was planning to ask for your hand in marriage at the end of the summer, and now it appears I ought not to wait.

"I am done with mining. I'm done with living here. I don't ever want to go back into a mine. They've furloughed us anyway because of the strike. To be honest, I don't know what I'll do—this is so fast. We can go to those islands—the San Juans. I'll work the lime kilns there. You know them? It's not far—sixty miles or so by sea. I'm told you earn a lot of money fast. Or something else. Something bigger. Better. But I am prepared to help you. I'll never let the doctor take your father to Steilacoom. Even if something happens. Do you hear me? I'll take care of Geordie, too. I'll treat you so well. I saved you before, from that cougar. I'll save you from every cougar."

Hailey stared at him, stunned.

She hardly heard him as he talked on, his voice growing more confident as she offered no objection.

"You can trust me. I went back into the mine. I found your father. He had powder with him. And a candle. An open flame. I don't know what he would have done to himself, Hailey. I saved him. I brought him out, for you.

"I'll keep you fine, my Hailey. I'll treat you like a queen. You and your family. One day you'll have a big house. The finest in Seattle. This proposal is not out of pity. You see, you are an obsession with me. I couldn't believe my eyes when I first saw you. An angel in my wilderness."

Throughout James's torrent, Hailey thought of Samuel. Samuel, whom she had wanted from the first moment she had seen him. Samuel, of whom she had asked, *Washington Territory*. But that was before she understood how far Washington was, and how far her past would fall behind her. How futile plans were. How desperate things could get.

"Marry me." James's blue gaze was unrelenting. "You'll never have to struggle. I've saved all my money. I'll find new work. I'll take care of you. Kiss me, will you?"

His lips were thin, unpersuasive, but he was deferential, grateful, mindful of Geordie, who was still playing with his soldiers in the corner. It went on for a long time, a dry, harmless thing that Hailey believed James thought respectful and that she could only think of as inevitable.

21

Samuel

THE NEXT MORNING, AFTER AGAIN LEAVING ALI-
son working happily in the kitchen with Annabelle, Samuel
hurried directly to the depot.

"No," the answer came from the same clerk. "Not today."

Samuel went to the post office, a freestanding structure on
the unburned side of Mill Street. The racket from the hammering and shouting nearly drowned out the disembodied voice
that yelled, "Shut the door quick, for God's sake, or the place
will fill with ash."

A large, heavyset man with a square jaw and bald pate peered
at Samuel with a distracted air. "Who are you?"

"My name is Samuel Fiddes. Are you Mr. Carr?"

"I am."

"I came to Seattle a couple of days ago. My sister Alison, too.
We're staying at Mrs. Barnum's on College Street. Can you
tell me—"

"Wait a minute." Carr pulled a pencil from a drawer and
sharpened it with a knife. Then he opened a ledger, his laborious
movements as protracted as if he were about to write down the
origins of the universe. "Barnum's, you said?"

"Yes, but—"

Carr held up one hand. "How do you spell your name?"

Samuel told him, the scratching of the pencil against the ledger aggravating his growing impatience. Finally, Carr adjusted his spectacles and looked up as methodically as he had done everything else.

Samuel said, "I'm looking for someone. A Scots family. They arrived maybe two months ago. They stayed at the American House. They might be here. Or in Newcastle. Or at another coal mine. But I don't know."

Carr finally set down his pencil and dusted the lead from his fingers as he peered at Samuel with a distracted air. "Name?"

"MacIntyre."

The postmaster turned the ledger pages one by one. "MacIntyre, MacIntyre. Lots of Scots over there in Newcastle. Lots here, too." But, no, he'd posted no letters to any Harold MacIntyre anywhere. But he had heard something about a new Scots fire boss out at the Newcastle mine. Was the MacIntyre he was looking for a fire boss?

"No, he would be a superintendent. He's an important man."

"Well, if he were an important man in Newcastle, I would have heard of him," Carr said.

"Are you certain?"

Carr raised an eyebrow. "Young man, I see that you're desperate. But I would know. I am Seattle's lost and found."

The man had taken such care writing Samuel's name in his ledger that surely if Harold MacIntyre had come anywhere near Seattle, the methodical Carr would indeed know. But it was possible that Harold MacIntyre had been here for too short a time to post or receive a letter. Or maybe, Samuel despaired, they had turned around and left, even gone back to San Francisco on a boat other than *Louisa*.

Heaving a sigh, Samuel followed Allaway's next advice and traipsed from saloon to saloon. He found several open and serving even at nine o'clock in the morning.

It was the same conversation, over and over again, all day.

There's a new fire boss in Newcastle. Named MacIntyre.

No, Samuel explained. *Harold MacIntyre would have been a superintendent.*

Oh, no. Charlie Shattuck is the superintendent there. Has been for a long time. If your friend was looking to be a superintendent, he would have gone elsewhere. Did you think of going up to Whatcom to look for him?

Whatcom, Samuel had learned, was nearly a hundred miles away. But before he went to Whatcom or anywhere else, Samuel would go to Newcastle and ask after the fire boss, just in case.

At the end of the day, the good news blazed through Seattle that James Colman had announced that the tracks were undamaged and the first train would run the next morning at six thirty.

SAMUEL ROSE EARLY to get to that first train, but Alison's needs kept him from it. She fussed around, asked for water to wash, begged him to braid her hair. Exasperated, he nonetheless cared for her, resolving not to miss the eleven a.m. She dawdled over breakfast as other boarders jogged off to various jobs. Alison was making it clear that she did not want to leave the table, let alone the yard. With her fork, she scraped syrup from her plate. Her doll lay sprawled on the bench beside her. She peered at Samuel with her bright blue eyes and smiled, pleased.

Annabelle carried a basket of eggs across the yard and set it on the table next to Samuel. "Heard the trains are running."

"Could you keep Ali again? I can pay you." He turned to his sister. "Would you like that?"

Alison grinned assent as Annabelle piled the dirty plates, balancing utensils on top. "Happy to," she said, "You know, "I took the train to Newcastle last month, for a dance at the Odd Fellows Hall. It's a nice ride above the lake there at the end. The town is ugly, though the people were nice enough. I want to go to the next one, but my mother says the boys there are no good. She didn't like the boys back home, either, so I don't know how I'll ever find someone."

Samuel sputtered with eagerness. "You've been? Did you meet a Scots girl named Hailey MacIntyre?"

Annabelle paused, thinking. "There was someone there called Hailey. Daughter of the fire boss. Everyone said she had her nose in the air, but she seemed lost to me."

The Newcastle fire boss named MacIntyre.

Samuel's heart leapt. *Hailey! His* Hailey. He jumped from the table, cupped Alison's face in his hands and kissed her, and then he tore toward town.

He had missed the six thirty and was too early for the eleven. He bought a ticket and began to pace beside the tracks. No time had ever moved more slowly. He thought he should go and help at Gatzert's, but he would only dirty himself. He watched herons picking at the edges of the water, and the Indians again, harvesting mussels and digging clams. The coal works smoked into the sky. Seagulls screamed overhead. The sun rose higher, flinging light onto the sculpted landscape, erasing shadows as it grew infinitely more cheerful and Samuel more morose. He had crossed half the world in less time than it was taking for that train to return from Newcastle. Maybe James Colman was wrong. Maybe something had happened to the tracks and no one would ever be able to get to Newcastle again.

In the distance, across the mudflats, a small speck appeared, spouting steam. The speck drew closer and transformed into a train. The piles supporting the tracks looked spindly and insufficient to shoulder the weight of the locomotive and its coal cars, but nonetheless it chugged toward Samuel and a now overflowing crowd impatient for its arrival.

An hour-and-a-half trip, the ticket seller had told him. An hour and a half seemed an eternity now that Samuel knew Hailey was close.

But soon. *Soon.* He'd done it. He'd found her.

THE TRAIN SQUEALED to a stop, and passengers poured out, blinking in the sunlight. More than two dozen men were being led down the platform, cradling bandaged heads and hands. The waiting crowd gasped. Some of the men were limping, but most could walk under their own power.

"What happened?" people called.

Samuel stopped a stout man as he shouldered past, ignoring everyone's cries, seemingly intent on getting to the saloons and whorehouses of Chinatown before anyone else. "Tell us, man."

Impatiently, the arrival hoisted up his pants and sniffed. "Explosion. Five of us dead. We struck, and now they've furloughed the lot of us, the bastards. Can you imagine? The lot of us, I tell you." He patted the shoulder of a passing man whose left eye was bandaged with gauze. "Bobby here got hurt bad. He needs the nuns and their hospital. But most of us—me—I'm headed for a drunk and a screwing that the bards will sing about forever, because by God it's been a live few days."

The man shook Samuel off, but before he could stumble into the morning's confusion, Samuel grasped him by the elbow. "Was a man named MacIntyre hurt?"

"MacIntyre? That daft idiot?"

Did a man call another man daft if he was dead? The wind had picked up, and the foul scent of the tideflats swept over the tracks. Samuel elbowed his way through the debarking passengers, but the conductor would let no one pass until the passenger car emptied.

A man on the platform cried out, "But who died? Do they have names? I'm going to see my brother. I've a right to know if he's alive!"

"I've got the list, but I'm not supposed to say. I'm walking it to the newspaper after I get the passengers settled," the conductor said.

He was drowned out by calls ricocheting through the crowd. "Read it aloud, man! Have you no heart?"

Over the hatted heads of the restless crowd in front of him, Samuel noticed that the last passengers were stepping off the train in twos and threes. A stocky, russet-haired man was helping a stooped, older man to climb slowly from the train car. A girl followed, holding the hand of a young boy in short pants. They huddled together for a moment, the older man leaning on the girl, the child hugging her skirts. Then the stocky man parted from them and went to the baggage bay of the car. The girl with the child and old man started down the platform.

Samuel stared, blinking.

The upturned nose, the wide, heavily lashed eyes, the pointed chin, the spill of curls.

Desire did that. Made mirages out of hope.

But it was Hailey. Unmistakably. She appeared not to see him.

She wore her green dress, a rosebud pinned to her bodice. She stopped and looked backward for a moment, then turned again and came down the platform, her pace slow, solicitous of her father and Geordie clinging to her. Harold MacIntyre hadn't died. They were fine. The MacIntyres were fine! And they were *here*.

There were perhaps ten feet between them.

Joy gripped him, turning him incoherent.

Hailey. "Hailey."

She looked through him, eyes uncomprehending. Had he changed so much in two short months? That eternity now seemed only the length of a breath.

"Hailey. It's me. Samuel." He wanted to shout to the heavens, *I found you.* "I came. To Washington Territory. I remembered. I'm here."

But she was a statue. Her eyes glazed as if she were fighting through a veil of fog.

His elation turned to grief. He had scared her with his mad dash across the world. Or she didn't recognize him. Or it was too much of a shock. Or maybe she had forgotten him. Maybe he had never mattered to her the way she mattered to him. He felt the swing of Damocles's sword, the strangle of disappointment, the crashing of all his dreams.

"Hailey." He wanted to shake her. "It's me. Samuel Fiddes."

Her face softened. "Samuel?"

He exhaled. "Yes." *Yes!*

"You came?"

"I came."

"For me?"

"For you."

He drank in her sublime face, her inviting lips, her blinking eyes. In them, he saw the love he needed to see, the flecks of gold like yearning, their depths the whole of his desire. He took her in his arms and lifted her to him and kissed her. His mouth claimed hers, and she responded with the same fervor that burned through him. She felt like a feather, like the embodiment of all his hopes. Whistles and the rustling of her skirts and the gasps of the crowd existed outside of them. He didn't care. The rest of the world didn't matter. He had found her. Against all odds, he had found her. Impossible. And now she was his. He would convince her parents and make a new life for them and by Jesus, Mary, and Joseph, and all the stars in heaven, he had done it. The conductor yelled, "All aboard," and people surged past them, but even then, he went on kissing her. He would never stop. Never. He would kiss her all day. All night. All year. All the rest of their lives, longer than anyone had ever lived.

When their lips finally parted, he lowered her to the ground.

She laid a hand to his cheek and said, "Samuel." Her touch was intimate and soft. "I didn't think I'd ever see you again."

"I coaled ships to get to you. I came around the world for you."

"You coaled from Scotland?"

"Yes. I went to New York. I worried you'd stayed there. I thought I'd missed you. Did you see the city?" He didn't know why he said this last. It didn't matter, except that he had accomplished a miracle. He had done it. All those worries—she could be anywhere in the world; he had lost her—but now she was in his arms.

"But when did you come? Why didn't I know?"

"Two, three days ago. I can't remember. I came and there was a fire. Do you know about the fire?" He waved his hand in the direction of the ruins. "The train wasn't running. And I didn't know for certain where you were. But then I did—an hour ago, Annabelle said she'd seen you—and I was on my way to you now. But here you are. You found me." He laughed. "You found *me*. It's a miracle."

"Yesterday? You could have come yesterday?"

"No. The trains weren't running because of the fire. But I'm here now. And Alison is, too."

The train was departing, steam billowing, the conductor obviously having trusted someone else to deliver the list of the dead. Samuel would cash in his ticket. He would cash in his ticket and their life together would begin.

Hailey kept glancing over her shoulder. The man who had helped them was piling trunks on a hand trolley. Samuel would tell him that he wasn't needed now.

"Here is Geordie. Won't you say hello?" Hailey drew the boy close, a protective hand on his shoulder.

Samuel forced himself back into time. There were other people to consider. He stooped and said, "Hello, Geordie. Remember me?"

But Geordie stuck his thumb in his mouth and disappeared into Hailey's skirts.

"He's tired. Please, Samuel. You have to understand. My father isn't well. There was an explosion. He hasn't spoken since. I think he's lost his mind."

Samuel stood and turned to her father, who he had forgotten even existed, and stuck out his hand, fully expecting Harold MacIntyre to take another swing at him for this second public kiss. But he remained motionless, a ghost in tweed. Samuel studied Hailey. He saw now how much she had changed. Her face, once so sweetly plump, was freckled and thin. Her dress was patched and torn at the hem, her sleeves frayed.

"Where is your mother?" Samuel said, alert now to something in the air.

"Mother left. She couldn't stand it here. She hated it. She took what money we had and said she was going back to Scotland, but I don't know where she is. Understand, I didn't have anyone. No one. Geordie and I were alone and there was no money—none—and I didn't know what to do. Please understand. I didn't know you were coming. And everything fell apart—"

Samuel said, "Your mother left? She left you and Geordie?"

Only a few debarking passengers lingered, organizing their luggage, and now they scowled as they pushed past. The barrel of a man came last, dragging a wheeled cart piled with trunks. Across one cheek, a long slash burned bright red. He stopped right next to Hailey. Something fundamental in Hailey's carriage changed. Suddenly she made a forlorn figure when she had never been one before. Always a spark inside her, always a defiant lift to her chin. Now she turned to wax. To glass. Nothing of her moved except her lips.

"Samuel," she said. "This is James Murray."

James Murray encircled Hailey's waist with a possessive hand. "That's not the whole of it, is it, now, my Hailey? Tell whoever this is who I am."

Later, Samuel would recall the way Hailey shut her eyes as she made the pronouncement, the small shudder of what he imagined to be revulsion, and her pleading look as she opened her eyes to meet Samuel's incredulous gaze.

"James is my husband."

"We married yesterday," Murray said. "So, whoever you are, you're late."

Part Three

✣

1879

Drink Home Beers
And
Keep money in the Country
At the
Tivoli Beer Hall
All the Puget Sound made beers are kept constantly on tap,
and none from California

~ADVERTISEMENT,
THE DAILY INTELLIGENCER,
1879

22

Hailey

HAILEY OPENED HER MOUTH AND OUT CAME NON-
sense. "James might try for work at the lime works on San Juan
Island. The island is somewhere north of here—not far. He's
good with a bludgeon, and they need rock fellers. It was uneasy
at the coal mines. There was an explosion. Did you know? Did I
say that already? The coal company furloughed everyone. There
is no work."

Hailey watched the light in Samuel's eyes extinguish as she
babbled on, his gaze roaming from James to her and back again,
seeking a disavowal of the marriage. After the first shock, comprehension seemed to flood through him.

He had come for her. Across oceans, across time, and now
she was flailing. She stared at his deeply chiseled frame. An ap-
parition. A mirage. The edges of her body liquefied. God, he
had grown strong. She had forgotten how beautiful he was.
She talked on, an impossible quest to reverse time. *One day. Just
one day.* Samuel's eyes dissected her appearance, her father's
alteration, Geordie's disquiet. She felt horror at what she had
done.

"That's enough," James said, ending her babbling. He steered her away, his hand firm at her waist, guiding her, dragging the luggage cart behind.

"Wait. Hailey—wait."

Hailey looked back over her shoulder, her feet stopping. Samuel's face had turned to stone, a marbled image of grief. She saw him struggle for something to say, to do. But how do you turn back time? How do you walk backward through the universe? She'd give anything—*anything*—to undo the past few days.

James pulled her away, fury in his touch. "Whoever he is, he's nothing to you now."

Hailey couldn't take her eyes off Samuel. "Samuel, I—"

James yanked on her arm, hauling her along, and she was powerless to stop him. Her father and Geordie trailed behind, and she soon lost sight of Samuel, who stood still amid the hubbub of burned timbers and new construction.

The day before, in Newcastle, within an hour of giving her consent, James had arranged the marriage ceremony. The minister hadn't left after Sunday services because the train still hadn't come, and for a fee of three dollars he ignored the sacrilege of marrying them in the immediate wake of five deaths. The ceremony took place in the chapel. Her father, Geordie, and Mr. Shattuck were the only witnesses. Bonnie didn't come, lost in grief at her husband's death. Hailey wore her green dress. It was the dress she had worn to the dance when she first met James.

Hailey and James spent their wedding night in an empty house. He arranged for a woman to stay in the MacIntyre house with Geordie and her father.

James showed mute reverence as he removed Hailey's clothing piece by piece, marveling at each layer of lace, no matter how ragged. She had wanted to wash and change into her nightclothes alone, but he said he could not wait. When she was completely naked, he took her hands and held them firmly in his, his face a mask of pleasure. She shivered. He tore off his clothes. She looked away, at the ceiling, out the window. With horror, she realized that there were no curtains. Anyone passing could have a look in. She sank onto the bed, covering herself.

He pushed her back onto the sheets.

He explored her body, pausing to cup each breast, exhaling with pleasure as he circled each of her nipples with his thumb and then leaned over and employed his tongue. At this, a bolt of incredulity shot through her. She had never imagined an act of such intimacy. Her back arched. He grinned and then paid attention to all of her, running his hands down her buttocks and her thighs, then turning her away and clasping her breasts from behind and then turning her to take them in his mouth again. His hands were busy in places no man should ever know about, spaces that were beginning to ache with fullness. He was rousing her, precipitating a response she could not refuse.

She cried out as he entered her. Her mother had never said a thing about any of this. Or about the pain. It ripped through her. James bucked on top of her. She endured this incursion with shock, holding back her cries. Miners on strike were shouting in the streets, music at the saloon blaring full blast. The rhythmic squeaking of the springs humiliated her. With every thrust, he hurt her.

Finally, he groaned and collapsed on top of her. Did she hear laughter? A cheer? It was too awful to contemplate. His weight pressed her into the mattress and he began to snore.

Once, after an evening in the coach with Samuel, she had woken in the night to find herself convulsing with unimaginable pleasure, her thighs wet, her breath coming in gasps. After it subsided, she never told anyone about it. It seemed shameful, and secret.

And wonderful.

None of that happened now.

They woke at dawn, and James left her so that she could wash. They gathered up Geordie and her father and made a foursome as they boarded the early train. There was no one to send them off. No wedding procession, no gift of a brooch or a wedding tea set or any of the other beloved traditions of a Scottish wedding. They joined wounded miners and furloughed strikers, nearly all of them hungover, to a man disdainful of her father.

Mr. Berg appeared at the train window. She'd searched for him yesterday but hadn't been able to find him. Hailey lowered the sash and said, "Where did you take my mother?"

"To Renton. From there, I don't know. She took her bag and walked off. I heard about your father. I'm sorry."

Then the train blew its whistle and started off, and Mr. Berg raised his hand in farewell.

JAMES TOOK TWO rooms at the New England Hotel on the corner of Commercial and Main, across from the burned district. The New England Hotel, which had survived unscathed, backed into the wharves and abutted a sausage factory that dumped its offal into the sea. Four stories tall, it was the kind of establishment where lumbermen and seamen kept a room. Each had a single bedstead pushed up against one wall, a table with an oil lantern, and an armoire.

Geordie cried that he was hungry. He needed a nap. He wept as he lay down on his bed. James left and returned with a tin of crackers, which Geordie stuffed into his mouth. Hailey tucked him in and asked James to leave so that she could sing him to sleep, but James refused. She implored her father to stay with Geordie, and he nodded absently, but she did not know whether he understood.

Hailey trailed James the twenty yards down the hallway to their room. It was noon, and the air was busy with the percussive pounding of nails and the water in the bay lashing against the wharves. Seagulls were screaming louder than the laughter rising from the dining room downstairs. The smell of butchered meat mingled with sawdust and ash. In the hallway, floorboards creaked as people walked past, chattering, their talk as audible as if the door to their room stood wide open.

But James had slammed it shut. He pushed her up against the wall, reached under her dress, found the split in her drawers, and fumbled with the buttons of his pants.

"Wait," she sputtered. "No—"

In the bright daylight, with the window open and the smell of entrails and devastation in the air, he took her. Urgently. Cruelly.

When he finished, he buttoned his trousers and said, "You're mine, do you understand? I don't want you to ever think about whoever that was again."

Stunned, she could barely speak. "He was no one," she finally said, hating the lie as soon as it slipped from her lips.

"I saw you kissing him. I saw you. Who is he, Hailey? Who is he to you?"

The man she loved. "Only someone from Glasgow."

"*Only someone*? I don't think so. That's not how you greet a person who is *only someone*, now, is it?"

She staggered to the bed and sat down, moving as if through mud. "He is a family friend."

"So you stuck your tongue down his throat in front of God and everyone?"

The vileness of the language struck her. She curled up on the counterpane. All she wanted was for him to go. "In Glasgow, he came to our house once for dinner."

James bent over her, pursing his lips, assessing. "*Dinner*, is it? Very fancy."

Clutching the pillow, she said, "He helped us. He saved Geordie from a runaway cart."

"Did he, now? Well, I saved your father. And you didn't stick your tongue down my throat in gratitude, did you? What's his name, Hailey? The next time I have to ask, it won't be so friendly."

It seemed unholy to speak Samuel's name now, but she did. Even to herself, she sounded reluctant. "Samuel Fiddes."

"Did he follow you? Did he come here for you?"

She shook her head, her curls obscuring her eyes. "I don't know." Though she knew, and so did James.

His blue eyes hardened. "Listen to me now, Hailey Murray. Don't turn your heart from me. I'm the one who married you. I'm the one who saved you from ruin. Your own mother ran off. I'm your husband now. Your protector. Don't forget that. And Samuel Fiddes, whoever he is, can go fuck himself." James smashed his hand against the pillow beside her head, the blunt impact crackling inside her.

Hailey flinched and edged away, fearful of a second blow.

She didn't recognize this man—this once taciturn, kind, awkward man who had pursued her, offering a benign life of security and boredom. Where had he been hiding this violence and jealousy? She understood that it had been a rude shock to find her kissing Samuel. Of course—it had to have been. But never before in her life had anyone been this angry with her. It felt as if the room had turned to ice, though outside the day shimmered with sunshine. She held very still as James yanked at his vest, a prideful assertion as he finished tidying himself. Then he insisted that they go to the dining room. He was hungry.

Hailey turned away, sick with pain. "What about Father?"

James stalked to the door and paused. "Your father should take care of himself. And I gave Geordie crackers. Now, arrange yourself. You look like you've been ridden hard." And he was gone.

After a long while, Hailey climbed from the bed. In the mirror, she saw that her hair had tumbled from its pins. Her face, grave and lifeless, stared back at her. The wavy glass broke her reflection into three pieces. She scrutinized the stuttering image. Where was the girl who had once defied everything and everyone in order to know Samuel? Where had her courage gone? The girl who had called, *Remember! Washington Territory.* Instead, she'd grasped at James Murray's offer as a drowning person grasped at a rock in rapids. Why hadn't she refused him? Taken the train into Seattle and found herself a job, a place to live? (Vaguely she thought, *With what money would I have done any of that?*) She ought to have written Samuel the instant they arrived in Newcastle. Told him where she was. (Would it have reached him in time?) A man who had coaled halfway around the world for her would have answered a letter. Knowing that he was coming, she would have outlasted anything.

But she hadn't done a single thing to save herself.

Oh yes, you did, she thought, staring into the mirror. You married James Murray.

But me and my true love will never meet again . . .

"Oh, Samuel," she whispered. "You oughtn't to have come."

23

Samuel

SAMUEL DIDN'T REMEMBER SAYING GOODBYE. ALL around him wafted the heavy smell of ruin from the fire, the stench from unearthed privies, the horse manure that no one ever seemed to clean up, the mildewed smell of wet sawdust, and the sour aroma of hops from a nearby brewery. Grief entered him like a fog, and for a long while he could not move. A lifetime without Hailey stretched before him.

He cashed in the ticket and waded through the fire's ruins to Our House, suppressing the thought that he ought to go home and collect Alison from Annabelle.

Big Bill took one look at him and sat him down and served him a plate piled with beans and pork. As Big Bill tended the cook fire and washed dishes, he eyed Samuel with concern.

Samuel said, "I'm thinking of going back to Scotland."

"Well, that'd be a shame, son, 'cause I like you. Mostly 'cause John Salvation and Pruss do. No higher recommendation exists. You haven't given Seattle much of a chance. And it's a long way home."

Samuel paid for his meal and went outside, into the terrible day, which had somehow turned into late afternoon. He stumbled into the Tivoli Beer Hall across from the Occidental Hotel, a ringside seat next to the fire ruins if there had been any windows in the place. In the dark, festering hole boasting of beers made in places like Milwaukee and Saint Louis, with names like Melhorn and Budweiser, he demanded oblivion. Samuel would not later recall how much ale he had consumed, but he drank glass after glass from a brewery in a place called Steilacoom, the home of the insane house. A choice that felt fitting. The ale went down easily, bitter as it was. As rain fell in a sudden, steady downpour, they fed him steamed clams and sardines and Russian caviar and bread, and when he was done trying to forget, he had spent all five dollars of the train ticket.

Toward nine o'clock he staggered outside into the newly sparkling evening and took the path down to the beach. Yesler's Wharf was behind him as he trudged north along Commercial Street and then down the path to where cliff cribbing reinforced the bluffs. On the beach immediately north of Yesler's Wharf and its raft of floating logs, he encountered a hulking, unfinished ship supported by rib braces, the hull black against the moonlight. The ship lacked her top housing, cabins, final decking, and sidewheel, but she looked splendid, if a bit forlorn. He turned, taking things in. This was apparently the neighborhood for shipyards. There were two other ships being built along the shore, a sloop and another steamship, seemingly in different shipyards. They were all wooden, Samuel observed, looking back at the looming hulk of the largest ship. A hundred fifty feet? How had he missed this? People built ships here? How had Allaway not named shipbuilding as one of Seattle's industries?

The bluff rose steadily beside him as he pressed on, past Indian shacks, their reef-netting canoes nestled up against the steep headland, his feet sinking into the shifting beach made up of stones and shattered shells. He passed under a collapsed wharf, its rotting posts throwing black, wavery shadows across the glimmering surface of the water. A barrel factory and pier under construction lay beyond that, and finally a deserted expanse stretched before him. Out on the water, shadows of vessels bobbing at anchor played on the surface.

He sprawled on a jumble of driftwood under the highest reach of the bluff and an impassible ravine that split it. He stared at the velvet black sky, stars winking like a million lanterns, and breathed in the clean smell of the salt water, the same water he had crossed to find Hailey, all oceans one vast connection, the water in Scotland the same as here, and he—he had washed up like so much flotsam.

We married yesterday, so, whoever you are, you're late.

One day.

The staggering joy of finding Hailey and then—blackness. On the way up the coast, the Milky Way had laced the churning water of *Louisa's* path, seducing Samuel into hope. Now the flung stars highlighted only blackness. This, Samuel thought, was what ale was made for. Revelations of futility for which there were no answers. Raw pain filled him again. He looked out onto the bay, a dance of white light on shadowy ripples lapping against the shore, eternity working its undulating handiwork.

If he didn't know what to do before, he was utterly at sea now.

Go home. Or stay. Those were his choices. Because any kind of choice about Hailey was no longer his.

Alison was the only one who mattered now, especially because he had dragged her all the way across the world for nothing. He scuffed at the rocks with his boots. He hadn't done a single thing right since he had taken Alison from Smyllum.

And because he'd stayed out tonight she was going to think he'd forgotten about her. He'd drunk up a good portion of their rent money. His head was spinning.

Remember, Samuel Fiddes. Remember! Washington Territory.

He relived their kiss. Hers was not the kiss of a married woman. Nor was it the kiss of regret. She had returned his passion in kind.

Understand, I didn't have anyone. . . . Geordie and I were alone and there was no money—none—and I didn't know what to do. Please understand. I didn't know you were coming. And everything fell apart—

What had fallen apart? The look on her face when she said, *My husband.* And her father. Absent. As if he were no longer inside his body.

Everything was corrupted by the fog of crippling sadness.

All he knew was that Hailey was never again to be his. She was what had brought him here, to this wild place, with its conflagrations and mountains and the beginnings of something out of nothing that could be extinguished again with the flick of a match.

Something out of nothing.

Samuel rose and walked blindly back toward town, which was finally quiet, not even a single loiterer. There were in Seattle, he thought, maybe a thousand structures, from henhouses and shacks to the university sitting high above him as he climbed back to Mrs. Barnum's. And then, through an open window, came an anguished cry. The broken sound arrested him. It was as if God had inflicted someone else with Samuel's pain, and he could hear his own heartbreak. The cries went on and on. He stood stock-still, listening, shattered by it.

Knock on the door? Call softly to the person from beneath the window?

He stood there a long time, listening.

Then, finally, whimpers, silence.

It was like pouring emptiness into emptiness.

Up he went, rising above Seattle's wide bay, climbing hills as if he were shedding pain. He slipped around the side of Mrs. Barnum's house along the uneven, dew-frosted ground, rounding a half dozen tree stumps as he made his way to the table in back. He wasn't ready to sleep. Across the street, the college building sat enthroned in a wisp of fog. No lights shone anywhere. Overhead, clouds drifted beneath the swath of stars and made a gossamer halo around the moon. The night air had turned crisp and heavy, redolent of sap and moist earth. Hooting owls yielded to chirping insects. Chickens rustled in the coop. Gone was the nuns' capricious brutality, Glasgow's relentless cacophony, the endless roar of ships' engines, and the awful, reverberating discovery of this morning. The night's brooding quiet hypnotized him. Even the vast and lonely oceans had not given him such a feeling of profound serenity.

Something out of nothing. That was who he was, wasn't it? A nothing from Glasgow who'd come in search of something. That something was Hailey.

What he needed now was to make a life. A life for him and Alison. In Glasgow, he would have made dinghies for the rest of his life, all the while worrying about Alison and living in the cold and soot, never having enough money to save them.

And now, in this place, he had a chance to save them. A chance to make Alison some kind of home.

Yesterday? You could have come yesterday?

He remembered the stunned sadness in her voice.

How do you live with unending heartbreak, when someone you love is no longer yours to love? Was this the way of the universe? Happiness only a fleeting illusion?

How had Hailey forgotten him so quickly?

I think he's lost his mind. Mother left.

Or maybe, he was the fool he had feared himself to be.

The drink had mostly left him now.

He felt the night veer away from darkness, felt a lightening around the edges of the world.

He'd survived before. He could survive again.

"Make a life," he said aloud. "Make a life, Samuel Fiddes, and live it."

24

Hailey

JAMES SMOLDERED THROUGHOUT THEIR MEAL IN the hotel dining room, while she avoided his eyes and tried not to relive what he had done to her. Then he disappeared without a word. Hailey went straight to her father's room to tend to him and Geordie, bringing them bread and butter she had tucked away in her napkin. She filled time by unpacking suitcases, distracting Geordie with games, finally going down to dinner. By nine o'clock she had settled them both in bed. Her father asked no questions and followed her about like a child. She found his mental absence unnerving. She longed to talk to someone—anyone—about all that had happened.

She had no idea when or even if James would return. He had been so angry. Her mind caromed between fear and the knowledge that Samuel was somewhere out there, alive and well, perhaps in as much pain as she was. He had come for her after all, only to find her married. A dozen times, she rose from her bed, determined to go in pursuit of him, only to sink back onto the coverlet, uncertain how to find him. People mostly lived on the steep hills above the town. She could go up there, but what was she supposed to do? Go door-to-door? Search the streets?

She didn't know the town. It was torture to know that he was close. He must believe that she had abandoned any thought of him when they left Scotland.

As the sky darkened, she paced, finally lighting a candle before the open window, as if its glow would somehow light Samuel to her. She wondered whether James's anger and absence now meant that he would leave her forever. She clung to that hope and paced some more, exhausted but unable to sleep.

At midnight, James burst into the room. His boots, covered in mud, tracked dirt across the floor. Glaring at her, reeking of alcohol, he wielded a metal flask and took a long swig. Never before had she seen him drink, and when he swallowed, his gaze turned wild, terrifying.

He took hold of her arm with a pincer grasp and drew her to the bed.

He struggled to keep from swaying. "Listen to me, Hailey Murray. I am not nothing. Do you hear me? I am not nothing. You could have said no. I didn't drag you to the altar. I asked you and you said yes."

She couldn't look at him, couldn't face the ruin of her life. "You hurt me today."

With one hand, he grabbed her chin and forced her to look at him. The crystalline blue of his eyes had turned rheumy with drink, and his voice boiled with indignation. "Hurt you? *You?* What kind of woman kisses another man the day after she marries?"

Hailey struggled to pull away, but he tightened his grasp. She said, "What kind of husband takes his wife in anger?"

"Don't you love me?"

"You're hurting me!"

"Tell me something now, Hailey Murray," James croaked.

He seemed to stop breathing as he stared, his face so close she could see every pore on his sweating face. "Tell me straight. If that man, that Samuel Fiddes, had stayed in Scotland, if you had never seen him again—would you be thinking of him now? Or would I be enough for you?"

She stilled. Sensing a lack of resistance, James loosened his grip. His features blurred as Hailey stared at him, trying to envision a life in which James could erase any desire for Samuel. Knowing that she would never see him again, reconciling herself to this new life, with time would she have banished Samuel to the past? Buried him in her heart? It was an impossible question to parse because it asked her to deny the miracle that Samuel had come. He had come for her. Across the world.

Tears welled in her eyes.

Even in his drunken state, James was no fool. He read Hailey's gaze and shook his head and slid from the bed to the floor. He reached one hand up and pulled her down beside him, gentle and solicitous now. "You don't love me."

Hailey shook her head. "No."

"You married me because you needed someone to take care of you. And your family."

Before she could answer, he seized her hands, crushing them. "Give me a chance. That's all I ask. I'll get money, and then you'll live the life you should lead, the one I promised you when I asked you to marry me, and then it will be all right. I can make you love me. Let me love you into loving me. Stay with me, Hailey. I'm sorry, my Hailey. I'm sorry. I don't know what came over me. You see, I love you so much. I'll never do you wrong. I promise on all the saints of Scotland that I'll never take you in anger again. I won't. I promise. Can you forgive me? Oh, please? I don't know what happened to me. I don't deserve you. Stay."

His pleas were heartbreaking, pathetic, this sudden, generous turn bewildering.

"James, you can't want me now—"

"I love you."

"You act as if you hate me."

"No. I love you. You're perfect. You're the most beautiful creature in the world. Give me a chance. That's all I ask. Let me try to make you love me. I was surprised earlier, that's all. You didn't tell me about him."

She hadn't, because what would have been the point? Had it been so wrong to conceal Samuel from James? It could even be seen as a kindness to not disclose it. And besides, even if she had dreamed of Samuel coming, she hadn't really believed that he would. What man had ever done what Samuel did? Crossed oceans? Had she owed James an explanation of a boy she thought she would never see again?

"I didn't know about Fiddes," he said, as if to underscore his point. "Seeing you kiss him was a shock. But you'll see. I'll not hurt you again. I promise. I'll work hard, and we'll live the grand life you ought to lead."

She was the dishonest one. She was the one who had concealed her love for another man.

His gaze grew soft, his drunkenness ebbing. "You married me. We're married now. You're my wife. Please, mo ghràdh, mo chridhe—my love, my heart . . ."

He was whispering Scottish endearments. Gaelic. As if he were reaching back through time to her life before, to remind her of the Scots girl she had left behind when the ship sailed away down the River Clyde.

"James, I—"

"You can still grow to love me." He began to kiss her nose,

her cheek, her neck. He could behave like an angel when he wanted to. "Give me time to make you love me, my lassie. My queen. I can do it. I can. You will grow to love me." All of his earlier temper had vanished. "I'm your husband. You married me, my love. We're married. You promised to stay with me until death. Stay true to your promise."

His lips were traveling the length of her neck. She stared across the room, at the dirtied floor planks and the armoire and the shadows of the candle dancing on the wall. James had saved them when they needed saving, even when he knew her father was sick, when loving her meant taking on Geordie, too. James's offer of marriage had been a generous, almost selfless gesture. Did she want to be the kind of person who turned her back on a man like that? Abandon James because he no longer served her purpose? No. She would not be. She had made a vow. She would not abandon him. She was not her mother. She stayed true to her promises, no matter the circumstances. For better or ill.

"Don't hurt me again," she warned.

James took this admonition as permission and undid the buttons at the nape of her neck, kissed her cheek, unpinned her hair. "We'll have money," he crooned. "The best house with the best view in Seattle. I'll build you a porch and a rocking chair and we'll fill the house with babies and your father will get well and Geordie will grow as tall as a fir tree and we'll live the best life, I promise, all of us. You, Hailey Murray, will live the life you were always meant to lead. I'll make you the queen of Seattle. You'll want for nothing. You must trust me. Let me take care of you."

She didn't care about money except that it would allow her to make a home for Geordie and her father—to give them something they had all lost. Wrenching herself from her past, the one in which she believed that you could dream something and it would be true, she let James do as he wished, closing her eyes as he blew out the candle and undressed her. She made another vow—one to forget Samuel, because she had to in order to endure this life she had brought on herself. She had no one else to blame for what had happened. She had lacked the courage to face the future alone, and this was the consequence. It was her own failing that had brought it on.

OVER THE NEXT weeks Hailey did her best to follow her resolve. She had a thousand questions for Samuel—why had he been waiting at the train? Had he been going to Newcastle to live? Was Alison well?—but she quashed every one. Still, she found herself looking for his face every time she walked Seattle's streets.

James found work at a warehouse on Yesler's Wharf, loading and unloading ships, shoveling hay, and heaving fifty-pound sacks of grain onto waiting freight wagons. Temporary work, he said, for a dollar a day, until he'd taken stock. His demeanor was affectionate, but sometimes Hailey caught him looking at her, and the possessiveness and suspicion in his gaze unnerved her. She was relieved of the endless chores of Newcastle, including the burden of cooking, because the hotel served meals in the downstairs dining room at regular hours, which James paid extra for. They ate passable porridge and boiled fish and coarse wheat bread, and were grateful for it. The luxuries of their Glasgow dinner table lay in her past, but she was encouraged to see Geordie's frame filling out again, and his cough was easing, away from Newcastle's dirty air.

Each morning and night, Hailey helped her father to dress and undress, discovering the dispiriting horror of taking care of your own parent as if they were a child. Hailey never knew what state she would find her father in. The doctor had said that he would never become fully himself again. He didn't speak. He could feed himself, though. Thankfully, he did not wet himself. But he rubbed the tips of his fingers together endlessly. The doctor called his state pathologic docility.

The deep affection her father had once carried for her had vanished. She missed his warm smile, the conspiratorial winks at the dinner table in Glasgow. She missed his unquestioning, generous love. She missed *him*. But that life, too, was in her past.

August in Seattle proved a revelation. The days grew warmer and the sky was constantly blue. It was as if the rain-soaked town lied to itself in other months about what it could achieve. Once a day, Hailey took her father and Geordie north along the beach to get away from the backwash of sewage in the bay and the persistent tang of dried fish and privies. They walked past a new barrel factory rising along the shore of the bay to a long swath of rocky beach where the Indians sometimes fished. The Indians were often there in the morning and didn't seem to mind Geordie's noisy capering among the crabs that skittered through the yellowed, slippery kelp tossed up by the tide. They shared salal berries and gave Geordie beaded toys. Most days, the mountain was out, as people said here, its towering beauty helping her to forget, for a moment, that she was unhappy.

Each night, she read to Geordie from books borrowed from the library. It had cost a whole two dollars to join, money she had let James believe had been stolen from him when he found it missing. But he never would have consented. Reading was a frivolous occupation, he said. Geordie still cried for their mother, and Hailey often wrapped him in her arms and sang to him, rocking him to sleep, more for herself than for him, because her mother had left this little boy Hailey loved, and the feel of his soft cheek against hers soothed her. James didn't seem to resent the hour at night she spent settling Geordie in. And every week, no matter what, he carved Geordie a new animal for his menagerie—a horse, a pig, a bear. James played long, complicated games of war with Geordie, the two of them concocting elaborate battle plans. He bought a rubber ball from Jennings' Dry Goods and played catch with Geordie in the hallway. Geordie soaked up the attention. He hadn't just lost his mother, he'd lost his father, too.

There was no more talk of the spectacular money James would earn at the lime kilns on San Juan Island. The kilns, he declared, were no place for a woman. And neither would he leave her in Seattle alone. He couched this decision as love, a need to never part, but Hailey suspected that he wouldn't leave her in Seattle because of Samuel's presence, not even for startling wages.

THE TOWN HAD already rebuilt itself. Within a week it was righted, the scent of newly cut wood wafting over a good portion of downtown. And Yesler's Wharf was back to its full operations. It was the heart of the city. Locations were measured from it—*A mile from Yesler's Wharf. Across from Yesler's Wharf.* It seethed with life: teamsters loading wagons, ships docking and departing, warehouse workers shifting goods.

One day after work, James was full of chatter as he pulled off his work clothes. "I've decided. I'm going to be just like that Yesler fellow. Most folks complain about him. They say he's a

tax cheat and a debtor, doesn't pay his creditors or city assess-
ments and argues with everyone about everything. But do you
know that he owns half the land in Seattle? He did something clever there. And everyone calls him the old pioneer. Have
you seen the beard on him? That gray carpet goes down to his
waist."

Hailey had seen Henry Yesler sitting on his porch at the
crossroads of the town, whittling and keeping an eye on things.
A friendly man, who nodded as she passed.

At the washbasin, James splashed some water under his arms
and dried them and changed into his good shirt, which he had
purchased with his first paycheck. "I'm going to save my money
and buy us some land and then I'll sell it and buy more and put
factories on it and in the end I'll be doing nothing but whittling
animals all day long, too."

Hailey didn't know much about money, but she knew that
wages of a dollar a day weren't going to achieve dreams of own-
ing any land.

"Listen to me, my Hailey. We have to save every penny. They
feed us here. We've got a roof over our head. That's all we need."

"Geordie needs new shoes. And I signed him up for school.
He'll need a slate and schoolbooks."

James pressed his lips together and shook his head. "I don't
think so, Hailey, my darling."

"But Geordie has to go to school."

"A family like yours, the life you lived, you expect that kind
of life—but it's not possible yet."

"But I've promised him—"

"Well, unpromise it, my Hailey. If we save our money, he
can go next year."

Hailey studied James in his new shirt, wondering how much

he had spent on it. "What if I buy his shoes and books on credit?" Like at the company store in Newcastle, it was a way to buy things when you didn't have ready money. "At Mr. Pumphrey's— we could start an account."

"Och, my Hailey, don't be running up any bills. I went barefoot as a bairn, and Geordie can, too. Cut holes in the tip of his shoes to free his toes. Or he can wear those rubber boots that he wore in Newcastle. Seattle's nothing but a sea of mud anyway. It won't hurt the lad." His voice was light, careless.

The humility of poverty. The humility of having to ask. "But Geordie can't go barefoot."

James whirled on her, his voice tight. "Do you want us to be out on the street?"

Fearful of this sudden flare, Hailey backed away, but even as she did, she perceived something vulnerable lurking beneath James's simmering temper. Embarrassment. James didn't have the money to send Geordie to school, and he didn't want to tell her outright. Pride, she was learning, ran though him like a fierce eddy. Any whiff of embarrassment would unleash a waterfall of anger.

James came to himself then, and blinked, and stepped away, wiping his nose with the back of one finger. He cast his gaze downward at the floor and mumbled an indistinct apology and slipped out the door.

She thought she heard shame in James's heavy footsteps echoing down the hallway, on his way to somewhere—certainly not dinner with them. She realized then that she had never questioned how much money he had saved. As a miner, living alone, without the expenses of a family, he had to have saved some. He'd said he had. Was he frugal, or were they really impoverished? Or had he lied? She sank onto the bed. How far did

James's responsibilities extend toward Geordie? Out of love for her, he was feeding and housing all of them. By her calculations, he had already spent twenty dollars on room and board. She hadn't even thanked him. And James was not Geordie's father. He had no real responsibility for him. She had made unfair assumptions.

They needed money.

There had to be some way to get it herself.

HAILEY, GEORDIE, AND her father headed down the beach on their daily route toward the barrel factory. It was always a hard walk on the rocks and around the driftwood and the shipyards, and so she didn't see the young woman and baby playing in a patch of sand until she was nearly upon them.

"Hailey?"

Hailey hadn't seen Bonnie since the day of the explosion, and she was shocked now to see that her friend's once pert looks had been drained of their merriness. Hailey remembered Bonnie's keening as her dead husband was carried from the smoking mine.

"Bonnie. Oh, Bonnie." Hailey sank down beside her.

"Hailey!" Bonnie was holding the baby in her lap, but the two women embraced around him, laughing when he complained.

"Are you living in Seattle now?" Hailey said.

"The company wouldn't let me stay in the house after Alan died. So I came here."

"How are you?"

Her already woeful expression turned even more mournful, and she burst into tears.

Angus reached up and pulled Hailey's hair, and she untangled his fingers. Her father had followed Geordie to the water's edge, where Geordie had taken up his new pastime of throwing rocks into the sea.

"I'm sorry for crying," Bonnie said, pulling away again and sniffling. "It's hard to have Alan gone. I miss him—and this one, he's a handful."

"Don't apologize." Hailey smiled at the baby, who was gumming his fingers, wrangling new teeth. Bonnie gave her son her own fist to chew. "Where are you living?"

"In a boardinghouse on Fifth." Bonnie had found work at Tierney's Pattern Shop on Commercial Street, where Mrs. Tierney let her keep Angus in a crib all day.

"I could use a job," Hailey said.

"But why? You have James. How is that brave husband of yours?"

Hailey automatically smiled. "He's fine."

"How's your pa doing?" Bonnie said.

"As you see." He was wandering at the water's edge. Here, but not here.

"Oh—did you hear? A mining inspector from San Francisco blamed coal dust for the explosion. So, it wasn't your father's fault, no matter what people said. You ought to tell him. Maybe he'll feel better."

Her father was eaten up by guilt and it hadn't even been his fault, and now he was gone. "I'll tell him, but it won't make any difference."

"What about your mum?"

This sorrow Hailey couldn't hide. She blinked back tears as she looked out at the bay, beautifully calm this hour of the morning. Gauzy clouds gathered over the hills of Bainbridge

Island. "I don't know where she is. I look for her on the street, but I've never seen her. I don't understand how she could leave. I could never leave Geordie, and I'm just his sister."

Bonnie laid her hand on Hailey's. They watched the waves rippling on the beach. "I'm dying to see my parents again, but I don't think I ever will. My parents haven't got the money to come up here, and I don't have the money to go back to San Francisco. They may never meet baby Angus."

"That's hard," Hailey said, thinking that everything was suddenly hard.

"I'm sorry she left you," Bonnie said.

Hailey laid her head on Bonnie's shoulder, and they sat watching the sunlight bounce off the bay, grateful to have found each other again.

25

Samuel

ON A SUNNY MORNING IN THE MIDDLE OF AU-
gust, Samuel, Alison, and Annabelle Barnum joined a crowd
milling on the shore immediately north of Yesler's Wharf. It
was the stretch of beach where Samuel had stumbled across the
dark hulk of a ship on his long night of reckoning. The hulk
turned out to be the future *George E. Starr*, an unfinished side-
wheel steamer, to be launched today. When Samuel heard that
a man named Shade had won the contract for the ship's fit and
finish, he had gone immediately to Pumphrey's to look in the
city directory for his address. There was no listing, nor did the
post office have it.

William Hammond, the current Inspector of Hulls, in
whose shipyard JFT Mitchell was building *George E. Starr*, did
not know where Shade lived, either. The shipbuilder said that
Shade had traveled from California for the job.

"Do you know if he's hired anyone yet?" Samuel said.

"Another Scot, are ye? Welcome. Listen, young lad, I haven't
got a job in the yard, but if ye want to try your hand at finishing
work, look for Shade at the launch."

So Samuel had come this morning in search of Shade. And,

as always, Hailey. One was his hoped-for future and the other his hoped-for past. It was odd that in a town with so few people—some said three thousand, some fewer, some more, depending on whether you counted the farmers in the Duwamish or the settlers on Magnolia Bluff or even the Indians—he hadn't caught a glimpse of her. Maybe her husband had taken them to the lime kilns after all. Maybe she was on her way back to Scotland. Maybe she was the girl he had heard crying that night. He hoped not, but he couldn't shake the worry that Hailey hadn't seemed anything like herself that day. In the wake of his grief, he had gone over and over that moment in his mind, her blunted gaze haunting him. It was terrible not to know where she was. He'd suffered the same dread from the moment he'd said goodbye to her in Glasgow. And now he feared that he wouldn't know if she needed him.

But Samuel was thrilled to see a launch, and it seemed that everyone in Seattle was, too. The burgeoning crowd vibrated with excitement. *George E. Starr* was not the first steamship fashioned in Seattle to make her watery debut, but she was the biggest so far. One hundred fifty-four feet long, with a twenty-eight-foot beam, even unfinished she was a beauty to behold. Everyone believed that the town's reputation and success hinged on the excellence of this new ship—a symbol of their birthright to be crowned the reigning metropolis of Washington Territory. Samuel had quickly learned that there was a collective boosterism to Seattle. Despite the fact that there were few graded streets, no sanitation to speak of, a patchwork water system of wooden pipes and private water companies, Seattleites were convinced that the town was primed for great things. And why shouldn't they be? No time had been lost in repairing damages from the fire. It hadn't even entirely been extinguished when a brand-new saloon had been built and stocked, and a temporary building to replace the McDonald blacksmith shop had its walls raised. Today was a fortnight since the conflagration, and to look at that part of town now, it was as if the fire had never happened.

Proof of Seattle's wily spirit lay in the new people arriving daily, who, while crowding scarce housing and complicating traffic, also validated the sacrifice of those already here. In pamphlets sent to Boston and New York, the town council boasted that you could plant a banana tree and it would grow, a wagon wheel and it would sprout, a seed and it would touch the sky. There were plans to run a horsecar line north and another east, over to Lake Washington, where a dock had been built to moor a little excursion steamer they were going to float in via the Duwamish. A telephone line had even been strung from the commercial district to the peninsula of West Seattle, where the pioneers had first landed. Seattle was on the rise. Seattle had plans.

And today, every possible vantage spot had been taken, even the flimsy roof of *The Daily Intelligencer*, while dignitaries climbed onto the deck of the new ship to ride her into the sea. On the wharf, Indians pounded drums and a dozen of their canoes waited on the sea for the "Bostons"—as the Indians called all whites—to launch their newest ship.

Alison clamored to see, so Samuel hoisted her onto his shoulders. She wore new leather boots from Schwabacher's— already completely rebuilt and restocked with new goods from San Francisco. Samuel had worked the last two weeks building around town after the fire, and it had paid well.

Samuel wiggled Alison's legs. "What do you say, wee lass?

Isn't it exciting? They're going to skid that boat right into the water."

He craned his neck to find Alison focusing all her attention on the candy he'd bought for her from a street vendor. He shook her legs again, and she looked down at him and beamed.

"Is it good?"

Her sunny smile broadened, and she went back to the work of making the candy disappear.

"She has her priorities," Annabelle said. She had abandoned the kitchen today and wore a gingham dress that showed off a narrow waist and slim hips. Annabelle came only to Samuel's chest and had to keep adjusting the brim of her wide sunhat so that she didn't hit anyone. She was the prize of staying at Mrs. Barnum's. Aside from being kind to Alison, Annabelle was a good cook, no matter how much she said she hated it.

She toggled Alison's new boots. "You're good company, little squirt. I'll be sad when I lose you to school."

In a couple of weeks, Alison was going to start at the Sixth Street School, a bare-bones building situated a couple of blocks up the hill from Mrs. Barnum's. Samuel had already bought her a slate and schoolbooks.

"Is that *Louisa* steaming in now?" Annabelle said.

He'd secured them a high-enough spot that they could see the bay. "It is. She's early."

The Inspector of Hulls had signed off on Samuel's work, and paint had magically been found and applied. Sooner than expected, *Louisa* had departed, taking with her Pruss and John Salvation for the last time.

Over dinner at Our House one night, Samuel overheard William Grose reveal to Pruss that Henry Yesler was going to sell him a few acres of land over the ridge. Grose assured Pruss that Henry Yesler was the kind of opportunist who saw no difference between a black man and an Indian man and a white man. He would sell to anyone, as long as they could pay fifty dollars an acre. But not the Chinese. Some Chinese owned land—a few farms in the Duwamish valley—but most lived within the enclave of Chinatown, in houses owned by Seattleites who kept ownership of the land beneath. Seattleites liked to keep the Chinese disenfranchised, corralled out of sight on the marshy slice of land near the tideflats. Before he left for San Francisco, Pruss had declared to Samuel that he was done with the sea and he was going to build a farm. Dirt was better than water because you could own dirt. And no one had let a former slave buy dirt in West Virginia, where he'd come from. But someday he was going to own land, and he was going to own it here.

"It's starting!" Alison shouted, beating her legs against Samuel's chest.

A protective cradle had been fitted around the ship, and the last of the ways greased. Men pounded away at wedges holding the stays in place. But before they knocked them completely away, little George Starr, the son of the owners, smashed a bottle of champagne across her bow. In a shower of bubbles and green glass, *Geo. E. Starr*, as she would ever after be abbreviated, glided stern-first into the bay. There was a collective holding of breath to see if she floated. Everyone knew that unless the seams between the planks had been well caulked to keep out the sea, the hull could leak and take on water. But *Geo. E. Starr* bobbed like a dream to raucous cheers.

Annabelle said, "That wasn't as exciting as I was hoping for."

"Did you expect a bigger splash?" Samuel said.

"I guess I did."

Refusing to come down from Samuel's shoulders, Alison twisted and turned, restless now that she had finished her candy.

Annabelle said, "Do you see the Lovings yet?"

"There they are!" Alison squealed.

Samuel, too, spied them wading toward them against the tide of the retreating crowd.

"Miss Barnum. Scotty. Miss Alison," John Salvation said.

"How in the world did you find us in this crush?" Samuel said.

"I looked for the prettiest girl with red hair," John Salvation said, teasing Alison. "Besides, where else would you be today?" With a solemn expression, he pulled a doll from behind his back. It was a real doll, with real hair and a porcelain face, wearing a dress made of calico.

Alison flung herself from Samuel's shoulders into John Salvation's arms. "Thank you, thank you, thank you! Did you see whales? Did you? Where are you going to live now? Come stay at Mrs. Barnum's!" She bounced between Pruss and John Salvation, telling them that she was going to go to school soon, and did they like her new shoes?

Annabelle said, "Mr. Loving, are you trying to steal Alison's heart from me by plying her with gifts?"

"If I can, miss. And Scotty, did you learn to speak English yet? 'Cause I still can't understand a word either you or Miss Ali says."

"How do you do, Miss Barnum?" Pruss said, addressing Annabelle with his usual dignity. "I expect your mother will be worried about you. Do you need an escort home?"

"Thank you, Mr. Loving, but Mother charged Samuel with taking care of me, and since he knows that she will evict him if anything happens to me, I am quite safe."

Together, they climbed the steep path to Front Street and Yesler's Hall, a public room Yesler rented out for plays and church bazaars.

Samuel said, "Could someone watch Ali for me for a minute?"

"I'll watch her, but only if she promises to show me her doll." Annabelle lifted Alison's chin. "And only if John Salvation will stay with me and keep us safe."

The two exchanged shy smiles, and Samuel thought that he saw them touch hands. Pruss caught the gesture, too, and shook his head.

Pruss said, "Where you off to, Scotty?"

"In search of a job."

Samuel pushed through the roistering crowd on Yesler's Wharf, aiming for the strip of dock where a short, grizzled man of about forty was pacing, monitoring the tug ship *Addie*'s halting progress guiding *Geo. E. Starr* to the dock. His air of distracted anticipation distinguished him from the drunken on-lookers.

Samuel shouted to be heard. "Mr. Shade?"

Shade turned. "Who wants me?"

"You're a hard man to find, Mr. Shade."

As Samuel talked, Shade seemed to only half listen, casting the occasional glance at *Addie* nudging *Geo. E. Starr* along. After a few minutes, he held up a hand. "You're telling me that you built ships on the Clyde? *The* River Clyde?"

"Well, dinghies. But I copied out plans for steamships for the architect. Studied them. And I rebuilt part of *Louisa* on her last trip when we hit a log."

"That was you? By God, Allaway was pleased. You should have heard him at Tivoli's. He said he'd give his right arm to have you as his ship's carpenter." Shade looked Samuel up and down. "And you can read and write, you said? Do math? Read drawings? You're not shiting me?"

"I know a little engineering, too."

"And where did you learn all that?"

"At an orphanage in Scotland."

"Catholic, are you?"

"No."

Shade sniffed, tapping his foot. *Geo. E. Starr* drew near, and he turned to catch a line. A torrent of words followed as he tied up the ship, detailing the terms of employment: "Three dollars and fifty cents a day. Show up or I'll hunt you down. Workday lasts from two hours after first light to just before dinnertime. Steal anything and you're dead."

Three dollars and fifty cents a day. Samuel could buy all the tools and clothes and boots he needed and still have money left over.

Waiting for him alone by Yesler's Hall, Pruss said, "Did you get the job?"

Samuel grinned.

"My son and Miss Annabelle took that sister of yours to Piper's Bakery to get some ice cream. It looks like we're going to have a celebration."

Samuel felt a breathless and uneasy spark of hope.

26

Hailey

"HOLY GOODNESS, MY HAILEY. DID I NOT TELL YOU that you can't spend a penny more than nothing?" James clutched the laundry bill in his fist, his face empurpled. "I pay for two rooms at this fancy hotel. I pay for board for four people. We can't pay someone to wash our clothes, too."

"But I can't haul hot water up four flights of stairs." While Hailey had grown strong in Newcastle, water was far too heavy to carry that far. "And you left our buckets and basins in Newcastle."

"The conductor made us choose between all that stuff we'd packed. So I gave up the laundry bins. Would you rather I left behind your clothes? The maid can haul the water for you."

"She won't. She said we have to pay for the hotel laundry. And Mr. Vacheux is cheaper than the hotel. I asked. I thought you'd be happy. I'm trying."

"Listen to me, my Hailey. I work all day to feed us and then you sashay yourself up to the fancy French laundry because you can't put your back into something?" His voice was part teasing, part exasperation and part tightly controlled irritation. "You have to do the laundry. You have to do your part. We're not worthy of your mother's china yet. But one day, you'll put it on a fine table. Until then, we need to save pennies."

James had been the one to insist they bring her mother's Doulton china rather than their laundry bins, a goal to work toward, he'd said. He leaned in to kiss her, tucking one of her curls behind her ear. Though she was usually able to hide her lack of enthusiasm, this time she couldn't. He pulled away and slammed the door behind him, his heavy boots clopping on the floor. She sighed, frustrated with both herself and him.

Unbeknownst to James, Hailey had been searching for work for two weeks now—at shops and factories, even the school, lugging her brother and father all over town. She had to implore Geordie to stay outside with her father while she inquired—in halting, humiliating speeches. She fit no necessary mold, possessed no necessary skills. She was prepared for nothing. There were only so many shops, so many places a woman could work, and it seemed as if all the positions were taken. Nor did she have the requisite sewing skill of a dressmaker to open a business out of their rooms. She'd been raised to make sparkling conversation around dining tables and to waltz in ballrooms, not to do anything practical.

Ruefully, Hailey thought how much she had once taken for granted. In Glasgow, their drawers and closets had been full of clothes that someone else had brushed and laundered for them. And though she had done their laundry in Newcastle, laboring over the boiling pots and scrubbing her hands raw, she had stupidly thought that living in a hotel would bring an end to the heavy labor of cleaning clothes. Now in late August she dreaded the return of the rains—any day now, people said—and the endless muck that would make for endless laundry.

It was six days until school began. Geordie needed school things, new shoes. And there was still no money.

She eyed the crate that held her mother's Doulton china. James believed it represented the kind of girl he'd married. Hailey hadn't told him that she'd tried to sell it to store owners, who rejected it as far too fine for a place like Seattle. Besides, they'd said, who wanted used dishes?

Hailey went down the hall to her father and brother's room and found her father asleep and Geordie playing with his toy soldiers and animals at the end of his bed. After she got her father dressed, all three went down to the dining room, filled with the unappetizing scent of boiled meat. After breakfast, they stepped onto the street. Today she would find a job, and if she didn't, she would beg on the streets to get the money for Geordie's school.

Crossing the intersection of Washington and Commercial, she spied Samuel entering the ship's chandlery. For a moment, she stood staring. There he was. Desire to speak with him boiled inside her. Clutching her father's and brother's hands, she ducked into Jennings' Dry Goods. She could not let Samuel see her, could not let him know how far she had fallen.

Fifteen minutes later, her courage rekindled, she peeked outside. Finding Samuel nowhere in sight, she marched to a saloon on Second Street, where a man wrapped in a damp white apron stood behind the bar washing glasses and chewing on a toothpick. Several customers sprawled at a table in a corner, nursing glasses of ale. She seated her father and Geordie in the opposite corner and strode to the counter.

No more hemming and hawing. It was this or look for work as a maid, and she wasn't ready to do that yet.

"You should hire me."

The aproned man raised his bushy eyebrows. "We don't hire girls here. And if you're too good for the Lava Beds, ask in a shop."

"I'm not a whore. And I've asked in the shops."

The man assessed her. "All those women in the shops are jealous of you, aren't they? All that pretty hair. And that shape. Are they making life hard on you?"

She fought a blush, but she was in no position to reprimand his impertinence. "I can't be a teacher because I'm married, and I can't work at the confectioner's because I don't know how to make candy and they haven't the time to teach me. I can't work at the cannery because they only hire Chinese. I've asked. I've asked everywhere. My little brother needs shoes. He needs schoolbooks. There are thirty saloons in this town, and I'm going from door to door today until someone hires me, because someone will. And when they do, they'll be the only tavern in town with a pretty barmaid. Which one will customers patronize, do you think?"

Blood was pounding in her ears. She tried to think of a time when this kind of speech had come from her mouth, and couldn't. She felt emboldened, and furious, too, that things had come to this. But how hard could it be to fill a glass with ale? She was tired of the restrictions—and the men—that told her what she could and couldn't do. She would do what she needed to, and she would do it now.

The man gaped at her, toothpick dangling from his mouth. The three men in the corner gaped, too, glasses mid-rise. The bartender said, "You look too fine for hard work."

"I may have been. Once. But I'm not anymore."

"You can handle men?"

"I'll learn."

THAT NIGHT AT dinner, James tipped back in his chair, eyeing Hailey through a narrowed gaze. "You did what?"

"I got a job."

"No wife of mine will work."

Hailey knew she ought to coddle him, highlight the advantages of the situation, soften the obvious shame he felt that he couldn't provide for them as he had promised. But today, she couldn't find it in her. She'd found a way to send Geordie to school, and she wasn't going to spare James's feelings. "We had no money to pay for Geordie to go to school. Or to buy shoes. I solved the problem."

James's face flushed. The chair fell forward, legs clattering to the floor. He leaned over the table and hissed, "I will take care of you."

"You've been so good to take care of my brother and father. But I want to help. It shouldn't be your burden alone."

"I forbid it."

For a moment, Hailey could not breathe. She had deliberately broached the subject in the hotel dining room, where the presence of others would dampen his fury. Geordie, ever sensitive to heightened emotion, pulled at her skirt. She handed him one of his toys. "Take Papa to the window to see how many seagulls you can count in the bay."

After they left the table, she said very quietly, "I will keep that job, James. Then you won't have to worry about my family."

"Go tell the man you won't be working tomorrow or ever."

Hailey stood. "I will. I will be working."

James seized her wrist and yanked her from the table and out into the hallway. She gasped in surprise and then choked with pain as he wrenched her arm behind her back and drove her into the wall. A passing maid hurried her steps.

"Don't sass me in front of everyone, Miss Glasgow," James croaked into her ear.

Hailey, flaming with exertion and fury, wriggled from his grasp and faced him. "I *will* keep that job. I *will* buy Geordie new shoes. I *will* send him to school. I am not Miss Glasgow. I'm a girl with a brother who needs to go to school. If anyone should feel badly about this, it's my mother, who's not here to take care of Geordie, or my father, who's lost his mind. Let me do this, James."

He stared at her for a long while, the clatter of dishes echoing in the background.

Finally, he said, "For what wages?"

"Seventy-five cents a day."

She didn't tell him that William Murphy, the saloonkeeper, had already paid her fifty cents for two hours' work after putting her to the test that morning.

"Fine, then. You'll be giving me that money, every night. Who will watch the bairn? And your father?"

"I'll work when Geordie's in school. Father can come with me."

James grunted his assent.

On this uneasy truce, they returned to the dining room. A hard-won victory that Hailey felt in her bones.

SEVERAL NIGHTS LATER, Hailey retrieved a bottle of ink, a sharpened pen, and vellum paper she'd purchased at Pumphrey's, where she'd gone that afternoon to buy Geordie shoes and his schoolbooks. She'd spent all the money she'd not handed

over to James, but a shiver of anticipation ran up her spine because soon there would be more. She'd lied to James. William
Murphy paid her a dollar a day, not seventy-five cents. It was as
much as her husband earned. She would keep the balance for
herself, for things her father or Geordie might need.

The work hadn't been terrible. It was less trouble than keeping house in Newcastle, and it would be even less if she could
dissuade Mr. Murphy from being so free with his hands.

She filled the pen with ink and put it to paper.

*Dear Samuel, I think of you all the time. I saw you in town,
but I didn't let you see me. It breaks my heart to know that you
are so near, but I am happy that you are. I hope Alison is
well. Yours, Hailey.*

She didn't dare write for long. James was unpredictable in his
timing when he went out. Nor would she send this letter. She
didn't even know where Samuel lived. But she needed some
semblance of a conversation with him. She'd been unable to
keep her vow to forget him; Samuel was unforgettable. She
could and would continue to avoid him to save them both the
pain of interaction. But her lifeline would be these secret writ-
ings, a record of her love for him. One day, she would send them
all, so that he would know that she had never wanted to let
him go.

She folded the paper and secreted it with the writing things
under a loosened floorboard at the edge of the armoire. At the
washstand, she scrubbed the ink from her fingers, then snuffed
the light in hopes it would deter James when he returned.

It was a ruse that rarely worked.

27

Samuel

SHADE OFTEN EXPRESSED ADMIRATION FOR SAM-
uel's work. They studied the plans together, poring over the
drawings of the *Geo. E. Starr*, trying to decipher the architect's
intentions when his schematic presented practical problems. The
architect was in San Francisco, of no use for day-to-day questions. Samuel had long ago learned that a design was a mix of
bible and suggestion. One day, they stood at the stern, studying
the door to the hurricane deck, positioned in the plans dead in
the middle of the aft saloon.

Samuel said, "If we move the door to the port side, it gives
us the whole length inside to fit the settee."

Shade said, "What about weight distribution?"

"I've done the calculations. It's no problem—and it will cost
less."

Shade raised his eyebrows. "Then do it." He threw Samuel a
respectful glance. "You know what you're about, Fiddes. You've
a talent."

"Thank you, sir. How long till we're done fitting, do you
think?"

"November or thereabouts. I'll be heading back to San

Francisco then. I've a commission there in the shipyards. Do you have a job after this, Samuel?"

Samuel shook his head.

"Well, if you come to San Francisco, I can keep you busy there in the Turner shipyard. They build the finest ships. It'd be steady work."

Samuel hesitated a moment. "If I were to go out on my own here—do you think someone would stop me?"

Shade stared at him, puzzled. "Why would anyone stop you?"

"Because—"

And then Samuel thought, *Why, indeed?* There was land everywhere in America, possibility everywhere. In Glasgow, a person might have to stay in their place, but not here.

"Thank you, Mr. Shade, for the offer, but I'll be staying in Seattle."

THE *GEO. E. STARR* attracted a lot of attention. People made forays to Yesler's Wharf just to watch her cabins rise. One day, a man stopped by and asked to board. He was pale and rail thin, with fatigue dancing at the corners of his red-rimmed eyes. He would have appeared distinguished were it not for his obvious illness. He roamed the ship in the company of Shade, who had little in the way of patience for gawkers, but for some reason had time for this man.

The visitor ran his hands over the paneling in the saloon, which Samuel had been working on for days.

"James Colman," Shade said, "let me introduce you to Samuel Fiddes, my excellent shipwright. Samuel, this, the man who designed the railroad to Newcastle, drove all the piles for the bridge across the tideflats himself. And he sometimes even drives the locomotive. He's going to build another wharf here to rival Yesler's."

"Someone has to rival that man," Colman said. "He thinks he owns Seattle. Is this your work, young man?"

"It is. Are you Scots?" Samuel said.

Colman broke into a grin. "I hail from Dunfermline. You?"

"Glasgow. Lanark, at Smyllum. Then Glasgow again."

"How marvelous. My wife hails from Glasgow. It's good to hear a bit of Scots spoken, isn't it? I hear it out at Newcastle, but we sou'easterners have our own way of pronouncing things, don't we? I can hardly understand a word some of those men say."

Seattle's perpetual complaint. The town was a polyglot place. While many spoke English, it came out of everyone's mouth a little differently. Samuel knew his Scots hadn't mellowed. Pruss and John Salvation spoke with that slippery slur of theirs. And everyone in Seattle worked hard to make sense of the singsong cadences spoken by the lately arriving Norwegians. Alison was already losing her accent. Malleable, the tongue of the young.

"Fiddes here worked on the Clyde, building ships," Shade said.

"Did you, now?" Colman said.

Samuel amended. "Dinghies, mostly. But before that I copied architects' drawings."

"Another engineer? Marvelous. I schooled in Edinburgh. You?"

"I'm not schooled, sir."

"Fiddes works by the seat of his pants, Mr. Colman," Shade said. "But he's got quite the eye. I rely on him."

Colman nodded. "Fiddes, if you need anything, come ask me. We Scots have to help one another."

IT SEEMED TO Samuel that all the business of Seattle took place on Yesler's lively, crooked wharf. From the deck of the *Geo. E. Starr*, it was easy to observe the goings-on. A few weeks into his employment, when he was fashioning the ship's paddle wheel, a fight broke out in front of Cosper's Warehouse, down the way.

It wasn't unusual for a fight to break out on the bustling dock, but this one was particularly heated. Samuel laid down his saw and went to the ship's railing to take a look. The fight was drawing onlookers. It seemed to be about the proper way to load a wagon. People were laying bets about whether the combatants would resort to fisticuffs. It was hard to see over the burgeoning crowd, but the raised voices carried.

"Shut up, you idiot. You think you know better than me?"

Samuel recognized the voice of Olaf Cosper, the Norwegian who owned the warehouse.

"Course I do," came the fiery return in heavy Scots. "What you've done is daft."

Samuel froze, then peered through the crowd and spied the russet head of the man who had married Hailey.

Murray was *here*. He hadn't spirited Hailey away from Seattle after all. Samuel had looked for her obsessively on the streets, but he'd never seen her. Not once. Now here was confirmation that she was still here.

"God damn you, James Murray, don't make me regret hiring you."

Murray spat, "If you let me use common sense, things wouldn't be in such a shambles—"

The benign Olaf Cosper had had enough. "Shut up, Murray,

and load the wagon the way I tell you to, or find work elsewhere."

To this, James Murray made no reply. Soon the crowd dispersed, disappointed that the fight hadn't escalated. All Samuel felt was relief. *Hailey was in Seattle.*

Over the next few days, Samuel kept his head down and an eye on Murray, who turned out to be a hard worker. Tirelessly, he did the heavy manual labor of both a stevedore and a warehouseman. He never got an order wrong and was jovial with the customers, often talking them into purchasing more produce than they wanted.

Once, Samuel and James arrived at the wharf at the same time, just past dawn.

"Samuel Fiddes."

Samuel was taken aback. So, Murray knew his name. Had he asked around, or had Hailey said something? What did Murray know?

"Are you leaving Seattle, I hope?" Murray said.

The SS *Dakota*, bound for Portland and San Francisco, was docked nearby and working up a head of steam, its line of passengers waiting to board winding down the wharf.

"I'm working on the *Geo. E. Starr.*" Samuel weighed his next words, but couldn't help himself. "How are Hailey and her father? And Geordie?"

"Go fuck yourself," Murray spat as a constable nearby upended a Chinese man's tall, lidded bamboo basket. This happened all the time—the constables were always in search of contraband opium. The basket tumbled to the wharf and out skittered not tins of opium, but huge Dungeness crabs, scattering the *Dakota*'s passengers along the slippery planks.

"No opium. No opium," the Chinese man screamed, scrambling to catch his crabs, some of which had already made it to the wharf's edge and were splashing into the sea below. "Wah Chong does not run opium."

Onlookers laughed. The uproar consumed the attention of everyone on the wharf, but Murray sauntered away, hands thrust in his pockets, his muscular shoulders tight with resentment.

Later that morning, Captain Allaway hailed Samuel from the pier. "Fine ship, Fiddes."

Captain Allaway hadn't wanted to sail the southern route, so he'd quit *Louisa* and purchased a small prop steamer in need of repairs—just a sixty-footer, but it was a fine ship that could easily handle the winds of the Strait of Juan de Fuca. He had preemptively christened her *Lady Barnum*. Everyone wondered why an oceangoing captain had stepped down from the heights to helm a jobber steamer, but Allaway argued that there was a lot of money in shipping on the sound. He also had reason to stay, in the person of Mrs. Barnum. It was no secret he intended to marry her.

"She will be fine when she's finished," Samuel agreed.

"You get tired of that work, you can always crew for me. You and Pruss and John Salvation."

The Lovings had gotten jobs working the coal tipples on Marshall Wharf, which John Salvation said was just about as bad as you could imagine.

Allaway sniffed. "I'm looking for James Murray. Do you know him?"

"You know Murray?" Samuel said.

"Met him drinking at the Tivoli. Say, did you know he married that girl you were looking for?"

Samuel directed his tortured gaze to the towering masts of a newly arrived sailing bark. He gestured carelessly to Cosper's as he turned away, ignoring Allaway's hollered thanks.

Within a few minutes, Murray and Allaway went off together, deep in conversation, headed for the Tivoli Beer Hall.

Samuel overheard them as they walked by.

"Do you need to stop by the New England, first?" Allaway said. "I'd like to see that beautiful wife of yours."

"My wife is busy," Murray muttered.

The New England.

Samuel told Shade that he was breaking for his noon meal. Shade waved him off.

The town, in a perpetually restorative mood, was planking Mill Street. Workmen's tools and a heap of sawed-off lumber blocked the walkway at the base of Commercial Street. Samuel darted around the mess and pressed on to the New England Hotel, where he stood behind a wooden pillar at Maddock's Drug Store across the street. As luck would have it, Hailey emerged from the hotel door with her father just moments later. She wore her green dress, and her hair was piled on top of her head under a straw hat. Samuel followed them at a distance. At Second Street, she stopped before the door of a saloon, one of those nameless establishments that never needed to advertise, for Seattle was a thirsty town.

To Samuel's great surprise, Hailey and her father passed through its swinging doors.

THE TAVERN REEKED of new wood, sawdust, urine, and yeast. The odor was overpowering. Dozens of men filled the saloon, vying for a spot against the bar, a slapdash stand of newly sawed wood that ran nearly the width of the building.

Behind the counter, Hailey moved with speed, filling glass after glass of ale in a determined, no-nonsense, let's-get-on-with-it air. She had removed her hat and stored it out of sight, and as always, her curls had tumbled out of their pins. She shrugged off the customers' leers and whistles, took their coins, and secreted them in a strongbox, periodically swabbing the counter and scanning the crowd. They were like baby crows cawing for her attention, holding out their emptied glasses, begging her to fill them. Her father sat alone in the corner, staring into space, unbothered by the hellaballoo. A sideburned, burly man with remarkably white skin weaved in and out of the crowd, changing out kegs and the water in the dish tubs behind the bar, circulating among the patrons, and disappearing from time to time into the back. Samuel kept an eye on the door, in case Allaway and Murray sidled in, truant from the Tivoli.

He glanced around the saloon, taking in the tawdry, unchinked clapboard. He remembered his room in Glasgow, its dank stone walls and gloomy light. He had a sudden memory of Hailey's charitable blindness in the face of those shabby surroundings. She moved now with her customary grace, but it was tinged with a grim efficiency. His heart broke to see it. She'd lost the softness that had made her so vulnerable, though there was something beautiful about this steely resolve. Independence, he hoped it meant. Or a will to survive. He didn't know their situation, but if Hailey was working here, he worried that things were very bad indeed. Her father, sitting in the corner with a blank stare on his face, convinced him.

Whenever Hailey glanced his way, Samuel ducked his head, trusting that the jostling crowd and his hat would disguise him. Her sweeping glances paid heed only to the necessities.

He got away with that for half an hour.

Then, as if a gong had sounded, the saloon's patrons slipped out of the tavern in twos and threes, heading back to work, half-inebriated. In the emptying tavern, Hailey glanced toward Samuel, and this time she saw him. Her eyes widened in surprise, and she held his gaze for a minute or more, as though caught in an illicit act. He came toward her and stood at the bar.

She lifted a hand. "Before you say anything, Geordie needed shoes."

"Does he have them now?"

"Yes."

"Because of you?"

"Yes."

"Good."

Perhaps ten men remained in the saloon, leaning up against the walls, intent on their drinks. Hailey filled a man's glass and took his money and secured it in the strongbox.

Turning, she said to Samuel, "Do you want something?"

"I'll take a pint." He would take a thousand pints if it earned him Hailey's attention. Her fingers, long and tapered, gripped the edge of the bar as she set down a glass of dark ale. Samuel took a sip. It was bitter and tasted of soap.

"How is Alison?" Hailey said. Her hands were trembling.

"She started school."

"Geordie did, too. He's at the South School."

"Alison is at Sixth Street."

"I wish they could be together."

"It's based on where you live, I think," Samuel said.

Hailey glanced away and back again.

"Alison was frightened at first, but now, apparently, she's a bit of trouble," Samuel offered.

This was inanity. What did it matter where their siblings

went to school or what happened to them there? It appeared they would talk about anything but themselves. What he wanted to say was that he missed her. That he was glad she was still in Seattle. That if James wasn't treating her well, he would murder him. Instead, he rambled on about Alison, how she liked school, but that last week her teacher, Miss Pierce, came to the house to complain that Alison was a bundle of sass. That week alone, Miss Pierce said, she'd spat water at a boy who'd called her names and thrown a shoe into the boys' classroom, earning her an hour in the corner with the dunce cap. The superintendent, on his weekly inspection of the four city schools, had observed the shoe incident and laid down the law: Miss Pierce must tame Alison's rascally ways. And so, Miss Pierce said to Samuel, *Tame her.*

When Samuel asked Alison why she had thrown the shoe, she said she didn't like boys. They smelled.

Hailey's guarded facade cracked into a smile. Through the opened buttons at the collar of her dress, her skin, once a lucent white, was dappled with freckles from the sun. He noticed that the lush curves of her body had diminished, too. The angles of her collarbones stood out. Her hands were chapped and red.

Hailey's voice turned wistful. "Do you think Alison remembers me?"

"We don't talk about you."

Her eyes dropped to the bar. "Of course not." Then she glanced at the door and back again with the darting vigilance of the wary.

"Hailey, I have to—I need to ask. Does Murray treat you well?"

Two millworkers covered in sawdust entered and pounded on the bar for service. Hailey poured their drinks, cleared the bar of discarded glasses, and dumped them into a tub of soapy water. She glanced at the door again and turned, pleading, to Samuel.

"Please go. Sometimes he comes in."

"Does he ever hurt you?"

"Please, Samuel, go."

"Hailey, I came all the way from Scotland for you. I have to know that you're all right. At least tell me you're all right. If you aren't, then—"

"You can't save me, Samuel."

The patrons hid their interest no longer; their curious glances became overt stares.

Hailey faltered, her eyes pleading. "I made the choice. I'm married now."

"I live next to the university," he said. "At the Barnum House. Sundays, we go to the Presbyterian church."

Hailey's cheeks flamed scarlet as she stared at him, her eyes flat and pleading for him to understand. "I can't."

"Where do you go to church?"

"I've given up on God."

"Listen. Anywhere, anytime, anything. If you need me, if you need—"

"Hey, Romeo. She doesn't want you. She wants me."

Laughter rang out, and the heckler waved his smudged glass to be refilled. When Hailey took it from him, the man grinned at Samuel as if to say, *See?*

A sacrilege to leave her here. She had never seemed more alone to him than she did now. And he knew the pain of being alone without help.

Against all his instincts, he turned and left.

THAT EVENING A letter came for him at Barnum House. It was delivered by a boy who thrust it into his hands and accepted a penny for his trouble. The lamplight was low in the parlor, and he could hear the thump-thump of Annabelle kneading bread down the hall. Alison had gone to bed, exhausted from a day of tamping down her rascally ways.

Dear Samuel,

Don't come to see me again. I suspect that you might, and I forbid you. I made my decision. Whatever circumstances I am in now, I've brought them on myself.

No matter what you may think of James, he has done wonderful things. He is a hard worker, and he says he loves me, so Geordie and Father and I will be all right. Geordie likes it in Seattle. The air is better here, and he is losing his cough from Newcastle. Father is better, too, though he is not entirely himself. But he has not lost his goodness.

Do not come to see me again.

I can't live the life I have to live if I see you.

Do you understand? Don't come to see me.

Hailey

Part Four

1880–1881

It is said by those who claim to know that shipbuilding will be more active on Puget Sound next year than ever before. During the past year or two but little has been done, not enough to make good the vessels that, by reason of disaster, have gone out of service. The trade with the Islands of the Pacific has increased immensely, and on the close of the war in South America there will be an enormous trade reopened there. Our builders will be called upon to supply the new vessels that will be wanted, and the Seabeck, Ludlow, and other yards will be taxed with work as never before. The Puget Sound Yards, however, are better prepared than before, and can turn out vessels more perfectly, more rapidly, and more economically than in years past.

~*THE DAILY INTELLIGENCER,*
SEPTEMBER 9, 1880

28

Hailey

AFTER AN OPPRESSIVE NOVEMBER AND DECEM-
ber filled with incessant rain, the whole town was astonished
when six feet of snow fell over a period of one week in mid-
January. The Indians had no collective memory of such an event
ever occurring. Outside town, barn roofs caved in, scattering
cattle, but in town, two hundred men were kept busy sweeping
roofs of snow to prevent similar disasters. The new opera house,
Yesler's Hall, and the cattle market were saved in this way, but
not the blacksmith shop of Mssrs. MacDonald and Hunt, nor
the pattern shop on Front Street. At Lake Union, north of town,
people starved until a hastily built plow was tied to six horses
and a road broken through. Blowing snow wormed its way
through chinks in house siding, and people in Seattle woke each
morning to find several inches of the white stuff on their
bedspreads—even at the New England Hotel. In the harbor, a
sailing bark sank under the snow weighing down its deck and
spars. And while James Colman managed to run his train out to
Newcastle to bring the town much-needed provisions, on his
return the snowdrifts stopped him at Steele's Landing, and he
had to walk the almost four miles back to the city.

But it wasn't all tragedy and destruction. Boys seized the chance to go coasting, rioting down Mill Street on greased crates, and pummeling one another in snowball fights. A few families hailing from Wisconsin and Michigan hauled out their snowshoes and glided atop the accumulation, earning the envy of everyone. Adults took to dashing through the snow in sleighs, runners quickly affixed for the occasion.

As Seattleites shivered and stoked fires and trimmed wicks and cleaned the chimney glasses of their coal oil lamps, talk turned to the wondrous news that a man named Thomas Edison had lit up an entire street in New Jersey on New Year's Eve with electric light bulbs. Envy reigned as the season of darkness and wet loomed over Seattle.

It took seven weeks for the snow to finally dissipate. When school resumed, Hailey trudged through the wet and drifts to walk Geordie there and back again. At night, she read to him by candlelight, and when the snow cleared from the beach, she and Geordie and her father resumed their walks to overturn rocks and catch crabs and poke at starfish and dig clams. Past the barrel factory, she spied a painted sign heralding Fiddes Shipyard. She stood in wonder—sheds, machinery, a keel laid on the beach.

Daily, Geordie practiced his numbers on a slate, already doing addition and subtraction. Hailey took solace in his kisses, and sometimes her father roused and Geordie climbed all over him, and their father laughed, rare breaks from his usual dull inattentiveness. In this way, she kept family life alive.

From time to time, they encountered Samuel on the street, but they did not speak. He had taken Hailey's letter to heart, it seemed, though she sometimes wondered if he went out of his way to encounter her. Mostly, though, Hailey was lonely. She was too tired to see Bonnie—and besides, she had no time for anyone besides her father and Geordie and work. And, Hailey admitted only to herself, her job as a barmaid shamed her. She walked around town conscious of the contempt of Seattle's better citizens, who disdained who she was and what she did. Especially the women.

Olaf Cosper had fired James in November after a second argument over something or other. James couldn't even say what the fight had been about. But overnight he remade himself. He purchased Judson powder from William Meydenbauer, the German baker on Front Street who sold the powder and cartridges and fuses for stump blasting out his back door. James began a business clearing farms of enormous tree stumps by blowing them to smithereens.

"It's a good business for me," he said, pleased with himself. "Miners know explosives. Have you seen those stumps around here? Some of them are twenty feet across—bigger, even! They must have been growing since Jesus's time."

Hailey perused the newspaper for him in search of invitations for bids. He won his first several contracts because he underbid everyone, though he barely broke even on the jobs. But he soon figured it out and earned a little more money than before.

But it was not enough. It was as if money did not stick to James. Hailey couldn't understand why, but he was always short. Throughout February and March, she worked at the saloon when Geordie was in school, buying him a new shirt and pants when he grew, and squirreling away the extra money she made in a box. She hid the box in various places. Lately, it sat on the top of the armoire, behind a decorative finial.

ON A MONDAY morning in March, welcome hints of spring hung in the air as Hailey walked up Commercial Street toward Front Street. The morning breeze also carried with it the sudden screech of the mail steamer as it rounded Alki Point, a noise that always startled her. Despite the misery of the past months, lightness quickened her step. After dropping Geordie at school, she was on her way to the dressmaker to get a new dress made. Hers were in tatters. The daily life in Seattle, with its mud and splinters, was hard on gowns made for Glasgow ballrooms. She had left her father in the hotel room. Lately, he'd taken to sitting very still in one posture for long periods of time. James thought it was funny, but Hailey found it unbearable.

The dressmaker's shop was on James Street. Every outing in Seattle involved mud and a climb, and today was no different. As she ascended the steep hill, Hailey pushed away a lock of hair and looked down into the yard behind the Occidental Hotel, where the building's stables and laundry stood. One of the maids was picking her way across the sea of muck, lugging a laundry basket of dirty sheets. Despite the mud, the maid walked with an elegant gait. Everything about her seemed elegant—the straight posture, the restrained way she carried herself.

Familiar, even.

Hailey's voice broke. "Mother?"

Her mother. The queen of Glasgow society, who had reigned over the city's best dinner parties, was wearing a maid's uniform and trodding ankle-deep through the Seattle muck, carrying other people's dirty laundry.

She turned and came toward Hailey as if through quicksand. Hailey edged down the steep slope into the yard, stuttering with incomprehension. Her mother had grown thin, thinner even than when she had left Newcastle.

"Mama? When did you come back from Scotland?"

Her mother glanced away and back again with a flutter of indecision. "I didn't go."

It took a moment for this confession to filter through Hailey's confused feelings. "You didn't go?"

Her mother's cheeks flushed crimson.

Hailey said, "You mean to say you've been here all this time?"

She gave a fatigued nod, as if she could not trust herself to speak.

"And you're working here?"

She lifted her chin, a stab at her old pride. "I am."

Hailey could not take it in. "You never left Seattle? You didn't go back home? You're a maid?"

"Yes."

"But why didn't you look for us? For Geordie? For Father?"

"I couldn't."

"You *couldn't*?"

Her mother's gaze dulled, her defenses rising.

"But," Hailey said, sputtering, "why didn't I see you? I've been in Seattle for months and months."

"I saw you."

"You saw me? And you didn't speak to me?" Her brain would not work. "Did you know there was an explosion at the mine?"

Her mother gave a half nod.

"Do you know how it's been, Mother? You left, and Father was sick, and Geordie was five. *Five.* Father can hardly talk. He's like a child. I married James Murray. I didn't want to, but I did. I had to."

Her mother took a step toward Hailey, balancing the laundry

basket on one hip. "Please understand, Hailey, I had no way of taking you with me. I was sick—broken. I wasn't myself."

Hailey began shouting. "Do you know, Mother, that on the day after I was married, I saw Samuel Fiddes. Here, in Seattle. He came. He came all the way from Scotland for me. All this way. Shoveling coal. I hear he is going to build ships now. Ships! He has his own shipyard. I've seen it with my own two eyes."

"I didn't know. I—"

"I had to tell him that I was married. *Married.*" Hailey whispered this last. "I married James Murray to keep our family alive. We needed that money you took. We had nothing. And all this time you've been here."

Hotel guests were hanging out the windows, attracted by the shouting. Others had gathered at the back door and in the kitchen alcove, all of them watching. On the street, passersby craned their necks. Her mother clutched the laundry basket closer, as if it could save her from this public scolding.

"I work as a *barmaid*, Mother. Because James doesn't make enough money to support all four of us. I fill glasses with ale during the day and look after your son and husband. That is why we have enough money to eat, why Geordie has shoes." Hailey knew she was making the kind of public spectacle her mother hated. She rejoiced as she watched her mother shrink with each hammer of her contempt. "And all that time, you've been here."

"I'm sorry—I couldn't. I didn't know how to face you."

"*Face* me?"

"Please, child—will you tell me—how is Geordie? Is he all right? How is his cough?"

Hailey backed away. "No. No. You don't get to feel sorry for yourself. You don't get to apologize. And you don't get to see him, either."

Heartbreak scrolled across her mother's face.

"Do you know how long Geordie cried for you? Well, he's forgotten you now. He doesn't ask for you. And I'm no longer a child."

Her mother's breath was coming in ragged gulps. "I'm sorry, Hailey. I'm sorry. I've been wretched without all of you."

"I don't *care*. You can't have Geordie, Mother. You can't have him. He is mine now. He is all I have left. I've lost Father. And I've lost Samuel—the man I truly lo—"

She caught herself. She could not shout the truth at the crossroads of Seattle. The story would soon be all over town, would reach James's ears by evening. She hurried on. "Don't take my happiness, Mother. Geordie is my last scrap of anything good in the world. Do you understand? You and Father—you ruined it all."

Her mother reached for her. "I promise I won't take Geordie. I'm so glad to see you. I've needed so badly to know if you were all right and now—"

"We are not all right, Mother!" Hailey whirled out of Davinia's reach, and as she did, her mother staggered backward and fell into the mud. The force of the fall caused the contents of the laundry basket to spill into the muck. Sprawled on the ground, her skirts and hands covered in mud, her mother struggled to rise. A chorus of screeching seagulls filled the air.

"You left us, Mother. You should have looked for us."

"I didn't have money—"

"That absolves you of nothing."

Her mother blanched. "Oh, Hailey. Please. I'm sorry. I want to go home. Don't you? I want to go home, back to Scotland. Let's all go home and then we can be together again."

"With what money, Mother? James pays ten dollars a week

to keep two rooms at the New England Hotel. And board on top of that. And he never lets me forget it. We have no furniture of our own. No cart, no horse. The only thing I have of any value is your china, but I can't even sell it. What use is Doulton china in a place like this? Go home if you want, Mother. Go back to Scotland. But leave me Geordie. Because, unlike you, he has never let me down."

Hailey turned and stalked off, heedless of onlookers, barely able to see the sidewalk through her tears.

29

Samuel

SAMUEL HAD BEEN LEANING AGAINST A WOODEN telegraph post on James Street, and now he waited until a blinded Hailey Murray marched away before he strode into the yard to help Davinia MacIntyre to her feet. He had come upon the explosive scene between Hailey and her mother as he was returning from Dexter Horton's bank, where he had signed on a second loan for his new shipyard.

I've lost Samuel—the man I truly lo—

And somehow, she knew he built ships now.

Samuel helped Mrs. MacIntyre to gather the spilled sheets and linens and put them into the basket. She looked at him dazedly, unseeing. He was certain that she didn't recognize him. She took the refilled basket from him and shambled to the barn and disappeared into it. After a short while, she reappeared. A light mist was falling from the sky, threatening rain.

"They're sending me home," she said. Mrs. MacIntyre seemed to be asking for help.

"Where do you live?"

She nodded down Front Street. "In a boardinghouse across

from the poultry yard. Mrs. Widger's. It's—it's awful. I can't go back there now. Not yet. I can't."

Samuel took her by the hand and tucked her arm under his. She was shaking, and he was afraid she might faint. With considerable effort, they made their way to the Presbyterian church on Third Street. A new brewery had been built across the street, and the frothy scent of yeast bubbled inside the sanctuary. He rearranged two chairs of the precise ecclesiastical rows so that they could sit across from each other. Sitting side by side somehow seemed too intimate.

Mrs. MacIntyre sank onto one of the chairs. Shadows filled the hollows of her face. The hem of her dress had been inexpertly repaired many times. She wiped her muddied hands on her skirts. Her regal bearing had vanished, and in its place was the breakage of a life.

"I couldn't take care of them. I could hardly take care of myself, but that's—" She broke off, shaking her head. "I didn't know about Harold. Not until Hailey told me now. I knew he was in trouble, but not as much as Hailey said."

Samuel nodded, keeping his expression impassive. Hailey's declaration reverberated inside him. *The man I truly lo*— Mrs. MacIntyre stumbled on, her eyes deadened with sadness. "I eat twice a day. I survive, but if the children were with me, we would run out of money weekly. And while I am prepared to let myself starve, I am not prepared to watch my children starve."

Rain began to fall in force, dimming what light had managed to penetrate the cloud cover. Someone had left a window open, an act of folly in a place where rain fell in waves without warning. In Seattle, you were always underwater. Samuel rose to shut the window.

"I am ashamed of myself every moment," Mrs. MacIntyre

said, holding herself rigid. "I took money from them. Harold said he had twenty dollars in gold—I found only five. But still. The trains weren't running. The fire. Mr. Berg took me on a donkey, and then I caught a ride in a farmer's wagon from Renton. I had enough for a week of room and board. I found a job—and then, I hid. I read in the papers what had happened. I thought they must have come to Seattle, and I didn't want Hailey to find me.

"The worst of it is, that if I'd had the money, I would have gone back to Scotland. And I would have been halfway to Glasgow before I regretted it. I'm ashamed to think now how fast I would have left. My mother once said that I was selfish in love. That I lived apart from everyone. I hated her for saying that, but I've learned that she was right. Do you know, it's horrible to find out who you are late in life? And then to discover that you have no capacity for change? It's a tragedy. And yet you live on, knowing all of it."

Still Samuel said nothing.

"I owe you an apology, too. I told her you wouldn't come. And look at you." She studied him with a rueful expression, seeming to mark for the first time that his clothes were newer and better cared for than hers. "I take it you make a living?"

"I've started a shipbuilding company." As the words emerged from his mouth, Samuel felt a great thrill. Back in December, he'd said nothing about his intentions to anyone except a trusted few—the Lovings, whose help he'd recruited, Mr. Shade, and Mr. Colman. Even though the reality of it was beginning to sink in, the miracle of it still staggered him.

Mrs. MacIntyre's eyes widened, and he was glad to say this to her, glad to force her to see him in a light that she had never imagined.

"And you know how to build ships?"

"I do."

"And is your little sister with you in Seattle? Alison, yes?"

"Yes," Samuel said, astonished that she remembered Alison's name. "She's in school here. No more factory work. I'm going to make certain that she's safe forever."

"You're like Hailey. She was far better with Geordie than I ever was."

Samuel let this confession go unanswered.

"Do you think she will always hate me?" Mrs. MacIntyre said suddenly. "Do you think that if I found a way to try to make it right, that she'd—but I'm not who I thought I was. When things got hard, I left my children. I'm ashamed. I've ruined everything."

"Maybe not."

"I don't deserve your kindness."

"Maybe you do."

"Why?"

"Because I miss Hailey, too."

SAMUEL WALKED MRS. MacIntyre down Front Street to her boardinghouse. The modest building stood opposite a mal-odorous poultry yard and a cigar store, a few doors down from the Jones and Brother Machinist's Shop, which exuded a pounding racket from six in the morning till six in the evening, except Sundays.

"It's not Glasgow's west end, is it?" she said at the door. A hint of dignity, a ghost of who she had once been. "Thank you, Mr. Fiddes, for escorting me home."

Samuel watched her go inside. Hailey's declaration roiled

through his mind, *The man I truly lo*— *Surely* she had meant *love*. And the memory of her letter: *I can't live the life I have to live if I see you*. And *I married James Murray to keep our family alive*.

He'd obeyed her. He'd given Hailey the space she said she needed. When he saw her on the street, he lifted his hat, but that was all. He'd not seen her much—Seattle's winter weather had driven everyone indoors. By circumstance and intention, he'd avoided her. He'd thought he had even found some clarity in this. He was making that new life he'd promised himself. He was caring for Alison. He had rented a house on Third Street. It was close enough to school for Alison and had a parlor and two bedrooms and an attached kitchen. And he had hired a Chinese man, Ah Sing, to cook and clean and to sometimes watch Alison after school. He'd even met someone promising at church, a young widow with a son, Bonnie Atherton. He was making a life.

But hearing Hailey's declaration, his heart had thrilled. She loved him still.

If Murray heard what Hailey had just declared to all of Seattle, he might retaliate. But if Samuel went to her now, it would be worse.

The calculations of love.

He ached to think of Hailey in such pain. And he could not go to her.

IT WAS SLIPPERY going down to the beach. High tides had reached the rocks and cribbing during the winter, and the storms had flung kelp everywhere. Samuel strode along, finally reaching the acre of shoreline beyond the barrel factory that he had staked off with twine and posts in December. A painted wooden sign declared, *Fiddes Shipyard*. Beyond it lay the work of the winter: a shed for an office, another containing a great worktable, another, larger, open-air shed with the steaming cauldron and vises, and the long skeleton of keel for Emile Clarkson's boat lying in her ways. The framing ribs curved like tentacles from the spine. With its surrounding scaffolding and bolstering stays, the new ship was a beautiful sight, and while Samuel sweated the details of each day, they passed in a breathless sprint, as time does when dreams are coming true.

Back in December, when Samuel had told James Colman that he'd gotten a commission from Emile Clarkson, Colman said, "Emile Clarkson? The first mate on the *Messenger*, the steamer that sails to Steilacoom three days a week?"

"He's wanting to run a new ship to Port Blakely and back. Eagle Harbor, too. Competition for *Success*. Just a small passenger ferry. No room for wagons or horses or overnight lodging or anything. It should be straightforward. V-keeled, not a flatbottom steamer like for the rivers."

"How on earth did you steal that business from Hammond and Mitchell?"

Samuel shrugged. "They're busy. Everyone on the sound wants a ship. And no one wants to wait three years for New England built. Or even San Francisco built."

"You must have done some talking, Samuel Fiddes."

"Not me. Allaway and Shade. Both of them. Clarkson hunted me down. It helped that the *Geo. E. Starr* is such a success."

"By God, lad, that's fantastic."

"It will be just fifty feet, with a small boiler, a single compression engine, a modest paddle wheeler. I've asked the architect of the *Geo. E. Starr* to design her. Wood, not iron."

Colman had recommended Samuel to Dexter Horton, the

banker, and Samuel had gotten his seed money for the saws, tools, and machinery he needed. In the wet of February they had laid the keel right on the beach.

Chin Gee Hee, the Chinese labor organizer whom James Colman recommended, found Samuel four good Chinese workers who knew how to steam and bend wood. After several sleepless nights, Samuel learned to trust the Chinese men. They were geniuses at reading the drawings, and together they worked out the day's tasks in a mix of English, Chinese, and gesture. A slight man with wide, large eyes and a smooth forehead, Chin Gee Hee provided Chinese labor in Seattle from his office in the Wa Chong store, where he held a partnership. He had sailed from China to the goldfields of San Francisco, abandoned them when he was mistreated, and found his way to Seattle after meeting Henry Yesler. Affable and easy in both Chinese and English, Chin Gee Hee wore western vests and suits with his traditional long queue and seduced the powerful men of Seattle with his competence. Thereafter, he provided Chinese laborers for hotels, the railroad, coal mines, and even farms—any concern that needed willing workers.

Samuel had begged Pruss and John Salvation to quit their jobs at the coal wharf to help him. They had given up the idea of buying a farm for now, as Yesler was still holding on to his land and no one else would sell to them. At first, the flip of responsibility between them was unwieldy. On *Louisa*, the Lovings had held seniority, but now Samuel was their teacher. Pruss, taciturn in the engine room, thrived in the out-of-doors and liked learning. John Salvation leaned into the wood, his eye especially good at choosing which plank of fir belonged where, which would best truss up the stern, or flank the starboard, or shore up the port hull. He had an eye for beauty and strength, for the taut fibers of a living thing, and he had the courage to question Samuel when they disagreed. Each day, the seven of them worked together cutting and steaming planks, bending them, and setting them in. Angles marked, bevels laid, ends scarfed, everything bolted in tight, the hull grew day by day. Caulking would come later, after the stringers had been set, the bulkheads inserted, and the hull fully assembled.

AFTER LEAVING HAILEY'S mother, Samuel approached the shipyard with his usual mix of terror and excitement.

Today, the world was slate gray. The water, the sky. If not for Bainbridge Island in the distance, Samuel would not be able to tell where the water ended and the sky began. Several schooners rode at anchor in Elliott Bay, their sails furled. A dozen steamers crisscrossed the choppy expanse, while southward, along the shoreline toward town, the roar of the open coal chutes at Marshall Wharf thundered over the bay and echoed in the hills, from Alki and West Seattle, where Seattle's pioneers first settled in crude wooden cabins, to Magnolia Bluff and Four Mile Rock, and even beyond, to the tidal inlet of Salmon Bay, where engineers were already scheming to dig a canal from the salt water to Lake Union. The clatter echoed alongside the searing roar of new foundries, the shouting of the new barrel factory, the chatter of fish canneries, the fiery clamor of the ironworks, and the whine of sawmills. It was the music of Samuel's new life, and he was growing to love it.

On the beach, a woman in a green tattered dress was sitting on a log in the rain. *Hailey.* He tamped down a surge of happiness, her words of that morning still singing in his ears. He might be able to live forever on that unspoken promise of love. And here she was, come to see him.

Hailey turned, the stress of her encounter with her mother still evident in her flushed cheeks. "Can we talk?"

He removed his mackintosh and laid it on one of the many rocks that littered the beach. He sat beside her, coatless in the wind.

"Geordie and I used to come walking here—before you made it your shipyard. It is my favorite place," she said.

So that, Samuel thought, is why he loved it here. "Hailey—"

"I saw my mother. I thought she had left us, but all this time, she's been here in Seattle."

"I know. I was there this morning. At the hotel."

Hailey turned crimson. "What did you hear?

"Enough to hope."

"Oh, Samuel. Please don't hope." She looked out at the bay. "We didn't choose this, you and I, did we? We didn't choose to come here."

He dug a toe into the rocks. "I did. You were here."

She looked at him with wide, sorrowful eyes. "I'm sorry for all of this."

"I'm just happy to know that I wasn't a fool for coming after you."

She bit her lip and looked away. The wind picked up tendrils of her hair and she brushed them back. "Oh, Samuel, do you remember Glasgow? How cold it was down on the Broomielaw? And the boys in the pasty stalls yelling, 'Warm one warm one warm one,' sounding like doves? And the grand buildings on George Square? And those rare days in summer, when it was as hot as a fire in hell and all the birds came out of hiding to sing and every hill turned emerald green and it was the most beautiful place in the world?"

Samuel said, "Don't forget the coal in the air, and the

shivering, and nowhere comfortable to lay your head. And the hunger. But I remember. I remember it all." His voice turned raw. "Hailey, I shouldn't have waited one second to follow you. I should have sailed the very day your family did, stalked you across the sea, followed you to Newcastle, and spent every second of every day begging you to say yes to me, your mother be damned, your father, too, everyone be damned but us."

Hailey reached for Samuel's hand and held it in her lap so tightly that he could feel the heat of her. "Oh, Samuel, I'm sorrier than I can say."

"I need to know—how is it with James?"

She produced a flat smile. "I don't want to talk about him." Her gaze drifted to his half-built ship. "Look at what you've done. Fiddes Shipyard. Samuel, it's thrilling."

He reluctantly let the swirling thoughts of James Murray go.

"I write to you," she said. "I write you letters."

"I received only one."

"I mean the others, the ones I don't send."

"Send them."

"They're nothing of consequence. I write about ordinary things."

"I want to read about your ordinary things."

"I'm happy for you, Samuel. I truly am." And without another word, Hailey stood and walked back toward town.

THAT NIGHT, JOHN Salvation came to dinner, as he often did. After Alison went to sleep, Samuel told him the whole story of his life. His family, the orphanage, everything.

"I chased Hailey MacIntyre all the way here," he finished, summarizing, taking another swig of the warming ale. Then he fell silent, spent and more than a little drunk. He felt exhausted, having confessed so much.

John Salvation said, "I saw her today at the shipyard. That pile of dark hair? A quick smile, like she wants to give you the benefit of the doubt? She was your girl? Her little brother liked to look for whales with me, like Alison used to, remember? She was the one you were after? Damn, Scotty, I'm sorry."

"She's married."

"Then I'm even sorrier."

"She won't ever be mine, will she?"

John Salvation made an indistinct sound of agreement.

It was suddenly clear in a way it had never been before. Samuel would never have Hailey. No matter how much he loved her, no matter how far he'd come, no matter that she wrote to him in secret, no matter that she had come looking for him this morning, no matter that he believed she loved him, he would never have her. She would never be his.

John Salvation's voice caught, and he stumbled over his next words. "I've got a girl I want, too, but Pruss says I'd be drummed out of Seattle if I even try. Maybe worse. But he doesn't understand that Annabelle's the most—"

"Annabelle Barnum?" Samuel said.

"Yes." John Salvation stopped himself. "You know that my father used to be a slave, but did I ever tell you I was born free? Pa lives in a different world. He warns me not to take a breath without thinking about what a white man might do to me if I ever let on about Annabelle. If someone found out, my life would be over. That's why Annabelle is never going to be mine. I think she'd like to, but I don't see how.

"Here in Washington Territory, they don't have laws like other places about marrying between blacks and whites, Indians and whites." John Salvation nodded toward the kitchen, where Ah Sing was washing the dishes quietly so as not to wake Alison. "Chinese and whites neither. None of them like it, but they won't string you up here for it. Not like back home in West Virginia. Most anywhere, really. But it doesn't mean they like it. When I took little Alison for ice cream when you got that job on the *George E. Starr*, I had to pretend I was Annabelle's servant. Everyone knows who I am, knows I worked on Allaway's ship, but they like it if you pretend. I can't walk around here with this color skin without being noticed for everything I do. Pruss and I counted once. There's eight of us black folk in Seattle. If we didn't have Big Bill, I don't know how we'd do. Everyone loves him. He's like John the Baptist in the Bible—the one that made way for Jesus. Like a crier, saying here we come."

A gust of wind rattled the windowpanes. Ah Sing was talking quietly to himself in Chinese. The beef he had cooked tonight carried a hint of orange and heat. Samuel didn't mind when Ah Sing fed him food from his homeland. He liked his strange, sweet sauces and rice. And besides, it was easier than trying to teach him how to cook anything resembling ordinary food, especially since Samuel couldn't cook.

Samuel wondered whether Ah Sing yearned for someone he couldn't have, too. There was hardly a Chinese woman to be found in Seattle. "Black people in Scotland keep to themselves, too. I suppose it's easier."

John Salvation squinted. "I'm goin' to ask—you ever wonder about me? Pa?"

"Wonder what?"

"S'not usual, hardly." He pointed at Samuel and then back at himself, suddenly wary, curious. "Us—different colors. Friends. Ever bother you, being seen with us?"

The shock of John Salvation's question unseated Samuel. It wasn't that he didn't notice the differences between them. But from the moment off the coast of Oregon when John Salvation and Pruss had saved his life at risk to their own, the fact of it had moved to the background. The Lovings had shown him and Alison more kindness than almost anyone in their lives. In truth, Samuel needed them. He needed their stalwart comradeship, their loyalty, their kindness. They believed in him.

And he believed in them. He feared suddenly that John Salvation and his father didn't know what they meant to him, didn't know how bleak those early hours in Seattle would have been if not for them.

Samuel considered carefully how to frame his words so that John Salvation would understand. He met John Salvation's wary gaze and sank back in his seat, folding his hands across his chest. "I don't know why you're not embarrassed to be seen with me. I'm far taller than you. Better-looking by a long shot. I show you up left and right. Don't know why you don't slink away with chagrin, or why you even show your face beside me, ever. It's a mystery, really. One for the ages."

After a brief interval in which wind battered the clapboards and filled the room with a cold draft, and Samuel feared that John Salvation had not understood the affection in his playful jibe, John Salvation finally keeled over laughing, his breath coming in quick starts and whoops. Samuel choked with laughter as John Salvation caught his breath and dried his eyes.

One eye cocked at Samuel, John Salvation said, "You ever have a friend? Be like this with anyone?"

Samuel shook his head, his voice now utterly sincere. "Never."

"Me, neither." After a time, John Salvation said, "You know what I think about? I think about a home. Papa and me—we left West Virginia, fast. Had to. I'll tell you that story sometime, maybe. Left my mother buried in a grave behind the little cabin where we lived. We've moved ever since—on one ship or another, up and down the Mississippi and up and down to California, until now. I'd like a home, you know? Somewhere that's ours. That's why Pruss wants land, if Yesler will ever sell. I'd like to know what that's like. A home, somewhere that's yours alone. You ever think about that, Scotty?"

"I do." But Samuel feared he would never have a true home, because, to him, home was always going to be a girl named Hailey.

30

Hailey

AT MIDNIGHT THAT NIGHT, JAMES BURST INTO their room at the New England Hotel. Wet through, he shed his jacket, stuck his hand in his shirt pocket, and whipped out a flask.

Hailey set down her pen and shoved the letter she'd been writing out of view. She was exhausted from the morning's blinding rage, the public shaming she had meted out, the joy and pain of speaking with Samuel, and the anxiety of awaiting James's reaction. After seeking Samuel at his shipyard, she had barely made it to her shift at the saloon. The patrons had been particularly thirsty today. And she never got to the dressmaker. Already, a waitress in the dining room had asked about her mother. She screwed on the lid of the ink and turned to face James, bracing herself.

The sharp scent of whiskey wafted from him. His boots, crusty with mud, had again tracked dirt across the floor. He often came home covered in wood shavings, but now he looked as if he'd dragged himself through a pit of sawdust. Taking another draught from the flask, he grinned and said, "Warmth for the soul. Did you get me dinner?"

Wary, Hailey went to the dresser and uncovered the dish of cold bacon and chicken she had brought upstairs from the dining room. She didn't like to keep food in the room, because it attracted rats, but James expected it.

Standing at the dresser, he wolfed down the food. A glint of excitement shimmered in his blue eyes. When he finished, he drew Hailey from her seat to the bed.

He grinned at her. "I have fixed everything."

Everything? Her loneliness, her mother's betrayal, her father's deterioration? "What do you mean?"

He leapt up and riffled through the pockets of his coat and withdrew a fine leather case with a strap and handed it to her, urging her to flip open the buckle that secured it. Inside, nestled in a felt-lined interior, was a pair of binoculars. She turned the heavy glasses over in her hands.

"What are these for?"

He watched her, his blue eyes glinting in the candlelight. "Can you guess?"

She shook her head. He was more animated than she had ever seen him. Was it possible that he hadn't heard about the argument with her mother? He grinned again, pleased to have stumped her.

"Captain Allaway hired me. He's carrying a certain kind of cargo these days, and he needs me to be his eyes. I'll get a cut of the cargo price when we land it. It's an impressive profit. It will be a lot of money, Hailey."

A certain kind of cargo. The number of industries in Seattle grew by the day. Now there were at least five major ones: coal, timber, fishing, shipbuilding, and opium. Opium was legal, sold everywhere. It was contraband only if it was smuggled. The tariff was two dollars a tin, payable upon import in Port Townsend at the customs office. Not paying the tax was the crime. Few citizens in Seattle condoned the opium dens, especially when sated men spilled onto the streets of Chinatown still intoxicated, and lay down on the sidewalk to finish their dreams. How much opium slipped past customs was anyone's guess, but there was a lot of opium money running through town, and Captain Allaway was said to be in the middle of it now.

"You don't want to blow up stumps anymore?"

"That's done. I'm never going back. I'll make us fast money, and then I'll be important—like Yesler—and then you'll finally be my queen. I'll make enough to build you a pretty house like I always wanted for you. Isn't it grand?" James peered at her when she said nothing. "C'mon, Hailey. Aren't you pleased?"

She had to be careful. His temper could flare in an instant. "Aren't you worried about the customs agents? About a trial? Jail?"

"They only go after the Chinese for that. And Allaway is no fool. . . ."

He talked on and on with growing excitement, but all Hailey could think was that James's scheme for prosperity offered no solution. No amount of money would make her happier with him. Rain was drumming outside, hard beads verging on snow. Hailey drew closed the shawl she had thrown over her nightgown and produced a wan smile.

The excitement drained from James's face. He studied her, gaze narrowed. "I don't relish coming home to a wife who doesn't love me."

Her heart caught in her throat.

"I heard. I heard all over town what you said about Fiddes. About me." His blue eyes turned ice cold. "Listen to me, Hailey Murray. Don't you ever tell anyone I can't make the money to support you. I live by my wits. I do what I can with what I've got. Not like Fiddes and his grand new shipyard. I hear he trained on the Clyde. Mr. Big Shipbuilder. He's had help. Not like me. I had nothing, and I've learned how to make my way in the world with no one's help. That's what makes *me* special."

She heard the envy in James's voice, the twisted logic about who had done what to save themselves.

"Do you even remember that I am the man who saved you?" he said.

"Of course I do."

"Have I hit you? Insulted you? Done one thing to injure you?"

She didn't answer. She could never erase from her mind the time he took her in rage after he met Samuel.

Abruptly, James rose from the bed and swept an arm over the things on the desk, smashing her bottle of ink to the ground. It shattered, and the puddling ink pooled in the grooves of the wooden floor. Her eyes followed the fluttering flight of the unfinished letter to the floor.

James narrowed his gaze until his eyebrows met, and after a moment, he followed her restless gaze to the half-written letter she had shoved into the corner of the desk. He picked it up, steady on his feet now. Holding up one hand to silence her, he read, his eyes stumbling haltingly over the page. He had so little education that reading was a challenge for him, but not an impossibility. He dangled the letter from his fingers. "You *write* to him?"

"No. I don't send them. It's nothing—I write about my life—"

"*Your* life?

She racked her brain, trying to remember what she had written. "Our life. About Geordie, mostly, and about how I spend my days. But it doesn't matter. I don't send them."

"Doesn't matter?" James said. "Doesn't *matter*? *I'm* the one who matters. *I'm* the one who helped you. *I'm* the one who feeds you. I *deserve* a wife who loves me." He stuffed the letter into his pocket and yanked her clothes from the armoire, searching the pockets of her aprons and dresses. She held her breath, terrified that he would find the loose floorboard where she had moved the box that held her money. But he found nothing. He pulled her from the bed, flipped the mattress over, and searched through the upended bedclothes.

Hailey flinched as he whirled on her. She backed against the wall.

"Does he write to you?"

"Please don't shout. You'll wake Father and Geordie."

"By God, I'll wake the entire hotel if I have to. Do you see him?" James screamed, grabbing her shoulders and shaking her.

She yelped in shock. Had anyone seen her at Samuel's ship-yard today? "Geordie will be frightened. Please stop."

"You go to him, don't you?" He shook her again and banged her head against the wall.

"No. Never. Not once."

"Are you lying?"

"No." *Only a little.* He released her and she sank to the floor, her dress billowing around her, the puddle of ink seeping into the hem. The bedclothes lay tangled around her as she began to sob. "He doesn't write to me. He came to see me once. At the saloon. I told him not to see me anymore. I write the letters as a diary only. It doesn't mean anything."

"You could have turned me down. I didn't drag you to the altar."

He'd said this before. And of course he was right. She had done everything of her own accord.

Sighing, James sank to the floor beside her. His tirade had exhausted him. "Do you love me even a little?"

She stopped her hiccupping, catching her breath before she said, softly, but with finality, "No."

It was the inescapable truth, and now their carefully constructed ruse collapsed. James had raged because he fully understood that she did not love him. And no amount of deflection on her part could conceal that fact.

"Everything I've done is for you," he said. "Everything."

She didn't doubt it. She pulled away. "James, did you know that my mother was in Seattle?"

He said nothing. She couldn't read him, couldn't tell whether he would tell her the truth. "Did you?"

"You have to stop this writing."

"But did you know?"

"What does that matter, Hailey? She left you. I haven't. I'm the one who stayed by your side. When everyone abandoned you, it was me who stepped up. *Me.*" He straightened, eyes glinting like ice, sorrow and fatigue erased. "Listen to me, Hailey Murray. You don't love me? Fine. But you're mine. Don't you forget it. And don't you dare embarrass me in public again. I'm going to make something of myself, and you will be on my arm every step of the way. You're my wife. You are Mrs. Hailey Murray. Never forget it."

His sudden coldness terrified her. He looked at her without warmth or sympathy, climbed to his feet, and held the letter to the candle burning by the bed.

Catching fire, it fell to the floor, and he stomped out the flames. The next day, Hailey burned them all.

31

Samuel

THROUGHOUT THE LATE SPRING OF 1880, SAMUEL
Fiddes built Emile Clarkson his boat.

By May, the hull was half-completed, and by early June,
Clarkson, who often came calling in between his runs on *Messenger*, was pleased that nearly the entirety of the hull had taken
shape. The long hours the new ship required kept Samuel from
Alison far more than he liked. More than one rainy night, he'd
returned home to find that she had already succumbed to sleep.
A lit pipe in hand, Ah Sing would report the events of Alison's
day in broken English, mostly along the lines of running rampant in the streets, petting stray cows, sliding down steep lots
on barrel staves, traipsing here, there, and everywhere, and returning home splattered with mud. He'd taken to giving her
cooking lessons to try to keep her home.

Samuel grew uneasy with Alison's hodgepodge existence.
He didn't like the absence of his governing hand. He started to
pay Bonnie Atherton, the widow he knew from church, to take
Alison so that she wouldn't run wild. Bonnie had tried to refuse payment, but he insisted, knowing how she and Angus
would benefit. For the remainder of the spring, Alison went to

Mrs. Tierney's Pattern Shop after school and played with little Angus until Samuel came to collect her.

He often lingered, chatting when Bonnie was free.

"Oh, it's *you*, Mr. Fiddes," she always said when he came in, flirting a little. "What a surprise."

She was easy to chat to. He liked how good she was with her son, how she never complained, even though he knew she must be exhausted. He knew, too, that she was lonely—she mentioned something about missing a friend from Newcastle, someone who seemed to have no time for her anymore. But she had a bright, winning way about her, and he found himself drawn to her. He'd seen little of Hailey—she seemed to avoid him completely now after that meeting in March. And though Bonnie wasn't Hailey, Samuel looked forward to seeing the pretty widow at the end of the day, a ritual that came to an end in late June, when school was dismissed for the summer and Alison spent her days at the shipyard instead.

She made a noisy, joyful nuisance of herself, climbing all over the ship and picking berries from the hillside and flinging stones into the sea. She plucked oysters from rocks and dug clams and fished for the tiny, black darting fish along the shoreline. On occasion, she invited troops of children to the shipyard, but Samuel put an end to that. The shipyard was alive with blocks and tackles, band saws and beveling machines, grindstone and emery wheels. The last thing Samuel wanted was for a child to lose a hand or an eye.

One day in early July, John Salvation and Pruss were fitting the decking subfloor, building it from bow to stern. There was the usual jumble of Chinese and English as everyone worked. A large gap remained at the stern, through which the engine would be lowered. They were almost finished, ready to launch the hull next week. Samuel had already rented dock space on the barrel factory's pier. The engine was due to arrive on *Dakota* this week.

"Samuel," Alison called. She'd been pacing the decking, counting up to a hundred and then beginning over again. She was doing a very poor job of staying out of everyone's way. "When the boat is finished, can I ride it into the sea? Will you name it after me?

"Alison," Pruss said, "watch where you're stepping. You see that big hole there at the back? You could tumble right into that." He had fashioned cushions out of burlap sacks to protect his knees, which made it awkward to move. "I can't move fast with these inventions on. Oh, child, you worry me."

"Ali," Samuel said, "she's not my boat to name. It's Mr. Clarkson's. Now, sit down before you test Pruss again."

"Come here, little one," John Salvation said. He had a knack for finding a way to keep Alison out of trouble. She danced to him, hugging the doll he had given her to her side, which she carried everywhere.

"Now," John Salvation said. "Lie very still next to me, point your face upward, and count those seagulls." The gulls had been wheeling overhead all day, fishing a school of herring. "And while you're at it, ask your brother if he's still going out tonight."

There was a dance tonight at the Parker House, the new hotel on the cliff above the barrel factory. Samuel had asked Bonnie to go with him. It would be their first time going out together. Samuel had resolved again to forget Hailey, to concentrate on the life he could make out of what was possible.

"Can you still take care of Ali?"

"I can, if this little one will do as I say." John Salvation poked Alison on her side, and she twisted away with laughter.

"Can I come, Samuel? Please, please, please?" she cried.

"Grown-ups only, but one day, maybe, when you're older."

"I don't know how to dance."

"Neither do I," Samuel said.

"I'll teach you," John Salvation said, and grabbed Samuel by the arm and joggled him all over the deck, carefully sidestepping the open stern and scattering tools and making Alison collapse into giggles.

THE PARKER HOUSE stood on West Street, a precipitous wagon ride north from Seattle over the steep road to Belltown, a settlement that teetered high above Samuel's shipyard. The proprietor, Captain Parker, eager to lure Seattleites to his out-of-the-way hotel, provided a steam launch to whisk his guests ten minutes along the shore of Elliott Bay instead of making them endure the rigors of the coach.

Samuel, though, walked up from the shipyard, having made a hasty bath from the spring that burbled from the bluff before he changed into a new shirt and pants in his office shed.

Bonnie was waiting for him on the hotel's wide porch, lit tonight with a welcoming lantern, an unnecessary courtesy since the sun hadn't yet dropped behind the Olympics. She was smoothing her hair, tied up tonight with a cherry-red ribbon to brighten her Sunday dress. She laughed when she saw him. "I haven't been on the water since I came up from San Francisco. I forgot how the wind has its way. Do I look a fright?"

The launch ride had pinkened her cheeks, and she looked beautiful.

"I promise I'll take the launch with you next time," Samuel

said. The Parker House had promised to hold a dance every other Saturday night.

Bonnie smiled at this mention of future dates and gave him her arm to be led inside. The ballroom was packed. The hotel was so new that its fir floorboards smelled of the forest and its flocked wallpaper the yeasty scent of the wheat paste that adhered it to the walls. Candles in two chandeliers flickered overhead, wax already dripping onto the floor. The Occidental Hotel's shabby ascendency and Yesler Hall's dinginess had been eclipsed.

Samuel had confessed to Bonnie when he invited her that he didn't know how to dance, but she had promised to teach him. When the band struck its first chords, she pulled him to the side of the floor and walked him through the steps. Soon he realized that dance was a pattern, and his mathematical mind seized hold of the intricacies. After several flawless turns, he boldly steered Bonnie into the stream of dancers and managed to maneuver without any collisions until she urged him to look at her instead of his feet, which caused him to stumble.

They laughed. Bonnie laughed a lot. Samuel felt a loosening of his spirits. The worries of work were being jogged free in this frivolous fun. The group re-formed for a reel. Bonnie kept him firmly in hand, whispering instructions for the steps and when to join hands and skip up the line. He whirled her through the next dance, a kind of quadrille, Bonnie explained, but westernized. Samuel didn't know what that meant, but he understood that Bonnie loved to dance, and when the reel ended, there was riotous clapping, and the caller declared a break. Everyone headed to the refreshment table.

Standing next to the punch bowl were the Allaways, the

captain and the former Mrs. Barnum, recently married, and the Murrays. All sense of happy abandon drained from Samuel.

It was hard to get used to the fact that James Murray and Captain Allaway were friends and, worse, that they worked together. He'd heard that James had abandoned his stump-blasting business to join Allaway. Everyone in Seattle suspected what they were up to, but so far they hadn't been caught. And it did seem that the Murrays had money now. Hailey no longer worked. Samuel knew this because he had occasionally walked by the saloon to check on her and recently he'd found her absent. He was no expert in dressmaking or expensive materials, but Hailey wore as fine a dress as any she'd worn in Glasgow, a deep red that set off her eyes. Trafficking in opium, he thought, must pay well.

James Murray took one look at Samuel and wrapped his arm around Hailey's waist, drawing her close. His eyes held a challenge and his mouth, condescension. Seeing them together in this way, Samuel fought waves of jealousy, though concern soon overtook the roiling envy. Hailey looked even more subdued and dispirited than before.

"Samuel Fiddes!" Captain Allaway boomed. "Dancing are you now, Scotty? And who is the young lady?"

"May I introduce Bonnie Atherton?" Samuel turned to make the introduction to Hailey and James, but before he could, the two women embraced. Hailey's face held an expression he couldn't interpret. James Murray's stony mask flickered into tenderness, and when the two women broke away, he took Bonnie's hand in his.

"How are you, Bonnie?" James said.

"Well enough," Bonnie said.

Then she explained to Samuel that she had known Hailey and James in Newcastle.

Samuel knew that Bonnie had lived in Newcastle. One day in the church's reception hall, she had told him how she had lost her husband in the explosion. But he did not know about this connection to James and Hailey. Bonnie had spoken about a friend from Newcastle, but she had never mentioned a name. Nor had Samuel ever mentioned Hailey to her. Why would he have? From the town gossip, Samuel thought now, Bonnie might have heard about Hailey's declaration at the Occidental Hotel. Crosscurrents were flying, and he couldn't straighten it all out in his mind.

Hailey fiddled with her purse. "So, Bonnie and Samuel, how do you two know one another?"

Samuel thought her voice sounded tight, though her smile for Bonnie was genuine.

Bonnie dimpled with pleasure, seemingly oblivious to the tension. "I take care of his sister. And we know one another from church."

Hailey forced a smile. "My family knew Samuel in Glasgow."

"Did you? And you're both here in Seattle? That's extraordinary. Did he come over with your family? I didn't know that. Hailey, you never told me you had a friend here." She looked from Samuel to Hailey with guileless confusion.

Before either Hailey or Samuel could answer, Mrs. Allaway stepped in to smooth the situation. Since becoming Mrs. Allaway, the former Mrs. Barnum had taken on a rather maternal affect. Samuel supposed it was the release from having to worry about money. She held out her hand. "It's lovely to meet you, Bonnie."

But her diversion didn't work. James broke in, a smirk contorting his already sour expression. "Fiddes didn't travel from Scotland with the MacIntyres. He came on his own, chasing after Hailey. Much good *that's* done him."

The shock of what he said silenced the group. James held on to Hailey like a trophy. Bonnie flushed and looked down at the floor, and Samuel wanted to wring James's neck, but this time Allaway stepped in, shouting over the clamor, clearly trying to create another diversion. Samuel reached for Bonnie's elbow to reassure her.

"Scotty, my friend, I bumped into Emile Clarkson on the docks. He raves about your work."

"I'm happy to hear Emile is pleased."

"Listen to me now, Scotty," Allaway said. "I need a new boat."

"Why? Did something happen to *Lady Barnum*? I watched her come into the bay just yesterday. She cut through the chop like a dream."

"That she does," Allaway said. "Didn't you see her tonight? She's tied up at the barrel factory. I brought our whole party over this afternoon. I have plans." He grew expansive and voluble. It was hard to know whether it was drink or truth that ruled his mouth tonight. "I need a *ship*, not just something to buzz around the sound in."

"He means he's already tired of me," Mrs. Allaway said, laughing. "A month of marriage and he wants to flee, wants to be a bachelor again."

"No, my darling. Scotty here will build me a captain's cabin like no other, won't you, Scotty? Room for both you and Annabelle, too, if she likes! Regular runs to San Francisco! A bigger life!"

Samuel eyed Allaway, assessing. "If you're serious, sir, I'd be happy to build you a ship. But it would take a while. I have to finish Emile's."

Allaway beamed. "Capital, capital."

A *ship*, Samuel thought. He wondered how large. And he wondered if Allaway would carry opium on this one, too, or if he would go back to merely ferrying passengers.

He could feel Bonnie shrinking beside him. Samuel said, "Bonnie is teaching me to dance."

James's voice dripped with delight. "Isn't that a wonderful thing, Hailey? Our Bonnie is teaching Mr. Fiddes how to dance."

Warm-up strains from the band spread over the ballroom, and Captain Allaway bowed to Bonnie and asked if she would honor him with a turn around the floor. She looked to Samuel for approval and Samuel nodded and Allaway took Bonnie in hand and swept her out onto the floor. James took Hailey by the hand and led her away.

"Don't mind James, Samuel," Mrs. Allaway said. "He can be crude. I am sorry, though, that he upset Bonnie. She seems a lovely girl."

"How did you know about—Hailey and me?" He watched as James swung Hailey around the floor, his jealousy rising again.

"Well, Hailey did make a fuss in public. And Captain Allaway hears a lot of things, and I do, too."

"How can I make it up to Bonnie?"

"Always be honest if you can." Mrs. Allaway followed his gaze and, understanding his pain, patted his hand to distract him. "Samuel, isn't this is a beautiful hotel? Captain Allaway rented us all rooms for the night, so we needn't go home. The captain wanted to make an outing of it."

Samuel forced himself to match her cheerful tone. "Didn't Annabelle want to come?"

"She said she was coming down with something. Pity, really. She would have enjoyed this."

On the other side of the room, James pulled a flask from his pocket and poured its contents into the punch bowl.

Mrs. Allaway said, "Samuel, did you know that Captain Allaway is building me a house in Belltown? It won't be ready for a very long time, but he doesn't mind. He wants a view of the sea—he can't be away from it for long. He's ordered all the furniture from the Orient. . . ." As the last strains of the polka died away, Mrs. Allaway talked about a pair of chandeliers she'd ordered, joyfully at ease with her new wealth.

Allaway came and pulled Samuel outside, where in the warm breeze of the July night they discussed the particulars of his new ship.

LATER, SAMUEL AND Bonnie joined the Allaway party at the midnight repast served in the dining room. Allaway was boasting to anyone who passed that the best new shipbuilder on Puget Sound was going to build him a ship. James was too drunk to notice much anymore. He had gone outside to the veranda, where he was smoking cigars with several men. Bonnie and Mrs. Allaway had fallen into deep conversation on the other side of the table, leaving Hailey and Samuel to talk on their own for the first time in months. Sitting beside her at the table, Samuel could almost pretend that things had turned out differently.

"I'm sorry about James," Hailey whispered.

Her expression was dull, flat, despite the music and dancing.

Samuel longed to draw her outside, to ask how she was, but he worried it would provoke a confrontation with Murray, and Hailey might pay for it later. He wondered what had been the repercussions of her public declaration in March. Did that explain her air of listless distraction? "Hailey, I have to ask. Are you all right?"

She turned to him. "I should explain to Bonnie about us. I would have before, except that I didn't know you knew one another."

"Please tell me how you are."

"I'm fine. Tell me about Bonnie."

Samuel gave in. "We met at church. Like we did."

"Is she—special to you?" Hailey said.

"I don't know." He abandoned any further talk of Bonnie for safer topics. "Where is Geordie tonight?"

"At the Meydenbauers'. He is friends with their son. And Father will be all right on his own—at least, I hope he will. I asked a maid to look in. So, you're going to build Captain Allaway a new boat?"

"If it's not just the whiskey talking. He wants a fast build, but it will be big. I have to find an architect to draw up the plans, and he has to approve them. He keeps neglecting the fact that I have to finish Emile's boat first." Samuel glanced out the window at James, whose face was blurred with the effects of his punchbowl doctoring. "Hailey, please, how are you? You seem—"

She was quick to interrupt him. "I'm fine. I am. James is happy these days. Money has a way of soothing all ills. Even if it comes from the wrong places."

So, she knew what James was up to.

Hailey looked at him from under her dark lashes. "I'm happy for you, Samuel. Bonnie's a good one."

He swallowed. So, the subject was not to be abandoned. "Is she?"

"She saved us in Newcastle. We would have starved without her."

Samuel nodded. What a tangled web. Sometimes, Seattle was too small. "I miss you," he whispered.

"Oh, Samuel." Her eyes filled with warmth. "I'm so happy to see you."

"And I you." He could kiss her, here and now, and no doubt she would revel in his embrace as much as he would. Under the table, he clasped her hands, and she let him, responding to the gesture with a squeeze.

Absorbed in each other, they did not notice James approaching until he slapped his hand onto the table between them, rattling the silverware and half-empty goblets, startling everyone.

"Goodness, James," Mrs. Allaway said, surprised out of her tête-à-tête with Bonnie.

"Having a chat, are we?" He was weaving with drink and slurring his words.

"Are you feeling all right?" Samuel said, rising. "Don't want to scare the ladies, do we?"

Hailey shook her head at Samuel, her meaning clear. *Don't start anything.* James looked between them, an inebriated lag in his understanding, then captured Hailey's hand. Samuel stifled an urge to knock it away.

He forced himself to say, "Bonnie, shall we? I think the steam launch has returned."

The captain's wife cloaked Bonnie in a smothering embrace, her maternal turn still in force. "Yes, certainly she's ready. Aren't you, Bonnie?"

A WILD AND HEAVENLY PLACE

He took Bonnie's arm, and together they retrieved her wrap. In suffocating silence, they descended the hotel's long flight of steps and walked across the beach to the pier, the hotel's gleaming lanterns guiding their way. The launch hadn't arrived—it had been too obvious a ruse, Samuel feared—but then he saw it approaching from a distance across the glassy sea.

Bonnie said, "There isn't a hint of wind."

He turned to her. "Bonnie, it's true that I came to Seattle because of Hailey. But I found her married to James." Even to him, his delivery felt awkward. It felt like yet another severing from Hailey. To voice it was to declare it true, yet again.

"You came all that way for her?" Bonnie said.

Samuel winced. "I know what it sounds like—"

She put her hand on his arm and spoke gently. "What a long way to come, Samuel. How difficult this must be. You know I lost my husband. I know what it is to lose someone important. It's a heartbreak that lasts forever."

Her unexpected kindness washed over him. "If I had known that you knew Hailey, I would have said something to you."

"I'm glad to know now."

"May I see you again?" It seemed suddenly important that he could. He would never have Hailey. Why did he have to keep learning this?

She considered this for a moment, waiting, perhaps, to make certain that he meant it.

The moonlight threw silver shadows across her face. It was shaped like a heart, he realized.

"I would like that."

The launch arrived and he helped her in, climbing in after. The engine was too loud to talk anymore. Samuel drank in the smell of salt and seaweed, recalling the look on Hailey's face when James slapped the table. She had startled and then smiled blankly, as if she were trying to erase herself from the world.

It was the first time he felt completely terrified for her.

AT HOME, HE found Annabelle Barnum and John Salvation asleep in each other's arms on the couch. Startled awake, John Salvation reared up, rousing Annabelle, who blushed and jumped to her feet.

She fumbled for words. "I brought some cookies over—for Alison—I wasn't feeling well. I must have fallen asleep." She smoothed her dress, flustered. "It was kind of you, John Salvation, to take care of me. If you'll excuse me," she said, and bolted from the house.

John Salvation rushed after her, calling, "You shouldn't walk alone."

And then he vanished into the night.

32

Hailey

FOUR MONTHS LATER, ON THE FIRST DAY IN NO-
vember 1880, Hailey stood with James, her father, and Geordie
in front of a pretty little house high on the hill on the road to
Lake Union. Hailey had learned that Seattle's terrain was made
up of north-and-south-running valleys and ridges, pocked with
lakes and laced by water and mountains. People built homes on
these precipitous hillsides, and the one they stood before now
was new, painted white, with a popped dormer window in its
roof and a porch in front, situated on a cleared plot of land
halfway up the hill behind Belltown—with a view to the valley
it sat above. Its relative elegance to the crude homes of Seattle
reminded Hailey of their home in Glasgow, though it was nothing like it, really—it was a cottage, if that. Still, its solidity rendered it special in this raw town of hastily clapped-together
buildings and houses. James beamed with pride as he unlocked
the front door and swept Hailey up in his arms and carried her
over the threshold to Geordie's squeals of delight. Inside, there
were fir floors, a table and four chairs, and an upholstered couch
and armchair. In the downstairs bedroom, an armoire was
pushed up against one wall and there were two beds with straw

mattresses in new ticking. A kitchen jutted off the back, furnished with a coal- and wood-burning stove, a counter, and open cupboards. Up a set of open stairs was a second bedroom under the slanted roof. A wide bed and a desk and chair took up the whole of the space.

"How?" Hailey breathed. James had kept all this a secret.

"I've leased it. And the rest—Hall, Paulson and Company," he said proudly. "All of it. The furniture, the mattresses, everything. I promised that you would live like a queen. Well, here you are."

There was no evidence of his temper, no smoldering impatience, not even with her father, who sank into the armchair and stared into the large, open room like a surprised child. And Geordie's fevered shrieking and marching around the rooms like a drum major earned not even a reprimand.

"There's a Turkish rug coming, too, for the parlor," James said.

A hired wagon arrived then, pulled by a team of horses. James had paid someone to pack their rooms back at the hotel, and their belongings were tucked in the wagon bed. Her heart in her throat, Hailey thought of the box in which she had hidden all her saved money. But the movers would have had to have known about the loosened floorboard, would have had to have known to look. Surely, they hadn't? Frantically, she formulated a plan for how to retrieve it. As she fretted, a whistling James unloaded, conscripting Geordie to carry in smaller items while he carried in the larger ones.

Setting down the crate of her mother's Doulton china, James said, "Now you can use these."

He produced new cast-iron cookware. The grocer's delivery boy appeared with two hampers containing enough flour and yeast and shortening to bake endless loaves of bread. There was bedding and toweling, all newly purchased, and other household goods that kept arriving, delivery after delivery. Her box did not appear.

When evening came, Hailey laid a side of bacon in one of the new pans. She would go to the hotel in the morning, explain to the front desk clerk that she needed to retrieve something. That was easy enough, wasn't it? People probably left things behind all the time. She would blame the movers. James watched her from the vantage point of the kitchen door, arms crossed, beaming as she lifted a lid to stir a pot of beans. She was roasting a pullet in the oven, too, because the butcher had also sent provisions.

So much plenty.

Hailey said, "We can afford all this?"

"I've bought some chickens for an egg house, too," James said. "The Barclay brothers promised to build us one tomorrow, if the rains hold off."

Hailey turned her back on the sizzling bacon. She knew she had to be careful how she asked this next question. "But—did we take on any debt for all this?"

James's smile turned quickly sullen. "Would you ask Fiddes the same thing if he'd provided so well for you?"

Startled—the accusation a surprise, as they always were—Hailey grappled for how to respond. Since the dance at the Parker House, James flared with jealousy at anything. He responded to innocuous comments with suspicious accusations that she had to defend against. The first time was the night of the dance, when up in their lovely room booked by Captain Allaway he'd yanked a fistful of her hair and driven her up against the wall, his knee forcibly struck between her legs, his face inches away. *You and Fiddes, whispering together in front of everyone. If I hear of you anywhere near each other when I'm away, I'll make you so miserable you'll be sorry you ever met him. I know a lot of people in Seattle, Hailey. Don't hurt yourself, you understand?*

Over time, she had become skilled at deflection. Today, though, she would be direct. She was genuinely worried. "My father lost everything. I don't want to go through that again."

James snorted with mirth. "Are you playing at ignorance?"

She started, relieved she had distracted him from thoughts of Samuel, but shocked at his mocking sneer. "I beg your pardon?"

"You know where the money comes from."

They'd spoken only obliquely about the smuggling. *I'm going to Victoria*, which was code for *We're off on another trip to obtain opium from the factories there, so don't say anything to anyone.* Since March, James had spent two weeks of every month away.

"You mean all of this is from—"

"Yes."

"This much?"

He grinned. "How do you think Captain Allaway is building his new house on the hill? On freightage fees? This is why I stopped blowing up tree stumps for a living. Look at all this, Miss Glasgow. I was a coal miner and a warehouse slinger and a stump blaster, and now we live here." Recently, he had begun calling her Miss Glasgow again—a sneer at her former wealth, the wealth he was so eager to provide her now. "It's for you."

It was one of his established tactics to remind her where they would all be without him.

"But what if—"

"You don't trust me." His eyes narrowed, the deep furrows of his forehead signaling imminent eruption. He spat out, "You think your father's money wasn't dirty? All those coal miners, dead on his watch? That explosion in High Blantyre? All that profit made on the backs of men like me? Why do you think he's gone off like he has? And now suddenly you're choosy about where your money comes from?"

It was as if he had slapped her. The man turned on a dime. Though her father had thought of his wealth in this way, she never had. She glanced quickly past James to see whether her father had heard. She couldn't tell if he had. But James wasn't wrong. Guilt had driven her father insane.

James began to shout, infuriated by her silence. "All I'm doing is not paying taxes. The only person I'm cheating is the government. And you know what customs does the second they arrest someone and seize their opium? They turn around and sell the stash and keep the money. What's the damn difference between us and them? But your father? He was making money off miners like me. Men who died. Nothing I do will hurt anyone. They sell opium outright in the pharmacy. Anyone can drink themselves into a stupor if they want. None of this is dirty money. I told you they only go after the Chinese anyway. They'll never put a white man in jail for this. The only way I'll be punished is if one of these days the Strait of Juan de Fuca gets angry enough to toss me in."

He rarely talked this much. His anger was usually swift, curt.

"I'm scared," Hailey said.

James softened, misunderstanding, believing what he wanted to believe, that she was worried for his safety and not terrified by his shifting moods. He pulled her in close. "Oh, my Hailey. Allaway can easily outrun the custom agent's cutter. It's a bucket.

And he is as careful as God himself in bad weather. Nothing will ever happen to me. I promise. And he says I'm a good sailor. I've captained a whole trip."

Hailey exhaled against his hard chest. She would encourage James to believe this delusion, when she was only fearful for her family, for her father and Geordie. Thank God he hadn't yet gotten her with child. If that happened, she didn't know what she would do. As it was, she felt immense relief when he went away on his trips. He was usually gone a week at a time—up and back twice each month to Victoria, with stops in between somewhere. It was all so vague. He'd never told her the particulars, but he did now, in an attempt to ease her fears, and perhaps because there was no one else to hear, no listening ears through the thin walls of the hotel.

He and Captain Allaway bought processed opium from the factories in Victoria that refined the tar from China. They snuck it past customs at Port Townsend by sailing at night, trusting the new Point Wilson lighthouse to keep them from the rocks, always on the lookout for the customs agent's cutter that patrolled the strait. After stops in Port Ludlow and Poulsbo, they stashed the tins in a secret place somewhere in Seattle and retrieved the opium to deliver later. Smuggling, James concluded, was such an easy business.

He unwrapped himself from her body with a pleased smile. "Ah, my Hailey, don't you worry. We're clever. I'll always come home to you."

Whistling, he went back to unpacking the crates in the parlor and she exhaled with relief, returning to her bacon, now on the verge of burning. She was tonging the rashers from the spitting fat when James appeared in the doorway, holding her box of money, the smile of pleasure wiped from his face. He had opened the lid.

"What's this?"

She froze. "Nothing."

"This is not nothing, is it, Hailey?" James said. His voice carried only a hint of the menace he had just extinguished, but she knew it would return. She looked into the parlor. Geordie lay on the floor by the fire James had built in the stove, absorbed in his animals. Her father sat placidly by, unperturbed. James always saved his wrath, meting out his anger only when they were alone, but now she grew terrified that was about to change.

"Were you keeping this from me?" he said.

"I was saving it, in case we needed extra money."

"Extra?"

"For Geordie's shoes. His clothes. I didn't want to bother you. And you asked me to do that, remember? You said I had to think of something. So I did. I got that job. We agreed." They hadn't quite agreed, but she prayed now that he would think the job had been his idea.

"But you gave me your wages."

"Our family was left with nothing when Father—I needed to make sure that if something happened—"

James's face crumpled in sorrow. "I haven't hidden a thing from you. I give you everything. I did all this for you. Why did you hide this?"

Hailey grasped for straws. "Bonnie's husband died and she's all alone, and I'm afraid if that happened to you—"

James advanced, shaking his head violently. "No, no, no. You were keeping this from me."

"I wasn't—I just . . . I didn't tell you." The bacon grease was still spitting on the stove, and she pulled the pan to the edge, burning her palm.

His suspicious gaze followed her every movement. "Your father kept money from your mother, didn't he?"

"Yes, but—"

"And she hated it."

"Yes, but—"

"Weasels, the both of you." James flipped the box, and the money scattered on the floor. He knelt down and counted it out. "Thirty dollars? What were you going to do with it?"

Hailey fought back tears. "I don't know." But she did know. It was security, a way out if she needed it. If she had ever been able to save enough. "I earned it."

"Well, look around, Miss Glasgow. I earned all this, too, and I haven't kept anything from you, have I? Not you or your dirty family."

"I'm sorry. Take it."

But James was already stuffing his pockets.

"You ruin everything," he said. "I love you, and you do this? Listen to me, Miss Glasgow, if you think you can ever leave me, you can think again."

He whirled back into the parlor and within seconds had yanked Geordie up and hoisted him onto his shoulders. This violence was because of her. He was threatening Geordie because of her.

With a whimper, Geordie grabbed James's head to steady himself. "Lailey?"

Trembling, she said, "James, put him down."

"What do you say, Master Geordie? Want to come to town with me?" James bounced around the room, dipping and weaving behind her father's chair as Geordie clung to James's head, his puzzled gaze locked on Hailey. He could tell there was something different about this play.

Hailey fought for control of her voice. "Put him down, please."

James made a show of considering her request. Then he lunged toward the door and ducked outside with Geordie still on his shoulders. Geordie crouched at the last minute to avoid hitting his head on the lintel.

Hailey dashed into the muddied yard behind them, the incongruous thought intruding that there would be ample room for a garden come spring. This was another terrible irony— planning for the future while she was mired in an intolerable present.

A hard rain was falling. James thrust his legs wide and with a wide grin rocked back and forth, gripping Geordie's knees. "You'll never leave me. Do you understand?"

Hailey nodded. "Never."

"Truly?"

She bit her lips. "Please put him down."

"I know where you go. I know what you do. I heard you were down to Jennings' the other day."

She had been—looking at boots for Geordie. How had he known? "Please, James, put him down."

It was a standoff. Geordie began to cry.

"Just so you understand how things are," James said, "I control everything." Then he lowered Geordie to the mud and was gone, his figure disappearing down the road, fog drifting in from the bay as the rain drummed her shoulders and ran down her forehead.

The land around them had recently been cleared. People were clearing land all the way to Lake Union, and bears had been seen wandering bewildered down the middle of the newly cut roads and emptied stretches of former forest, heads swaying.

Danger lurked everywhere.

Hailey led Geordie back inside and knelt beside him, straightening his shirt, smoothing his wet hair. "Did he hurt you?"

Biting his lip, he said, "He only scared me."

"But you'll tell me, won't you, if he ever does? Promise?"

Geordie bobbed his head, and she pulled him to her as her father blinked, then resumed staring off into the distance, a distance that now seemed to stretch into forever.

LATER THAT NIGHT, James stumbled back into the house. She had kept a lantern burning for him outside, and she heard him snuff it and set it down and then his heavy steps as he climbed to their bedroom. He plopped on the edge of the bed and kicked off his boots. She'd been sitting up, waiting, but as soon as he came in, she'd slid onto her pillow and feigned sleep. She smelled no alcohol on him. He was as sober as a day in church.

"I know you're awake. Don't try to pretend. I spent all your money, Miss Glasgow. I bought rounds and rounds of drinks for everyone at Tivoli until it was all gone. Every cent. That's what deceit earns you."

She swallowed and said nothing. *All her money.*

"Maybe I'll take Geordie with us to Victoria next time."

Hailey froze. Geordie, out on the seas, in the winter winds, away from her? She pictured him on that small boat, the waves tossing him about in the cabin, calling for her. She rose to her elbows. *Say anything*, she thought. *Say anything so that he'll leave Geordie alone.* "I'm sorry, James. I truly am."

"Don't lie to me. Don't say you're sorry if you're not."

"I *am* sorry. I didn't do it to hurt you."

There was a muffled sob, and then he collapsed next to her and pulled her to him, his tears running into her hair. "I love you, my Hailey. I do. I love you more than anything. Everything you said before—I've loved you into loving me, haven't I? You love me now, don't you?"

She knew what he wanted. "Yes, James. I do."

33

Samuel

THE NEXT MORNING, NOVEMBER 2, JAMES GAR-
field was elected to the presidency and Samuel Fiddes delivered
Emile Clarkson's fifty-foot passenger ferry in a deluge that
pounded Elliott Bay into a choppy mess. The season's change
had long been in the air. Autumn days dawned cold, the evenings closed crisp, and Samuel could feel the grip of the gathering fog that plagued the late autumn and early winter dawns
of Puget Sound. But Seattle's intrepid mariners and ships swam
in any weather, so Clarkson and Samuel took the newly christened *Arrow* out for her sea trial anyway. Her timbers creaked in
three-foot swells, but Clarkson wanted to measure her against
the days when the chop would grow even more fierce. The engine balked initially, then hummed with power even through
the worst of it. Samuel and the engineer, trailed by the new Inspector of Hulls, Captain H. E. Morgan, a taciturn man given
to scratching comments in a notebook, roamed *Arrow*, eyes
peeled for leaks and strain.

Before a single hour was up, Clarkson grinned and said,
"Well, Fiddes, seems you've made me a fine craft. The nimblest
girl I've driven yet. That is, if she doesn't sink."

A WILD AND HEAVENLY PLACE

Samuel said, "If her hull weren't tight, she would have sunk when we launched her."

But his glib answer belied the gravity of the moment. The launch of *Arrow* had been nothing like the *Geo. E. Starr*'s. No fanfare, no bugles, no cheers during her unheralded slide into the sea. But as *Arrow* cut through the waves, Samuel felt an enormous swell of pride. He had done it. Not even a year and a half after arriving in Seattle, he had built a ship. He had accomplished what he had set out to do. And she wasn't just any bucket. *Arrow* had the sweeping, graceful lines of a waterbird. She was a gorgeous swan, and when she sailed past, he would be able to point to her and say, *That's mine. I built her.*

Last night, even Alison—standing still for once as rain fell around them—was almost reverent. "Are you going to make another one?"

"I am, wee one. I'm going to build a ship for Captain Allaway."

"And after that?"

"I'll build another."

"For who?"

"I don't know yet, Ali, but I'll find someone. And then it'll be as if we moved the Clyde here."

Samuel and Clarkson spent the whole rainy afternoon at sea, steaming first to Port Blakely, then into the tricky entrance to Eagle Harbor, where Clarkson made the tight turns negotiating the shallow inlet, then back into the heaving sound and along Bainbridge Island up to Port Madison. They executed sharp turns, varying the speed to test the capacity and response of the engine, crossing their own wake at top speed to see how she handled. The fir yawed and heaved without complaint. The boiler took the increased pressure just fine, and over the hours, *Arrow* met every challenge posed. Toward late afternoon, as even blacker clouds blew in over the Olympics, they docked at her new berth on the Marshall Wharf. Morgan declared *Arrow* sound and turned an admiring eye of respect on the nascent shipbuilder, who'd failed to provide him any reason for a write-up.

Clarkson and Samuel stood on the dock, tilting their heads in unison as they took in her beautiful curves and timbers. "I'm going to claim she's Clyde built," Clarkson joked. "You've done Scotland proud."

That afternoon, at the bank, Emile Clarkson paid Samuel his last installment, which Samuel paid right back to the bank to satisfy his own loan. Building *Arrow*, Samuel had cleared very little profit, the vast majority of which he had used for his living expenses. The outlay for the machinery he'd had to purchase and sheds he'd had to build had eaten up the rest, along with payroll. All these costs would amortize over time, but it meant that now Samuel was in need of a new loan to float the initial purchases for Allaway's boat.

Clarkson's boat cost less than half of what Captain Allaway's would. For Allaway's ship, the seven hundred thousand feet of lumber needed would cost thirty-five thousand dollars alone. The steam engine and casings and piping and all the rest would cost much more. It was astonishing the kind of numbers Samuel was beginning to toss around. He didn't think he'd ever get used to it.

He was floating these initial costs because Captain Allaway had said that he needed to shift some funds in order to pay him. Because Samuel had the signed the contract in hand at a cost of just under seventy-five thousand dollars, he felt only a minor twinge as he signed the loan for the first thirty-seven thousand dollars with Dexter Horton, who was happy this time to lend money to Seattle's up-and-coming shipbuilder. Samuel had proven himself to the world. Like Clarkson, Allaway was going to pay in installments, and a full half of the bill wouldn't be due until after the sea trial. This first thirty-seven thousand dollars would cover the initial costs. There were so many shipyards on Puget Sound now. Places like Port Ludlow and Port Townsend and Olympia and Seabeck, to say nothing of the shipbuilders farther south in Portland and Coos Bay. Allaway could have chosen any one of them. Though the margin and profit would be tight, Allaway's ship would be Samuel's second calling card. After that, he could charge more. And he trusted Allaway. He'd been good to Samuel from the start. Now Samuel could be good to him. Despite the rumors running around town about the source of Allaway's new wealth, he was as straight a shooter as anyone Samuel knew.

As they exited the bank, Samuel said to Clarkson, "See you tonight? Our House?"

"Wouldn't miss it."

SAMUEL WENT DIRECTLY from the bank to James Colman's office on the corner of Commercial and Mill, in the block of brick buildings Colman had built after the fire.

Colman was in a meeting with several lawyers, something to do with his troubles with Henry Yesler and the sawmill that had burned down during the fire, which Colman had been leasing in order to purchase. Their voluble talk drifted through the open door. More than one year after the fire, Yesler was demanding that Colman still buy the now-burned-down mill, and Colman was refusing. It was an ugly, public, never-ending argument.

They shifted discussion to the recent sale of the S&WWRR

to Henry Villard and his Oregon Railway & Navigation Company, now to be called the Columbia and Puget Sound Railroad Company. This had been the cause of huge celebration in Seattle, for finally, it seemed, a railroad company would figure out a way to get a train across the barrier of the Cascade mountains into Seattle. Currently, the only way to get rail-shipped goods across the Cascades was to float them down the Columbia River, a route fraught with perils that added cost and time. For passengers, it would be grand to step on a train in Seattle and debark in Manhattan City. This was one topic on which everyone could agree.

Colman brushed off these concerns the minute the meeting broke up and he saw Samuel. He pounded Samuel's shoulders to congratulate him. "When people see *Arrow*, they'll want more. Mark my words, Samuel Fiddes, you'll never need another thing from me."

"Actually, I do need something, Mr. Colman. Could you build me a dock? The moorage fees at the barrel factory are crippling. And now I'm going to build Captain Allaway a much bigger ship. A hundred feet, twice the size of *Arrow*. Paying moorage is out of the question."

Building the dock would incur even more debt, which Samuel didn't like, and would necessitate another loan, but he was learning the meaning of the adage that you needed to spend money to make money. "A hundred, hundred twenty feet long, just far enough out into the deep where a hundred-foot boat with ten feet of draft will be safe at lowest low tide?"

"Ten feet of draft? What was *Arrow*?"

"Four and a half."

Colman beamed. "That's it, my boy. Well done. You're on your way."

"It felt good to deliver that boat."

"I bet. Where will you be getting your timber?"

Samuel cocked his head. "You?"

"We can do it. And we'll start soaking new piles in coal tar for the dock tomorrow. The coal tar will deter the teredos, so no need for wharfing underneath. That takes a bit of time, though, and then more time to drive in the piles. Winter's not the best season for that on the sound. Are you in a hurry?"

"By April, at the latest."

"I'll send a contract. Then let's talk tomorrow about your mill order. And see you tonight for the party. Mrs. Colman and I are looking forward to it."

LATER, AT HOME, Ah Sing greeted Samuel and said that he'd pressed and laid out his new suit, as Samuel had asked him to do. Alison was already working on a plate of beef with one of Ah Sing's special sauces.

There was a letter from school. Alison eyed Samuel as he read it, a sly smile dancing on her face.

He folded the letter and added it to the stack of others the school had sent. "Alison, you have to stop poking the boys with sticks."

She thrust out her bottom lip. "They throw rocks at me."

"Then be smarter. Poke them when no one is looking so you don't get in trouble." Joining her at the table, he lifted his fork. "We're going out tonight, remember? To the party Big Bill is throwing for us for finishing *Arrow*. The Lovings will be there."

Alison squealed. "Annabelle, too?"

"Of course."

"She and John Salvation are sweet on each other, aren't they? Like you and Bonnie?"

Samuel cast a quick glance at Ah Sing, who was washing dishes, oblivious to their chatter. "Why do you think that, wee one?"

She giggled. "Because they are. I see them, all the time. When they're here, and everyone goes inside, they stay outside and talk. And sometimes they sneak kisses."

Eyes sharper than anyone's, Samuel thought. "Don't say anything about that. It's a secret."

"But why?"

"Because her mama wouldn't like it."

"Why not?"

"She just wouldn't. Don't say anything to anyone. Promise me?"

She sulked. "Yes."

"Good. Now get yourself into your nice dress. And don't poke any boys with sticks at the party."

PEOPLE FILLED OUR House, which Big Bill had shut down for the celebration. James and Mrs. Colman, Dexter Horton, even Henry Yesler stopped by to pass congratulations. Big Bill held court, as he always did. He was as venerated a figure in Seattle as Chin Gee Hee. There was something intoxicating about the kind black man whose restaurant had fed Seattle for so long—and whose word was gold. The difference was that the eminent people of Seattle socialized with Big Bill, while no one ever socialized with Chin Gee Hee. That is, they socialized with Bill at his restaurant, and on the street. Whether he had been to anyone's house for dinner was a matter never discussed.

Still, people felt warmly toward him. He had given Seattle a sense of community before anyone else had.

People milled about, parishioners from church, Captain Morgan, fending off criticism for hobnobbing with the shipbuilders he was supposed to be inspecting, the very reason Hammond had lost the position. Emile Clarkson held down one corner, accepting his own congratulations, as Bonnie beamed from another, watching with glowing eyes as everyone clapped Samuel on the back. John Salvation had firm custody of Alison, who in her capers had already turned over Pruss's glass of ale. Annabelle seized the opportunity to help John Salvation clean up the mess and then stayed by his side. Mrs. Allaway, who had come to the party though her husband was away, seemed to miss the electric sparks running between her daughter and the young black man who would help build her husband's next boat. Even Mitchell and Hammond, the two other major shipbuilders, along with John Yarno, who kept a small boatyard for rowboats, stopped by to celebrate Samuel Fiddes—the handsome, promising shipbuilder who had grown in stature and was seeing the young, pretty widow.

"We'll be watching you, Fiddes," Mitchell said.

"May the best shipbuilder win," Samuel said.

"To the sea and all the men who love her!" Hammond shouted, raising a glass.

At this, Clarkson raised his and bellowed his thanks from across the room, and the whole place fell into laughter.

When it died down, James Colman raised his glass. "To Samuel Fiddes. My fellow Scot. Come an orphan to these foreign shores, and now a shipbuilder par excellence. To his new life! And his continued success!"

Samuel basked in the praise. Bonnie shyly sidled next to him, putting her arm through his, claiming him in front of everyone. Samuel eased away and climbed onto a chair, shouting for attention. "I want to thank all of you for your kindness in helping me to celebrate tonight. Thank you, Big Bill." He raised a glass to Bill, who smiled back. "And thank you to every single one of you for welcoming us to Seattle. Had Ali and I stayed in Scotland, we'd have lived a friendless, desperate life. All of this, you—you fine people who have put your trust in me, who helped us and welcomed us—I thank you. In the dark gloom of Glasgow, I never dreamed that this kind of life was awaiting us. I will ever be grateful. And to you, wee Alison, thank you for being the feisty lass you are and for braving the Atlantic and then the Pacific and then only minding slightly when we turned up in a burnt-out town with nowhere to call home."

Lifted high on John Salvation's shoulders, Alison whipped her red braid over one shoulder and beamed.

"And to Mrs. Barnum—sorry, Mrs. Allaway—thank you for taking us in when we must have looked like the cat had dragged us in for a meal."

Laughter all around.

"And to Pruss and John Salvation, whose friendship I couldn't do without. You deserve as much credit for *Arrow* as I do."

Was there a slight flicker of hesitation as people raised their glasses? Samuel owed his present well-being to these friends of his—these black men who looked uncertain in this crowd of Seattle's high folk. Absent, of course, were the Chinese who had helped build *Arrow*, and whose presence Samuel knew would have complicated the delicate nature of Seattle's social intricacies. But he was grateful to the Lovings. So grateful that he wanted the whole town to know. He waited until all the glasses in the room were raised, then Samuel saluted his friends again, and they saluted back.

Samuel said, "One last thing. Tomorrow, I begin building a new ship for Captain Allaway, who ferried us up from San Francisco on *Louisa*. I'll be eternally grateful to him for driving *Louisa* into a log in a storm so I could show him that I could rebuild a ship from nothing."

Cheers rose and chatter resumed, and Samuel stepped down from the chair, reflecting with pleasure that he was a lucky man. He had nearly everything he had ever dreamed of.

Nearly.

As he walked home after dropping Bonnie at Mrs. Widger's, Alison half-asleep on his shoulders, Samuel wondered what building a ship for Allaway would be like. It would probably mean closer proximity to James Murray. And perhaps to Hailey. He hadn't seen much of her, not since the dance in July—by her design or his, he wasn't certain, but they rarely met now, and when he did see her on the street, she shied away. He worried for her. He could sometimes go an entire half day without thinking of her. But he would have loved to have her there tonight, to have her by his side at his triumph, to share in it.

All of life is yearning, he thought. Every hour, every minute, every second. Would it never end? Anything could set it off. The scent of rain on the streets, smelling like Glasgow. The flicker of the gas lamps on Commercial Street, like the ones near St. Enoch's train station. The organ at the Episcopal church when its player practiced and the strains billowed down the hill, reminding Samuel of the city and church where he had first met Hailey.

Words came to him now, words from a song he remembered that his mother used to sing to him.

O the summer time has come
And the trees are sweetly bloomin'
And the wild mountain thyme
Grows around the bloomin' heather
Will ye go lassie go?

I will build my love a bower
By yon cool crystal fountain
And round it I will pile
All the wild flowers o' the mountain
Will ye go lassie go?

If my true love she won't have me
Then I'll surely find another
To pull wild mountain thyme
All around the bloomin' heather
Will ye go lassie go?

If my true love she won't have me, then I'll surely find another.
Was that what he was doing with Bonnie? Was she just a sub-
stitute for Hailey? Samuel pushed the unwelcome thought away.
His heart, he feared, would break forever.

34

Hailey

THROUGHOUT THE WINTER OF 1881, HAILEY GREW
ever more astonished as new arrivals crossed Seattle's watery
threshold and stayed. Homesteaders had moved farther north
than Lake Union, on land grants surrounding Green Lake, a
tired little pond that bloomed algae like the sky bloomed stars.
The coal mines were churning out sixty railcars of coal a day
now. More and more steamboats skimmed like mosquitoes
across the sound, ferrying people here and there on important
business that could not wait. Colonel Squire's new opera house
on Commercial Street was keen competition for lowly Yesler
Hall. Indians still canoed from one hunting or fishing ground to
another, expanding and decreasing the town's population by a
good hundred on any given day. And weekly, oceangoing schooners sailed in from the Sandwich Islands and China with exotic
goods for trade, giving the region the illusion of a burgeoning
cosmopolitan metropolis.

In March, in the midst of this boom, Bonnie sent her a note.
Would Hailey meet with her at Piper's Bakery?

They hadn't seen each other in the eight months since the

dance at the Parker House, so Hailey was eager to see her. As she pushed open the door, Angus was wiggling on Bonnie's lap at a little marble table filled with slices of cake and tea. He'd grown so much. Hailey and Bonnie embraced, tentative, but grateful to encounter each other again.

"How old is Angus now? Two?"

Bonnie smiled. "Yes. And he's still quite the handful, but I don't know how I'd live without him."

Bonnie asked after James, who Hailey said was delivering something to the coal mines at Nanaimo, as he'd instructed her. These lies bothered her, but she couldn't very well say, *Oh yes, he's off to Victoria, smuggling again!*

Hailey shared with Bonnie about their new house and she exclaimed over Hailey's luck and how good James was to her. Unknowing, because how could she know? Hailey wanted to tell Bonnie, but all she could see was Geordie, terrified, bouncing on James's shoulders, out of her reach.

Then Bonnie revealed the reason for her note. She'd moved recently, too, to Mrs. Widger's boardinghouse, where, it turned out, Hailey's mother also resided.

As much as she could, Hailey had put her mother from her mind. She'd had to. It was the only way not to live in perpetual loss.

Bonnie described how Hailey's mother would take Angus from her in the evening when he was fussy and tell him stories in the parlor. It was maddening how much Hailey missed her mother, despite everything. It ached to hear of her little demonstrations of kindness to someone else's child when she had been so cruel to her own.

"There's something else," Bonnie said.

What else could there possibly be? Hailey thought.

· 312 ·

"Samuel visits her." Had been, apparently, every week for nearly a year. He took her out walking with Alison and asked what she needed. He took care of her.

Hailey swallowed, feeling struck. "He does?"

"I wanted to tell you," Bonnie said, "but he asked me not to say. I only learned because I moved there."

The pain of it was almost too much for Hailey to bear. Bonnie had everyone—her mother, Samuel, Alison. All of them, together. All she had was Geordie and a father whose needs would keep her tied to James forever. Bonnie was living the life Hailey should have had, if only she'd been braver.

"I have to go."

"Oh, Hailey, I'm sorry—"

But Hailey rose to her feet and fled.

AS THE LENGTHENING days of the spring of 1881 trudged along under a perpetually dismal sky, Hailey still felt the pain of that loss, like a bruise that wouldn't heal. Meanwhile, everyone in town—everyone, that is, but her—fell in love with a game called base ball, an amusement that apparently resembled cricket. James had, too. He'd joined a team in Newcastle, called the Newcastle Boys, and when he was in town he often took the train over to Newcastle to practice.

On a weekend in the beginning of June, a kickoff tournament took place, and so on a Saturday morning Hailey and Geordie and her father rode one of three special trains of the Columbia and Puget Sound Railroad twelve miles south to Renton. A base ball diamond had been scythed from the late spring grasses near the Cedar River, which was siphoning snowmelt from the Cascades into the Black River and the Duwamish beyond.

The Newcastle Boys were one of eight teams from across the sound. Four games were to be played today, the victors playing Sunday morning—churchgoers given dispensation—and the final championship game to be played Sunday afternoon. All of this for a thousand-dollar purse. The order of play had already been set. The Newcastle Boys would play the Elliott Nines first. Samuel and John Salvation played on the Nines. James was relishing this matchup, but Hailey dreaded it. Both teams had already assembled on the field by the time Hailey arrived. Samuel was easy to spot, as always, handsome in his rugged clothes, his face brown from the sun. James, swinging bats for practice, was throwing taunts his way. Since November, James had seen a lot of Samuel. He went frequently down to the shipyard to inspect the ship that Captain Allaway was calling *Lady Allaway*. Hailey knew Samuel's success bothered James, but he kept his simmering envy quiet, fascinated by the new ship in spite of himself. Returning from the yard, he spoke in awed tones about dimensions and hull shape, rudder size and side wheels, boilers and engine fit. Occasionally, when James was away on a trip, Hailey hid in the cover of the barrel factory to observe the progress. It was indeed a thing of beauty to watch a ship rise from nothing. She could hardly contain her pride for Samuel. She was careful never to be caught near the shipyard. Since that awful day when James had threatened to take Geordie out to sea with him, Hailey had done everything she could to make certain that the thought never occurred to him again.

The field was teeming with life. At ten cents apiece, tickets had been snapped up. Every hotel in Seattle overflowed with players and visitors, who had steamed in the day before despite a lingering fogbank. The sheriff, Louis Wyckoff, was snapping up one of the peach pies the Women's Suffrage Society was selling at a table. The Colmans were keeping a healthy distance from Henry Yesler, who was lapping up liquid refreshment from one of the Tivoli Beer Hall's ten kegs. Hailey spotted Bonnie with Angus in her arms, supervising Alison, who had organized footraces for the children and was bossing them all about. Hailey didn't know if Alison would even recognize her now. But she didn't want to go over there. Recently, James had gleefully reported to her that people in town were gossiping that it was high time that Samuel Fiddes asked that sweet widow to marry him. They'd been stepping out for nearly a year. Bonnie had divulged nothing about it in their visit. Since the meeting at Piper's, their friendship had cooled. Bonnie was a reminder to Hailey of all she had lost, and, being the sweet creature that she was, Bonnie sensed it, and made no demands.

Hailey chose a spot next to the Allaways, away from William Grose's camp kitchen, where he and Pruss were already cooking sausages. Now that James and Captain Allaway were working together, Hailey had gotten to know Annabelle a little. But the relationship was only cordial. Hailey sensed that Annabelle's friendship with Samuel made her cautious of her. The link between all of them was Samuel. She settled her father and let Geordie run off to play with the other children.

The Elliott Nines were up first. With a crack of the bat, they hit their first run, and everyone cheered. Hailey understood the game a little, but in time it was easy to see that James was blistering the Elliott Nines with his pitches. John Salvation was pitching for the Seattle team, and he was just as good. After three innings, the score remained low, 2 to 3, in favor of the Boys.

After a while, Mrs. Allaway spread out their picnic of succotash salad and Hailey's bread and scones. Captain Allaway purchased sausages for everyone, except Hailey, who refused.

For four months now, she had subsisted on oyster crackers and chewed ginger root, sipped diluted wine and chamomile tea, and occasionally boiled water mixed with bicarbonate of potash, which the dry grocer had recommended after he postulated the reason for her biliousness. That communication had been fraught with awkward exchanges and flushed cheeks and Hailey's hasty exit from the store. She had said nothing to James. She was grateful that he was away so much that he never asked about her courses. The baby was a problem she didn't know how to solve. After two years of marriage she'd begun to believe that she wasn't capable of having children, a circumstance she'd never mourned. Not when it meant she wouldn't be having James's baby.

No one had ever told her a thing about how her insides worked, but she thought it was possible that she may have lost babies before. Twice she'd been a week late, and when the flow finally came, blood coursed out of her in a torrent. Maybe those had been lost babies, she didn't know. And recently things had become irregular again, but she'd still had a monthly flow, though far less than usual. She had not been one of those young girls who had dreamed of the babies that she would one day have. But soon this nausea would turn into flesh and blood.

In the next several innings, things grew heated. After a flurry of hits by both teams, the score climbed to a dizzying 24 to 18 in favor of the Nines.

At the bottom of the seventh, the Newcastle Boys had two outs when James came up to bat.

John Salvation pitched, and James missed.

The umpire called a strike.

James snarled, "I know it."

After two more strikes, James spat and threw his bat to the ground.

The next inning, John Salvation hit a home run, and James, now relegated to catcher, shed his glove and blocked home plate, legs flung wide, arms crossed.

The Nines shouted for James to yield the base.

James didn't move.

John Salvation rounded third and raced toward home, barreling into James and sending him flying into the dust.

James scrambled to his feet and launched himself at John Salvation, shouting a vile epithet. The foul word reverberated through the crowd, sending a wave of inhaled shock that reached as far as Pruss and Big Bill, who looked up with alarm from their sausages sizzling on the grill. Rarely voiced in Seattle, and definitely not at a public event and most certainly not in front of ladies, the insult and impact of the two men sent a shudder through the crowd.

Fists flying, the two men wrestled each other, getting in the occasional blow, grunting and rolling around, trying to gain advantage.

Pruss and Big Bill dropped their utensils and ran toward the field. Geordie came running, and Hailey scooped him onto her hip as if he were a three-year-old. She grabbed her father's arm; he had risen to follow her. "Wait on the blanket. Wait for me here." She could hear her own voice turning frantic, but he nodded dully and sat back down. There was no one to ask for help, because the Allaways had already run toward the field along with everyone else. The sheriff screamed for everyone to stand down.

Before anyone else could intervene, however, Samuel pulled James off John Salvation.

James hurled a string of Scottish epithets unintelligible to nearly everyone but the Scots in the crowd: *"You doaty bamput bassa, get offa me."* Then he turned and hit Samuel squarely in the eye.

Samuel landed several blows in turn.

John Salvation and a half dozen players wrested them apart. James broke loose and hurled himself again at Samuel.

"What the hell, Murray?" Samuel shouted, springing up as James was pulled off him again.

"Loving ran into me, you idiot."

Sheriff Wyckoff thrust himself between them. "That is enough! I don't want to be arresting anyone on my day off."

The umpire put an end to the fracas by calling the game for the Elliott Nines. The Nines gave a grim cheer. Flushed with shame, Hailey turned away without seeking out James. Out of the corner of her eye, she saw Annabelle Barnum run to John Salvation. Bonnie had taken charge of Alison. Hailey gave her a limp wave.

Geordie chattered at her. "Why are they fighting, Lailey? Why are they mad?"

She returned to their little camp of blankets and picnic baskets. Hailey prepared to pack up and leave, hoping to get away before James came looking for her. She wondered when the next train would run and whether she would be able to carry everything on her own. She was on her knees, gathering up the corners of the blanket, when she realized that her father wasn't there.

Then a shriek of horror ricocheted from the riverbank.

PEOPLE SURGED TO the river. Hailey picked up her skirts and ran, Geordie following and calling after her.

Her father lay facedown in the tall grasses at the edge of the river, his body twisted like a jackknife, his legs pointed down-

· 318 ·

stream, his tweed jacket billowing. Four men waded in and hauled him out, carrying him waterlogged to the shore. They set him on the grass. Hailey sank to her knees. She'd left him for mere minutes. Geordie was crying, "Papa, Papa."

A group of little girls stood nearby, crying. "We found him. We were making stick boats and we found him."

It seemed to Hailey as if her father wasn't finished dying, as if he was still deciding whether to go.

She laid her head on his chest. "Is he breathing? Listen! I think—oh, someone help me! I think—"

But his chest was still. He smelled of the river. Of must and earth. All the strain of his life had vanished. It looked as if he were asleep. As if all he had to do was wake up. Isn't that what people say of the newly drowned? That they look as if they are sleeping?

Mud had lodged in his ears and nose, and it made a brown smear across his lined forehead. His jacket had been pulled half off and was bunched under his back. The buttons of his shirt had come undone. She had buttoned those for him that very morning. She had wanted him to look his best. She picked up her father's hand and held it to her cheek. It was warm, inexplicably. She felt for a pulse, hope against impossible hope.

Oh, the futile gestures of the bereaved.

Someone said, "Come with me, Hailey. The men will bring him. Come on, now."

Mrs. Allaway was lifting her, embracing her, steering her back to the train. Hailey was stumbling along, past the staring, murmuring crowd. She couldn't see. She was breathing in gulps. Nausea crippled her.

"Geordie?"

"I have him. I have him right here." James's voice came from behind, and then Geordie's protesting cries: "Lailey! I want Lailey."

Bonnie hurried beside Hailey, Angus on her hip, from time to time catching her hand. Alison had taken hold of Geordie's hand, and kept saying, "I'll stay with you." The thought occurred to Hailey that Geordie and Alison hadn't seen each other in two years, not since Glasgow. Did Alison remember him, or was this innate kindness?

"Mr. Colman is going to drive the train back," someone said.

Things happened without Hailey doing them. She was helped into the train car. Her things were piled at her feet. Bonnie murmured at her from the seat behind her. Geordie was set in her lap. He was crying now, too, his palms on her cheeks, turning her face to make her look at him.

"What's wrong with Papa? Lailey, Lailey, don't cry."

Hailey could hear the boiler in the locomotive spitting and hissing. How long did it take to ready an engine?

"They have him now," James said. "They've laid him on a bench in the back of the car."

She turned, half rising. In the rear of the passenger car, a protective ring of grim-faced men stood guard. It was every member of the Elliott Nines and the Newcastle Boys, Samuel towering above them, Pruss and John Salvation hanging back. Half of these were men who moments ago James had insulted beyond measure. Hailey handed Geordie to James and lurched down the aisle. The men parted for her. Her father lay crookedly on the bench, his right arm dangling to the floor and his long legs jutting into the gap across the aisle.

"Does someone have a cloth? Can't we at least wash his face?"

Someone produced a blanket. With its edge she wiped away the river silt. There was silt in his beard, caught in his eyebrows.

"Oh, help me," she cried.

A hand reached out. "Give the blanket to me."

It was Samuel. He wiped her father's face. The railcar jerked underfoot and began to steam faster and faster. Soot and ash sailed past the windows, casting little shadows across her father's cheeks. Samuel kept wiping with the blanket edge. Alison was gripping his shirttails, crying, Bonnie trying to comfort her.

"I have her, Fiddes. I have her now," James said, crowding into the circle, Geordie in his arms. "I have her."

The men stiffened at James's intrusion. Several bruises had blossomed on his face. One eye was beginning to swell shut. Samuel's eye was purpling, too, but the tension between them had dissipated.

"Lailey, Lailey, what's the matter? Why is Papa sleeping? Why is he wet?"

"Come on, Hailey," James coaxed, in a voice barely audible over the clatter of the rails. He reached out and touched her elbow. "Come sit with me. Sit with Geordie. Your brother needs you."

He led her back up the aisle. The Duwamish was running beside the train, emptying Lake Washington, carrying the Cascades' fresh water to the sea. If those little girls hadn't spotted her father, he would be floating away now, lost forever. She crushed Geordie to her chest, this time burying her face in her little brother's shoulder.

"I'm here, darling boy, I'm here," she whispered into his ear.

In the seat behind her, Angus was crying, but Bonnie kept saying, "I'm so sorry, Hailey."

James Colman did not stop the train for passengers waving

him down at Steele's Landing. He sped on. She remembered nothing of the trip home: the hired hack, the wagon following, carrying her father's body with the picnic blanket flung across him, a sleeping Geordie cradled in her arms, the jolting ride up the hill, her father carried into the downstairs bedroom by Samuel and John Salvation and Pruss, their terse questions and James's bitten replies, the tension and unreality of it all, the sense that everything was broken.

Her father lay still, his disarranged clothes sodden, one shoe gone. The ghosts of High Blantyre would trouble him no more. He could meet them on the other side, tell them that he was sorry. And he could apologize to the Newcastle dead, too. Tell them that no one knew that coal dust was so much trouble in the Northwest. *This must be how the dead spend their time*, she thought, *begging for forgiveness for their misdeeds on earth.*

"I'm sorry, Papa," she whispered. "I'm sorry I left you alone."

The house was full of people. She heard Angus crying again, and Bonnie searching in the larder for something to feed him. Hailey went in and pulled a canister from a shelf.

"Fresh biscuits. I baked them yesterday. We have butter and jam. We should give the children something."

Bonnie grasped her hand. "I have it, Hailey. I have it."

It was dark now. How had it gotten dark? It was June. It was almost the longest day of the year. She went back into the bedroom. In the corner, Alison was embracing Geordie. Then she took his hand and they slid down the wall to sit beside each other on the floor. Geordie was looking at Alison as if she were an angel. Bonnie appeared with the biscuits, Angus on her hip. He was chewing on one, crumbs all over his tear-traced cheeks.

Samuel appeared in the doorway behind her, his eyes filled

with sorrow and kindness. For once, James provoked no confrontation.

Samuel came toward Hailey and said, "It's not your fault. You were good to him, Hailey. You were."

"No."

He folded her into his arms. She leaned against his chest, breathing in his scent, wishing she could stay locked in his arms forever. The world around them stilled. His strength, the feel of him, was so familiar to her. She shut her eyes, wishing she could lay her head against his chest every night.

Reluctantly, she pulled away. "Would you go to my mother, please, and get her for me?"

"Bonnie told you that I visit your mother?"

She nodded, and Samuel disappeared, John Salvation and Pruss trailing behind him, Alison saying good-bye to Geordie with an expression of real grief, followed by Bonnie, whose evident distress made Hailey realize that the embrace and words she and Samuel had shared had been public.

James jerked his head after them. "How does Fiddes know where she lives?"

"Do *you* even know?"

His voice turned surprisingly gentle. "If you think about it, Hailey, this is for the best."

"How can dying be for the best?" Her head was a confused fog.

"Your father belonged at Steilacoom."

In her agitation, Hailey was unable to place the word. "Steilacoom?"

"The insane asylum," James said. "He wasn't well. That's why he wandered off today. That's what happened. I was going to send him there."

Hailey could hardly breathe. She stared at James, at his deep blue eyes. And then she remembered where she had heard Steilacoom before.

"You *promised*. You promised that you would never send him there. The doctor in Newcastle said he would, and you *promised*."

"And now I don't have to."

"Then why even say such a thing?" But she knew the answer even as she asked. This was revenge for Samuel's embrace.

James said, "But now we don't have to worry about him anymore, Hailey. And we won't have to argue about sending him there. The problem has been solved for us. You have to admit, he was a lot of trouble."

She stared, anger welling. "He's my *father*."

The father she had left alone in an unfamiliar place near a fast-flowing river. Hadn't she railed against her mother for leaving them alone? Well, now she'd left her father, too, hadn't she? She'd left him alone and unprotected, a man as incapable of fending for himself as Geordie.

"It's for the best, my Hailey."

It was the stupidest thing people said to the grieving, yet people said it all the time.

"Leave me alone, James. Just leave."

Sullen, he withdrew as she leaned over her father and kissed his cold forehead. "Sleep, my papa. Sleep."

She picked up Geordie and carried him into the parlor and explained to him that their father had died. And then that their mother had come back. Several times, Hailey had hesitated before the door of Widger's boardinghouse, Geordie in hand. She didn't know if it had been right to withhold Geordie from their mother, though in the end, she'd decided it would be too confusing for him to see her, because it was too confusing for her.

Stroking Geordie's hot forehead, she said, "Do you remember Mama?"

He nodded solemnly.

"What do you remember?"

"That she left."

Hailey nearly wept. She swallowed back a rising lump in her throat. What had she done? "Well, she's in Seattle, and she wants to see you."

"But you're my mother now."

Hailey pulled Geordie close and shut her eyes. "You'll always be mine, Geordie, my love, and I will always be yours. That will never change."

James, lurking nearby, turned away, yet she read the hurt in his eyes. She had never once said anything like that to him, ever.

At midnight, Hailey washed her father's body. A drenching rain began to fall. The wind whistled around the eaves, found its way inside, lifted the curtains from the black windows. She knew then that her mother would not come tonight. His daughter would be the one to put her father to bed one last time.

Later, Hailey lay next to Geordie, who slept between her and James. She'd had to convince James that Geordie could not sleep in the same room as his dead father, and for once James conceded. To the sound of James's even breathing and Geordie's quiet exhalations, Hailey mulled over the terrible ironies of life. Her father's death would reunite her with her mother, and might have yielded Hailey freedom to escape James's control, except for Geordie. Now there was a new shackle, made of flesh and blood. She would have to tell James about the baby soon.

35

Samuel

WHEN SAMUEL, ALISON, BONNIE, AND ANGUS reached Mrs. Widger's boardinghouse after Harold MacIntyre died, it was midnight, and the full moon had disappeared behind a wall of clouds. Just as they stepped into the parlor, a heavy rain began to fall. A stoating rain, they'd called it back in Glasgow.

Inside, Bonnie took charge of Alison and Angus, but not before putting a hand on Samuel's chest and saying, "I love you, Samuel Fiddes."

It was the first time she had said that to him. He bent and kissed her on the forehead, unable to respond in kind. But the moment was wrong, the discussion too intense for a fraught time like this. He put her declaration away to examine later.

Samuel knocked on Mrs. MacIntyre's door.

Mrs. MacIntyre, awakened from sleep, did not at first comprehend what Samuel was saying. Her disheveled hair, lately streaked with gray, was tucked in a sleeping cap, which she pulled from her head to hold at her throat as he repeated that her husband had died and that Hailey was asking for her. Samuel caught Davinia MacIntyre as her knees buckled and lifted her onto her bed, sitting beside her in intimate silence as she convulsed with tears. *This is how reprieve manifests itself,* Samuel thought, *with great sorrow and overwhelming relief.*

"I thought I'd see him again," Mrs. MacIntyre said when her sobs subsided. "I blame him, but . . ." She didn't finish. There would never be an end to that sentence, Samuel thought. Davinia MacIntyre would always blame her husband for what her life had become, and that would be their ending. Would his ending with Hailey be the same? Regret and sorrow?

"You're sure Hailey wants me? She asked for me? You're sure?"

By now, wind was slashing at the window, drumming on the roof. Who was he to say, but he said it anyway. "You ought to wait until morning. Rain is guttering down the hills. You'd be drenched, even if you could make it through the mud."

She protested, rising to change her clothes.

"It's as dark as dark can be out there. Dawn is only four hours away. I'll take you the second the sun rises."

Reluctantly, she conceded. Alison was tucked into bed with Bonnie and Angus. Samuel sat up all night in the parlor. Davinia MacIntyre appeared at his side the moment the sky breathed light. It was still pink with newness when they knocked at the Murrays' door. The moment Mrs. MacIntyre was admitted to the house, Samuel stepped away and left them to whatever would come of Hailey's grace. He returned to the boarding-house to collect Alison. It was Sunday, and they had to change to go to church. The Elliott Nines had withdrawn from the tournament, but the streets were already alive with everyone heading toward the train.

Trudging up Second Street, Alison said, "Why did that man hit you?"

"We disagree about things."

"I don't like him. He's a bad man. I see him doon the water sometimes. He's always putting something into a little boat and then he goes out by himself."

Samuel smiled. Still a bit of Glasgow in her. *Doon the water.* "I don't like him either, wee Ali. Best to stay away from him."

"He wasn't very nice to that lady."

"That lady is his wife."

"But isn't she the lady from home? The one who brought us food and picked me up in the carriage? And we saw her at church, and we went to her house and ate once?"

Samuel stopped dead. "You remember her?"

"What happened to her?"

"You know what happened. Her father died."

"She was sad before that. But back home, she used to be happy."

"Yes, my wee one. She was."

"Why is she here?"

"What do you mean?"

"It's a long way to come."

Samuel squatted and looked Alison in the eyes.

"Did we come here because of her?" she said.

Samuel nodded.

"But now we're not friends?"

"No."

"Why not?"

"Because she's married."

"To that bad man?"

Samuel nodded.

"Oh." Her voice was soft with pity.

"Ali, lass. Tell me. Do you still think of Scotland as home?"

She peered at him, eyes sharp with thought, her tangled

braid heavy down her back. "John Salvation and his daddy don't live there. Bonnie doesn't live there. They're our friends. We wouldn't see them if we were over there. And it's nicer here. I'm not hungry anymore."

Samuel stared, overwhelmed. He might not have Hailey, but Alison was safe, and fed, and loved. He had taken her out of the orphanage, out of the grime and the factory. She had grown a foot. Her eyes were bright, her cheeks full. The nuns had vanished from their lives. This much he had accomplished. And it was more than much. It was very nearly everything, at least of the things he could attain.

He turned so she could climb onto his back and he piggybacked her up to the house, where Ah Sing was frantic with worry but had cooked morning sausages just the same.

SEVERAL DAYS LATER, Samuel climbed into the half-built hull of *Lady Allaway* under a thinning afternoon sun alongside John Salvation, Pruss, and a dozen others who had begun corking the planks in the bow. All around them, musical Chinese chatter echoed in the hull, interspersed with an Irish lilt and a Swedish singsong and even the butter of a newly arrived Frenchman. The thing about Seattle, Samuel thought, was that you didn't have to travel anywhere to see the world. The world came to Seattle, delivered by the sea.

It had been a fast build. From the second week in November of last year, when they started, until now, they had been working for seven long months. Samuel had expanded the shipyard, erecting more sheds as necessary. He had purchased more tools, too, and calculated and recalculated the amount of fir he would require, and even increased his workforce by a dozen, hiring men away from Hammond's and Mitchell's shipyards. Long after quitting time sent everyone else to saloons in the Lava Beds, Samuel, Pruss, and John Salvation worked on through the evening, even in driving rain, doing what they could to advance the work. There were so many details to keep track of that sometimes Samuel thought his head would explode. The most daunting aspect was the size of this ship, though every time he worried, he broke the project down into manageable parts. Lay the keel. Erect the ribs. Bend the planks. And so on. Samuel was looking forward to the moment when the ship slid into the sea, but that wouldn't happen until after the engine had been set in. The engineer who had fitted the *Geo. E. Starr* was coming up from San Francisco to do it. They could launch as soon as late August, almost three months from now, and would tie her up at the new dock Colman had put in. The paddle wheel was already under construction. They could build out the cabins and pilothouse by the end of September. "She's not as big as *Geo. E. Starr*," Samuel had said to Allaway, "but she'll be livelier." As always, Allaway had nodded, pleased, and said nothing about the money.

Allaway was behind on payments. He'd given Samuel only half of what he owed from the first installment, promising more in August. Samuel didn't know what to do. For a man who seemed to have a lot of money, Allaway didn't want to part with it much. Maybe it was Scots parsimony. But interest was building. Samuel would have to talk to the bank to see if they could fold that into Allaway's next payments somehow. He thought he'd made it clear to Allaway last week when he had visited and Samuel had given him a report.

"Captain," Samuel said, "I was hoping that you would make

your payment. I've had to run more credit than I like with the chandler."

Allaway did not acknowledge Samuel. Instead, he looked up at the boat and caught sight of Pruss leaning over the hull, observing. The captain laid a proprietary hand on Samuel's shoulder and boomed, "Doesn't our Scotty here have a knack for boat-building?"

"I tell him that every day."

"Captain," Samuel said, "I'll need that money soon."

"Of course, of course." Then Allaway shook Samuel's hand and strode out of the yard.

Samuel was thinking about this as he corked another plank. Alison was playing on the shore. She was too old now to stay inside with Bonnie. He would have to think of somewhere else for her to go this summer, because the work on the ship would only intensify. Or maybe he would give up and let her run loose in town with the other children to pick berries and fish and clam and traipse across the tideflats on the railroad tracks, which seemed to be Seattle's definitive rite of passage.

A loud hail came from outside. *Dear God*, Samuel thought, *not Allaway again.* His visits always interrupted the flow of work. Samuel sighed and threw a leg over one side of the hull and clambered down the rope ladder. It was indeed Captain Allaway, standing in his wide-legged stance as he ran his hand over the lapped planks of the starboard hull. He was joined by James Murray, who was giving off an air of ownership, imitating Allaway, making a show of assessing the latest progress. His right eye still bore the purpled imprint of Samuel's fist.

Allaway said, "Coming along, Fiddes. She's tight, I'll say that." The captain walked to the bow and ran his palm along the chine, squatting to see whether light shone through the joint. "Tight, too. Clench nails look flush. Nice work."

"Yeah. Nice work," James said. He wore his squashed woolen hat that Samuel was always surprised he hadn't lost to the sea.

Ignoring him, Samuel said, "How can I help, Captain?"

"I need a word with Pruss."

Before Samuel could call, Pruss and John Salvation appeared, having recognized the captain's booming voice.

"Pruss! Can we talk, friend?" Allaway said.

Pruss and Allaway walked toward the high shed where the slats of the paddle wheel were being measured out. They talked for a while. Mostly Captain Allaway talked, until he turned and lifted a hand in farewell, leaving James behind and Pruss staring after him.

With Allaway gone, Samuel turned to James. "You're not welcome here without Captain Allaway."

"I've got something to say to you, Fiddes."

"Is it that you're going to help me get my money from the captain? Or do you want to insult John Salvation again?"

"Out on the dock," James said, and strode off.

Samuel watched Allaway amble across the littered rocks and sand as Pruss returned.

"What did he say, Pruss?"

Pruss exhaled. "Nothing. But Captain Allaway's nothing is always a whole lot of other people's something." He jutted his chin in James's direction. "You need help with him?"

"No. Keep an eye on Ali for me?"

"Always," John Salvation said.

As Samuel strode after James, he noticed that Pruss had pulled John Salvation away from the boat. His voice carried on the wind, farther, Samuel was sure, than Pruss wanted.

"Captain Allaway says you've been seeing Annabelle on the sly?"

"No, Papa."

"Listen to me, son. Listen to me like you just grew ears. You stay away from her. I don't want Mrs. Allaway to suspect anything, think anything, you understand?"

"Papa, I—"

"Don't you go uttering any more words. Not a breath. Not a *thought*. Murray turned on you because you hit a home run. What do you think the world would do to you over a white girl?"

"It's not like that here. You know white men marry Indians. That black man came all the way up from Oregon and bought all that land, and he married a Chinese and—"

"Have you hurt yourself? Have you lost every bit of your brain? By God, I'll not lose you because you can't think straight."

"But—"

"No buts."

Samuel heard nothing more as he walked down the dock toward James who had stopped halfway down the pier.

"Stay away from my family, Fiddes."

"Her father died."

"Don't touch my wife again. Don't come to the funeral. Don't think about her. Don't even look at her."

"Harold MacIntyre—"

"Harold MacIntyre deserved no one's respect. Long as I knew him, he was a crock of loony. His dying saved me the trouble of sending him to Steilacoom."

Without a word, Samuel punched James across the jaw, hard. The force of the blow sent him tumbling into the sea. The dock stood twelve feet above the surface. Not until James splashed solidly into the black void did Samuel wonder whether the man could swim. It was June, but the blistering cold of the sound took a man's breath away no matter the time of year.

James did not surface. Samuel counted to ten, fifteen. James's hat bobbed up in a circle of foam.

Swearing, Samuel kicked off his boots and plunged in feet-first. He gasped as the water closed around him, momentum carrying him deep into the frigid darkness. Panicking, he struggled to the surface and flailed, circling in place, looking for James through the frothing water.

He found James under the dock, clinging to a barnacled pile, coughing out seawater.

"You fucking Scot," James sputtered.

"Can't you swim?" Samuel said.

"No, ye scabby roaster. I cannae." He lunged at Samuel, encircling his neck, trying to pull him under. Samuel kicked him away and James floundered back to the pile.

A rope hit Samuel in the face. Through blurred eyes, he saw Pruss and John Salvation lying on the dock, extending the rope, anchoring its end. Fighting to stay above the water, Samuel pushed it in James's direction. James released the crusted post and snaked one arm into the knotted loop and then, swearing and swallowing more water, wormed it over his head, squeezed his other arm in, and shrugged the loop around his torso. He bobbed there, supported by the strength of the Lovings. The hemp strained under James's sodden weight. They kept several dinghies now on the beach, and someone climbed in and rowed toward them. James went limp and white as he was inched up to calls of "Steady, steady," as workers—carpenters and barrowmen from the barrel factory, a dozen Chinese, and even the chandler's boy, newly arrived in a skiff from town with a delivery of brass fittings—dragged him over the dock's edge. James was disentangled and the line lowered again for Samuel, who was clinging to the dinghy. He, too, was lurched upward to the dock. James, still heaving, crawled to his knees and swung at Samuel, but he missed and collapsed belly-down onto the slick wood.

Samuel's eyes streamed with seawater. "You malign the Mac-Intyres or my friends again and I'll do worse to you."

James's hair had matted on his forehead and dripped into his eyes. "She is *my* wife."

He lurched to his feet, soaked through. His wet shirt clung to his hard body as he staggered toward land, stopping only to erupt in spasms of coughing. No one helped him. Alison, who had run onto the dock, stepped warily aside to let him pass.

Pruss propped one foot on a dock cleat and studied Samuel. "Didn't know you could swim, Scotty."

"I can't," Samuel said.

Part Five

1881–1882

All the important towns in Western Washington are situated on Puget Sound, one of the most magnificent inland seas in the world, and probably the only one which commands such noble views of water, forest, and snow-capped mountains. It has been called the Mediterranean of America; but the metaphor, though good, is misleading for while the European sea reveals only scenes identified with man and civilization, here all is primeval expansiveness and rugged grandeur.

~*RAMBLES IN NORTH-WESTERN AMERICA: FROM THE PACIFIC OCEAN TO THE ROCKY MOUNTAINS* BY JOHN MORTIMER MURPHY, 1879

36

Hailey

ON A WEEPY JUNE DAY IN 1881, A LITTLE MORE than two years after they had arrived in Seattle, Hailey and her mother buried Harold MacIntyre in the Seattle Cemetery, north of town, near the grassy prairie leading to the Salish's summer grounds. At the graveside, Hailey's mother stood dry-eyed, grimly presiding over her family's ruin and her children's grief. She had arranged for the minister to say the burial, had contacted the undertaker, had paid the twelve dollars—all her savings—for the plot, finally taking from Hailey the burden she was never supposed to bear. Hailey, her mother, and Geordie tossed daisies, picked outside the cemetery's derelict fence, onto the lowered coffin.

There were eight mourners: Hailey, Geordie, their mother, James, Samuel, Bonnie, and the Lovings.

Samuel and James each bore bruises, which Hailey suspected had arisen from yet another altercation between them. Yesterday, James had barreled into the house after a visit to the waterfront, soaked through, his boots a muddy mess, his hat missing. He was shivering and livid.

"By Jesus, Mary, and Joseph, that bloody Scot." James yanked off his suspenders and unbuttoned his flannel shirt. "I'm changing and then I'm taking the evening train to Newcastle and I'm going to get a job. I'll hire on with the coal company and I'll keep working with Allaway. I don't bloody care, but we are leaving. We are never living in Seattle again."

Panic washed over Hailey. "But Geordie's going to start school again in September, and my mother and I just reconciled—"

"Geordie can't live with us anymore. He stays in Seattle with his mother."

"No," she said. "No, no, no."

James's face screwed into a knot of rage. She'd never fought him like this. "What did you say?"

To tell him would make it real. There would be no going back.

"I'm going to have a baby. I'm with child."

For a long moment, James said nothing. Then he crossed the room and lifted her into his arms, his demeanor utterly changed. He murmured over and over, "A baby, a baby."

Not this way, she thought. *Not this man.*

He was gleeful, crowing. "We are making a family. Our own. You're *my wife*."

"Of course I'm your wife."

"Don't forget that."

"I never forget it."

"Some people do."

"What do you mean?"

He wasn't listening. "We'll stay. I was just upset."

"But what happened?"

"No matter, no matter," he said, and went upstairs to change, whistling.

AT THE FUNERAL, James remained solicitous, his rancor abandoned for the moment in the wake of the news of the baby. He was being careful with her. He had hired a teamster named Frank Poole to ferry them back and forth to the cemetery, even paying happily for her mother. Samuel, the Lovings, and Bonnie had walked from Seattle. After the service, they followed Poole's wagon for a brief time before Bonnie headed toward town and the rest turned off for the shipyard.

Later, James, too, went off to town, mumbling something about an appointment with Captain Allaway. Geordie darted outside and Hailey was making bread to distract herself. Davinia lingered at the doorway, keeping a wistful eye on Geordie.

Hailey and her mother were trying. It had been only natural to send for her mother after her father died. Standing over her husband's body, her mother had held Hailey up, knelt to dry Geordie's tears, and wept tears of her own when Geordie would have nothing to do with her.

"Mother," Hailey said, her elbows deep in bread dough. Their conversation until now had been desultory, polite. "I need to know something."

Her mother stiffened. She had worn a perpetually wary face since their reunion, ever on alert, Hailey knew, for the moment of reckoning. So far, she and her mother had negotiated their reconciliation by not speaking of what had happened.

"I need to know . . . if you wanted me," Hailey said.

She startled. "I beg your pardon?"

"When you found out . . . when you knew . . . knew for certain . . . that I was coming. That you were going to have me."

Her mother's gaze grew focused and alert. "Hailey?"

"I'm with child."

With child. Hailey had said it to herself again and again.

A grave expression, mixed with something else, something indiscernible, blossomed on her mother's face.

"Please, Mother. I need to know. Did you want me?"

"Oh, Hailey. *Want* you? I *knew* you. You lived inside me. I felt every tumble and roll, every hiccup. I knew when you slept and when you woke. I counted your heartbeats when I couldn't sleep. I talked to you."

"But," Hailey persisted, "did you want me? Want Geordie?"

"I wanted you more than I wanted to live."

"You and Father were—"

"Happy. We were, back then, before everything. Oh, Hailey. Are you sorry?"

Hailey sank onto the kitchen stool. That was it. The indiscernible thing in her mother's gaze had been perception.

"Listen to me, Hailey. You could leave James. People do here. I see the divorce announcements in the newspaper all the time. No one needs to state a reason. It's easier to divorce here even than in Scotland, where, God knows, people fly apart left and right. You and Geordie could live with me. We could pack you up right now. We could send someone for the things we can't carry. We'll put extra beds in my room."

The heady scent of moist dough was causing wave after wave of nausea to wash over Hailey. *Divorce.* It wasn't as if the idea hadn't plagued her. She'd read those papers, too.

"Do you think I can just leave James? That I could walk out the door and be free? He will never let me go. He watches me. He knows where I've been, what I've done. He'll never let his child go, either."

"Listen to me, darling. What I did—leaving you—was despicable, unforgivable. I am sorry. I am sorrier than I will ever be able to say. But I don't want my mistake to mean that you live in unhappiness."

"Your *mistake?* Oh, Mother." Rage bubbled up, threatened to undo all their progress. "Leaving us was not a mistake. You left because you couldn't imagine a life other than the one we led in Glasgow. But I could, Mama. I imagined one with Samuel. I married James because you left us alone to fend for ourselves."

"I was wrong, to my everlasting shame. I did the worst thing. I broke the bonds of motherhood, and I hurt you and Geordie—but this—this is different. You don't love James."

"Do you think Samuel would have me now? And James's child? I wouldn't ask it of him, Mother—even if he'd take me, even if he still loved me, James would always be in our lives. He'd make everything miserable."

Eyes tearing, Hailey dipped her hands into the bowl of flour and coated them, readying to knead the wet dough, but her mother took her hands, held them, looked in her eyes.

"Hailey, darling."

Hailey made a last plea for understanding. "James saved us. He helped us. After you left, when Geordie and I were all alone? He helped us. He was the only one. I forget sometimes, and I shouldn't. I didn't know Samuel was coming—I shouldn't have married James. It's confusing—I know he can be cruel, but did you hear that he went back into the mine after the explosion? He brought Father out. He can be a good man."

"Can be, or is?" Davinia said.

Hailey shut her eyes. Her mother had left them, had failed her family at the most crucial juncture of their lives. She shook her head. "It would be wrong to leave."

"Wrong or impractical, Hailey?"

"Both," Hailey snapped. "What would we live on? I had money. He took it. We'd both have to work. Who would take care of the baby? Or Geordie? It's not possible. It's wrong *and* impractical."

"But you don't love him."

Hailey finally spoke the awful truth. "Mother, it would be *dangerous*. There will be no unshackling. He will never let me go. He will never let me leave with his child. He will make our lives hell, he will threaten us, he will hurt Samuel."

Her mother put her hand to her mouth as Hailey fought back another wave of nausea.

"I'm carrying James's child. I can't, Mother. I can't. That's all."

Silence fell. They could hear Geordie outside, singing to himself.

Her mother said, "Do you want the baby?"

Hailey gave a scornful, exhausted laugh. "You ask as if I have a choice."

"Hailey, what you want does matter. Even without choice, desire still matters."

Such irony, given that her mother had stolen choice from her.

But suddenly, Hailey knew. Knew without a single doubt. She wanted this baby growing inside her. Wanted it fiercely, and absolutely. But she dared, finally, to say, "But it's James's child."

Her mother was quick. "And you're grieved it's not Samuel's."

Hailey could no longer hold back the tide of nausea. She bent and retched on the floor.

SEVERAL DAYS LATER, Hailey left Geordie in her mother's care and went to Front Street, just to get out of the house. Her mother had begged time off from the hotel, and miraculously, they had given it to her, the new widow, though no one had known that she was even married. Hailey spotted Pruss Loving mumbling under his breath as he leapt over one of the dozen potholes on the street. The endless June rains had rendered all the roads a sloppy mess. For months the city council had been dithering about extending road improvements this far north. But any decision that required consensus—or taxation—engendered endless deliberation and indecision, and in this case had perpetuated the northern stretch of Front Street as a soggy nightmare.

Pruss said, "How do you do, Mrs. Murray? It's hard goin' today."

Hailey liked Mr. Loving. She liked his calm, deliberate way and how he always seemed pleased to see her.

"Hello, Mr. Loving. Where are you going?"

"The chandler's. There's always something you're needing when you're building a boat, ma'am." His gaze slipped past her. Hailey turned to see Bonnie, Alison, and Samuel coming toward them, Angus riding on Samuel's shoulders.

Everyone said hello. Suppressing a wave of jealousy, Hailey kissed Bonnie and nodded to Samuel. "Thank you for coming to the funeral. All of you."

"We wouldn't have missed it," Bonnie said, reaching out her hand to take Hailey's. "How are you?"

"Well enough, thank you. You're not working today, Samuel?"

"I'm just taking a wee break. We've been to Piper's to celebrate. Angus got another tooth."

Hailey took Angus's little hand and said, "Congratulations to you, little Angus."

Angus ducked his head with shyness as Alison said, "I remember you. I remember when you took care of us."

Hailey smiled. "Yes. A long time ago. I'm very happy to see you again, Ali."

"I'm sorry about your father."

"Thank you, Alison."

For a moment no one said anything, though Samuel seemed to be groping for words. Finally, he said, "Bonnie, could you excuse me? I'd like a moment with Mrs. Murray."

Bonnie hesitated. "Of course."

Samuel handed down Angus to her. "Pruss? Could I impose on you to escort Mrs. Atherton and her son and Alison home for me? I'd really appreciate it. I'll meet you at the chandler's in fifteen minutes."

"It'd be my honor," Pruss said.

Bonnie released Samuel's arm. Forcing a smile, she turned to Pruss. "Thank you, Mr. Loving, that would be so kind."

"I'll come by later, Bonnie," Samuel said, his voice full of empathy, knowing, it seemed, what it cost Bonnie to leave him in this moment. "After dinner, as usual?"

As usual.

With one last lingering look, Bonnie went with Pruss down the sidewalk, Alison lagging behind.

Hailey called, "Alison?"

The little girl turned.

"I really am glad to know you again."

Alison answered with a broad smile.

Samuel steered Hailey away from Front Street. They climbed Seneca, keeping to the edges of the road, where there was less mud. Here and there, a few modest houses stood on cleared lots. In one, a dairy cow chewed her cud, observing them with a placid gaze. Samuel stopped beside a whitewashed fence.

Before he could say anything, Hailey said, "Did you go at it

with James again? He came home sopping wet and furious before the funeral. He almost moved us to Newcastle."

"Did he hurt you? He was furious when he left."

Hailey put her hand to her belly, feeling the sudden tugging
of something inside. "So something did happen. Couldn't you
just not talk to him?"

"He starts it."

"I know he does. But it doesn't help me. Please, just ignore him."

"Is that what you do?"

"Samuel, you have to let me go. My life gets worse every
time he sees you. He threatened not to let Geordie live with us
anymore. Though maybe it's better for Geordie—I don't know."

"Did he hurt you?"

Hailey took a deep breath to quell a sudden, sharp pain in
her abdomen. "He's fine to me without you. He is. He can be
nice. It's you who makes him crazy. It's you who makes it worse,
do you understand? You make my life worse."

"I've stayed away, Hailey."

She'd never felt such pain before. She held her stomach,
flinching with each new wave.

"When I have the baby—"

"A baby? You're having a baby?"

The pain was constant now. "Please, don't defend me, don't
talk to James about me, don't do anything. Don't try to make
things better. I don't care if you hear that I am dying. Leave me
be. We're back to where we were before—do you remember? At
the saloon? I told you then that I couldn't talk to you anymore.
Please. Go ahead and marry Bonnie. It's clear she wants you.
Find happiness. I'm not the answer for you."

"I don't believe you."

But she didn't hear him. The pain in her abdomen consumed her. She grabbed Samuel's hand as her knees buckled. This was not the cloying nausea that had dogged her for months. This was something terrible.

"Hailey!" Samuel cried as he lifted her into his arms. "Hailey, what's the matter?"

She protested that she could stand, though in truth she couldn't. He wouldn't set her down, and it felt so good to be cradled in his arms as excruciating wave after wave tormented her. He carried her down Front Street, where he hired a teamster at the Occidental Hotel to drive them to her house, but first he sent word to the doctor and her mother.

HAILEY WAFTED IN an out of consciousness. Her screams came from forever. She pictured them tumbling down the hill to the waterfront and casting themselves out over the sound, mingling with the screaming of the gulls. Someone held her hand, and she felt a caressing graze against her forehead.

Darkness closed in on her. Her bedclothes were soaked. She was thirsty, but she couldn't speak. It was hard to get air somehow. Her throat was failing her. She knew the baby needed air and water. The baby couldn't go out and get it on its own. Poor baby, she said.

Someone took her hand. "Hailey. It's your mother."

Mother. But Hailey was deep under now and couldn't open her eyes.

At length, there came a second voice, male, unfamiliar, gentle and authoritative. It seemed that she was further along than she knew, or that's what the voice said. A feminine gasp, but not hers. Bonnie's? She couldn't tell anymore, because she was drowning. And she was tired of trying to make sense of everything. She didn't know what was real and what wasn't. Did they remember she had a baby inside her? She tried to tell them, but words wouldn't pass the murky, impenetrable surface between her and the world.

"Will she be all right?"

"I don't know," said the male voice. "It depends."

There was more prodding and then nothing. It was getting harder and harder to stand the pain.

After an eon, again came the same male voice: "She's bleeding too much."

The shivering of labor fell away. She relived every day of her life. One by one, the separate, vivid hours came to her. A first pram ride, a picnic on a rocky lakeshore, plucking her first daisy, a long walk in some towering woods. A frightening day at a seashore when she tumbled over and over in a vigorous wave and dreamed of death before her father snatched her out and made her learn to swim. Waltzing at balls, the beautiful house in Glasgow, London and the Crystal Palace, Edinburgh, and finally Samuel in the church mezzanine. The ocean voyage and Newcastle and the fire of loss afterward. And then losing Samuel again, after he had found her. Even when he had crossed oceans for her. And since then—oh, well. It didn't matter anymore.

The baby, though. Could the baby breathe? Was there air enough for two? How much air did a baby need inside? She pictured the child, floating. She had a sea inside her in which her baby floated. The baby swam in a sea. Could they both drown? If she drowned, would the baby be safe?

Oh, new sorrow. Not for herself. For the baby. She apologized. *I'm sorry I'm failing you.*

What a trickster time is. It stops, restarts, and, most cruelly, slows in pain. Seconds pass like hours. Days like years.

Now she dreamed Samuel's voice. In her ear. At her side. Calling her name. Telling her he loved her. Calling her back. Oh, how she wished it *were* him. It was so hard to climb out of the drowning without him. She had made him leave her. It was the right thing. But now the moment of eternity beckoned. It would be easy to let everything go, to drift. She was on the cusp of resolution. People died all the time. It could be her turn now. Funny, to have a choice, to remember what it was like to have one.

Choose, Hailey. Stay or go.

SHE CAME BACK into her body. It was a hard thing to do, her head heavy on the pillow. Daylight filtered through her closed eyelids. It had been dark for so long. Not dark, *exactly*. More like old light that had already expended itself.

Her mother was there, and James. James knelt at her bedside as her mother slipped away. Had she called for him? She didn't want her mother to go. She lifted her hand, reaching for her, but James took hold of it instead.

"I love you, Hailey. I do." It was a question, not a statement. *Do you love me, too?*

When she didn't answer, he said, "Why was Fiddes the one to come get me?"

His voice insinuated, invaded. Her baby was gone. Life was an empty cavern.

"I was at Tivoli," James said. "Fiddes found me."

She lifted her head. "Where is my baby? I need to see my baby."

"Why were you with Fiddes?"

"Mama," she called.

"I told Fiddes to stay away from you."

"I need my baby. I need to see my baby." Only this mattered. She was weeping. "Please let me see my baby."

James gaped, twisting the bedclothes between the fingers of one hand. "No, no, no, my Hailey. You don't want that. The doctor took it away."

"Is it a boy or a girl? Did you see? Please let me see."

"Hailey, the baby died."

"Died?"

"I'm quitting Allaway. He doesn't know it yet, but after I do my next deliveries, I'm done with him. We'll have enough money. I'll find some other work. And we can try for another baby and be a real family." He stroked her forehead. "Doesn't that make you happy?"

He was echoing her father, who had once told her mother, *We'll make a life away from everything that went wrong.*

"James Murray, if you love me, you will go now and get my baby for me. Get me our baby."

Our baby. She'd been saying *our* all along, hadn't she?

He rose and left her and returned with the baby wrapped in toweling. It was barely there. It weighed nothing. A girl. She could pick out the eyes, the tiny, spindled hands and feet, veins like strands of hair under translucent skin.

"We'll have another, my Hailey," James said.

She gave the baby over to James, and he accepted it with reverence. Then he laid his head on her shoulder and wept.

37

Samuel

HAILEY'S SCREAMS PENETRATED THE THIN WALLS of her bedroom as the doctor delivered her of her dead infant. Samuel and James were pacing in lockstep in the front room. The second Samuel had pulled James off a barstool in the Tivoli Beer Hall and explained what had happened, James's combative air turned to confusion and then heartbreak as they raced each other up the hill. The doctor admitted James to the bedroom, but Samuel was barred. The fact that he was not Hailey's husband struck Samuel with terrible force. He shuddered as each of Hailey's anguished cries pierced the afternoon. She had been feather-light in his arms. He'd cradled her head in his lap as the wagon climbed the steep hills, suffering each jolting shriek. Now he might lose her. The screams were terrifying. How could such a tiny being cause so much trouble? Samuel prayed, summoning the Catholic practice of his past. *Not Hailey. If you let her live, I'll give her up. Just let her live.*

As if Samuel had ever had a claim on her.

To prove the folly of this notion, Mrs. MacIntyre emerged from the bedroom and asked Samuel to take Geordie to Bonnie.

Geordie had been cowering outside, and Samuel scooped him up and took him back down the hill, leaving him with Bonnie and Alison, who asked a thousand questions he could not answer. When Samuel returned to the house, James was waiting for him.

"How did you know Hailey was in trouble? Why was it you who came for me?"

Samuel took it as a mark of James's true distress that it hadn't occurred to him to ask before. "Bonnie Atherton and I were walking on Front Street with Alison and Angus. We came upon Hailey and Pruss." He included Bonnie and Pruss to mute James's heavy suspicion. "Hailey collapsed. She told me then. She had to." Samuel had rearranged the chronology—collapse, then revelation, rather than the other way around—so that James wouldn't think Hailey had confided in him.

"Then why didn't Bonnie bring her?"

"Bonnie could hardly have gotten her home. Did you want me to leave Hailey on the street?"

A high-pitched shriek exploded the air.

James clutched the back of a chair, eyes glazed, undone by fear. "Get out, Fiddes."

Samuel stood his ground. "I'll leave only when I know that Hailey is safe."

Toward late evening, Hailey's cries ceased. The two men eyed each other, fearing she was dead.

After several minutes, Mrs. MacIntyre appeared again at the top of the stairs. "She is asking for you, James."

James loped up the stairs as a dagger sliced into Samuel's heart.

Mrs. MacIntyre came downstairs and embraced him. "Thank

you for bringing Hailey home. Thank you for my daughter's life. It seems that you've saved both my children."

"She'll live?"

"She's lost a lot of blood, but the doctor says she will."

"Did she ask for me?"

Mrs. MacIntyre hesitated. "She was delirious. Not in her own mind."

"But she'll live? You're sure?"

"Yes."

He let out a deep sigh.

Mrs. MacIntyre said, "She's deeply grieved. She wanted the child, but—"

Samuel interrupted her. Of course she had. And she had turned to her husband in her grief. He offered swift condolences to Davinia and bade her good night, then flung himself into the wet night.

It was intolerable to know that at her worst, after losing her child, Hailey had asked for James. The cold fact of it crippled him. She was someone else's and he knew it now. She had lived, and he would keep his promise to God. He would give her up.

If only a soul didn't need love. That was the crux of it.

His mind echoed with her words. *I can't live the life I have to live if I see you . . . I don't care if you hear that I am dying. Leave me be . . . Samuel, you have to let me go.*

Every word had been chiseled into his heart.

He reached Commercial Street and strode on, down its uneven, planked walkways to Chinatown.

The parlor of Holiday House was a shiny jumble of red velvet and rich fabrics, stuffed with armchairs, a player piano, and heavily framed paintings of naked women. It was appalling and sumptuous, and he paid for Gabrielle, a French girl who steered him to her room.

He had given Hailey to God, had made his vows. He would keep them.

Gabrielle's lithe body was no answer to his ills, but it proved compensation enough for an hour.

A WEEK LATER, Samuel put his hand to the small of Bonnie's back and steered her upstairs to the second floor of Yesler's Hall to see Queen Kittie White, the celebrated traveling dwarf who was singing in the show *Sundown Seas* before voyaging to Port Townsend. It was stiflingly hot in the airless hall. Samuel, sitting through every song, heard none of the nuance of her famous phrasing, nor a single note. Miss White finished her songs and bowed her way through two standing ovations, and Samuel escorted Bonnie outside into the swelter of the July evening.

It was ten o'clock, and the last purple light of the sunset shimmered over the Olympics. They strolled back to her boardinghouse.

At the door, Bonnie lifted her gaze, her golden curls framing her heart-shaped face. "Samuel Fiddes, I want to say something to you. This might shock you, but know this: I am not a virgin you need to be careful of. I know the delights of the bed. I know what pleasure we could share."

She put her hands to his face and kissed him. She pressed against him, emitting a whimper of pleasure, holding his lips to hers, imbuing her body with the kind of softness that made him understand that he could do anything he wanted to her. Her body was ripe and luscious and consuming. Lust suffused him. Hadn't Hailey so much as ordered him to marry Bonnie?

When she broke off, she seemed to revel in satisfaction that he had to take a moment to recover himself.

He began, "Bonnie, I've been unfair to you when you've been so kind—"

Her breath caught and she backed against the door, holding up a hand. "Please, don't. I love you too much to hear what you're going to say next."

"Someday, someone—"

"Stop." Bonnie's eyes grew dark in the face of his obvious preference for the girl he could never have. Offering him everything had been her final, desperate gesture.

Samuel said, "You've saved me from loneliness—"

"Don't you dare. Is that all I've been to you? Someone to keep you company? Someone to distract you from Hailey? Everyone thought—*I* thought—I *believed* we were going to marry."

Samuel had believed they would marry, too. But when she had made her offer, her body ripe against his, he'd suddenly known that he would never love her as he loved Hailey. He could not marry this lovely, affectionate woman. And it wasn't until just then that he'd understood this, understood that even if he had given Hailey up to God, he could never forget her or his love for her.

"Bonnie, you're good and generous—"

"Stop it. Just stop. I can't hear any more of this. Not a word. Leave. Just leave."

She was kind and pretty and good and she loved him. And he ought to love her. But he knew that he would never be able to

get Hailey out of his mind. The injustice of his actions morti-
fied him.

She stood there, watching him, and he turned and left. He
knew too well what it was to love someone you could not have.
He knew, too, that devastation and hopelessness wanted no
witness.

38

Hailey

HAILEY RECOVERED SLOWLY. IN THE DAYS IMME-
diately after the birth, when she dangled her legs over the bed, she
grew dizzy and had to lie back down. Her heart raced. The doctor
recommended beef broth and greens and if she could tolerate it, a
trip to the butcher for a glass of blood. She recoiled at that.

James's promise to quit, so fervently made, was forgotten.
He was solicitous of her, but distracted, talking about how good
the money with Allaway was. And so a week after she delivered,
he packed his duffel while Hailey shivered in bed, sipping tea.
She was always cold now. James tucked a hot brick at her feet
and sat on the edge of the bed, holding her hand. He seemed
awed by her frailty, tentative and unsure after the loss of the
baby, and more than relieved to escape back to the sea. She
didn't resent him for it. She was glad for him to go. She knew
what he was capable of, and what he wasn't. His presence was an
irritant. Davinia had moved temporarily from her room at the
boardinghouse to take care of her, and she was downstairs now,
cooking the midday meal. Hailey had to admit her mother's presence was a salve. She and Geordie and her mother together—it
was a semblance of the distant past.

James was pulling on his boots, preparing to leave. "You don't mind that I'm going?"

"It's fine," she said.

"You going to be all right?"

"I'm fine."

"Do you believe that I love you?"

"Yes."

Hailey was still shivering, so she crawled to the trunk at the end of the bed and pulled out another blanket, climbed underneath it, and shivered some more. She cared little about anything. She wasn't sure whether she wanted to live. She missed the child. She couldn't remember all of what had happened the day of the miscarriage. *Miscarriage*—a strange word, as if she had dropped the baby and it was all her fault. She remembered being held in Samuel's arms as pain first racked her, the comfort of his presence. Her mother told her that Samuel had brought her home. She shuddered to think what would have happened to her if not for him. She pictured the child, floating in the sea inside her. She apologized. *I'm so sorry I lost you. I'm sorry I failed you.*

BY THE FIRST week of July, she could take short walks on her mother's arm, and toward the end of the month brief excursions outside. Her mother tried to keep her inside, but when the weather was so warm, the sun beckoning, Hailey insisted. She grew physically stronger by the day. Her mother did all the housework, spoiling her, taking care of Geordie, force-feeding her broth and meat. James came and went, if not on *Lady Barnum* to Victoria, then in a rented steam launch to do whatever it was he did around Elliott Bay. In early August, James and Allaway took a longer trip, up to the coal mines at Nanaimo, and across the Georgia Strait to Vancouver in Canada with a stop at What-com on the way back. A lot of money to be made there, James said. They'd be gone as long as three weeks.

The promise of three weeks apart from James worked on Hailey like a tonic. Sitting outside in the splendor of the summer heat, the totality of all she had suffered struck her. Leaving Scotland, losing Samuel, her mother's abandonment, her father's gradual erasure, her awful marriage to James, Geordie's prolonged bewilderment, and the loss of the baby. Hailey let herself weep. She wept until she was hollow, and when she finished, her pain was spent.

She went inside to get a wrap and told her mother that she was going to walk. Davinia called after her to wait, but Hailey was already down the road, already letting her footsteps carry her toward the water. She emerged from the valley and rounded Belltown hill and found her way down a new stairway from the Parker House to the beach and Samuel's shipyard.

Lady Allaway's hull had been launched. She was tethered to the dock, her white paint as bright as snow, fittings gleaming in the summer sun. The length of her was astonishing. She took up nearly the whole of Samuel's new dock. The pilothouse, under construction, sat rounded and prominent on the second deck, just behind the bow. The brig masts had been erected, and the funnel had been raised. The walking beam engine had been installed, too, and its iron elbow jutted high into the air. Her paddle wheel was nearly encased. She was breathtaking.

Samuel had done it. He had made this beautiful thing. The impoverished orphan from Glasgow had made a ship of incomparable beauty.

Samuel, emerging from his office, stopped when he saw her and then strode toward her. Without speaking, he took her elbow and steered her through the yard to the bluff behind, where the spring splashed out of the cliff. She and Samuel sat on a silvering log. The spiders were already anticipating autumn, stretching white webs in hollows where they could lie in wait. Gulls circled overhead. The day was crisp, clear. Perfect in the way that incomparable beauty always breaks your heart.

"You told me to stay away," he said.

"Yes, I did." She nodded at *Lady Allaway*. "She's stunning."

"She'd be more stunning if Allaway would pay me." Samuel searched her face, his dark eyes filled with concern. "Hailey, are you well? Should you be out?"

"I'm getting there. Thank you for taking me home that terrible day."

"You remember?"

"My mother told me. It's been hard these last weeks—my father, the baby. I already loved the baby, before it was even born. I don't know what I'm supposed to do with all this love. It doesn't disappear. It's always there, and you think, you wonder, who would the child have been? Sometimes, I see her in a field of daisies, and the sun is shining, and then—an echo . . . stillness. All the beautiful possibilities of life extinguished." She had begun to weep.

"Oh, Hailey. I'm sorry." Samuel pulled her to him, his encircling arms powerful, the warmth of the splendid summer on him, his voice full of tenderness. This was what she had missed. Kindness in the voice of a man who cared about her. James claimed to love her, but did he *care*? To him, she was a possession. Someone to be controlled, to keep. She laid her head on Samuel's chest. She wanted to bury herself inside him. His embrace, his breath on her hair, the kiss he planted on her head—it was like going home.

She pulled away. "I need to go away with you, Samuel. James and Captain Allaway are gone for three weeks. We can leave. Go somewhere. We can be together. At least for a time. After that—I don't know, but I want to go away now. I need to go away."

Samuel held her face in his hands, his eyes boring through her. "Are you sure?"

James would punish her somehow. She tried to imagine him acquiescing to a divorce and couldn't. He would rip Geordie from her. "There has to be a way out of this—"

Samuel's response was urgent, swift. "I won't let him hurt you." He studied her, black eyes newly flat with—regret? anger? "When you almost died, I made a vow. I told God that if he let you live, I would leave you alone. That I would give you up."

"It's not your choice, Samuel Fiddes. Or God's. I don't even know if he cares whether I live or I die. The choice is mine. I choose you."

"But your mother said you asked—that you asked for James when you lost the child. That's why—oh, Hailey. I'm sorry. I thought you would ask for me. I've thought all this time that you really loved me, and then when your life was in trouble, you wanted James."

Hailey touched his face, caressed his cheek. "I don't know who I asked for. I was sick. Exhausted. Are you taking that as revelation? Here's a revelation. I love you, Samuel Fiddes. I want you. *You.* No one else. And I want to go away, somewhere, any-where. With you."

She fell into him, and they rose, fused together, in desperate need of grace—and each other.

39

Samuel

SAMUEL AND HAILEY STOOD AT A WINDOW OF
the steamer *Dispatch*, hands clasped, bodies touching, bracing
themselves as the vessel edged along Cattle Point, the hilly hook
at the southern end of San Juan Island in the Archipelago de
Haro. A fast ebb tide was barreling through the narrow chan-
nel between the point and another island, colliding with an
opposing wind that was stacking waves into a four-foot chop.
Passengers clung to anything nailed down. And then, suddenly,
Dispatch rounded the hook and glided into the wide inlet of
Griffin Bay. A haven of unruffled tranquility, there was no
sound except the exhalation of excess steam as the firemen
damped *Dispatch*'s fires and the captain dropped anchor a hundred feet from shore.

Samuel gazed at the rocky shores festooned with driftwood.
With its wild beauty, golden hills, and lapping seawater, the
island was as reminiscent of Scotland as Captain Allaway had
said. Alison would love it here, Geordie, too, but Hailey's
mother was caring for both children. Davinia had sanctioned
the journey, a glint of reprieve in her eyes as she wished them
well and bade them be careful. The Lovings were in charge of

the shipyard. Samuel's absence would delay delivery of *Lady Al-laway*, but if Allaway wasn't going to pay him, then he could wait.

On land, a figure swung a lantern next to a derelict pier extending into the water. Beyond the pier stood a whitewashed warehouse, and, beyond that, weather-beaten shanties and false-fronted cabins lined a wagon trail rutting into a grassy meadow. Samuel had asked James Colman where he ought to take Hailey among the islands, and he had suggested San Juan Town, where the American army had camped during a recent border dispute with Canada called the Pig War. Most of San Juan Town was deserted, but there was a store and an inn and a post office to service the archipelago's farmers, who inhabited a number of the larger islands.

Samuel helped Hailey over the side of *Dispatch* into a dangling skiff. They were lowered to the still waters, followed closely by two more skiffs ferrying their bags and crates of goods loaded at Port Townsend. Sailors rowed the three boats ashore, leaving rippled wakes. When their skiff beached, Samuel helped Hailey out, and they climbed the rocky beach strewn with ribbons of kelp to the man with the lantern, who greeted them in a heavy German accent.

"Mein name ist Israel Katz. I run a store here und vun in Port Townsend. I have rooms. Do you need? Gud. First, I see about my crates."

After Katz's goods had been unloaded and carried to the warehouse, Hailey and Samuel followed him to the back of the old warehouse that contained his store, then climbed an outside stairway to a second-story landing that opened to a central hallway and a half dozen doors. Katz unlocked one, revealing a simple room that housed a bedstead and dresser.

Katz unrolled a feather bed and pulled linen from a dresser drawer. "I'll leave you the lantern. Rent is two dollars for a week, including meals. I need nothing in advance."

Then he left, shutting the door behind him.

Evening light edged around them, shining off the lapping sea.

They entwined hands. Samuel sat on the bed and drew Hailey onto his lap. The intimacy intoxicated him. He had longed for this for years, dreamed of it, needed her in every way possible. And now she was his and her yielding warmth sighed against him. He touched her face, traced the supple line of her cheek to her lips, and she turned breathless, her eyes glinting with warmth. They were together and free and alone and he could not believe his luck. He nearly wept with happiness.

They kissed, hungry as only the starved can be. They came up for air, then kissed again, and Samuel lost himself in Hailey's scent, her soft lips, the tendrils of the curls falling across her face. He swept the locks away, laid his hands on her cheeks, kissed her again.

If kissing alone could sustain them, they would live forever.

"Are you certain?" he said. "You've been sick—"

Wordless, Hailey stood and turned, and bade him to untwine the ribbon from her hair. He untied it, and her locks loosened.

She murmured, "My buttons."

One by one he undid them, remembering the time in the carriage in Glasgow when his hands had found his way to the tiny pearls at the top of her beautiful gown. Down his hands went, following the placket of her dress, until her back and corset were exposed.

"Unloose my ties."

The flat strings posed some resistance to the unthreading. Inch by inch his trembling hands bared her back, and then she turned to face him as the bodice fell away. The air was velvet around them.

"Hailey," Samuel said, hoarse. But he could say nothing more, and nor could she, for nothing else mattered, not the past, not the future, not even the marriage vows Hailey cast aside without a thought.

AFTERWARD, THEY LAY face-to-face, bodies entwined, moonlight silvering the window, flung open to the soft night air and the lapping sea.

"I remember the first moment I saw you," Samuel said. "You were so beautiful. I knew then that I loved you. I hadn't even spoken to you, but I wanted you more than I wanted life. And then you asked me to your family's home, and you were so caring and looked after us. You changed me—just the possibility of you changed me. You made me hope. I hadn't hoped before. I had nothing and then there was you."

She cupped his face, tears falling, and kissed him, a soft crushing of his lips. He pulled her closer. He didn't ever want to part from her again.

Hailey kissed him again and whispered, "When I saw you, up there in the mezzanine, I thought you were the handsomest boy I'd ever seen. And then you saved Geordie. How could I not love you? And then, to my utter joy, you turned out to be you. Clever and kind and responsible and persistent. Oh, why did I ever leave Scotland? Leave you? *Years*, Samuel. It's three years from the moment I first saw you, and I've wanted you every second of that."

"I couldn't believe I missed you by one day—"

She lifted a finger to his lips. "You came. I saw you and I thought, 'He loves me.' Oh, how I wish—"

It was his turn to quiet her. "No more regrets. I have you now, Hailey, my love. I have you." He was suffused with joy. He pulled her even closer, until there wasn't a part of him that wasn't touching her.

"You've made me whole, Samuel Fiddes. I'll never let go of us. Never."

They fitted together as if they had been made from the same fragment of eternity. Their limbs entangled, they breathed astonishment at their mutual pleasure, the brilliance of their joined selves. To be parted was to feel pain, so they did not part. Only hunger sped them from their bed to eat, and a different kind of hunger sent them back.

SEVERAL DAYS AFTER their arrival, Samuel and Hailey climbed up and over the southern ridgeline's tawny fields, passing a farmhouse whose mistress waved from a wide veranda, and descending to a long, wild beach that stretched along the island's southern hook. A westerly was sending white spray across the water. In the distance, the Olympics climbed to the sun, while Mount Tahoma blinked in a milky haze and Mount Baker—another cone of splendor—shimmered pure white. They walked along the hard sand, palming flat rocks as they absorbed the spectacular sunlight bouncing off the expanse of sea and sky. After a time, they stopped at an uprooted, silvered tree, flung there long ago by some raging storm, its roots a petrified star, its dry wood holding the warmth of the sun. They slipped down to the sand, with Samuel's back against the driftwood and Hailey cradled between his legs, her head lying against his chest.

"You once said you wanted to go back to Scotland," Samuel said, his gaze fixed on the splendor.

"Oh, Samuel, but this place is like Scotland. This is our home. I declare it." She twisted to look at him. "Our own Briga-doon. The place where time stands still. You know that story, don't you? The town that appears every hundred years in the Highlands? You can only stay if you fall in love." She gazed at him. "Let's make time stop. I want to exist only in this moment. Forever."

Samuel, too, felt the march of the clock. They were pitting themselves against their eventual return to Seattle. But they had a week yet.

"You're not like James," Hailey said. "Not in any way."

They hadn't yet spoken of James.

"Maybe in one way. We both love you," Samuel said.

"It's not love that James feels for me." Hailey looked out at the Strait of Juan de Fuca, the skittering sunshine, the leaping fish. "I think I needed to believe that he loved me. That's what happens to women. We emphasize the good and accept the bad. It's our way to survive. But you?" she said. "You're mine. Do you understand? This place—this moment—is ours."

They basked in the sunlight. In the distance, a schooner, its sails billowing in the capricious wind, beat its way southward toward Admiralty Inlet, crossing wakes with an ocean-bound sailing bark loaded with timber. A dozen flat-bottomed Indian canoes paddled past. In one, they had laid flat stones for an oven and were baking salmon, fragrant smoke trailing behind, ward-ing off voracious bald eagles that dove and harassed them. They had learned that the Indians were assiduous students of wind and current, and that islanders hired them to ferry them across to Victoria in the fierce drifts of Haro Strait. It was lovely to watch the canoes on their travels, their sleek, formidable craft framed against the vast waters and the snow-topped Olympics.

But for Samuel and Hailey, nothing was as attractive as the lapping shore and the bright sky and their languid hours together.

Hailey said, "We could live here. We could buy some land from Mr. Katz and build a house and have a garden. Alison and Geordie, too. All of us, together." Mr. Katz dabbled in everything, including real estate, but he was experiencing stiff competition from a Mr. Sweeney, who was laying bets on a place called Friday Harbor, north of Griffin Bay.

"We could have a family, and—" Samuel stopped himself, suddenly worried that voicing this desire after her terrible loss would hurt her.

She turned to him, a fleeting look of sorrow crossing her face before she raised her eyes to his, filled with emotion. "A baby with you? I would love it."

Samuel exhaled with relief. "I'm sorry, I—"

"I want another one. I do." She sank against him again, and for a long time, she said nothing as the breeze bore the scent of the sea on the undulating waves. Then, "We could buy a cow. And keep chickens."

His voice vibrated with hope. "And a horse. And a wagon."

Neither mentioned the myriad obstacles that stood between that dream and now, though they were ever present in their minds. They kept this a time apart, in which anything was possible.

The next afternoon, they borrowed a skiff from Israel Katz, and Samuel rowed north along the shoreline of the bay, past rocky beaches and tall forests edging the water, skirting the tiny islands close to shore, and beaching the boat on the bay's northern arm, where houses from the old fort had been floated, though no one had yet come to live here. Samuel and Hailey climbed onto their wide verandas and peered into the windows. They would put a rocker in that corner there, a cabinet along that far wall, would stoke the stove until it glowed, would listen to the winter winds rattle the window glass, would revel in the isolation. They trekked north across a peninsula jutting into the sea and came upon a sheltered cove. This was Friday Harbor, where Joseph Sweeney wanted to build his town. The southern shore lay bereft of house or farm. Samuel's keen eye traversed the gentle slope of the bank. He imagined a shipyard. A stone house perched above, built with his own two hands. A home.

They borrowed bedrolls from Israel, bought a skillet and cof-feepot and groceries, and returned to camp for several days in one of the empty houses. Mornings, under the dawning sun, they dug for clams and snared crabs and baked them on flat rocks like the Indians did. Afternoons, they sat on the veranda steps and watched the south light shimmer across the bay. Nights, they made love under a spray of stars and listened to the calls of whiskery seals hauled onto the beach.

Samuel said, "You've erased my loneliness."

She said, "I didn't know what it was to be happy."

Occasionally, Hailey wept. Frail still, she would plunge into sleep, cradled in the crook of Samuel's arm. They still did not acknowledge the ticking clock. In a few days' time, *Dispatch* would call for them.

One afternoon, lazing along the shore, the tide slowly rising, Hailey said, "You unbroke my heart, Samuel Fiddes. I'm leaving James. I'll apply to the courts as soon as I get home."

Samuel took in the curve of her cheeks, her sun-kissed skin, her gaze, newly direct. Over the past week, he had waited. He had not pushed. He had not asked.

"You either break or you live," she said. "I want to live. Will you have me? Will you make a life with me?"

Her voice shook, but in her tremulous notes Samuel heard the Hailey of old, the girl who had appeared at his doorstep in Glasgow, had kissed him in the church courtyard to the shock of everyone, who had said, *Remember, Samuel Fiddes. Remember! Washington Territory.*

He said, "I've wanted nothing and no one else since I met you. I'm yours. Forever."

Joy seized them, and they came together, taking heed of nothing but their happiness.

40

Hailey

IN SEATTLE, THEY WERE CAREFUL TO LEAVE THE
ship at different times, though whether the ruse would keep them
safe from gossip was hard to know. Samuel had given Hailey
money for a wagon to drive her home so that she wouldn't have
to trudge to the house with her bag, an uphill walk of a mile and
a half. She was going back to the house first, as it was midafter-
noon and her mother would be at the Occidental with Alison
and Geordie. Hundreds of gulls were diving for herring in the
bay, a cacophonous, vicious undertaking, more slaughter than
feast. The ugly noise followed Hailey up the road toward the
house that she hoped never to share again with James, who was
expected back in a few days' time.

She had no lies prepared. She would pack her things and
stay with her mother at the boardinghouse. Davinia had kept
the children there as a measure of security—there were other
people there. Then Hailey would plan what next to do. She
would never again have to come to the house. Never. She was
leaving forever.

But as she approached, she found a note tacked to the front
door in James's crude lettering:

I know you went away with Fiddes.

She dropped her bag. James and Captain Allaway had returned early. They were *early*. She ran breathless to town, down the rutted road skirting Belltown's high hill, the bay glimmering far below, the beauty in sharp relief to the terror rising inside her. A schooner was unfurling its sails, a tug nudging it out into the sound, the gulls screaming and diving.

She tried the boardinghouse first, but her mother hadn't yet returned from work, so she dashed to the Occidental Hotel. To Hailey's great relief, she found her in the laundry barn, along with Alison and Geordie. Her mother was ironing sheets, and Alison was chattering away about how a boy at school had once erased all the teacher's arithmetic problems from the blackboard and he had to sit in the corner for the whole of the day, and—

"Geordie!" Hailey said, her hand to her throat. Geordie skipped toward her and engulfed her in a hug, thrilled to see her.

"Hailey! You're back!" Her mother beamed and set the iron in its tray and embraced her.

Breathless, Hailey said, "You're all right? Alison is all right? James hasn't been here?"

"No. And we're fine. Why? What's the matter?"

"James is back. He left a note. He knows. I don't know what he's going to do—" She broke off. Neither Geordie nor Alison needed to hear any more. Her hair was in disarray and her hands shook. "I have to warn Samuel."

Sharp as always, Alison's restless eyes darted between Hailey and her mother. "He's a bad man."

Hailey hesitated. "Who is?"

"Mr. Murray."

"Why do you say that?"

"He hides things at Samuel's shipyard."

"He does?"

"Burlap bags filled with tins, on the bluff, up high where I pick salal berries. I saw him."

Hailey exchanged a glance with her mother.

To Alison, Hailey said, "Does Samuel know?"

"Not about the tins. I didn't want him to get mad. Samuel always gets mad about him. The base ball game scared me. I don't want Samuel to fight anymore."

Hailey knelt down and took Alison's hands. The girl looked as vulnerable as she had when Hailey first knew her, when she was just five and hungry and needed help. In Seattle, she had grown strong and vibrant—but not now. Now she looked fearful. "I'm glad you told me. That was the right thing to do. We can tell Samuel together."

Alison nodded, and Hailey embraced her as Geordie sidled over and took Alison's hand, standing solemnly at her side.

Hailey said, "I'm going to find Samuel. I'll go to the house and then the shipyard. Keep the children, Mama?" She had to warn Samuel. He had to know that James knew.

"I want to go," Alison said.

Hailey touched the girl's hair. "I'll find your brother and bring him to you."

"I want to see him."

Hailey felt a flood of guilt. They had been away two weeks— the longest amount of time Alison had ever been separated from Samuel. She wasn't even sure if Samuel had told Alison he was with her.

"Did you miss your brother, Ali?"

Alison bobbed her head.

It was evening. The light changed abruptly this time of year.

Day one minute, night the next. They could be wandering around in darkness soon. But Alison looked so bereft.

Hailey took her hand. "Come on. Let's go find your brother."

They went first to Samuel's house, but he wasn't there.

A yellow ribbon of sunlight lined the Olympics. There was time to check the shipyard.

Alison was a fast walker. They hurried down the path to the beach. Hailey hoped James was drinking away his fury at the Tivoli. She feared an encounter. She reminded herself that he wouldn't know when they were coming back. Unless, of course, he had someone watching the docks. She couldn't believe what her life had become.

Hailey drew Alison close to her side as they turned the corner at the barrel factory onto the shipyard beach.

41

Samuel

SAMUEL WATCHED HAILEY FROM A DISTANCE TO make sure she got safely into the wagon. She was going to go home to pack and afterward go straight to her mother's. She would be safe now. What obstacles were coming—the divorce, James's fury—they could face together. Samuel could not remember being so happy. Light in his step, he went directly to the shipyard. *Lady Allaway* looked breathtaking in the afternoon dazzle, the sun bouncing off the water, everything aglimmer. He felt a sense of great contentment. Joy, even. Everything had fallen into place. Overhead, squawking seagulls circled and dove for herring in the bay. They could be mutinous with one another, but today their noise seemed a celebration.

Pruss and John Salvation were sanding wood on *Lady Allaway*'s afterdeck, readying to apply the first coat of varnish. Samuel noticed that in his absence the last of the hardware had been fixed in place, the brass bell secured by the pilothouse. Enough done so that he could hold Allaway accountable for his next payment.

The two men shot to their feet when they saw him. "Have you seen Murray?"

Samuel went cold. "Why?"

John Salvation said, "He got back yesterday, went raging through town. He heard somehow. I don't know how, but he did. He came by here this morning, furious. We told him you'd gone to Port Blakely to see about some more fir. He watched us like a cat. After a bit, he stormed away like he was going to murder someone."

Samuel felt himself pale. "Stormed where?"

"We couldn't tell once he got past that old coal wharf. We didn't know when you'd be back or we would have met *Dispatch* and told you."

Samuel swallowed. *Hailey.* His mind began to work, trying to guess where a man like Murray, crazed with jealousy, would go.

"Pruss? John Salvation? Could you search the waterfront— taverns, docks, everywhere? If you find Murray, keep an eye on him."

HAILEY'S BAG HAD been dropped in the yard. The note on the door fluttered in the breeze. There was no answer to Samuel's knock. He pushed open the door and listened, alert for the slightest breath. Nothing. He padded from room to room, keeping his footfall light, fearful of what he might find. But there was no sign of either James or Hailey, no sign that she had been inside. James's bag was tossed and open on their bed, the bed-clothes unmussed.

Samuel ran toward town. He strode through the commotion of Yesler's dock, skirting off-loaded livestock and trundling wagons in search of *Lady Barnum*. Why hadn't he looked for the boat when he and Hailey disembarked *Dispatch*? What a care-less fool he had been. Too elated, too happy to do the essential thing. Hailey had said James wouldn't be back for days, but he ought to have thought, ought to have looked. The wharf was lively with activity. No fewer than five barks were tied up and loading lumber. Sometimes it seemed as if Washington was shipping its forests to the entire world, tree by tree. A steamer from Honolulu was unloading coffee and sugar. *Dispatch* had already moved to the coal dock to refuel.

He found *Lady Barnum* moored to the last cleats at the end of the crooked wharf, out of sight around the long wharf's dogleg.

Allaway was attending to *Lady Barnum*'s lines.

"Fiddes!"

Allaway always seemed genuinely glad to see him, blithely unconscious of Samuel's frustration about his delinquent payments.

"Is Murray here?"

"Hello to you, too."

"Is he here?"

"All business today, are we?"

"Where is he?"

"Don't tell me you two are at it again. When will *Lady Allaway* be finished, Samuel? Make good progress while we were gone?"

"She'll be finished when you pay me, Captain, and not before. Where does Murray like to go?"

Allaway shrugged, unperturbed. "He's fond of the Tivoli. And the Aurora. You could also try the Eureka. Or the Boomerang. I've supped there with him a time or two. And lately, he's been known to frequent the Holiday House for, shall we say, satisfaction, while his wife recovers from—"

"Holy hell, Allaway."

He shrugged. "It's hard on a man, a wife under the weather like that."

Anywhere. Murray could be anywhere. Samuel turned on his heel as Allaway called after him, "I'll be paying soon, Samuel, I will."

The late afternoon sped by. Samuel made a thorough search of Seattle's taverns, elbowing through crowds. The gaslights on Commercial were already being lit as he hurried to Davinia's boardinghouse. Maybe he should have gone there first—if just to see Alison—but the sight of Hailey's dropped bag and the note had spurred him to this goose chase. He ran into the Lovings, who hadn't seen anything of Murray, either.

Davinia answered her door at the first knock. "Samuel? Oh, thank goodness." She craned her neck to look behind him. "But where are Hailey and Alison?"

He recoiled. "What do you mean?"

She turned to the Lovings. "Didn't you see them?"

Pruss said, "See them where, ma'am?"

"Samuel's house, the shipyard. They're looking for you, Samuel." Davinia beckoned them in. Geordie was lying on the bed on his side, playing with his soldiers. She told them what Alison had said about James and his hiding place. "James knows about your trip."

"I know. When did they leave here?"

"Two hours ago."

It was eight thirty, growing dark. The sky had begun to leak rain. Samuel sprinted toward the shipyard.

42

Hailey

THE SHIPYARD WAS EMPTY, THE BARREL FAC-
tory shuttered for the night.

"I'm sorry, Alison. It looks as if your brother is somewhere else. Maybe back at your house. Maybe we missed him." The light was failing. She would take Alison back to her mother—and after that think what to do.

Before Hailey could stop her, Alison had slipped from her grasp and was scrambling up the steep rise of the bluff, through the scrub and salal bushes.

"Alison, come down. We'll tell Samuel tomorrow about the hiding place. We need to go home."

But Alison did not heed her. She was already halfway up the bluff.

With a whoop, she called out, "I have one!" and hoisted a burlap bag bulging with opium tins over her head.

"Thinking of joining me in the trade?"

Hailey whirled. James, a peculiar smile of gratification lighting his face, stood behind her.

She swallowed hard. "Alison was showing me where she likes to pick salal berries."

"Near my wee hiding place, is it?" He called to Alison, "Come down here, lass."

Alison dropped the bag and obeyed. Silently, Hailey urged her to run, but the moment her feet touched ground, James snatched the girl in a vise grip. Alison kicked but couldn't free herself. Hailey admired her spirit even as her heart hammered in fear. A Scots lass. The kind of rebellious girl she had once been.

James's expression and manner remained calm as Alison's fists beat against him. Hailey would have preferred his eruptive anger or wheedling pleas. Those tactics, at least, she recognized. This serene turn was terrifying.

James said, "Hailey, climb back up and fetch the bag she dropped, would you?"

"Don't hurt her, James."

"Such a worrier, you are. The girl's merely insurance."

Twigs grabbing at her skirts, thorns grazing her knuckles, Hailey groped her way up the bluff, hauled out one unwieldy bag filled with tins, and shimmied down. "Now will you let her go?"

"Follow me." He started toward shore, a firm grasp on Alison, who dragged her feet and made miserable work of it for him. In one move he slung her over his shoulder. Hailey had forgotten his strength. She followed behind, dragging the clanking bag of opium tins through an empty shipyard, the machines hulking in shadow. *Lady Allaway* floated black and imposing at the dock. On the beach, she could see one of Samuel's dinghies had been turned upright, its oars fastened into the oarlocks, tiny waves lapping at its bow.

"Alison and I won't say anything about any of this," Hailey said. "Let her go."

"Throw the bag into the dinghy."

The Parker House's lights were burning, and strains of lively dance music floated out over the beach. Hailey craned her neck and looked back at the little hotel.

"No one's going to save you from giving me that bag," James said.

"You're going to take her with you, aren't you?"

"Yes."

"Take me instead."

"And let this one run and fetch her meddlesome brother?" He tossed Alison onto the floor of the dinghy, manhandled the bag away from Hailey, and with one swift motion, pushed the boat into the water and scrambled over its side. Hailey splashed into the water, her skirts dragging. With one hand she caught the stern of the boat and somehow hauled herself in.

"Welcome," James said.

Hailey realized that James had wanted her to get in, and to spite her had intentionally made her wade through the frigid water. Within seconds, he had rowed them thirty feet from shore. Hailey pulled the frightened Alison into her arms.

"Can you swim?" Hailey whispered. A futile question, because if Alison were to go over, the water would be too cold for someone as small as she was to survive.

Alison shook her head. She said nothing else—out of character for the girl who led a troop of children through the streets of Seattle like the Pied Piper. The only sound was the dip of the oars into the flat calm of the water, grown smooth as a millpond. Over the eastern hills an orange moon burned through the evening mist. It was much colder out on the water than onshore. Neither she nor Alison wore a coat. The sound's icy temperature penetrated the floor of the dinghy.

At first, James said nothing, and the oars dipped in and out in rhythm, drops flinging as he swung them in their locks. Then he began talking as if he were a tour guide. "First, we'll make a delivery at Smith's Cove. Hermit there likes his opium. Then we'll go around Magnolia Bluff past Four Mile Rock. A pair living on the beach flats around Sandy Point are fond of it, too. Then we'll work around into Salmon Bay. There's a whole settlement of Chinese at that new sawmill. Did you know that? First sawmill in Seattle not on Elliott Bay. Progress."

It was a trip that would take all night. "James, row to shore. Put Alison off. She's shivering."

"Do you know how many nights I've shivered out here? For us? You never asked me if I got cold or uncomfortable."

"She's a little girl."

"She's Fiddes's sister."

Hailey, too, was shivering. Her skirts were soaked. She feared the hours ahead and the currents that ran through Puget Sound. James would have to stay strong to row against them. He usually took a steam launch. What if he grew fatigued? But she quieted her fear, thinking that when he beached the dinghy at Smith's Cove to make his delivery, she and Alison could get out there. Hide. Wait out the night. James couldn't deliver opium and keep hold of them both. In the distance, back toward the barrel factory and the hotel, she could see lanterns bouncing along the shore, hear faintly strained voices.

As if he had seen them, too, James said, "Come to think of it, I'll stop at Smith's on the way back."

He turned the boat west, following the curve of the shoreline at a hundred feet out. Already, it felt like big water. Fear bit at Hailey as she clutched a silent Alison to her, trying to keep them both warm. It was monstrous to take a child out onto the sound at night. Hailey cast around for something to say, some way to help James understand what he was doing, that he was better than this, that he was endangering a child. And her, too. Rowing to Salmon Bay as the tide ebbed? At night? It was too far, the currents too strong. Their added weight would fatigue James, allow the currents to drive them north.

"Remember who you are, James. A hero. You're the man who went into a burning mine. You saved Father. You saved me and Geordie."

"I want him to suffer."

He could only mean Samuel.

Hailey said, "It's me you're upset with. Not Alison. Me." There was the distinct sound of another set of oars—or was there? She was growing desperate. "I'm the one you should be angry with. Leave Alison out of this."

Alison was mute, huddled on Hailey's lap. She made little animal sounds as she shivered.

James had the work of oaring to keep him warm. His voice showed no trace of bother. "I want to take something precious from Samuel. So he knows how it feels."

Hailey said, "I'm the one who left you. Please take Alison to shore."

James stopped rowing. Above the eastern hills, the orange moon had risen higher, showering the water with licks of light. His face was full of fury. She could see everything of him now. His neck thick with years of labor, his eyebrows straight as the horizon, his stolid cheekbones heavy. Miners' bones.

"You're nothing but a slut."

She expected a blow next, and waited for it, eyeing the distance to shore, blessing her father for the summer visits to the loch, where he had taught her to swim. But was she strong enough to carry Alison with her? She feared that the cold would defeat her, too. She tightened her hold on Alison, sorry the girl was here, sorry she was subjected to this.

James resumed rowing, hard, his face cold now, all sympathy gone. "I loved you."

Someone had once told her that a man would hurt a woman the moment he was certain he would lose her. She gambled. "I owe you an apology."

He looked up, forehead wrinkled with pain.

"I shouldn't have married you. I was afraid and I needed help. I had Geordie and my father to take care of." She'd confessed this before, but it seemed as if it were new information to James. "And you asked, and you promised to take care of them. I believed you."

"I meant it."

"I know you did."

James exhaled and let the boat glide. A slight wind had picked up and he let it carry them, the ebb tide sailing them out. Alison shifted in Hailey's arms, wordless, trembling. Hailey wanted to whisper reassurances in her ear, but she feared drawing attention to her. What did James plan to do? Throw them overboard? That would be insane, but why else drag them out here? She was apoplectic with fear. She had just reclaimed Samuel, her happiness—and now? She was going to lose everything. And Samuel would lose Alison. She fumbled for what to say next.

Before she could utter another word, he said, "You used me."

He started rowing again, out to the wide depths of the sound. She could see lanterns shimmering off the water behind them. Indians, fishing for salmon. She swallowed hard. She didn't know what was dangerous to say now and what wasn't. James was like black powder, volatile with possibilities.

ROBIN OLIVEIRA

The truth, she thought. More of the truth. "I did use you."

"You want Fiddes."

"I can't help how I feel about him. It's the way that you can't help how you feel about me."

James peered at her, eyes steady with something she could not read in the dark.

"Our baby . . ." he said. He let *baby* hang in the air, revealing a deeper anguish than he had shown before.

"I know."

"We would have had a family."

"I ache, too, James."

He let out a sob, mourning the ghost of their impossible future, the lost baby. He collapsed over the oars, the skiff drifting. And then, abruptly, he leapt to his feet, sending the dinghy wobbling from side to side. Hailey gripped Alison and implored James to sit down. It seemed as if he were going to swing at her, at both of them, upending them all.

"It's your fault," he shouted. "If you hadn't left with Fiddes—"

And he did swing, lunging at them both, scrambling to get ahold of Alison.

Hailey wrested Alison away—she didn't know how. She thrust the girl behind her as the dinghy rocked perilously. Then she seized the bag of opium tins and heaved it over the side. It was an instinct, a way to distract him for a minute, a diversion. She would think of what to do after—grab an oar, fight him off, she didn't know.

But before she could do any of it, James cried out and, with a wild look, leapt after the opium. In a second, he disappeared beneath the water, black as coal, while above the moon exploded with light. Hailey gasped and reached over the side, grappling, reaching for James's hand, his shirt, anything. The shock of the cold water froze her hand, and she yanked it out and instead fumbled one of the long oars out of its lock, shouting at Alison to lie flat on the bottom of the dinghy and stay there. Obediently, Alison dove to the floor.

Hailey sat in the stern and bobbled the oar and finally managed to stick the paddle deep into the water, imagining that James would reach for it. She shouted his name again and again. A head popped up, but it was only a seal's sleek canine shadow, its whiskers skimming the water. She thought she heard a faint voice calling her name, the sound of oars.

"James," she screamed.

Someone called her name, but then, nothing. The moonlight danced on the waves—flickers of orange light. Was it the moon? Time slowed. The reflections on the water were playing tricks. She twisted in her seat, searching. Where had James gone in? Had they drifted? "Alison, help me. Do you see him?"

Alison popped up, clung to the gunwales, and scanned the dark surface of the water. She shook her head, her lips pressed tight, eyes wide with fear.

"James!"

A coarse shout: "Hailey!"

She twisted again. "James?" But it wasn't James, surfaced and breathing. It was Samuel, with John Salvation and Pruss, rowing toward her, lanterns held high. They came alongside and took hold of the gunwales of their dinghy and brought the two boats together. Samuel clambered over the side into theirs. Alison flung herself into his arms.

He inspected Alison to see if she was hurt. "Ali, lass. Oh, Ali."

"He was taking me and Hailey climbed in . . ." Alison babbled the story while Hailey sat in shock. She was shivering uncontrollably. Her skirts were soaked, her hands numb from the water. She laid the oar down, tried to slow her heart.

John Salvation and Pruss were talking to her. "You all right, Mrs. Murray? You all right?"

She couldn't answer. Samuel was hugging Alison close, pressing her to him. "Tell me true, wee Ali. You sure you're not hurt?"

"Yes."

"Then sit up there in the bow while I take care of Hailey."

Samuel clambered over the seats to Hailey and sat beside her and engulfed her. "My love, my love, my love. Oh, my love."

He was warm and strong, and he had her.

"I thought for sure—I thought I wouldn't get to you in time. I thought—I thought I would lose you—like before, but worse, but—I've got you, I've got you, I've got you." Samuel rocked her back and forth, kissing her, enfolding her against his chest. He was warm from the exertion of rowing hard across the waters of the bay, and Hailey sank into his warmth.

Pruss was murmuring to Alison, John Salvation pulling off his shirt and wrapping her in it.

"I've got you," Samuel whispered in Hailey's ear.

Just in time, Hailey thought, shutting her eyes. *Just in time.*

He released her—reluctantly—and fitted the freed oar into the oarlock, turned the boat for shore, and rowed as fast as he could. Pruss and John Salvation stayed behind to search for James.

But Hailey knew it was no use.

ON THE SHORELINE, her mother and Geordie waited with the sheriff.

"I went for him," Davinia said. "I didn't know where you were. I was so worried." She wrapped her coat around Hailey and pulled Alison to her. Geordie flung himself into Hailey's arms. She knelt down and kissed him.

"I'm fine. I'm here," she said.

Samuel got a fire going using scrap lumber from Allaway's boat and fed it into a leaping, roaring thing. They had to back away because it was so hot. A bonfire. Brighter than the lights of the hotel above. Hailey knew it would serve as a beacon for Pruss and John Salvation.

The sheriff was asking questions. Alison, calm now and eager to show the sheriff the cache, led him past the hulking ways and the shipyard's many sheds, his lantern tracing their path toward the bluff.

All Hailey could see was the coal-black water and James disappearing into it. The salt water was evaporating from her skirts. Samuel was standing close guard, hands on his hips. Her mother stepped from her side, taking Geordie by the hand and leading him away. Samuel pulled Hailey into his arms. Out on the water, she had felt near death, on the brink of never. The whole of what had happened finally hit her. Every muscle in her body ached. Drifting out on the sound, she had felt helpless.

Samuel engulfed her. Her voice was muffled in his embrace. "How did you know?"

"Pruss told me. I went to your house. I saw James's note. We looked everywhere for you, for him. Your mother told me you were here. We could hear you on the water." He pulled away. "I almost lost you—again. *Again.* Oh, Hailey."

The Lovings rowed up and beached their dinghy. They walked up the beach, shaking their heads, confirming what Hailey already knew.

"James didn't deserve that. Whatever else he was—he didn't deserve that."

"No," Samuel said.

The fire roared and crackled. The sheriff's lantern was dancing up the bluff, Alison calling directions to him from below. The others left Hailey and Samuel alone.

Samuel said, "Is it true? Did you force your way into that boat?"

"He was so calm—I would have been less afraid if he'd been screaming. I couldn't let him take her. I waded out after them and climbed in."

Samuel said, "What would have happened to her without you?"

"I knew it was me he wanted to hurt. He was furious at both of us, but he knew that if he hurt Alison, it would pain me doubly, because it would hurt you, too."

"So brave."

"I'm not. I was terrified."

He held her tighter still, pressing kisses into her hair.

"Samuel, do you have to build your ships here? I can't stay here. I can't stay in this place where everything has gone wrong." She pulled away and seized his hand. "Let's begin again. You and me. And Geordie and Alison and my mother and the Lovings. Let's go, let's build a shipyard. A place for us. All of us. A wild and heavenly place."

"All of us?"

She nodded. She never wanted to be separated from anyone she loved again.

Samuel grinned. "Anywhere. Anytime. Anything."

Epilogue

EIGHT MONTHS LATER, UNDER A DRY APRIL SKY, Samuel Fiddes stood admiring the house he had spent the winter building.

A stone cottage by the sea, dreamed of when he was a lonely boy in an orphanage and now come to life by his own hands: eight windows, four on each floor, with arched window frames festooned with egg-shaped rocks Alison had gathered on the beach. A rock fireplace stood at either end. A woodstove in the buttery—a Scottish word that pleased him, but their buttery was only a corner of the one large room downstairs. He had roofed the dwelling with slate bought from the quarries on Vancouver Island. He had built furniture and sent for mattresses from Katz's in Port Townsend, and linens and dishes, too. The glazier in Victoria had sent windows to Samuel's measurements, and these he had fitted one by one.

The house occupied the swath of land on the southern shore of Friday Harbor that he and Hailey had discovered. Joseph Sweeney had given Samuel good terms, because he was eager for someone—*anyone*—to make Friday Harbor their home. Samuel would begin his new boatbuilding business now that he had finished the house. He would start small this time, crafting the popular sailing sloops that could navigate the raging current around the islands and across Haro Strait to Victoria. Maybe steam launches, too.

James's death had shocked Seattle, but, remarkably, Captain Allaway was not charged with smuggling, because no opium was found on *Lady Barnum*. The sheriff was satisfied by Hailey's story of what had happened out on the bay, especially after he found James's cache.

The day after James's death, Samuel went to the shipyard at dawn and dug his heels into the rocks, taking it all in. He wanted to say goodbye. It seemed that Seattle had always been and would always be in the business of reshaping itself. Samuel had been, too. Over and over in his life, any sense of home had been ripped from him. His family, the inhospitable cruelty of Smyllum, the cold indifference of Glasgow. Seattle turned out to be a raw, ambitious, contentious place where the tides of fate had fractured so many of his hopes. He looked out over the open-air sheds, his office, the steam engines and pulleys and winches, the saws and the lathes and everything else, and finally *Lady Allaway*, tied to the pier that Colman had built him. It had been a beginning he had believed in. One he had made for himself, a consolation when he had lost Hailey.

But now he had what he wanted most.

Samuel marched to Hammond's Shipyard, where he had once watched the launching of the *Geo. E. Starr*. Hammond pledged on the spot to buy Samuel out, lock, stock, and barrel, thrilled to be rid of his most skilled competitor. The older ship-builder dropped his tools and marched with Samuel in his work clothes, sawdust in his eyebrows, to visit Dexter Horton's bank. From the sale, Samuel garnered just enough money to buy the materials for the house, keep him and Alison in food, and fashion a nest egg to begin his next business.

A week later, he and Hailey wed in a small ceremony attended by her family, the Lovings, the Colmans, and Big Bill. And today Hailey and her family were coming to Friday Harbor to begin their lives. Pruss Loving, John Salvation, and Annabelle had moved here, too. In January, Pruss had put in a contract at the land office in Olympia for 160 acres on the island, having lost patience with Henry Yesler, who hadn't yet divided his parcel in the valley behind Seattle. Pruss bought good farming land, and he and John Salvation had already purchased oxen and a plow and had sown their fields with wheat. They lived over the hill, in the abandoned wood-frame houses that Samuel and Hailey had camped in.

John Salvation and Annabelle Barnum were wed in Port Townsend by a Methodist minister who saw no reason that two people who loved each other couldn't marry. There were no laws against marrying between races, but it was safer here on the island, where so few people lived. Mrs. Allaway had not come to the wedding, but she hadn't stopped it, either.

Down the beach, Alison bent over an open fire, coaxing the halibut they had purchased from some Salish in anticipation of their guests. She remembered Ah Sing's lessons and had become a good cook. School on the island ran from May through September, when the roads and footpaths dried out enough for travel. Over the winter, Alison had lived a vagabond life, helping Samuel to build the house and suffering through his math and reading lessons by candlelight, under night skies splashed with stars.

"Is *Dispatch* here yet?" Pruss called to Samuel from the beach fire, where Annabelle was setting the table with the cooked potatoes and bread and jam she had brought to complement the halibut.

"Taking her sweet time," Samuel returned.

But then *Dispatch*'s unmistakable form steamed by. Samuel ran to the waiting skiff he had built in the evenings and rowed up the harbor, past the shore filled with towering fir trees, and the many bobbing seals, their gleaming heads turning as he skimmed by. Waterbirds ignored him, intent on fishing. It was a mile to row, and with every dip of his oars the distance seemed to grow longer. *Dispatch* rounded the harbor's guardian island and glided to a stop at the floating platform anchored just off the little town growing on the shoreline. The town consisted of a few houses and an outpost store owned by the industrious Katz. Samuel glided to a rest across the platform from *Dispatch*.

Two weeks ago, Samuel had sent a letter: the house was ready; it was time to come. And now here Hailey was, along with Davinia and Geordie. Hailey's gaze locked on Samuel's as the lowered skiff creaked ever downward to the harbor's black surface. He rowed close and pulled his skiff next to theirs, and he and Hailey grasped hands across oar and gunwale and the endless three months since she had last visited. Now she was here forever.

It was unwieldy to change boats, and so Hailey stayed in hers as Samuel piled their things in his. Then the crewman and Samuel set off, the only sounds the oars splashing the water and the wind in the trees and Geordie's exclamations over the seals and *Dispatch*'s exhalations. Samuel craned his neck to look at Hailey, and she kept her eyes on his, unable to stop smiling.

The skiffs drew side by side onto Samuel's beach. Alison was jumping up and down and Pruss came and lifted Geordie and carried him ashore, and John Salvation stood in the cold water to give a hand to Davinia. The sailor unloaded their bags as Samuel went to Hailey and gave her his hand and she stepped off the bow.

The others walked ahead, leaving them alone. Hailey entwined her fingers with his. They stood face-to-face. His nights had been full of the memory of her face, her shining eyes, her dark, untamed curls.

An osprey's high-pitched whistle wafted over the water.

Samuel said, "Come with me?"

"With you where?"

"Home."

She exhaled, as if she had been holding her breath for a very long time. They picked their way up the perfect sloping beach to the clearing where he had built the house. The others, still discreet, had wandered even farther away to remark on the perfection of the cove, standing by the firepit to hear Davinia describe their voyage. Alison had taken Geordie by the hand and the two were skipping rocks across the water, their happy chatter wafting down the beach.

Samuel led Hailey under the heavy lintel into the hushed quiet of the new house. Suddenly, he worried that the timber and stone were too crude—an echo, perhaps, of the wretched room in Glasgow where he and Alison had once lived. She ran her hands over the chairs and table he had crafted, the new cooking stove, the stairs ascending to the second floor, which she climbed. She explored the three bedrooms, each with a Turkish rug and window. He had built a vessel for their lives, for Alison's and Davinia's and Geordie's, too.

In their room, Hailey half turned, her gaze still wandering, finding the candle sconces on the wall, the brass doorknobs, the white linens on the bed. "You did all of this?"

"Yes."

She went to the window, from which you could see the entire cove. She looked out over the seascape, which Alison had already grown so fond of that she had declared she would never leave, ever.

Hailey turned to him. "Our wild and heavenly place."

The light on her face gave a golden aura to the rooms that Samuel had crafted with such hope. Hailey filled them in a way he hadn't even dared imagine.

Samuel said, "You are my wild and heavenly place, Hailey. You. You always have been."

She came to him and put her arms around him, and Samuel kissed her. It had been so long, but she was here now.

They went outside. There was no wind.

An eagle lifted off a nearby branch and soared out across the flat water of the harbor. The clear light peculiar to the islands cast shimmering reflections across the sea, which lapped against traces of the past and the future. Such a tangled path their lives had taken, but now they were together, and it was slack tide, and all was still, not a ripple to mar the world.

The first gimmer of this novel began years ago on San Juan Island, a gorgeous rocky isle situated in the Salish Sea in the state of Washington. On the island's northern tip lie the ruins of a stone house. This house—its gray stone, its architecture—is unique to the islands. For thirty years, my family has vacationed near that haunting skeleton, and every time I pass by, I wonder who might have built it, who had lived there, and why it lies abandoned and unheralded today. When I couldn't uncover its history, I imagined one.

For more than a quarter century, I have made my home a hundred miles south of there, on Cougar Mountain, a part of the Issaquah Alps, a three-mountain grouping just east of Seattle. Through its sedimentary and volcanic underpinnings run the abandoned tunnels of a defunct nineteenth- and twentieth-century coal mine, named after the Newcastle mines of England. Once, the mine caught fire, and people say that the mountain's frequent mists are really smoke from the black rock still smoldering deep in the earth. Wildlife lingers. I still encounter cougars, bobcats, bears, coyotes, and deer.

The last spark for this novel is rooted in my heritage. My family—the Fraziers—hails from the Highlands of Scotland, outside Inverness. At the end of the nineteenth century, my great-great-grandparents immigrated first to West Virginia and finally west, where my grandfather became a physician in a mining camp.

These deeply personal elements began to coalesce, and, in search of a story, I traveled to Scotland for the first time. The moment I set foot on Scottish soil, I was struck by three things: how at home I felt, how closely the landscape resembled that of Western Washington, and how its marvelous stone architecture instantly recalled my beautiful ruin on San Juan Island.

I would soon learn that emigrating Scots in the nineteenth century departed from Glasgow for destinations across the globe, and a good number of those Scots traveled to Seattle, where some worked in the coal mines a mile from my home. An epic love story began to percolate as I explored Scotland. I pictured a Romeo-and-Juliet tale, born in Glasgow and ending in the Pacific Northwest, with young lovers pitted against poverty, family ties, shipbuilding rivalries, racial tensions, environmental catastrophes, economic greed, an illegal opium trade, and the early, unheralded industrial history of Seattle.

Three notes: While a disastrous mining explosion and several minor ones did occur over the years in the coal mine in Newcastle, Washington, none occurred in 1879. I modeled the explosion in *A Wild and Heavenly Place* on the largest, which happened in 1894 in a different mine shaft, though I altered its magnitude and outcome. I also moved the location of Samuel and Hailey's "new" stone house. The ruin on San Juan Island is in a different location than in the novel. And while many readers may be aware of the famous 1889 fire in Seattle, in this novel I wrote about a different fire, which occurred in July 1879.

A Wild and Heavenly Place is less a summary of historical events than it is a chronicling of human desire—the impossible, the terrible, and the beautiful—in a time before Amazon, Microsoft, and Starbucks, when coal, timber, and shipbuilding ruled a rollicking, raucous town of immigrants on the make, hungry for profit, but mostly hungry for home. This novel reflects my love of place most of all, but also a sense that everyone is in search of home, and love, and that when they are the same, we reach a wild and heavenly place.

ACKNOWLEDGMENTS

I could not have written this book without the invaluable help of my virtuoso agent, Marly Rusoff, who believed in this story from the beginning and whose faith in me did not flag through many early drafts.

I am thoroughly indebted to my editor, the eminently competent and brilliant Tara Singh Carlson, who fell in love with Samuel Fiddes and Hailey MacIntyre and who helped me to craft their story into its best and fullest incarnation.

The entire team at Putnam has been welcoming and helpful. Thanks to Ashley Di Dio, Aranya Jain, the marketing and publicity team, and my skilled copyeditor.

I am eternally grateful to my friend Rich Farrell, who read more early pages than I can count and who gave me endless encouragement, nudging me forward whenever I doubted myself, which was often. I am grateful for his companionship and kindness. My thanks as always to dear friends Rena and Scott Pitasky, who read an early version of the novel and offered great suggestions. And thanks to them for the loan of their son, Samuel, who bears more than a passing resemblance to our hero.

Rendering crucial assistance, writer and naturalist David B. Williams, author of *Too High and Too Steep*, spent hours explaining to me the complicated geography of Puget Sound and Seattle, connected me with invaluable research documents and maps related to the early infrastructure of Seattle, and went out of his way to hunt down answers for me.

Many members of the Newcastle (Washington) Historical Society lent me their expertise. I referred often to their fascinating book, *The Coals of Newcastle: A Hundred Years of Hidden History*. Several members took extraordinary personal steps to help me. I would like to especially thank Michael J. Intlekofer, who extended me many hours of instruction, answered countless questions, sent me maps and documents, hiked with me throughout the mountain, and toured me through the organization's collected artifacts. In addition, Susan Day, Raymond Lewis, Kent Sullivan, Russ Segner, and Carla Trsek offered their varied expertise. And finally, I'm very grateful to Pam Lee and her family, whose privacy I inadvertently invaded one Easter afternoon in my eagerness to view a restored miner's home.

I am very grateful to Vicki Heck, King County librarian at Coal Creek Library, who made the introduction to the Newcastle (Washington) Historical Society members.

Deep gratitude to Trevor Brice of North Pacific Yachts, who knows boats and how to build them, and whose deep intelligence and goodness is reflected in Samuel Fiddes.

My many thanks to Jill Anderson, assistant archivist at King County Archives; Elizabeth Steward of the Renton History Museum; the Orcas Island Historical Museum; Boyd Pratt, architectural historian on San Juan Island; Áine Allardyce and Claire Daniel of the Archives and Special Collections of the University of Glasgow; and Jeannie Fisher, reference archivist, Seattle Municipal Archives.

The many resources I consulted include but are not limited to the Library of Congress (American Memories, Chronicling America), the British Newspaper Archive, the Seattle Municipal Archives, the Renton History Museum, the 1879 King County Census, the Seattle Room at the Seattle Public Library, MOHAI, archived Sanford Fire Insurance Maps, Seattle City Directories, the National Library of Scotland, the National Galleries of Scotland, Archives West, and the UW Libraries Digital Photo Collections.

The nonfiction books I consulted are too numerous to list. Of note are: *The Coals of Newcastle: A Hundred Years of Hidden History*; *Seattle's Black Victorians*; *Seattle Now and Then*; *Emerald City*; *Exploring Washington's Past*; *The Black West*; *Washington Territory*; *Too High and Too Steep: Reshaping Seattle's Topography*; *To the Ends of the Earth: Scotland's Global Diaspora 1750–2010*; *Washington: A Bicentennial History*; *Early Schools of Washington Territory*; *Pig-tail Days in Old Seattle*; *Native Seattle: Histories from the Crossing-Over Place*; *The Forging of a Black Community*; *In Search of the Racial Frontier*; *Rambles in North-western America*; *The Annals of the Chinese Historical Society of the Pacific Northwest*; *Seattle and Environs, 1852–1924*; *History of Seattle: From the Earliest Settlement to the Present Time*; *Historic Photos of Puget Sound*; *Ship's Fastenings*; and *Hearts West*.